SULTANA KOSEM

IN THE HAREM

Part One – of the Magnificent Century TV Series

DEMET ALTINYELEKLIOĞLU

Paperback ISBN: 978-1-945544-43-9
ePub ISBN: 978-1-945544-42-2

Written by Demet Altınyeleklioğlu

Published by Royal Hawaiian Press
Cover art by Aziz Hicham
Translated by Wieslawa Mentzen
Edited by EV Proofreading
Localized by Glenys Dreyer
Publishing Assistance by Cheeky Kea Printworks

Originally published in Turkish by Artemis Publications as W Haremie Sułtanka Kösem, #1.
Translated and published in English with permission.

First Edition

Presented By Royal Hawaiian Press

www.royalhawaiianpress.com

Dedication

For Doğy and Seymena

Prologue

There was darkness everywhere. Inside, there only one candle burned.

"Salkım Efendi doesn't like light," said the man.

"Salkım? An Efendi, a Lord? Who is he?" the woman whispered.

"The most powerful of the djinns – the Ruler."

The man narrowed his eyes. He clasped his hand on the golden bowl full of water, that stood before him. He mumbled under his breath. His voice rose like a wave.

"Salkıııım... Salkıııım... Are you on Mount Kaf, on the moon, or maybe on Venus? Where are youuuuuu? Wherever you are, come. Get on the backs of the waves during the storm or fly on the bird's wings... Look! In front of me is the ocean, the sea. Come! Salkıııım... The storm starts at sea!"

Out of fear, he released the bowl from his hands. He opened his eyes wide. He was terrified. The tiny eyes of the man stared at the burning wood, that threw sparks around. Although no one was touching the golden bowl at that moment, the water in it raged like a sea during a storm. It waved, foamed, and spilled on all sides.

"Welcome, Salkim..." The low-pitched, horrifying voice of Hüseyin Efendi suddenly changed to the voice of a little boy. "You brought a relief..."

It seemed that the man heard someone. He nodded his head approvingly.

"Is there anyone who is not afraid of anger, Salkım Efendi? We shudder at the very thought of anger... But this woman needs anger, magic. Do you know her?"

Hüseyin Efendi, the Safranbolian Hodja, began to shake and clench his teeth suddenly as if something squeezed his chest.

"No!" The scream come out of his larynx. "No, it's not like that!" All his hair stood on end, even his beard. He continued to nod his head as if he were listening to someone and was pretending to understand. He began to breathe faster and faster. "No," he said in a hoarse voice. "I, of course, am the guarantor."

Hüseyin Efendi began to tremble and utter strange words.

"Tarismai... Budos gari! Eloy, eloy! Eloy!"

At that moment, the Safranbolian's darkened face seemed to be radiant again.

"Lefajel Salkım Efendi," he muttered. "Lefajel domas!"

"Tell him," the man then whispered. "Tell him, and fast... Salkım Efendi doesn't like to wait. Please beg him."

"Son," the woman said. Suddenly, she was filled with fear. What if the djinns didn't like such obscene conversations...? About women, about matters that are private for every man? And if Salkım didn't like them either, wrath would fall upon him, would break his head...

"Speak," Hüseyin Efendi said in a childish voice. "Tell him... Tell him everything, but I beg you, hurry!"

The sea in the golden bowl continued to wave, but the woman had no choice. She didn't even think to escape.

"How to put it, son... The lady doesn't allow us to approach her in any way. We have tried everything. Nothing works. Hüseyin Efendi said that your strength is immense, unlimited. Please, give her strength, kindle the fire in her, blow life into her..."

The water in the golden bowl suddenly stopped whirling.

"He left," the man said. His face was sweaty. "Salkım Efendi left." His eyes remained fixated, staring, in the gold bowl with water.

"What's going to happen now?"

"It will be!"

"Oh, Allah!" Happiness gave the woman wings. "These magical words again... It will be."

When Hüseyin Efendi returned home, he begged his wife for a glass of water. "For Allah's sake, a sip of water!" he shouted. He was completely pale. He trembled all over. His eyes were bloody and his nails blue.

As he drank the water that his wife hastily brought him his hands trembled so much he spilled the drink on himself.

"Salkım Efendi," he moaned. "Why did you do that?"

"What did he do?" she asked, irritated. "How many times have I told you, Hüseyin Efendi, not to play with fire and not to call that damned djinn? One day he will take you; he will kill you."

Despite his fatigue, the man thrashed around on the mattress. "Not me, he won't take me," he mumbled with difficulty.

"Then whom will he take?"

The hodja narrowed his eyes. "There will be blood... Blood will flow in the quantities the Ottoman Empire hasn't seen yet. A betrayal."

New Palace, Harem Chambers, Şimşirlik

After Evening Prayer - September 2nd, 1651

When Meleki Kalfa reached the door that led from the rooms of the Valide Sultan—the mother sultan—to the inner courtyard, she stopped to take a deep breath. She'd managed to get that far unnoticed and unheard by anyone. But at that moment, she was in much greater danger. If she pushed open the heavy door leading to the courtyard, it was very likely that she would meet the harem guard. A great misfortune could fall on the head of a girl who was in the service of the great lady and outside the room after the evening prayer, and who, also, went out into the courtyard.

"Oh..." she sighed. It's was all because of the Bosnian Hüseyin, with his beautiful eyes. When he was on duty, she could hardly wait to reach the place where his company was stationed because of her excitement and longing for him. For weeks, she'd waited for the meeting, dreaming of Hüseyin's hands touching the most sensitive parts of her body. As soon as his guard duty began, she ran to him, out of breath, to quench the flame of her longing as soon as possible. Seeing in him the same flame fed by lust, they didn't waste time. He kissed her hot mouth, neck, and she begged: "Let's not waste time. I can't wait anymore!"

The very memory of this storm of feelings that she had experienced aroused lust in her.

"Now you can't go back, Meleki, not after all that has happened," she muttered to herself. "You are playing with fire, but let it be. You are already burning, anyway. Either here, or in Hüseyin's arms. Open this damned door already. Fly into the arms of your beloved man like a free bird!"

She pressed the handle made of bronze and pushed the heavy door gently. She slipped her head into the crack in the door and listened intently.

Nobody. There is nobody there, she thought. *Come on, find the Bosnian quickly and extinguish the flame of longing. Otherwise, it all will end up with you stuck in the half-open door.*

She pushed the door open with her arm and slipped outside. She paused and waited a moment. She couldn't be seen until she reached the stairs used by the coachmen and horse-boys. When she got down the stairs, she found herself in a place full of rooms and dark corridors, but Meleki knew them by heart. She could find her way even with her eyes closed.

She stopped to catch her breath. Her body strained like a string. Suddenly, Meleki relaxed. She flew away like the bird she had created in her imagination. She went to the first door in the corridor and leaned back against it.

Nothing happened. I've succeeded, she thought. Her body began to burn with lust again. *I'm coming, fair-haired Hüseyin! I'm arriving all hot!*

As soon as she took the first step, she was consumed by darkness. She wasn't afraid. She counted the steps.

One... two... three... seventeen... eighteen. Stop! The steps are over. Now turn into the corridor on your right. Well. Now go ahead. Count forty-two steps!

Even if she was sure at that moment that no one was able to hear her, she continued to move silently.

One step... another step... eleven... twelve... thirteen... fourteen. I'm almost halfway there, she thought.

Her heart again started to beat like crazy. But she knew that this time, the cause of the accelerated heartbeat was not fear. It was a storm of feelings raging in her heart and arousing lust in her. She felt her nipples harden. She was close to madness.

Who knows what he will do to me this time? She chuckled under her breath.

Suddenly, she stopped.

She heard something. Every part of her body was on alert. Something like a clang... No, it was probably a voice...

I've been discovered!

She was covered with cold sweat. She couldn't catch her breath. Someone was there. The sound came from the third room to the right. Now she was sure someone was in the room.

She'd counted her steps, so she knew she was close to the door. It would take just one step to get to the wall. Then she could hear the voices coming from behind the wall much better. Maybe she could also see who was inside there through the barred window.

"Where are you?"

She could hear the whisper of a woman. The answer came almost in the very same second.

"Here. On the right."

A sound again. Something dropped to the ground with a thud.

"Damn it!" a man growled.

It might have been a very tiny object, but it frightened Meleki as if a ball had burst right beside her.

"Shhh!" the woman's voice was heard again, "careful."

In one second, she recognized the voice. She covered her mouth with her hands so as not to scream.

Allah! Her heart almost popped from her chest. *It's her! I recognize her! That's her voice! The great lady is inside!* The thoughts whirled in her head.

"Did you have a good look around, Üveys? I hope no one saw you coming down the stairs here."

Üveys? That is, Üveys Pasha? Is my lady talking to him? It is impossible.

The great lady and Üveys Pasha! After the evening prayer... Together. And in the farthest and darkest corner of Şimşirlik! What can they do here?

Maybe... maybe she's just like me...No way! she told herself. *She's over sixty years old. Okay, maybe there's still some little flame in her. But to quench it in a dark corridor? Impossible! No, definitely not,* Meleki continued to convince herself. *Then what is she doing here?*

She was overwhelmed by fear. The premonition of danger flowed all over her body. Waiting for the warm kisses of Bosnian Hüseyin, she felt the cold breath of death on her face.

Run, she told herself. *Turn around and run. You are in a place where you shouldn't be! You heard things that should've never reached your ears! Run away!*

But she didn't do it; she did not run away. She crouched under the barred window and listened carefully.

"Was everything done according to our demands?" The whisper of the great lady seemed almost like screaming to Meleki.

"Without the slightest fault."

"The barracks?"

"There's nothing to worry about," the man muttered. "The military is loyal. Additionally, Siyavuş—"

"Shhh!" the woman warned him. "Careful!"

"No one will hear us here. Please don't worry."

"Pasha, we ourselves are witnessing the reign of the fifth sultan already! That we were able to stay alive, we owe only to the fact that we didn't trust even the stone walls. In the place we call the palace, even the right eye shouldn't trust the left one."

"There was a split in the army," the man whispered. "We have taken all possible preventive measures. We moved one company of cavalry and two companies of artillerymen there. We've been told they got orders. But if it comes to a fight—"

"I see," the woman interrupted.

The lady knew what was going on, but Meleki couldn't understand anything from what she heard.

She began to doubt whether these were actually the people she thought they were. After all, the voices might be similar. There was certainly more than one person in the world with the name Üveys.

But the woman called him Pasha, she thought. *If he is Pasha, and his name is Üveys, it changes things. Despite the size of the city, it would be hard to find another Üveys Pasha.*

That was it. He was the lady's weapon. When she imagined his face, she shuddered with fear.

There was silence. *What happened? Why have they stopped talking?*

"What is it?" the man broke the silence.

"You'll need them tonight," the woman replied.

It was silence again. After a while, a strange clang, like glass objects bouncing against each other, could be heard.

"What's in them?" he asked.

"Sorbet!"

The tone of the lady's voice made Meleki start to tremble with fear, like a lamb's tail.

"This..." the woman hissed. She lowered her voice so that it could barely be heard. "Add this to the sorbet for the child."

For the child? What child?

"The child won't be suspicious?"

"You fool!" The woman's voice cut through the air like an arrow. "Do you think I haven't thought of that?"

"Oh no, not at all. But—"

"There is no taste or smell. The color is exactly the same as the sorbet made from tamarind. It is impossible to tell the difference."

Meleki, trying to understand, once more repeated in her mind everything she just heard. *No taste, no smell... color... Tamarind! Allah... It's the sultan's favorite sorbet!*

The girl shuddered. She had a muddle in her head. She couldn't think logically.

What could be in the bottle that the lady gave to Üveys if they met secretly? No taste, no smell. The color and texture of sorbet. Impossible to tell the difference...

Poison!

Fear overwhelmed her.

"And for whom is the other one?"

"You are asking me?" After a moment's silence, she heard hissing from the lady. "It's not good to separate a mother from her child."

Oh no! Oh no! Oh no!

"Add this to her water," the woman said. "And don't worry, she won't notice anything, either."

The man muttered something under his breath, but Meleki couldn't hear what.

"The child first," the woman said slowly. "Until this is taken care of, we can't continue to work. When this happens, we must be ready immediately. Do you understand?"

Again, she couldn't hear Üveys. Or maybe he didn't say anything, just nodded humbly.

"Who will bring him to Eyüp Sultan for the ceremony?"

What? A ceremony? At Eyüp Sultan?

At that moment, Meleki solved the puzzle. She had accidentally witnessed a conversation about a terrible ruse. They were going to kill the sultan and his mother. Poison for the child. Poison for the mother. Don't separate the mother from her baby! On the throne, in place of the sultan, they wanted someone else. But whom?

Allah, she thought, *why did you make me witness to this talk of bloody treachery? Me, a poor maid. Why did you bring me here? What am I supposed to do now?*

And how is this your business? Turn on your heel, go away, her inner voice suggested. *Or continue your journey; find solace in Hüseyin's arms. As soon as he catches you and touches your hips, you'll forget everything. Nothing will remain in your memory—neither poison nor sorbet. Hüseyin will take you up to heaven.* That would be the best way out. She saw nothing, heard nothing. After all, she wasn't even sure if these were the people she thought they were! Maybe her lady was sleeping soundly at that moment, covered in a satin duvet.

Don't talk nonsense! You can't do that, said the voice of conscience. *You know it's them in there. They will poison the sultan and his mother. They will make someone else the sultan! And while they commit this cruel murder, you will throw yourself in the Bosnian's arms, right? Shame on you! And your name Meleki means Angelic? It should be Satan, girl! Satan!*

She imagined the sultan's face. The laughing face of a child who tried to be serious. Someone once told her that sultans don't smile. But he was still a child; he couldn't stop himself. The dimples that appeared on his cheeks when he laughed were ready to show themselves at any moment, he was so fast to laugh...

Allah! He's only nine years old. How can they do this to the innocent nine-year-old child?

Now she saw the delicate silhouette and the pink cheeks of the sultan's mother in her mind's eye. She walked so gently that she seemed to hover over the ground. Meleki's conscience spoke again: *She isn't even twenty!*

Her heart quivered. A thought that she ought to warn someone about the ambush dashed through her head like an arrow.

"Did you understand what I said, Üveys?" The woman's voice snatched Meleki out of her thoughts and brought her back to the earth. "We can't waste time, pasha. Let everyone realize this. We risk a lot—it's sink or swim. Everything should be done by the morning ezan, the morning call to prayer."

By the morning ezan... They aren't wasting time!

A noise came from the room.

They are leaving!

Pushed by fear and excitement, Meleki moved ahead in the dark corridor.

The last thing she heard was the lady's voice, "Finish it, Üveys. Show me what you can do. In the morning, come to me as the second vizier."

The rest she didn't manage to hear. *What should I do now?* she thought continuously.

Where should I go, whom to warn? Maybe I should forget about everything, pretend that nothing happened and continue living my life or...

Meleki had made a decision even before she realized it.

Turhan Valide's Room

September 3rd, 1651 - Midnight

"Turhan Valide! Wake her up!"

She remembered – as if through a fog – the two servants of Turhan Valide surprised and running in her direction. Her knees bent under her, and she fell to the ground just before the door.

She couldn't remember how she got there. The only thing she remembered was the orders and commands she gave herself: *Run, run. Do not stop. Run!*

Even if someone would stand in her way and try to stop her – it didn't matter.

In order not to cross her lady's part of the palace, she slipped through the back door used by the servants. As she ran, she thought about making everyone jump to their feet in the middle of the night by shouting, 'Ruse!' Maybe then the insidious hand of the killer wouldn't reach its victim.

A ruse! Murder! Wake up! Get up! They're going to kill the sultan!

Or maybe she would become a victim – they wouldn't hesitate to behead her.

But, reason told her the right thing to do. She would barely take two steps, and either an arrow would pierce her, or someone would stab her with a sword.

One of the maids of the sultan's mother ran to Meleki and fell to her knees next to her. "What happened?" she asked in a breathless voice. The second of the servants joined them.

Meleki's lungs wanted to burst from her chest. It didn't matter that she could take in more and more air in with every breath, she could barely breathe. "Wake... up!" Everything became black in front of her eyes.

"Oh dear, she's fainting... Lay down here, like this. Take a deep breath."

One of the inner doors opened. Two other servants who'd heard the anxious voices came to see what had happened. When one of them realized what was going on, she poured water from a glass carafe on the table into a cup and ran to the group sitting at the door.

"It's Meleki. She serves the great lady."

One of the girls, hearing that Meleki was the great lady's maid, puckered up her lips. "Then what is she looking for here? She can get away from here and faint at the great lady's feet," she mocked.

Meleki took a sip of water. One of the servants poured a few drops of water into her hand and moistened Meleki's face and hair, and she began to slowly recover.

"Wake up. Before it's too late..." she moaned again.

"Who are we to wake up?" one of the maids who came later, asked surprised.

"The sultan's mother."

"What? Has Meleki gone crazy? We are to wake her up in the middle of the night? Bah!"

Meleki tried to explain to them, but only a wheeze came from her throat.

"Rest now. You almost fainted. Turhan Valide gets up before the morning ezan, then..."

The morning ezan!

These words kept ringing in her ears. The morning ezan! It was supposed to be over by then.

Suddenly a strange feeling struck her. A suspicion. Maybe these girls were going to be involved in the murder... maybe they were all conspirators? Maybe they'd betrayed the Valide Sultan?

Her reason objected, but the seed of uncertainty was sown. *Why not? Have I not betrayed my lady, running here, head over heels? She could have bribed them.*

She thought of another possibility. In order to poison the Valide Sultan, Üveys Pasha would need to enter her bedroom. He must have an accomplice there; he couldn't do it himself...

Allah, oh Allah, one of these girls will poison the Valide Sultan!

Meleki herself didn't know how she managed to stand on her feet in her condition.

"Run!" she said in a hoarse voice to one of the servants. She reached out her hand and grabbed her collar.

Meleki's face, which had just been as white as the wall, was now flushed. "Awake her! Take me to her! Or..."

While the other servants struggled to free their companion from Meleki's grip, she screamed, "Or... or she will not see the sun anymore! She won't hear the morning ezan!"

The Valide Sultan hurriedly put on her clothes and sat on the edge of the ottoman.

One of the servants put the night slippers on her feet. She looked at the girl walking toward her with astonishment, but also with interest.

Meleki's gaze rested on the decanter on the nightstand next to the Valide Sultan. She saw one of the servants, at a sign from her mistress, fill the cup with water.

"No!" she cried. "Don't drink it!"

In an instant, Meleki broke free from the hands of the girls holding her, crossed into the bedroom, and knocked the cup out of the servant's hands, who, surprised, froze like a pillar of salt.

"Hey!" Turhan Valide raised her voice suddenly. "Why did you do that?"

Meleki knelt at her feet. "Send them away," she asked, and because her face was squeezed into the carpet, her voice sounded as if she were suffocating. "Send them all away."

"Excuse me?"

"Quickly. Time is running out. We have very little of it. The morning ezan is approaching. You have to listen to what I have to say."

Turhan Valide felt a shiver pierce her. Her heart started beating harder with anxiety. "Does the lady know you're here?"

Meleki, without rising from the carpet, turned her head once to the left, then once to the right. "Quickly, the morning ezan is coming. Make them all leave."

The woman hesitated for a moment. "I hope you will be able to explain your impudence somehow. Otherwise..."

Meleki raised her head and straightened up. "Listen to my words, please. Then you can do with me whatever you want. But now, quickly... quickly..." She turned to the surprised girls watching and said, "Get out! Get out of here!"

The sultan's mother nodded, giving the servants the sign to leave the bedroom. "What is going on? Tell me what happened."

Meleki did not look away from Turhan Valide's eyes until she heard the sound of the door being closed. When the sound of the latch came from the outside, she threw out on a single breath, "They'll kill you and our sultan!"

Turhan Valide bent down in panic, grabbed Meleki's hair, and angrily pulled her head toward herself.

"Girl, tell me immediately – who wants to do it? Who wants to betray our sultan?"

"The great lady... his grandmother!"

Meleki told her everything, and Turhan Valide listened without interrupting her once. She imagined the great lady's face. *Satan, a pure evil,* she thought. When the girl finished talking, the Valide Sultan stood up and headed for the door. She turned back and looked at the servants who followed her. Most of them came from the same place as her. The Crimean khan chose the most beautiful girls, and he sent them to the palace as a gift. She trusted them all. But man learns from the mistakes made by his predecessors.... She should be careful.

"Tatiana," she whispered to the head servant. "Lock all the doors. Don't let anyone go outside, and don't let anyone in."

Next, she grabbed Meleki's wrist and pulled her behind herself. "And you," she said. "Come with me."

They walked through a door Meleki had never seen before.

"Run!" Turhan Valide cried. "Even Satan himself can't see us here. Run! Pray that it is not too late."

Meleki didn't stop praying. Being late would be the end of the road for her. She would pay the price for the betrayal. She heard Turhan Valide calling after her...

"Run!"

That night she kept dashing somewhere – as if she raced with Azrael, the Angel of Death himself. Either she would outrun him and save these two souls, or she would lose her own life.

Turhan Valide stopped suddenly. Meleki noticed that the woman groped for something on the wall in the dark. Then she hit at it.

Knock... Knock! Knock, knock... knock! Knock, knock, knock!

Is that a password? Meleki wondered.

The wall moved. She saw the figure of a big man in the impenetrable darkness.

"Go."

As they squeezed through, the wall closed behind them. They walked, sliding their backs on the damp walls. Another door opened in front of them and they entered an antechamber lit by countless candles.

The sultan's chamber!

In front of them stood four armed guards with crossed spears, behind whom were huge double doors.

The guards didn't even budge at the sight of Turhan Valide.

"Move away," she said, walking toward them. "I have to see our sultan. Immediately. Let me pass."

But the guards continued to stand in their places.

"Son, get up!" Turhan Valide said, this time in a much louder voice.

"The Sultan is sleeping."

Both the Valide Sultan and Meleki quickly turned their heads in the direction from which the voice came. The nursemaid!

The woman was surprised to see the sultan's mother in such a condition. "Our Sultan is sleeping now."

"In that case, wake him up!"

"I can't do that. He... he is the Sultan."

Meleki was screaming inside. *What if we are too late?*

The Valide Sultan's face flushed red. She was certain that exactly the same thoughts whirled about in her head.

"Nursemaid!" Turhan Valide screamed in a terrifying voice. Her voice expressed everything she felt at that moment – fear, pain, anger... "Woman, wake my son. Wake him up and bring him to me. Otherwise..."

Her voice stuck her in her throat, and despite all her efforts, tears flowed down her cheeks in streams. "The empire is in danger."

At that moment, they noticed a boy standing in the doorway, his hands rubbing his eyes.

Allah! That's the sultan! Meleki wanted to shout.

Mehmet, the nine-year-old sultan, looked at them, puzzled.

Before the Morning Ezan

September 3rd, 1651

"My Lady, My Lady... wake up, please."

The servant leaned over a woman who lay in a beautiful, wide bed, covered from head to toe with a red and green satin duvet.

"Wake up please, My Lady."

Finally, the duvet moved.

"Shhh... stop yelling," the great lady reproached her, straightening herself. "I heard you... What time is it?"

Why would she have to wake up; she hadn't even closed her eyes that night. She hadn't even removed her clothes.

"The morning ezan is approaching. There are a few moments left."

A few moments. That means it was all done! Thanks to her, there would be a new sultan.

So, what? she asked herself in spirit. *Is it easy to be Valide?*

She stood up. She spread her arms, a sign to the servant to help put on her caftan. She loved it – it was almost as black as tar. The golden thread that it was embroidered with flashed in the darkness. The second servant, who rushed to the great lady in a hurry, put feet flat-heeled slippers with curved noses on her feet, decorated with golden thread just like the caftan.

It was still dark outside. The sun had not yet risen. There would be an uproar after dawn at the Eyüp Sultan. He came to the war as the son of the Sultan, and he will leave it as the Sultan himself. *Long live the Sultan, long live the Sultan!*

Her eyes brightened. She sighed. She wiped her face with water brought in a copper jug by one of the girls and dabbed it with a decorated towel. She sat on the edge of the ottoman and rested her back on the pillows.

"Oh," she sighed. "This stomach ache will kill me someday."

She felt strange, thinking of death. Those two were already dead.

Or maybe not just those two... maybe a lot more people had lost their lives.

The whole population of the empire should pray for your health, Mahpeyker, she thought. *See what you've done again. How many sultans have you already given to the empire? Five? Six?*

The brothers Mustafa and Osman must also be included. If we count them, too, Suleiman will be the seventh. Well, let's say that wasn't me that made Ahmed the Sultan; Suleiman will be the sixth one I took in my hands and sat on the throne.

She smiled to herself. Destiny. Who would think that another sultan would come out of the Chamber of Şimşirlik after Ibrahim?

"Emine!" she called the servant. "Find out if Saliha Dilaşub has come from the Old Palace already."

The girl ran out.

The mother of the new sultan should be here by now. That was the custom. Immediately after planting her son on the throne, the Valide Sultan moved from the Old to the New Palace.

"Dilaşub doesn't resemble the Moscow viper in any way," she snapped. "She doesn't have to be reminded twice. She will come to show her respect and kiss my hand, even before the ezan."

Emine stood in the doorway. The expression on her face was disturbing. She didn't understand why Dilaşub would be in the New Palace at this time, but nevertheless, she bowed to the great lady and said, "She has not arrived yet."

Siyavuş had probably planned everything this way, she thought.

While reading the ezan, the new sultan and his mother, Saliha Dilaşub, were to be together. The sun just rose over their heads. She was going to be the queen again. *This time they will call me Sultan Mother. Saliha will certainly show respect. Why hasn't the girl come to kiss my hand yet?* They probably decided that bringing her during the prayer would not be right.

Now she started to think who the Grand Vizier should be. *Maybe Tarhoncu Ahmed Pasha. Üveys certainly isn't good vizier material. Probably the best solution would be Siyavuş again. We'll see. If all goes well then yes... and if not, he will learn the hard way what Sharia law means.*

Suddenly there was noise from the outside – footsteps on the floor.

They are coming, she thought. *The whole group is coming. That means everything is done already. The new sultan has been sworn in. They are leading him to me.*

The footsteps got nearer. A thought came to her mind that Üveys Pasha might say that it would be safer to lead the new ruler to his chambers by passing this way. They were about to turn right, and the sounds of the steps would start moving away.

But the people didn't turn, and the footsteps were not moving away; on the contrary, they started getting very near.

"Allah!" The sighs could be heard in the room.

They are bringing the new Valide to me, of course. "Emine, they are bringing Saliha Dilaşub. Have the girls pull themselves together. And you, put my headscarf on."

Emine ran toward the inner door. As the footsteps approached, she heard the girls talking in the adjacent lounge. The steps went silent, having stopped just before the door to the room.

They have arrived.

She sat in the middle of the ottoman, her hands on her lap. She put the sullenest expression she could on her face, but she still couldn't help but smile slightly. The new Valide Sultan was ready to show acceptance, understanding, and support. The great lady was ready to finally welcome the new Sultan Mother.

She heard the door to the room open. A scream pierced the air.

It is probably one of the girls happy to see Dilaşub, she thought.

"Emine!" she called. "Let her inside. Let's not make her wait."

Emine didn't reply. The great lady heard a strange sound as if a lot of people suddenly began to trample on the carpet lying on the floor. They stopped in front of the door.

"Please come with us," the man said gravely. "We are waiting."

Both wings of the huge door opened loudly.

Chapter One

Island of Milos
June 1601

The scream of a man driving a wagon, as big as a giant, pierced the sky like thunder. "Come on, stop screaming like that!"

Nastya shrugged and ignored the next slap on the face she got and started shouting even louder, "Leave me alone! I want to go back to my village!"

The driver's bald head appeared between a dirty, thick veil that separated him from the girls. The other girls, seeing the man's eyes bloodshot with anger, huddled even closer. They looked at Nastya with eyes that begged her to stop, but she continued to shout. "I command you! Take me back! Immediately!"

"Hahaha! Her majesty commands!" He burst out laughing, then his head disappeared behind the curtain again.

The screams of one of the girls could be heard behind him: "Killer... criminal! You are even worse! You are a devil!"

Hmm, Satan... thought the coachman. *The girl is about right. I'm a devil.* He liked that comparison.

"Hey, Aristides! Cyprian!" he called to the men riding horses. "Did you hear? The lass called me Satan!"

They laughed. One of them held the horse. He waited

until the wagon passed by him, then he approached its back. He parted the covering and looked inside.

Seeing him, Nastya took out a crucifix and started screaming once more, "Don't hit me! For God's sake, don't hit me!"

The other girls also raised their voices.

The man looked at them. He burned with lust. His eyes wandered among the imprisoned girls' slender wrists, ankles, and their shapely legs, bound with a rope. He shuddered.

"Don't even think about it, Cyprian," the man in front of him said. The whole wagon shook from the coachman's laughter. Grumbling, Cyprian climbed into the seat.

"Let me out!" Nastya shouted, almost choking. She tried to stand on her feet. "I beg you... isn't there any bit of pity in you?"

"Shut up!" the man thundered and slapped her face.

The blow was so strong that Nastya fell. She crouched and began to sob.

The girl who sat next to her whispered, "I beg you, Nastya, don't cry. Don't provoke them to beat you."

When the wagon swung around and stood still, there was no hope anymore.

"Hey, Tasula! Where are you, old woman?" the coachman shouted.

"Shhh!" Cyprian turned to the girls, putting his finger to his lips. "We've arrived at the han. Be quiet. I'll untie your legs. If you try to escape, I swear I'll break your legs."

All the girls looked at him.

Nastya felt some hope – a han, or caravanserai was a roadside inn with a courtyard, rooms, shops and a mosque. Perhaps...

"Quiet or I'll cut your tongues off," he growled, and the dagger's blade flashed in the sun.

The girls began to shake with fear.

The man leaned over and freed the girl sitting closest to the end. She tried to straighten her numb legs and started to rub the red marks left on her ankles by the tight rope. A grimace of pain twisted her face. When he started to untie another one, they noticed that his hideous hands slipped over the girl's thighs and breasts.

"Mother of God. Jesus. Help us," Nastya sighed.

At that moment, they heard footsteps coming from outside.

"It must be God punishing me for something," a woman's wheezing voice said.

It had to be Tasula, called by the driver.

"First a bunch of Ottoman dissenters, and now you... All Saints, what a cursed day is that? I no longer have any people to allocate to you."

It was clear that the woman hated them. Nastya thought about calling for help. Maybe if she found out that there were five girls abducted from one village imprisoned in the wagon, she might help them... And then, there were also Ottoman Turks in the han. Maybe they...

"Go on, hurry up!" The cutthroat who walked over to the wagon cut in. "Stop standing and talking like this. I'm dying of hunger. Only some well-done meat and wine will save me from death."

Exactly at that moment, Nastya felt an ice-cold hand of a man on her leg. *Even if a snake had crossed my leg, I wouldn't bristle so much*, she thought.

Cyprian pretended he was trying to untie a knot. One of his hands moved higher and higher. Finally, he stopped fighting with the knot and started to run his arms around the girl's legs. Nastya was terrified. She tried to pull away from him as far as she could.

"Don't touch me!" she hissed. "If you don't stop, I'll start screaming. All the Ottoman soldiers will run here."

The man stopped his hand on her knee for a moment. Their eyes met.

Nastya was frightened by the flash of lust she saw in his eyes.

"Just try!" he said, and his hand began to move up lasciviously under the girl's long skirt.

Nastya squeezed her legs as hard as she could and trapped the snake. She felt the man's breath, accelerated with anger, on her face.

"Before they get here, I'll have plenty of time to rip you apart," he said and pushed his hand that was stuck between the girl's legs, even higher.

She felt his tongue in her ear. When she realized he was trying to catch her earlobe with his teeth, she withdrew her head. This time he touched her neck with his tongue. She thought she was losing her senses. Then she thought that the best way out would be... to go crazy. She moaned and pulled her head away even further.

"Slut," Cyprian said. "You like it, don't you? I noticed at first glance that you were excited. Don't worry, you'll get what you want... and even more."

He clung back to her neck. Nastya moaned again.

"Anastasia! My God, how can you do this?" It was Katerina. It was certain that she thought her friend had given in to the man.

Wait. Wait, you'll see what will happen next, Nastya thought.

The man pushed against her more and more. As he twisted his head to get his lips to hers, his ear touched her lips. Agitated with lust, Cyprian lost all his other senses. He didn't notice that she opened her mouth. He didn't notice her white teeth flash like daggers. They were like a snare waiting for the victim – a snare that snapped greedily.

A horrible scream ripped out of the man's throat. "Aaaaaaaaah! Damn slut!"

He gripped his cheek below the ear she'd just bitten. He felt a warm and thick liquid on his hand. Blood! Cyprian was seized by panic. He caught Nastya's throat with his other hand.

Outside the wagon, the girl heard the woman, the owner of the han, shout, "What's going on here?"

The other girls began to cry.

The coachman shouted angrily, "Cyprian! You are finished!"

Nastya felt her breath getting weaker and weaker. She seemed to hear the fluttering of the wings of the arriving angels. *That would be it,* she thought. The short life of Anastasia Vasiliades, the daughter of the orthodox Kostas Vasiliadis, ended here.

Chapter Two

Ugrularin Elinde
Haziran 1601

The man took the hand off his cheek and grabbed Nastya's hair. He twisted her neck with all his strength. "Let go of my ear or I'll break your neck!"

The blood that dripped from between his fingers left red streaks on the girl's hair.

Her lungs burned with live fire, but the need to take a breath won over her anger. *Bite even harder. Rip, tear!* her mind told her, even while her teeth parted of their own will.

Cyprian moved away from her, howling with pain. The hand that had been ready to break Nastya's neck went to his torn ear. He looked at his bloodied fingertips in panic and anger. Nastya saw the man raise his hand, but she didn't see him lower it. The blow that struck her was so strong that it knocked her down as if a missile had hit her in the right cheek.

The blood flowing from Cyprian's ear quickly covered almost his entire face. His eyes looked like two big, scary white hollows. His hand covered his ear again, while blood spurted between his fingers. In his other hand, he held a dagger.

"Slut!" he yelled. "Bitch! I'll skin you piece by piece! I will drink your blood instead of wine!"

The other girls began to sob. And the woman running the han shouted, "Hey, they're killing the girls! Quickly!"

When the coachman tried to silence her, a shrill scream sounded.

"Aaaaaah!"

Immediately after, the moans of girls imprisoned in the wagon were also heard. The dagger that Cyprian held pierced the body of one of the girls, who'd tried to hold him back.

"You spawn of Satan!" the coachman yelled. "If you did something to even one of them..."

He glanced quickly around the wagon, trying to find Tasula.

She'd fled and ran towards the han, waving her hands.

The second coachman, trying to calm the horses, shouted, "Damn fool!" Going to the back of the wagon, he added, "You want to destroy us..."

"Enouuuuuuuugh!" Cyprian thundered. "Stop, Dimitri! Don't even try to face me!" His voice resembled the roar of a bear that had not eaten for months. Soon after, he burst into terrifying laughter. "Wait for your turn. First, I'll tear the lungs out of this slut. You will be next. I'll rip your gut out. I swear, I'll do it!"

The coachman saw him reach his hand towards the girl who lay on the ground. Her nose and mouth were covered with blood. She'd been the one who'd cried all the way, the most troublesome of them all. The other girls tried to stop Cyprian and grabbed his legs. The girl in whose arm he'd stabbed with the dagger tried to frighten them all and screamed incessantly as if she lost her mind.

Nastya peered between the legs of the man and saw the coachman trying to get inside. She struggled to push away the girl who'd thrown herself on her in an effort to protect her from the blows.

"Let go of me, Katerina," she begged. "Pray to Mary for a place in heaven for me."

Not even two steps separated her from this monster. She was surprised when she realized she wasn't scared at all. She couldn't believe it. The man whose ear she'd torn and enraged, headed toward her to kill her. He extended the hand with the dagger in it toward her. A few seconds more and he'd raise it up and lower, exactly as he had done before with the blow on her cheek. But she wasn't afraid.

Among the cries of girls, she heard the voice of the coachman, "Stop it, don't do it. We should leave here immediately."

Nastya opened her eyes. Between the bloody face of the man and his arm, she noticed that the coachman had taken a step toward them. He held a huge knife and shouted, "Stop! Stooooop!"

"Go ahead, stop me," Cyprian said, contorting his face into a scornful smile. "Come here and stop me!" He quickly turned toward the girl lying in front of him. He raised his hand higher and higher.

Nastya looked into her killer's face. *Holy Mother...* she thought. *Take Nastya to yourself.*

The coachman shouted, trying to stop Cyprian. The girls cried.

And those will be the last sounds I'll ever hear in my life, thought Nastya. But no, they weren't the last ones. Among the screams, she heard something else – a sighing breath.

Nastya opened her eyes. The man's hand was still in the air. When she wondered why he hadn't lowered it, she noticed the expression on his face... a face seized by fear. Nastya quickly turned to the side. Cyprian fell face down to the ground. The dagger he held dug into the wagon's bed under the pressure of his body. He was dead.

The coachman had driven his knife between the ribs of the man, all the way to the handle.

"Silence!" the coachman growled. He pulled another knife from his scabbard. He slid aside part of the curtain and stood still.

"Whoever dares to shout, I will cut their thro—" He was cut off mid-word.

He'd heard a whistle. When he turned around to see what was going on, an arrow pierced his neck. The coachman felt the sharp-pointed arrow pierce and rip to pieces the veins and cartilage of his throat. The blade went through to the other side, tearing a piece off his neck. For a moment, it seemed that the coachman wanted to hold to the curtains, then his hand slid down the material, and his body faltered. He fell out of the wagon.

Screams came from outside the wagon; all kinds of blasphemies and curses mingled with each other.

"Hey, you, thief!" roared the man. "Are you kidnapping them from our lord's land? Don't you know that here, even a flying bird in the air belongs to him?"

Nastya wasn't fast to feel overjoyed, and in a single moment, she understood that she was right. *My God...* she thought. *And now the Ottoman soldiers!*

The girls heard a clang of steel objects striking each other. Someone was dueling. It didn't last for long. There was a scream, and then everything went silent.

They heard steps. A torchlight approached the gap in the curtain, and the curtain parted.

They saw a head wrapped in red cloth.

The man frowned his black, thick eyebrows. The light of the torch made it seem that his eyes sent sparks. Nastya could swear she had never seen such a terrifying man in her life. She could have also sworn she hadn't seen a more handsome one.

"What's going on here?"

They thought it was the sky thundering. He stretched his hand with the torch slightly ahead. He looked at the crying girls. Nastya noticed that the expression on the face of the man – menacing just a moment ago – softened.

"Why are you screaming like that? We came on time, didn't we?"

Chapter Three

Kumanovo, the Estate of Ibrahim Karayelzade
January 1602

"Damn it!" sighed the woman. She opened her eyes with excitement. "And then? What happened after that? Tell me!"

"You know what happened next. And now I'm here."

"My God, Nastya, I can't believe it. What does it mean, 'And now I'm here'? Eh," she sighed. "You barely began to enjoy the fact that you were liberated, when you got into even bigger misfortune. You fell into the hands of the corsairs."

She and the other girls had thought the same, seeing the Ottoman sailors with their bushy mustaches and naked calves. But contrary to what could be expected, they weren't scared. First, they made a trip across the sea. Later, at the slave market, each of them was sold to a different buyer. Nastya was bought by a man named Ibrahim Karayelzade. She was separated from her companions, which very much surprised and troubled her. The man who made the deal counted the coins, packed her on a dilapidated wagon and took her for a long journey. Passing through the mountains, the valleys, and crossing the river, they finally reached here. What else could she say? "Now I'm here."

And she was here – in a place called Kumanovo, which she had never heard of before, at the estate of Ibrahim Karayelzade, whose face she hadn't seen so far, although she had been here for many days.

Beautiful, rebellious Anastasia from Milos. Now she was a servant. And from the day she came here, she had told her superior her whole story, from the beginning to the end. Her supervisor, Mirna, opened her eyes wide with astonishment and sighed every time, "My God!"

That day, too, she listened to Nastya's stories with fear. "Corsairs! Damn it! Misfortune one after another..." She stopped silent at that moment.

Nastya looked her over from head to toe. She dared not ask directly.

But despite this, Mirna said, "Ottoman corsairs. Who knows what harm they must have done to you?" She shuddered with fear at the thought of the horrors that came into her head.

Harm? They didn't do anything to us, Nastya thought. *But if I answer like that, I might disappoint her.* Mirna was sure that the girl had to have lived through terrible moments. That is to say, according to her, it had to be so. Someone who fell into the hands of the corsairs, shouldn't get away from them in one piece.

"Nah..." Nastya said quietly and shrugged. "They put us on the ship. They led us down into the hold."

"Mother! And there they..."

Nastya realized that the woman had imagined a scene of rape.

"No, Mirna, nothing like that happened."

Mirna again put her hands to her chest. "Fortunately," she said.

Nastya liked Mirna. Plump, always smiling, caring for everybody like a mother. She'd accepted her as if they had known each other for years, and she hadn't allocated work to her immediately after arrival. Right from the very start, a bond was created between them.

"Come. Straight to the bath! Take these rags off and throw them away. They are all torn. I'll find you something to wear. Then come to the kitchen. You will have a proper meal, and we can talk."

Mirna watched the girl absorb food with a huge appetite.

"What's your name?" The woman's voice sounded friendly.

"Anastasia, but everybody calls me Nastya."

"How old are you?"

"Thirteen." In fact, she'd added one year to her age.

"Oh, child, you're so young. Where are you from?"

"From far away."

"Tell me anyway."

"From the island called Milos. And you, where are you from?" She immediately noticed the sadness in the eyes of the woman.

"You could say that I'm from far away, too. They call the city Belgrade. This means that, like you, I come from across the water."

"From across the water?"

"Yes... You are a girl from across the sea. I am a girl from across the river. I came from a place where the Sava and the Danube meet, from a place that doesn't resemble Kumanovo. Belgrade is a city of rivers, not mountains and valleys... Do you know what the Sava and the Danube are?"

How could she know? Nastya shrugged. "Have you ever seen the sea?"

"The sea?" The longing in the woman's voice was overwhelming. "The sea?" She sighed again. "No. But I know what it is."

"How can you know what something is if you've never seen what it looks?"

"From the stories," Mirna muttered. "From my grandmother's stories."

The woman fell silent and began to unfold bedsheets. For a while, they kept doing their work quietly, and Mirna hit the pillows as if she wanted to unload all the anger and regret that filled her. Then she turned to the door still without speaking.

She stopped in the doorway. "A man may also know things he has not seen," she said as if to herself.

She didn't turn around and look at the girl. But Nastya understood that Mirna didn't turn around, not because she'd hurt her, but because she wanted to hide the tears that flowed down her face.

"Everyone has their dream ship, Nastya. As soon as you step on it, you are ready to spread your sails and sail away." She turned the doorknob, and the door opened. "I am the captain of my dream ship. I sail on the seven seas." She crossed through the door and gently closed it behind her.

A dream ship, Nastya repeated in her mind. What a beautiful term. She decided to memorize it. *Dream ship...*

She went to the window. There seemed to be nothing but snow outside. The pines looked like brides in white dresses, waiting in silence.

In the next instant, Nastya imagined the hot, blue Milos sky before her eyes. She sighed. She remembered the visible white clouds, sprinkled here and there, so thin and wispy that they looked like tulle in the sky. She loved to watch the sky become golden, and the clouds turn into red and purple blots. Later, she used to run to the shore, holding a piece of freshly baked bread made by her mother, to sit on one of the stones hit by the waves and stare at the view which stretched in front of her.

Now she was doing exactly the same thing in her imagination. She sat on the same stone again. She could feel the waves stroking her feet, and she heard their noise. In the distance, in the place where the sky meets the sea, the ripping waves were merging with the sun that was changing their color to red.

She recalled Mirna's voice. *Everyone has their dream ship, Nastya...*

It must have been the ship that Mirna mentioned. She also had to have her own. She was also the captain on her ship. But she was just a poor maid. She was lonely and in a situation without any way out. Without hope. She had a past, but was there a future for her? She doubted it. But with her ship, she could open the sail both for the past and the future.

Suddenly, she felt her sadness fly away; it left her heart like a leaf caught by the wind. Her body may be imprisoned, but her mind was free, as long as she could dream.

It was the only freedom she could taste here. Memory! Dreams!

Hope!

"Come on, Captain," Nastya muttered. "Put the sails on!"

After that sad conversation, Mirna began to think of Nastya as her relative. They were both girls from beyond the water.

"You will call me 'sister,'" she announced one day. "Sister Mirna."

This invented relationship raised her spirits and protected her from the loneliness and darkness she hid inside.

Mirna pressed Nastya to keep telling what had happened to her.

In the evenings, after finishing work, she took her to the side and asked, "Tell me, please. How did they kidnap you?"

And Nastya told her. Mirna would either let out a word out of fear or cursed. Nastya sat all the nights long, talking about the three days she had spent in captivity with the three thieves.

"Oh, mother!" Mirna shouted. "May Hell devour their souls. They led you to the cave?"

She had told it so many times, but the woman exerted so much pressure on her that she was forced to go back to the beginning of the story. Ten times she repeated the story of how the three thieves had been killed.

"The robbers got what they deserved!" Mirna clapped her hands and straightened up. "Wait, I'll bring you some burma. Don't even think about going to bed, girl from across the sea."

"Burma? What is it, sister?"

"A kind of cookie, pastry with walnuts and syrup. You won't be able to resist it. But now, quiet. You will still talk about what happened at sea."

"Okay, but in return, you tell me the stories of your grandmother."

Mirna answered something in a low voice, but Nastya didn't understand.

Burma was something really wonderful. Although she ate three large pieces, she would've had no hesitation to enjoy more if anything had been left. But Mirna was losing patience.

"Come on, come on, tell me," she said.

She wanted to be told, in the smallest details, how the corsairs managed to free the kidnapped girls and how they took them to the ship. She also didn't forget to ask if they were handsome.

She leaned over. Her cheeks were red with excitement.

"And Kemal—"

"Who is Kemal?"

"The one who killed the second thief in the wagon and saved us was Kemal, sister." Nastya felt a pleasant shudder at the memory of Kemal's black eyes, and black eyebrows and mustache.

"Oh, I understand." The woman chuckled. "And then? Come on, tell me. You boarded the ship. And then?"

"They put up the sails."

Mirna looked at the girl as if she was making fun of her. "You sailed... And then?"

Nastya didn't want to talk about those terrible days at sea.

Three times she'd stood face-to-face with death; the third time God forgave her. She didn't even want to remember those three days when the giant ship was thrown like a toy by the rough waves that raised it so high that it could touch the clouds and dropped it back down a moment later.

She thought again of Kemal, the handsome dark-haired man. Even during the horrific storm, he did not forget about them. Whenever he had the opportunity, he went down to the hold and tried to lift their spirits.

"Don't be afraid," he'd say. "This ship survived the war. She is guarded by the souls of the heroes who died here. Nothing will happen to us."

It turned out he was right.

"How many days were you at sea?"

"Probably longer than a month. At sea, a person loses the sense of time."

"Where did they take you?"

"Kemal called the place where they landed us, Aidipsos. It's somewhere to the north of Milos."

"And what happened there?"

Nastya, like a disobedient child, swept her finger through the sweet syrup on the plate where the burma had been previously. Her eyes were stuck to the floor.

"There we parted," she said sadly.

She felt as if she was aboard her ship with dreams. At the memory of that day, she felt pressure in her throat.

"That's it," Kemal had said. "Now everyone will go their own way, following their own destiny."

Own road, own destiny? At that moment, she had only one question in her mind, and she still did. There was no such thing as her own way and own destiny. She no longer had any road to make or destiny which she could face.

She heard again Katerina's sobs rumbling in her head. Their tears mixed.

She felt their salty taste in her mouth. She saw Helena before her eyes, trying to free herself from their embrace. She heard Maria's pleading. She heard the whip hitting Eleni.

The separation was terrible. Like death.

Until that moment, it never occurred to them that one day they would be separated. They felt that they would be together forever. They had got used to each other; they had become a family, created by the misfortunes that were thrown upon them by fate. A family without men. Five girls. Five sisters. Five orphans. Without fathers, without mothers.

And one day, they were forced to part.

Separation meant loneliness. Lonely, helpless, without hope – Nastya thought then: *The real bondage will begin only now.*

They clung to each other. They twisted their hands so that they couldn't separate them. Every time they dragged one of them away, terrible screaming and sobbing sounded around the neighborhood.

"Eleniiii!"

"Katerinaaaa!"

"Mariaaaa!"

"Helenaaaa!"

"Nastyaaaa!"

The leader of the corsairs assigned Nastya to Kemal. He was the one who took her to the slave market and handed her over to the buyer. He didn't anticipate that it would be so difficult for him to part with her.

"Nastya," Kemal said in a subdued voice. He was ashamed to look her in the eyes. His eyes were fixed on the ground as if he searched for something there. He had always had a problem with conversation. But that day, it was even worse. He suffered with every word spoken.

"If I could... take... you... back... home..."

"If you could..."

That day, for the first time, Kemal raised his head and looked her in the eyes. He didn't look away.

"Eh, if we didn't have to separate..." His voice trembled. "The fates will show... You will see, one day... we will see... each other... again."

They both knew it was impossible. It seemed to the girl that his eyes fogged.

"Eh," he sighed in the end. "I have to go back. Time is running out for me." He looked her in the eyes for the last time. "I wish you all the luck. I heard that the man who chose you is a good man. I hope that is the case."

Then he turned and walked away.

Nastya remembered how she wanted to cry with all her might at that moment, 'Kemaaaal!' but her voice choked in her throat.

She returned to reality, to hear Mirna's voice.

"Come on, tell me what happened after you separated." The woman suddenly looked into her eyes. "Hey!" She grabbed Nastya's hand and shook it. "Are you crying?"

Nastya shook her head. *But my inside cries with sad tears,* she thought. It had been weeping since the day of her departure from Aidipsos. *Why should I stop myself from crying?* she repeated to herself all the way from Aidipsos. *I was right. The true bondage began when I was separated from my companions. I'm lonely. There is no hope in me. No one is at my side. I'm powerless.*

Apart from that, the most painful thought was that she didn't know what awaited her.

Every time she thought about it, she wanted to burst out with a terrible laugh. *You don't know what awaits you, Nastya, huh? Of course, a brutal, coarse, dirty type! Some simple landowner! What else can happen to you? You're just a slave they buy and sell.*

"Here, here," Mirna whispered. She brought Nastya's head to her breast. "Don't cry anymore." She began stroking her head. "You know what, girl from across the sea?" she whispered, "You must know that he is Turkish, he is a dissenter, but the lord of this land is really a good man."

The fact that the woman was so excited about the owner of the estate made Nastya doubtful. Without lifting her head, she stared uncertainly at the woman's eyes.

"How old is he, sister?"

"Who?" asked Mirna, thoughtfully.

"The lord of this property. How old?"

The sound of the girl's words surprised Mirna. When she understood the allusion, she blushed.

"No, no, no. None of these things," she replied with fake anger. "Crazy, what else could he be?" She looked at Nastya. "I don't want to see you crying anymore, understood? Every day, God creates the world anew. He rewrites freshly what is intended for each one of us. Every morning, we wake up in a new world. That is why we can't know what will be tomorrow."

Chapter Four

Kumanovo: the Estate of Ibrahim Karayelzade May 1603

Any time Nastya asked, 'When will I see the owner of the estate?' Mirna always answered, "Wait a bit more. Everything in its due time."

Hours, then days passed.

The most common answer was, "But the lord is not at the estate right now. He doesn't come here often. It is like this... He summoned soldiers from his lands, took some of his belongings and left. Probably a war is coming again."

Mirna also didn't allow the girl to go upstairs. Almost immediately after Nastya's arrival at the property, she took her to the big double door and said: "What is behind that door is forbidden to you."

"Why? What's behind it?" asked the girl. *God, what could be upstairs? Why couldn't she go in there?*

One night, between dreaming and waking, she thought, *Harem! Yes, the owner of the estate must have a harem upstairs. Men in the Ottoman Empire took a lot of women. They locked them somewhere, would come to them, and then go.*

One day she asked Mirna, "Is there a harem on the second floor?"

Mirna almost dropped the plate she was carrying.

"What kind of an idea is that?" she reproached her. "You can't talk about such things."

Nastya didn't talk about it again. However, she thought she was onto something with solving the mystery of what was on the second floor. Those who went upstairs had access to the lord's bed. Dear mother... When she thought of it, she felt a burning red blush.

She wondered how many women he had. Were they beautiful? Did it mean that since she couldn't go upstairs, they couldn't come down? Had they been imprisoned there?

So, one day when Mirna said, "Come on, let's go upstairs," Nastya was very surprised.

"But I'm not allowed."

"You are now."

They stood in front of a pair of large, white double-leafed doors. Mirna took in her hand a bunch of keys, which she had strapped to her belt, then took one key off and opened the door.

In one instant, Nastya was in a panic. *We are entering the harem!* A cold shiver went through her. Her heart resembled a bird trapped in a cage, flapping its wings – it beat so strong and fast. Sweet Jesus! They will lock me up in the harem! But... But I'm too young! "What will we do upstairs?" she asked in horror.

"The Lord wants to see you, Nastya."

Mirna's voice echoed in her ears. *The Lord wants to see you. The Lord wants... The Lord...*

She turned her head away, afraid to look. She lost all sympathy and trust she had for Mirna. The woman had set a trap for her, played cat and mouse with her. *So that was the reason she looked after me,* thought the girl. *Of course! Why didn't I realize? It is easy to trap such a young country girl and prepare her for such a man.*

For months, Mirna had taught her proper behavior, good manners, and showed her how to behave – not like a maid, but rather like a lady.

"Sit down like this, Nastya... And you should get up like this... That's how to hold a fork... Eat with your mouth closed... do not mumble... bravo, that's right... you catch things quickly... but there are still a lot of things I have to teach you."

Of course, there were still many other things. She hasn't yet shown me how to do 'it'!

Fear rapidly grew in her.

Or maybe that was just what the lord was supposed to teach me? So, that's what Mirna meant by saying that everything had its due time. And it was now that time. The man waited for her in one of the rooms at the end of the dark corridor which she now stood in.

She realized that she didn't at all want to see the place she had been so curious about for so many months. She thought about running away. Well, but where would she escape to?

"Come on, Nastya, go. You have been tormenting me for months. What are you waiting for...? Go up the stairs. You can't make the lord wait. It's a shame."

"What shall I do there?" she asked without looking at the woman. But Mirna grasped her chin and turned her head toward herself. She looked the girl carefully in the eyes.

Nastya tried to look away. *Again, with these false looks,* she thought. *How can such a fantastic, friendly person suddenly become so evil just like that?*

"Nastya. Look at me."

She glanced at Mirna.

Mirna noticed the fear in the girl's eyes. Nastya almost fainted.

Mirna didn't need much time to understand what its cause was. She laughed. "There's nothing to be afraid of," she said. "I will dust. And you will help me. Then the lord will have the opportunity to see you. Maybe he'll ask you something. But remember not to speak without permission." She looked carefully at Nastya to check if she'd managed to get rid of the fear visible in the girl's eyes. "Just don't look at him as if he were your enemy, the way you are looking at me right now. Come on, go in."

The hallway was bright. There was no one there but them. Silence.

Where were the women, then? Mirna turned to the room in front of them. She knocked several times and waited, then she gently opened the door. She moved to the side and let Nastya in.

The lord was there. He didn't even look at them.

As soon as Nastya saw his huge figure, she was frightened almost to death. *Are all the Turks so big?* She shuddered. Weren't there any men with a finer structure here? Kemal was like this. Of course, compared to the lord, he was a slim man, but he was still definitely on the larger side. Master Ibrahim, whose name she heard several times a day and whom she had only now the opportunity to see, was completely different. He was so huge that everyone who worked at the estate knew where their master was at any given moment. As he stood up and began to move, the walls trembled.

The giant sat with his legs crossed on a low cedar seat covered with a rug.

Nastya didn't step away from Mirna and pretended to dust. But her thoughts circled around the lord. He had terrifyingly large hands – but his eyes seemed to look friendly. *He doesn't look like a bad guy,* she thought. Even the terrifying tar-black beard was unable to change his gaze. He tried not to show it, but he also followed every move of the new girl.

Clink... clink... clink.

Sometimes the sounds could be distinguished, one clink after another. Sometimes they accelerated so that they merged together.

Clink, clink, clink, clink!

And then they slowed down again.

Clink... clink... clink.

Nastya realized that she liked the sound. It was also possible that every clink slowly killed the fear in her. The clinks of the tespih, her Master's Muslim prayer string with it's 33 beads, seemed to her a harmony, giving rhythm to the life at the top of a mountain.

"Is that the new girl they bought at Aidipsos?"

Mother of God... Was that the Lord's voice? She was surprised that the voice of the giant man, from whom she expected a thick, thundering voice, was so delicate – all kind of surprises.

Mirna caught her wrist and led her in front of the lord.

"Yes, sir," she said, not letting go of the girl's wrist and forcing her to bow.

"When did they bring her?"

"Over six months ago."

"Has she learned anything?"

Nastya shuddered. *Like what?!* she cried in her mind. *What was I supposed to learn?* Out of the corner of her eye, she glanced at Mirna. She talked with the lord without lowering her head. Nastya was about to straighten up, but the woman felt it and tugged at her wrist – so she bowed down again.

"She's learned a lot of things, sir. She is smart. All I have to do is show her something just once, and she already knows all about it. I took her in with me so that the other girls wouldn't tease her."

"You did well. She's still young."

There was silence.

"How old is she?"

"She said she is thirteen, sir."

"Ah!" came out of the Lord's mouth, hidden somewhere between the lush beard and the mustache. "She's still a child. It's a sin."

Now I will surely look, Nastya promised to herself in her spirit. *Enough of this looking away. After all, he won't punish me with death just because I looked at him.*

So, she did. She looked up. She glanced at him.

His head was huge, but he had no hair on his head. A wide forehead, and dark brows that were so close together that they almost joined. Eyes almost as black as the eyebrows. The mustache and the beard had started to turn gray here and there. She stopped her eyes on the man's hand which rested on his knee, in with he moved the tespih with large beads, once up, once down. She was interested in something about how the big, heavy fingers moved around the beads. She couldn't believe that such huge hands could look so gentle. But that's how it was.

The fingers began to move again. One bead entangled in a string and struck another one.

Clink...

"Allah protect me," Master Ibrahim muttered. "What's your name, girl?"

"Anastasia, sir."

"Where do you come from?"

"From the Island of Milos."

Although a beard covered almost his whole face, Nastya noticed an expression of surprise on it. "From the Island of Milos?" he wondered softly.

"So far, our people have not gone to the Aegean islands, but... Eh. Apparently, it was bound to happen. The days have come that the prices have doubled. It seems that money is becoming more important than honor... They've started kidnapping children."

"She wasn't kidnapped by our people," Mirna interrupted. "She was abducted by people from her own island."

"Yes?" There was relief in the man's voice. "I'm sorry," he continued. "Our people, since the times of Sultan Mehmed the Conqueror, have not harmed the people of the islands..." He turned and looked at her. "Especially children."

Nastya felt herself boiling with anger. She couldn't hold her tongue behind her teeth. As usual.

"These were your people," she began, clearly uttering every syllable, "that kidnapped me and my companions from our people. They killed everyone. They took us to the slave market..."

She didn't finish. Mirna, trying not to be noticed by the master, grabbed the girl by the arm and squeezed it tight.

"I see," the man said. "I see, girl." He lowered his head in pain.

You are no different from these robbers, Ibrahim Karayelzade, she reviled him in her thoughts. *They kidnap and take us to the market, but you buy, counting the right amount of money. Wasn't it you who ordered your people to bring the girl you called a child to the property?*

"Fine," said Master Ibrahim and straightened up. His voice sounded strong as if he'd made a decision. Nastya noticed a wrinkle on his broad forehead. *Was it there just a moment ago?* She didn't know the answer.

"Let the girl stay with you, Mirna. Teach her everything. Later, she will begin to come upstairs. She will serve here."

Nastya felt her legs tremble with fear. What did it mean that she would serve upstairs?

When Mirna pulled her arms and led her to the door, she looked at the man for the last time. If Master Ibrahim hadn't turned toward the window at that moment, he would surely have seen fear and hatred in the girl's eyes.

She will serve here.

What kind of service was it supposed to be? When the woman pulled her toward the doors of the room, she thought she had been right to have doubts. *Dusting. And I was supposed to help. What a lie.* She let herself be caught.

When they reached the stairs, she managed to free her wrist from Mirna's hold.

"Nastya, what's going on? I was dying with the fear that the lord would realize..."

"You were lying. From the very beginning..."

Mirna put her finger to her lips with fear, "Shhh... don't yell. He will hear us..."

Nastya lowered her voice and continued, "You were lying from the beginning... And I trusted you. Wipe the dust, huh? You made it up just to get me to the harem later, isn't it true?"

"To the harem?"

"Well, to the harem... Me..."

"For God's sake, Nastya, speak quieter. He'll hear..."

"Let him hear!" Suddenly, tears began to flow down her cheeks. "I was going to learn what the rules were in this property, and I was also to be a lady... He just gave away his lie. Teach her everything. Then she will come upstairs. She will serve here. What will you teach me?"

She couldn't finish. Mirna made such a quick move that the girl couldn't react.

"Harem, right?" she snapped. "Now I will take you to the harem; you will see!"

"Let go of me!" Nastya tried to free herself from the grasp.

"Come!" Mirna struggled with Nastya.

"Where do you want to take me?"

"To the harem!"

All of Nastya's efforts were unsuccessful. She couldn't resist the strong Serbian, and Mirna pulled her up to the last room in the corridor.

"Let me go!" Nastya whined. She stopped when she suddenly heard muffled voices coming from behind the door. First, it was a voice of a woman. She probably belonged to the harem. Soon she was going to be one of them. The Lord's voice resounded in her ears again, 'Teach her everything. Later she will come upstairs. She will serve here.' It was behind that door that she would serve. This was where the giant's bed was located. God!

Suddenly, a delicate, affectionate, yet emotionally charged voice came from behind the door. A high feminine voice. One of the women was singing. Struggling with the sobs that shook her body, Nastya raised her ears. What a beautiful voice it was. The woman, whose voice was so delightful, had to be beautiful. She couldn't understand the lyrics, but the moving, calm melody immediately calmed her down.

Mirna gently knocked on the door, then opened it slightly. She pushed the girl toward the crack at the door. "Go in," she whispered. "See what the harem looks like!"

She couldn't believe her eyes. She counted at least six women in the room.

One was looking for something in the cabinet, another worked, another sat somewhere in the corner. Exactly opposite the door was a window that stretched almost from the floor to the ceiling. Despite the grille covering its lower part, daylight came through the upper part, decorated with colored glass, creating red, purple, green, and yellow spots on the floor and throughout the room.

Right next to the window there was the largest bed Nastya had ever seen. An angel with silver hair laid in it.

Yes, she could be an angel, she thought. In order to feel comfortable in a reclining position, she had ordered others to put several pillows under her back. Thick – although unhealthy looking – hair was gathered on one side and spread on the pillow. Despite the light coming into the room, she looked pale. Nastya wasn't able to determine her age. Was she elderly? Not really. Young? Not quite, either. But it was certain that she was as beautiful as an angel. She couldn't see her eyes. They were closed. Either she slept, or she listened with her eyes closed to the song sung in the beautiful voice by a girl who sat at the bedside.

"So?" Mirna whispered. "Have you had enough of watching the harem?"

She pulled her out of the room and closed the door behind her. The beautiful voice stayed behind the door. Nastya couldn't speak at first.

"Who is she?" she asked quietly. "The woman lying in bed?"

"Ibrahim Karayelzade's lady."

"His lady? What does it mean?"

"His wife. Sick... or rather paralyzed. These women take care of her."

Nastya regretted her words so terribly. She was ashamed.

"Poor thing," Mirna whispered. "It's been four years that she has been in that state."

"The lord has no other women?"

"No. Why would he? He is madly in love with his wife."

Nastya felt hidden jealousy in her voice. It was obvious that Mirna was as madly in love with him as he was with his wife.

"Every night," Mirna continued, "Master Ibrahim goes to her room. He spends hours by her side. He talks to her... We don't know if she hears or understands anything, but he talks as if she understands everything."

"What does he do later?"

The woman was surprised at this question. "What should he do? He goes to his room and goes to bed."

"Does it mean he doesn't have a harem?"

"Akinji lords cannot have a harem," Mirna muttered.

"Why?"

"They pass their lives on horseback, that's why. Our Lord is one of the most famous Ottoman Akinji. He is Ibrahim Karayelzade."

"Karayel... what?"

"He comes from a long line of Akinjis. Their nickname is Karayelzade. Both the grandfather and father of Master Ibrahim were Akinji. His grandfather was like the northwest wind – that's what people say. That is why his children and later grandchildren were nicknamed Karayelzade, which means son of the northwest wind. Master Ibrahim is just as scary as this strong wind. Forget the wind... my lord, riding a horse, resembles a cyclone! You blink, and he's already left the courtyard of the property, rushing down the road to the mountains, and a ton of dust rises behind the horse."

The woman went silent. Nastya realized that when Mirna talked about Master Ibrahim she did so with a spark in her eye, and she tried to make her feel the same way. Mirna burned for him.

So, this is what love looks like... Nastya thought. *It hurts rather than brings happiness. When you have no hope for fulfillment, you burn.*

Mirna had fallen in love with the sun. Was that possible? What could she hope for?

She was the superior of the servants, but she was one of them, anyway. Ibrahim Karayelzade wouldn't look at her.

Anastasia, Nastya... Who are you? she asked herself. *You are only a wretched slave. An ugly cleaning lady waiting by the door. A freckled stable boy. A blacksmith's son. This is your future. Don't even look at the stars, the sun.* At this point, she made a decision – she will not burn like Mirna. Never, never!

She grabbed Mirna's hand and smiled.

"Come on," she whispered. "Let's go. Teach me everything, sister."

On some days, the tap of horseshoes would suddenly clatter into the courtyard. Master Ibrahim would immediately leave, welcome the guests, and later invite them to his room where they'd talk for hours.

Nastya, who entered the room from time to time to bring refreshments, always tried to eavesdrop, even though as soon as she opened the door all of them would suddenly go silent. However, she did manage to catch a few sentences now and then.

"Our business is not going well, gentlemen."

"The capital is meddling in our affairs again."

"The society is getting poorer."

"They take bribes and disappear."

There were also several names on their lips. They mentioned Sultan Mehmed. And a woman: Safiye... Nastya heard this name very often. But neither Master Ibrahim nor his guests liked this woman.

Ever since she could go upstairs, she became like a watchdog. She liked the long hours of waiting in the scary, mysterious corridor, lightly lit by the flickering candle flames. She could stay alone with herself. The darkness seemed to open its arms so that she could solve the problem of irritation that she had felt recently – but didn't know what she was dealing with or why she felt that way.

She wanted to blow out the candles and dive into the darkness like in the dark sea.

One night, she awoke full of fear. She was surprised why she hadn't seen it until now. She took out a crucifix. It was only now that she realized that when she was ripping Cyprian's ear when he tried to touch her, she'd felt nothing. Later, when she pushed aside the limp body of the attacker – she'd also felt nothing. Nor when the coachman, pierced by an arrow, fell near her feet. When the other girls were screaming their heads off, she just watched. She wasn't terrified, not even for a moment. She didn't feel even the tiniest repulsion as she looked at the lifeless bodies. Eleni vomited immediately. Helena was fine only until she got out of the wagon.

And Nastya – well, she'd just stood impassively and stared at the corpses. It was as if something had left her. As if she'd lost something irrevocably. Compassion had died in her. No, no – maybe all her feelings had died.

Or maybe she sinned?

That was when she got scared. This question stuck in her mind all day. She hadn't been to church for a year.

One morning she ran to Mirna. "Sister, I..."

Mirna was all red with anger. "I'm going crazy because of them... I'm gonna lose my mind!" she shouted. She turned to the other side. "You can be happy that Nastya has come. Otherwise, you would be much less lucky. Go on, everyone to their duties."

The servants scattered, looking gratefully at Nastya.

"Yes? You need something upstairs?"

"I want to go to church, sister!"

The woman threw the cloth she held in her hand and stared at it. She was silent for a moment. Later, she picked the cloth back up, squeezed it, and started to straighten it.

"Is it forbidden?"

"Nooo... You saw it, too. Everybody goes freely to the church near the bazaar."

"We'll go together, sister."

Mirna hesitated. "I converted to Islam, Nastya," she said.

What? When? Nastya shuddered. *She became a dissenter! Mirna left our religion.*

"Oh, poor sister, who knows how much they tortured you to make you convert to their religion."

"What tortures? None of those things." Mirna tried to smile. "I wanted it myself. Islam has greatly influenced me. That's all. I thought about it for a long time."

Nastya understood that she had wasted her breath for nothing. She would never understand this decision.

"I'll tell them to assign someone to you," Mirna said.

Nastya started to walk toward the door, her feet stomping loudly on the floor. "I don't need you to. I know the way to God." She opened the door and crossed the doorway. "I will also pray for God to forgive you!"

Now Nastya felt she'd lost something. She thought that nothing would be the same between them like before. She was the daughter of Aziz Peder Kostas Vasiliadis. She couldn't be friends with a dissenter.

The church was small but very nice and clean. It was on a tiny hill with fifteen steps that led to it.

Nastya knelt down before the altar and lowered her head. She didn't know how long she knelt there, but when she got up, she felt light and as free as a bird. She was rid of all fear, anxiety, and longing. She looked at the Virgin Mary next to the altar for the first time.

"Our Divine Mother..." she whispered. "Help me. Protect me."

She couldn't forget her memory of the bloody bodies... the view of which had driven her to this madness. On top of this, there were her mixed feelings about Mirna. She couldn't admit it even to herself, but she'd looked at her as at an enemy. The worst thing was that Nastya knew she was wrong. How could she become an enemy of a woman who had shown her so much love and had done so much for her?

But she renounced her faith... she's now a Muslim, she thought.

Was it really so? Maybe it was the master who forced her to change her faith. Maybe they'd tormented her, and she doesn't want it to come to light. Perhaps they'd threatened to kill her? She couldn't confess the truth out of fear.

I heard it myself. She wanted it. She herself wanted to leave God. She became a heretic. A heretic! The thoughts spun in Nastya's head. If she weren't in the holy place, she would probably have silenced the voice in her head.

Quiet! Her heart and mind rebelled at the thought that Mirna had become an enemy. She began to cry. She didn't try to stop the tears. Maybe the tears that flowed down her cheeks would take with them the feelings of hostility toward Mirna, that had sprouted in Nastya. She looked at the Virgin Mary with teary eyes.

"Show me the way, Holy Mother," she whispered. "From that terrible day, strange things have happened to me, I know. From the day I was kidnapped by robbers, something has been slowly dying inside me, but also something is being born. I feel my heart is cooling, Mother. A different 'me' is coming into the world."

She flinched at the sound of footsteps. The priest's helper lit the candles on the altar.

Nastya straightened up. She wiped the tears from her cheeks with the back of her hand. For perhaps the last time, she took out her crucifix and headed for the door. Maybe she would never go to church again. Who knows?

When she'd entered the church, it was still daylight. Now the foggy navy blue of the evening sky had begun to envelop Kumanovo. Candles and lanterns were lit on the second floor of the Karayelzade Estate on the opposite hill. It was Master Ibrahim's wife's room.

I'm late, Nadia thought. Instead of the bazaar, she headed straight to the stone stairs on the slope. The streets were still crowded. People heading home, who decided to buy something on the way, haggled with the sellers. The villagers were reluctant to return home with their merchandise, so they screamed, trying to sell the last of their goods.

As Nastya passed a blind beggar sitting on the last step, he turned to her.

"You are her."

"Her? Who?"

"Just her," the man said without raising his head. "The Queen."

Nastya was completely surprised.

"The queen?" It was so absurd that it didn't even occur to her to laugh. Every beggar had a certain method of 'hunting.' Apparently, this was his. The three coins that

Mirna had given her a few weeks earlier, and which she was supposed to spend on donations, were still in her pockets. She took one of them and dropped it into the box in front of the man.

The beggar immediately took the money into his hand. He raised his head and looked at Nastya with narrowed eyes.

"May you have luck in life, beautiful Queen," he said.

"Queen?"

"Yes," said the man, who kept blinking. "Thank you, beautiful Queen."

This time, she couldn't refrain from laughing. "I thought you were only pretending to be blind, beggar. But you really do not see. Otherwise, you wouldn't call a servant a queen."

The man's face grimaced. "But you will become one."

"What? Aren't you ashamed to say lies, sitting right in front of the House of God?" Nastya snorted.

"It is not a sin to tell what is certain to happen."

Oh, what rubbish this beggar is saying, she thought. But still, she had a whirl in her head. *Ha, ha, Queen!* She sighed. *The Queen of servants!*

Despite it all, she liked the fact that someone called her a queen. He'd won her sentiments that way. She put her hand in her camisole's pocket. She found the other two coins, but she didn't throw them. She leaned over the man and put them in front of him.

"You are a liar and blind. I am a slave and a maid. By what miracle could I become a queen? And how do you know I'm beautiful?"

The beggar suddenly opened his eyes wide, which he'd had closed from time to time before. He grinned in a smile. He winked. Then he closed his eyes again.

"Your Majesty, when I see a beautiful woman, my eyes open immediately."

A queen then? And a beautiful one at that!

That night, when she got back from the church, and for a few more nights when she waited, sitting on the mattress at the door of the lady's room, she thought of the words of the beggar. *Where did he get this 'queen' nonsense from?*

Don't be silly, Nastya, she reasoned to herself. *Who knows to how many women he's said exactly the same thing to. He probably tells the men they will someday be kings.*

But it should be like that. In order to get some money, he had to feed their pride.

And her answer? How should this be assessed? 'You really are blind. Otherwise, you wouldn't call a servant a queen.' The beggar didn't care about her sharp words and answered without hesitation:

"But you will become one."

This was certainly one of his tricks. *Of course,* said the voice of reason. *Certainly, a trick. Well, he caught a wise girl like you. He won three coins. Liar.*

That was it.

Still, Nastya liked it. "The queen, right?" She spoke to herself. "He even addressed me as 'Your Majesty' and 'beautiful Queen.'"

One morning, when Nastya, was in the lady's room, she looked at her own reflection, in the mirror with a silver handle, that lay on the table. She was beautiful. That she could be sure of. She knew that the suffering, the despair, and the anguish she'd experienced during the abduction had made her lose something irretrievably, but in spite of this, the girl who looked back at her in the mirror was still very, very beautiful.

As she looked at her reflection in the mirror, she imagined she had a crown on her head.

"Your Highness. You are beautiful; a Queen."

She looked at herself for a long time. Did the crown fit her? Of course!

Once, Nastya's grandfather summoned all the children from the area and told them the story of Queen Theodora, the beautiful and wise consort of Emperor Justinian.

"The queen had such a beautiful crown on her head," he said, "that when she put it on her head at night, everyone in the Byzantine Empire thought the sun was rising. Over the course of the day, the shine of Theodora's crown embarrassed the sun, which hid behind the clouds."

Nastya dreamed of such a crown. About a crown that would shame the sun!

She put the mirror back on the table. She turned back. As she walked toward the basket in which Master Ibrahim's paralyzed wife's undergarments were kept, she thought, *I'm not crazy. I am a queen. The Queen of Servants, who brings dirty clothes to the laundry!*

Two days later, she went with Mirna to the bazaar. There was a distance between them now that both tried to hide. Nastya was embarrassed that she had hurt her sister Mirna, whom she loved and felt obligated to. She also thought Mirna was ashamed of straying from the path leading to God. At least, she would like that to be so. But Mirna didn't make such an impression at all.

When Mirna was shopping, Nastya looked for the beggar. He wasn't sitting on the stairs. She thought maybe this time he'd sit somewhere else, but he wasn't anywhere.

The next day, she went to church again, and again, she didn't find him on the stone stairs.

On Sunday, this time with the consent of the master, she set out for church. She was sure she would meet him that day. Of course, on Sunday, the church would be crowded. It was a good time for beggars to collect money, calling everybody queens and kings.

But he wasn't there.

After the Mass finished, she left. She looked around for him, but she didn't notice anything. Eventually, she walked over to a man who had set up a little stall at one of the steps and sold toys. She saw him here sometimes. He had to know something about the blind beggar.

"Yyy..." she began. "I've been looking for a blind beggar on these stairs for a few days. Is he ill?"

"Blind?" questioned the vendor.

"Yes. Blind... I mean, a beggar."

"A beggar?" asked the stunned seller. His facial expression spoke for itself, and Nastya understood that he was really surprised.

"Yes... He sits on the last step and asks the passersby for money."

The toy seller shrugged.

"I haven't seen either a blind man or a beggar. Come on, go away from here. I'm losing customers because of you."

Now she stood stunned. He told the truth and hadn't seen him.

But I saw you both on these stairs... she thought. The toy vendor had been on the edge of the third step. And the blind beggar sat in the middle of the lowest step.

When Nastya descended the stairs, she had a huge muddle in her head. *Maybe it was a dream? Did I imagine it that someone called me a beautiful queen?*

In her life, there were no emotions, no colors, no changes. After all, what could happen in the life of the maid other than the ordinary everyday work?

But it happened. Kumanovo suddenly came to life. A huge cloud of dust rose from the hill opposite the Karayelzade Estate.

Master Ibrahim hadn't been at the estate for several months, so Nastya thought he was coming back, but so far, his return had never aroused such excitement. A group of his people had never stirred up so much dust on the road. The sky and earth mixed with each other, and dust covered the surrounding area like a cloud. It even absorbed the pine forest on the hill. The cloud approached them. Later, the noise and the clatter of the horse's hooves could be heard.

Nastya ran to the window that overlooked the courtyard. *My God, the end of the world is coming*, she thought. Downstairs, she saw Mirna run to meet the newcomers.

"What's going on?" she called to someone. "What's the buzz?"

"Soldiers." Then the man ran to the entrance without further explanation. He tried to hastily close the great double-winged gate, but he couldn't manage to do it. "Hey, look here! Make somebody come and help me. Let's close it, or the looters will get inside the estate."

"Get somebody go to the bazaar!" Mirna shouted. "We need to find out what's going on."

One of the men ran to the street.

Nastya ran downstairs. "What's going on, sister?" she asked Mirna anxiously.

"Soldiers. Come with me. We will see everything better from the window overlooking the street."

So, they did. Horsemen were coming.

"It's our people," Mirna whispered.

How much Nastya hated that word. 'Ours?' Meaning who? Christians or Ottoman soldiers?

"Janissaries. Spahis," the woman whispered as if she'd heard the girl's thoughts.

Turkish infantry and cavalry, Nastya translated to herself.

Nastya didn't know who was more tired, the horses or the riders. They were all dirty. Black beards and mustaches already covered their faces, which were now also covered with dark dust. Then she saw the others. The wounded – some had bandaged arms or legs, other heads. Some had their whole chests was wrapped in bandages. Blood soaked through all layers of material. Their galligaskins were jagged, and bloodied wounds could be seen through the holes. They looked as if they were ashamed of the curious crowd who began to gather on both sides of the street.

"They were defeated..." Mirna moaned, and she covered her mouth with her hand fearfully.

So, this was the way a defeated army looked.

Nastya suddenly understood what that meant. Since they were defeated, ours won.

The war was won by Christian soldiers. Good, but why wasn't she happy? Why she didn't shout to upset Mirna, 'Hurrrraaay! Our soldiers won, your men were defeated.'

There were also carts seen moving among the horses. Their wheels rattled over sharp stones, and one could hear their creaking. Each cart was full of wounded soldiers.

Finally, at the back walked the infantry. Their condition seemed to be even poorer than the cavalry going in front. Some of them, exhausted, leaned on their companions and thus tried to move forward. It was an image of despair.

Still further behind them, huge horses and oxen pulled cannons. The oxen, as if they also felt the pain of failure, drew the guns attached to them, sadly shaking their heads side to side.

The servant, whom Mirna had sent for reconnaissance, brought the news an hour later.

"The military is retreating," he said. People came over and encircled him, waiting for information. "The heretics of Nemçe, which they call Austria, occupied two castles. The Grand Vizier left us and escaped – one of the wounded told me. Only they had been saved. The rest died."

Nastya asked the question at that moment, which everyone had in their mind, but no one had dared speak.

"What about our master? What about..."

She didn't finish. Mirna's eyes silenced her like a knife.

Master Ibrahim returned two days later, during the afternoon ezan. His condition wasn't very different from the rest of the army that had passed by. Without speaking to anyone, he went upstairs and locked himself in his room. Mirna and Nastya immediately prepared something to eat and drink and ran upstairs. The door was locked.

Mirna knocked. After she tapped the third time, they heard a tired voice:

"What is it?"

"We brought food, sir. A little soup..."

"Put it in front of the door."

So, they did. But the door didn't open. The tray with food stood on the floor all day.

At sunrise, a week later, hooves could be heard in the courtyard again. Everyone at the property was excited. Was it the invincible Austrian army this time, in pursuit of the defeated Ottoman army? Nastya, along with Mirna, stood by the window that overlooked the courtyard.

Six horsemen arrived. When the pennants fluttering on the sticks held up by the first riders grew visible, all the grooms began to rush toward the courtyard. Several people caught the reins of the mount that stopped first. One of the grooms helped the man get down off the horse.

Someone from below shouted, "Wake up the master and pass him the message!"

Nastya noticed that the soldiers arriving weren't in such a state as those who had passed through the town a week before.

"Who is he, sister?" she asked Mirna.

"It's the Beylerbey, the Provincial Governor of the Ottoman Empire!" she replied. "He's never come here personally before. The Beylerbey of the Rumelia province. They call him Çivici Pasha. The groom is right; we should immediately notify the master."

But there was no need for that. Master Ibrahim's had already opened his door.

"Mirna!" he cried out. "Before I finish dressing, run and open the door at the stairs."

Nastya also started to run.

"Give the news to the kitchen!" the master shouted behind them. "Let them prepare a meal worthy of pasha. At least you won't let me down in these difficult and sad days."

They prepared a large table in the master's room almost at the speed of light.

The visiting beylerbey was almost as huge as the owner of the property, and even when he sat down at the table and removed the kavuk – his turban-like headgear that Ottoman dignitaries always wore – from his head, he didn't lose a touch of his seriousness and majesty.

They both had sullen faces and wrinkled brows.

The first words that Nastya managed to hear didn't sound comforting:

"The news is not good, Ibrahim. As if the defeat on the Austrian front wasn't enough, it's not good in the capital, either."

As she entered and left the room, she also heard:

"When Vizier Yemişçi Hasan Pasha left the army under the command of Lal Mehmed Pasha and fled to the capital, everything got complicated. Sultan Mehmed has given him a death sentence."

"Did he make a mistake? After all, he left the soldiers on the battlefield and escaped."

"Of course, he was right. But if you want to know my opinion, it wasn't the Sultan who issued that death sentence, but the Valide Sultan. You know that Safiye Valide can't stand Yemişçi Pasha.

That woman again, thought Nastya, leaving the room. *People are talking about her again*.

Master Ibrahim nodded in agreement.

"But he got used to running away, Ibrahim. The spahis, despite their victory in the skirmish, had to retreat to escort him. He ordered the soldiers in the harbor to escort him all the way to the Suleiman mosque. This time, the Sultan was frightened and also sentenced to death the Kaymakam Mahmut Pasha. He also removed Shaykh al-Islām Sunullah Efendi."

Nastya didn't know who a Kaymakam was, but later found out that he was the official who stood in for the Grand Vizier during his absence, due to illness, travel or during the intervals between the dismissal of one and the appointment of another.

"What does Shaykh al-Islām have to do with it all?"

The beylerbey laughed sadly. "He did not resist when the soldiers gathered in the courtyard of the mosque."

He stopped and took a chicken leg from his plate. He drank ajran poured into a bowl decorated with colorful stones before he continued:

"They closed the gates of the capital. The leader of the janissaries, Ferhad Aga, urged Yemişçi Pasha to take him down, and attacked Kurşunlu Han, where the spahis gathered."

"Many of them lost their lives there."

"May they rest in peace. That news made me very sad."

"Wait, that's not all yet... Wasn't it the Sultan Mehmed who agreed to meet these thugs Poyraz Osman and Öküz Mehmed, and bargain with them?"

"He ordered to kill them both. Later, the Sultan sent spahis to kill Yemişçi Hasan Pasha and ordered their leader

Hüseyin to report to him. Poor Hüseyin thought the Sultan would issue a new order. He waited patiently when the executioners entered. They strangled him. Yemişçi Hasan Pasha once again appropriated all power."

"Unbelievable, Pasha. How is that possible at all?"

"It happened, unfortunately. This fugitive, Yemişçi, has ordered his men to hang all his enemies. I won't be surprised when my turn also comes."

"Don't say that. What kind of idea is that? Who would raise a hand to Çivici Pasha?"

"Then go and convince Yemişçi Pasha. The people I sent to find out about the situation in the city say he has lost his mind completely. We don't know who'll be next."

The beylerbey put his hands on his belly to show that he was full, and said, "May Allah make your lands fertile, Ibrahim. Delicious food and the opportunity to talk honestly made my soul feel a little better."

"What can I say, Pasha. May Allah have pity on the Ottoman Empire, and on its people. Just give your order, and I will go to the capital. I will take the life of this traitor Yemişçi Pasha, such is my great resentment toward him. I can't forgive him for having left us in the face of danger. He wasn't afraid of the subjects... will he not fear Allah, either? Didn't he think that when hundreds of men were dying on his orders, the army would scatter when he left the battlefield? Just give your word. I will set off immediately to take his life. And then let happen whatever is to happen."

"Hold on, Karayel," the beylerbey said. "Not only you resent him. Those who brought the news also say that Safiye Valide is just waiting for the opportunity, too. Apparently, she said to the Sultan in front of the mass of the subjects, 'The Sultan, who tramples his own orders, will be trampled down himself one day. While Yemişçi Hasan Pasha is alive, no one will look at you as the ruler.'"

The man paused for a moment.

"Well, that's the situation," he continued. "I'm afraid that until we get rid of him, the Ottoman Empire will not be strong enough. The Sultan is not himself. Since even his mother thinks so... I will do it."

"But Pasha..."

As if he didn't hear him, Pasha nodded and continued:

"I swear to Allah, Karayel, I will kill him... But you hold for a while. We will see what happens, what we will hear yet."

Nastya's heart caught in her throat. She couldn't believe what she had just heard. In what world did they live? Their lives were full of competing sultans, queens, viziers, and rulers who, without mercy, just like that, could sentence someone to death.

They led a fabulous life. These realities were addictive. But also, scary. Power and death went shoulder-to-shoulder. People who live in glamor and splendor can lose their lives in an instant.

When Nastya served the beylerbey a bowl with hot water and rose petals so that he could wash his hands, her mind was in the new world she had just discovered. It was a scary world from which she should stay away. Dangerous. Sinister.

Her world wasn't full of glory or rich, unlike their world. Up until the time she was abducted, there were only God and servants in the reality she had lived in. They were called villagers, workers, slaves, and servants. To fill the pots, everyone was forced to work. In the world from which she came, there were also the stories grandparents and grandmothers used to tell children gathered around the stove on winter evenings, about kings, queens, and palaces. But here, in the world on whose shore she had been thrown, she learned that everything she believed belonged only in the stories, really did exist.

It surprised her most that the two completely different worlds, like black and white, could exist next to each other. How come she hadn't noticed that until now?

This should be a new story, full of heroes and traitors. The two men who sat at the table were part of it. And at the end of the story, they were about to disappear.

And Nastya would go back to her life.

That night, while Nastya guarded Master Ibrahim's wife's door, she thought about what she had heard. About the horrible realities, these people lived. There was always someone lying in wait to take their life – because there were dangers and enemies everywhere – they couldn't trust anyone. Of course, no one trusted them, either. Everyone could count only on himself.

When she felt her eyelids close involuntarily, she shuddered. Her eyes widened when a question appeared in her head.

Was there any passage between the world of slaves and the world of queens?

Nastya held her breath. She remembered the words of the blind beggar. Slowly, a smile appeared on her face.

"A queen then, right?" she whispered. She looked down the corridor, which looked like a long tunnel in the light of the slowly dying candle. *What seed have you put inside my head?* she thought.

Chapter Five

Istanbul, the Palace of Siyavuş Pasha
December 18, 1603

"The Sultan is dying."

"Spit those words out. Allah forbid."

"Allah doesn't defend killers, Hodja Efendi. Am I wrong?"

"Not at all, Kasim Pasha."

The elderly man sat down comfortably on the ottoman. "I know, what I know," he said. "Sultan Mehmed won't get out of bed anymore, because he was cursed."

A young man sat next to a brass stove in the middle of the room. "Allah protects me," he said calmly. "It's a sin. Don't say that, Kasim. You must not invoke the curse," he nodded as if approving his own words. He grabbed one of the coals from the stove with tongs, blew the ash off it, placed it next to his lips, and blowing on it, lit it up. A few sparks fell from the charcoal, so he blew on it more and more until it glowed.

"Well, what was I supposed to say, Hodja Efendi?"

The man flinched. "Just don't say that, Kasim Pasha. What is left for us? Since the Sultan has dismissed us and has made Mustafa of Arabia, called Ebulmeyamin, the Shaykh al-Islām, I am just Sunullah." He suddenly fell silent and angrily nodded his head. "Do not say that, for Allah's sake. Someone might hear. Allah forbid... If you can't pronounce my name because of respect, it will be fine if you just say Sunullah Efendi."

Kasim Pasha nodded. It was obvious that what the man just said had entered his head through one ear, and left through the other.

"The damned throne, cursed throne," he muttered. "Didn't Sultan Mehmed give an order to strangle his nineteen siblings on the day he took the throne? There were small children among them. Isn't that a sin? Can the assassination of nineteen innocent people bring any good? It didn't. The empire hasn't been able to get rid of the curse from that day on."

Sunullah Efendi sighed. "What can you do? This is the order of the world... Sultan's ancestor is Mehmed the Conqueror..."

Kasim Pasha, who had been the vizier's special foreign diplomat with full powers to represent their government due to his participation in the Egyptian expedition of the Grand Vizier Yavuz Ali Pasha as a kaymakam, grew angry.

"Don't even try to mention his name along with the name Mehmed the Conqueror, Hodja Efendi. What can he owe to him? And leave the world order alone, too. Two hundred years ago, everything was different. Is it the same now? For Allah's sake, what world, what sort of order? Can there be any sort of order under the rule of a sultan who finds a thousand excuses not to go on an expedition?"

"You are unjust in your assessment," protested Sunullah Efendi. "I still remember the words of the Sultan that he said at the council meeting, 'From Osman to our great-grandfather Suleiman, all the sultans set out on the expeditions together with their army. This custom was discontinued by our grandfather Sultan Selim and our father, Murad. We made a mistake at the beginning that we didn't participate in the expedition, either. Our soldiers want to see us at their side. We have decided that we will also set off in the near future.' You were there too, Kasim Pasha. Didn't you hear what the Sultan said?"

"I heard it," the pasha snapped. "He had every word memorized – his mother made him do that. Later, she got up and tried to interject, but the Sultan shouted with anger, 'Valide, Valide!' As if he said to his mother, 'We are a family of sultans. If we don't fulfill our duties, on what purpose did we swear on that sword? The decision has been made, we will embark on an expedition. We can't sacrifice our country for the throne.' That's it. Or are you so naive that you have been cheated, Sunullah?"

Kasim Pasha stared at him and waited for him to say something, but Sunullah was silent. The sultan was still alive, and when the power in the country was stable, conversations in such a tone were dangerous. The walls had ears.

"But he kept his word," muttered Sunullah. "Together with the army, he set off on an expedition."

"Right, he set off," the pasha confirmed. "The army was defeated in Mezőkeresztes in two days. The dissenters took our banners and, showing their intimate places, started dancing like some women. While our soldiers were fleeing, cooks, grooms, and cleaners rushed at the enemy. They started fighting with whatever they could lay their hands on – axes, pokers, sticks. Thanks to that, the Sultan saved his own life, and we miraculously defeated the Austrian army. Otherwise, Sultan Mehmed would have either died there or been captured. Or he would have returned to the capital defeated."

He stopped for a moment and looked at the man sitting opposite. "Why?" he asked. He didn't give Sunullah a chance to answer. "It's all because of that curse. He had the viziers and advisers killed. It is certainly because of those crimes, Sunullah Efendi. The little Prince Cihangir, who, extending his hand to the executioner, said, 'Please, help yourself with some chestnuts,' brought about this curse. Because it couldn't be the mute executioner!"

Sunullah Efendi nodded, the sign that he agreed. He added, though, "But don't use that word anyway."

"The curse has been hanging over the capital for years. The Sultan spared only his sisters."

"The girls don't aspire to the throne."

"And do you aspire, Sunullah Efendi? Nothing else comes out of your mouth, except 'Allah' and 'Qur'an.' What did he want from you? You barely survived, too. Your daily prayers have protected you."

The man began to shudder at the memory of the days of fear when the Sultan removed him from the office of Shaykh al-Islām. Those moments when he hid in the pantry when horsemen arrived at the house, flashed before his eyes. Hadn't he had enough fear when he thought every time he heard the horses in the courtyard that soldiers were coming to take his life?

"Allah protects me," said Kasim Pasha, looking at the ceiling. "The horrors that he has done to so many people are not irrelevant. Have you forgotten, Efendi? When the army revolted and headed for the palace, what did the Sultan do? Didn't he soil the honor of the homeland by inviting those two rebels, Öküz Mehmed and Poyraz Osman, to the palace for a conversation? Wasn't it because of the slander of two thugs that he had innocent people killed? Can't that be the cause of these misfortunes?"

"You know that Yemişçi Hasan Pasha forced the Sultan to do most of these things, simply because he is a Vizier and thinks he has some power in the empire."

"Apparently he was tired of all this killing. He found someone even more bloodthirsty than himself. Sunullah, these two... You, too, were there... when after leaving from the council, they gave an order to kill Tirnakçi Hasan Pasha. You have seen everything with your own eyes. Has the empire seen such cruelty before?"

He didn't know what to say. After all, he couldn't say he hadn't seen anything. He moved his head. Ten assassins attacked Tirnakçi Hasan Pasha. The Sultan hadn't even left the council yet. One of them threw a loop around his neck, another pierced his stomach with a spear, the third cut his throat. But that wasn't enough – they then pushed the body down the stairs, kicked it, and wiped the blood from their hands with bits of fabric they had torn from his clothes.

"See, you too have nothing left to defend him. There hasn't been such a bloody ruler in the empire until now. But let's forget about it already, Hodja Efendi." He leaned towards Sunullah. "The last of his sins," he whispered, his face twisted in disgust, "being a killer of his subjects wasn't enough for him, he committed infanticide."

Sunullah's face turned pale. His heart almost jumped out of his chest when he learned that the Sultan had ordered the killing of Şehzade Mahmud. He looked around with fear.

Pasha nodded. *He's right to be afraid*, he thought. *The real cause of Şehzade Mahmud's murder was Safiye Valide.*

Şehzade Mahmud's only fault was that he was the son of the chief consort of Sultan Mehmed, Halime Haseki.

Safiye, whose original name was Sofia Baffo of Venice, envied Halime, whose name was Sirindella Violetta of Austria. She wanted revenge. There was no trick that Safiye wouldn't have imagined so that the throne wouldn't go to Halime's son, Mahmud. Slander, rumors, witchcraft, incitement – all of this with the help of Yemişçi Hasan Pasha made her succeed in persuading the Sultan to kill the prince.

Actually, right from the day Mehmed got on the throne, it wasn't sure who was in charge – he or his mother. The orders didn't come from the Sultan, but rather from his mother. The viziers said after the council "Our Sultan's mother has surpassed even Nurbanu Valide. Until now, the Ottoman Empire hasn't seen a sultan who would rule under such a great influence of his mother."

"If your head is still in place, Kasim, it's only because you are one step ahead of Safiye Valide in the competition with the Sultan," Kasim Pasha said, mostly to himself.

He was a wise man. Everyone said so. Through his spy networks, he watched India, Yemen, and Rumelia. He could do the impossible. Despite the incitement of the mother of Sultan Mehmed, he managed to twist him around his finger. *What will happen later isn't importan*t, he thought. The Sultan's days were numbered. The most important thing was to drop anchor in a safe place. But, in which harbor was he supposed to drop it, in the city where several heads fell every day?

Şehzade Mustafa or Şehzade Ahmed?

It is not a desire for power, but to survive, he thought to himself.

Kasim Pasha extended the tongs he held in his hand toward the stove. He made a movement as if scattering ash. Then he froze in place – it was certain he was thinking.

Sunullah Efendi knew how it was in the difficult days. "Hold the compass and the pliers well, Kasim!" the Pasha suddenly said.

Sunullah was surprised. "What pliers?" he muttered. "What is he talking about?" Then louder, "What was it, Kasim Pasha? Did you say 'pliers'? I don't understand."

But the Pasha's thoughts were elsewhere. He didn't hear the question. His eyes were fixed on the ashes. Sunullah realized it was some kind of message, but he couldn't decipher it. What could a compass mean?

Kasim Pasha scratched his head thoughtfully. If he doesn't stick to the compass, he'll be alone, he'll get lost. He didn't want to wonder about who would get the throne. How many nights had the question whirled in his head: *Why did Allah give me reason?*

Who could become the Sultan?

Mustafa was crazy. Although... it was said that he wished to take over the power, and only pretended so that his father wouldn't have him murdered.

Ahmed was still a child. As soon as he heard from someone that he was going to be the Sultan, he looked for a place to hide.

Actually, it didn't matter to him who would become the sultan. If he'd managed to stay alive and even became a kaymakam, it was only through politics. But times had changed. He couldn't continue to play this game. Everyone chose allies first and set the rules of the game later. You have to make wise choices. The possibilities were many. If you choose the wrong path, an executioner waits at its end.

He shouldn't ask himself who would be a better sultan... but what would be better for him?

He thought all the days and nights, pondered all the pros and cons, until one morning as he left his house, he thought: *Ahmed*.

This decision, however, wasn't caused by the expectation that the prince might be a much better ruler in the future, but by his knowledge of Safiye Valide's actions. He was sure she was preparing Ahmed to take the throne. A few months ago, she said to the pasha, "Kasim Pasha, in recent days the Sultan is not feeling well. He is pale and exhausted. I'm afraid he may leave us. Fortunately, Şehzade Ahmed is in good health, may Allah protect him."

Wasn't that clear enough? But how could this woman predict the death of a healthy thirty-nine-year-old Sultan? What was she scheming?

Safiye Valide wanted to put Ahmed on the throne – and she'd surely considered every way to do it.

Since she said that the Sultan may soon leave us, she certainly had some information upon which she'd deduced that. And where else would she find such a quiet and controllable woman like Ahmed's mother, Handan? Pasha knew Safiye could easily wrap Handan around her finger and control her every movement. If Ahmed gets the throne, Handan will become the Valide Sultan... but the strings will still be pulled by Safiye.

Sunullah noticed a slight smile on Kasim Pasha's thoughtful face. This time he stared at the Hodja, but he could promise that pasha didn't see him there.

I, too, should keep myself on Ahmed's side, and Handan will be easier for me to steer, too. But only on the condition that I get rid of Safiye, thought the Pasha.

How would I do it, though? There had to be some way. There's no one in the empire who doesn't burn with hated for Safiye Valide. All the pashas, the viziers, the agas, have their hopes associated with the innocence of Handan. If one could get rid of Safiye after Ahmed's enthronement... Some kind of dagger, a poison... even Handan might like this idea – after all, she's still a kid; she would be easy to convince.

Yes, sighed Kasim Pasha in his thoughts. *A drop of poison. Handan certainly wouldn't do it selflessly.* He had already decided a long time ago what the prize should be for that. Would there be a better candidate for the position of the Grand Vizier?

He flinched. He was impatient. In order to implement all his plans, he had to get rid of Mehmed first and then Safiye. The Sultan was ill – very ill. The doctors were reluctant to provide information on his condition, but he had already made the diagnosis: plague!

"The killer deserves such a punishment!"

"I'm sorry, Pasha? Did you say something? I didn't understand."

The words of Sunullah ripped Kasim Pasha from his thoughts. Apparently, he'd blurted out some uncontrolled words. He pulled himself together. He smiled. "No, nothing. A thought came to my mind."

In fact, he hadn't called Sunullah Efendi there tonight to talk about the sins and murders of the Sultan. The conversation wasn't supposed to be about the past. Whatever would happen, the Sultan would die, and his mother would live. For the good of the empire, but above all for his own good, Kasim Pasha had to take some precautionary measures.

"Anyway, Sunullah Efendi, let's leave the past and talk about the future. In my opinion, after the death of the Sultan, we should put Ahmed on the throne."

"Ahmed?" Sunullah Efendi was surprised.

"Yeah. Well, certainly not Mustafa."

"No, no..." The hodja suddenly became afraid. He was scared that when Ahmed became a Sultan, he would no longer be needed by anyone. "But he's still a baby."

"And Mustafa's gone crazy!"

"This is the truth. As Allah is my witness..." Sunullah sighed to himself. Şehzade Mustafa was crazy. How many times had he seen him try to talk to the walls? He asks them questions, expects them to speak to him, but when he doesn't get an answer, he starts laughing. Of course, if you can call it laughter – more like a crazy scream; the type of scream that gives you goosebumps. Sometimes he also ran after the servants, shouting: "Valide, valide!"

His heart ached. *Ah, Osman,* he thought, *get up and see what state the empire you have created is in. The empire will be governed either by a child or by a madman.*

"Say it!" Kasim Pasha rushed him. "Ahmed is the right candidate, isn't he? He is still a child, but most importantly, he hasn't lost his mind."

"Yes," answered Sunullah thoughtfully. "A child. An uncircumcised child!"

"Oh, don't worry," said the Pasha. He chuckled. "We'll take care of that. As soon as he takes power, we will do a snip, and it's done!" He raised his right hand and made a scissors-like motion.

But he failed to show that he didn't hesitate. Sunullah, seeing this, asked, "What? Something's wrong?"

"No, but..."

"Come on," he urged. "Since we got rid of Yemişçi Hasan Pasha, there is something that keeps bothering you.

Do you think that the Grand Vizier Malkoçoğlu Yavuz Ali Pasha and the great Admiral, Kapudan Ciğalazade Sinan Pasha, would oppose putting Ahmed on the throne?"

"They won't object."

"Are you afraid of janissaries – those elite household bodyguards of the Sultan?"

"No, why should I be afraid? They back whoever will give them money. Same as the spahis."

"Then what is it about?"

Kasim, kneeling, moved slightly towards Sunullah. He took a blanket and spread it. He didn't say anything until he sat comfortably. He had to choose his words carefully.

"It's about that woman again," he whispered into Sunullah's ear.

"About Safiye Valide?"

Kasim nodded his head.

"What about her?"

"Which one of the grandchildren does she prefer?"

Sunullah Efendi was surprised. He hadn't thought about it at all. It wasn't without reason. They said that Ahmed was the son of Handan. Mustafa's mother was Halime.

"Ahmed," whispered Kasim. "A child, and also, as you said, still uncircumcised. Think of his mother – she is also still a child, too. How old can Handan be? Twenty-six, twenty-seven? Her son has just turned fourteen. Mustafa is crazy, but his mother is a bit older. She is probably about thirty-five years old."

Although Sunullah Efendi was totally focused on the pasha's statements, he didn't know where he was going with that. "So? What do you mean?"

"This is what I mean – which grandson, together with his mother, would she prefer to twist around her finger? A sultan who is still a child, and his still-innocent mother? Or the sultan who has lost his mind, but his mother is a mature woman? What would you say to that?"

It had never occurred to him at all, but he decided to answer the question anyway. It wouldn't be good for him if Kasim presented him in a bad light tomorrow, in the presence of the Grand Vizier, claiming that he was useless. A new sultan, new hopes, new office.

"In my opinion," said Sunullah, "she would choose the madman and his mother."

"Why do you think so?"

"Because of the nickname, he will be given – The Mad. He personally doesn't think... he doesn't say anything that would be worth listening to. Even if he talks, no one listens to him. As for Halime, if Safiye would make her son a sultan, she would be grateful to her for the rest of her life. And obedient. That is why I think Safiye Valide would prefer a sultan who has lost his mind."

"You're wrong."

After a short while, Kasim Pasha rose from the mattress he had been sitting on. "You are wrong, very wrong. According to me, she will choose Ahmed. Because a crazy sultan means trouble. After a few days, the uprising would begin. Rebels from all over Anatolia would stand at the gates of the capital. Lots of other worries would fall on her head, and she would not want to fight with them. Ahmed is still a kid. He will obey her. Handan is just as naive. Although, in fact, she will really benefit from this... she will become a Valide Sultan, but she won't be able to carry the weight. She will do whatever she is told by Safiye, who will be able to control both of them this way."

"How can it be? After all, when Ahmed becomes a sultan, Safiye Valide will no longer have any power. It will go to Handan Valide."

"Your reasoning is wrong, Sunullah. She will certainly find a position for herself that will give her power. Higher than Valide Sultan. For example, for example..." Kasim Pasha thought for a moment. "For example, Valide-i Muazzama. What do you think? Safiye, the Great Sultan Mother."

"She may order the people to address her however she wants. But, according to custom, she will have to return to the Old Palace. You know that once someone is sent there, she never comes back."

Kasim Pasha circled the stove, then suddenly stopped and said, "What did you say, Hodja Efendi?"

"What? What did I say?"

"Say it again."

The man was confused. *What did I say that made him panic so much?* "Once someone is sent to the Old Palace, she will never return." There was fear in his voice.

"And you say you don't know about these things? You have just found a solution. We have to do this. As soon as his father dies, Ahmed should be enthroned as the new sultan, here in the palace, so that there will be no need to take him to Eyüp Sultan. The first thing we should do is to send Safiye Valide to the Old Palace – before she makes him issue a proclamation ensuring her authority in the New Palace – so that she won't ever leave it."

From the place where he was sitting, Sunullah managed to see that the pasha's eyes shone.

Of course, he thought. *He wants to send Safiye to the Old Palace just to be able to twist the new sultan and the new Valide Sultan around his own finger.* A grinning smile of admiration for the pasha appeared on his face. He pointed his index finger at him.

"And the second thing we should we do right away?" He made a scissors-like motion with two fingers – snip, snip. Circumcision.

Kasim Pasha chuckled. He clapped his hands. He asked the servant for a piece of paper and an inkwell. Then he leaned over the table and began to write.

"To His Majesty, the Grand Vizier Malkoçoğlu Yavuz Ali Pasha, bravely fighting on the Egyptian expedition..."

The second letter he wrote to the Kapudan of the fleet, Ciğalazade Sinan Pasha.

There were only three sentences in the letter.

"It's time to celebrate. It will be as we have established. I look forward to your quick return."

Chapter Six

Kumanovo, the Estate of Ibrahim Karayelzade
December 20, 1603

"I am overflowing with pessimism, sister."

Mirna turned to Nastya, who stood looking at the hills outside the window. "Why, my beautiful Nastya? See, the snow is falling. By Christmas, it will be white all around."

Nastya shrugged.

"This weather drives me crazy. How many days have passed since the last time the sun came out? There is darkness everywhere; the hills are barely visible. See what happens? The pines were first covered by the clouds, and now they've disappeared under the snow."

There was silence. They both knew that. They knew that it was not the weather that caused Nastya's pessimism.

"The Lord agreed," Mirna said suddenly. "A table for non-Muslims will be set at Christmas near the stable. Master Ibrahim said, 'Let them celebrate and have fun in whichever way they want.' You should go, too. You may cheer up."

"You won't go?"

Suddenly the room got cold. Mirna wanted to say something, but she finally gave up.

Nastya, who understood her mistake, muttered without turning away from the window, "I'm sorry, sister. I didn't mean to grieve you. Forgive me."

Mirna decided it would be better to behave as if nothing had happened.

"You will come to the celebration, won't you? There will be lanterns hung and candles arranged in the courtyard. We'll prepare them together with the other girls. Let's hope there will be no snow or gale. You will come, won't you?"

Nastya didn't speak, so they both remained silent for a moment.

"Also," Mirna broke the silence, "there's supposed to be music, too. The son of the head groom is to bring his two friends. I don't know what they are going to play. Maybe you can dance, too, huh?"

Again, the girl didn't reply.

"Don't think I don't understand," Mirna chirped. "Slobodan doesn't take his eyes off you. I bet the boy won't dance with any other girl except you."

Slobodan? The head groom's son was still a child. *He must be only about four or five years older than me,* thought Nastya. Black hair fell over his forehead and reached his brows over green eyes. They said that whoever looked into his eyes would feel as if they were walking in a green meadow on a sunny day. She'd never tried, but she heard the other girls whispering among themselves. He had a delicate mouth and a strong jaw. His only shortcoming was his height – he was tall and as skinny as a pole. Either Nastya would have to climb on her toes, or he would have to stoop for her to be able to see his face. If that would be enough, of course.

He didn't show his feelings on the outside – or rather he thought he was succeeding in that – but Nastya was aware of his interest. Slobodan invented thousands of excuses to see her. As soon as he'd find out she'd gone down to the kitchen, he would come running as fast as he could. He had to have spies among the servants. As soon as they passed him the information, he'd drop everything and run to see the girl.

"Nastya, can I get a cup of water?" he'd ask. "Could you give me a slice of bread?" he'd try the next time. One day, he came to the kitchen with a small white flower in his hand. "Nastya, look. I picked it for you."

She reached out, and Slobodan placed the flower on her palm.

"What is it? It's the first time I've seen something like this. Flowers like this don't grow where I come from."

At that moment, Slobodan's eyes – green like a meadow – shone with joy. "A snowdrop."

"It's beautiful."

If Mirna hadn't entered the kitchen at that moment, Slobodan would surely have said something else.

Afraid of being caught in the act, he began to walk toward the door, but as he passed by Nastya, he whispered into her ear: "Not as beautiful as you, though."

She admitted to herself that Slobodan's interest flattered her, but every time she thought about it, she also told herself that he was just a groom. A groom, son of the head groom. There were also times when she reproached herself, "Well, so what that he is a groom? And you... who are you?"

Exactly, God couldn't be expected to send a prince to a simple servant. That was the way things were. So what, that she was beautiful? The world is full of beautiful women. She was a slave. All the rest was a lie. Her future was covered by black clouds, like her soul now. She'd had enough of this darkness – of these black clouds. She wanted to see the sun on the horizon. She missed the light. She missed everything she had left behind.

Mirna walked up to Nastya when she noticed her start to drift away somewhere in her thoughts.

"What do you say? I'm sure you two are a good fit. Nastya, I swear, all the girls will die of envy. Sister?" As the girl turned, Mirna whispered, "Nastya? You are crying again?"

Nastya suddenly did something that the woman didn't expect. She stretched out her arms and threw herself on Mirna's neck. She hid her head in her friend's open arms.

"I'm homesick, sister. I miss my village. My mother. My father."

The woman stroked her head timidly. From the day she'd confessed to becoming a Muslim, she had been afraid to show any feelings for Nastya.

"Don't cry, darling..."

Nastya didn't even hear her. She began to sob, "I miss the sun, Mirna..."

Mirna took the girl by the arm and sat her down beside her.

"I know," whispered Nastya, "that you have been resentful since that day."

"Nastya..."

"I couldn't understand it. I didn't know... I was unfair to you. I thought you would distance yourself from me just because you are different. Or that I should keep my distance from you because our religions are different..."

Mirna grabbed her chin and turned her head up. She looked at Nastya's tearful face.

"It seems so," she said as she wiped the tears from the girl's cheeks. "Our God is the same. We both believe in the same God, we pray to him, we turn to him. And besides, I already forgot what we were talking about that day."

Nastya decided she would also forget. She snuggled closer to Mirna.

"I want to tell you something else."

The woman liked the expression of a naughty child that Nastya put on her face.

"Ah yes? I'm listening then. Tell me."

"I..." She stopped suddenly. *I wonder if she'll call me crazy*, she thought. But she had no choice if she wanted to break free from that burden. "I hid something from you, sister."

"What? Just don't tell me you are in love."

Nastya shook her head. "No... nothing like that."

"So, what's going on?"

"I... I... I saw a beggar. On the steps in front of the church."

Mirna was really surprised. She stepped away from the girl and looked her in the eye. "A beggar?"

"Uh-huh."

And what is there to hide? Mirna thought, excited. "What happened next?"

"I know you'll think I'm a candidate for a crazy person, but so let it be. When you hear what I have to say, you'll probably decide that I went crazy a long time ago. The beggar told me that..." She didn't know how to express herself.

"Nastya, please don't stutter. What did he say? Something bad?"

"No. He called me... a queen."

Mirna opened her mouth with the intention of saying something but quickly closed it. She asked about the first thing that came to her mind. "A queen?"

"Uh-huh. He called me a beautiful queen."

"He was right. You are a queen. You are the beautiful queen of Karayelzade's Estate, Nastya."

"I laughed when I heard it. I'm only a servant and a slave at that. I asked him if it was possible for a maid to be a queen. And this time... this time he said that..."

"For Allah's sake, Nastya, what did he say?"

"He said I would become a queen."

Mirna couldn't find an answer. *It must have made a big impression on her... and on whom wouldn't it?* she thought.

"Let's hope," she said. "Allah surely told him."

"You know what happened? He wasn't blind at all – he pretended to be. He blinked at me."

"So that's how he sets the trap to get money. A queen, right? I would give him a few coins, too, if he called me that..." Mirna muttered to herself.

"That's not all," Nastya continued. She said what happened later.

"Can you imagine it, Mirna?" she finished with a mysterious smile on her lips. "Nobody else has seen him, besides me. Even the man who was selling toys on the steps that day when I was talking to him. How many times have I been to the bazaar...? I've searched almost all of Kumanovo. Nobody saw a blind beggar, or even one who pretended to be blind, nor a true one."

Mirna thought it must have been one of the wandering beggars. Most of them were thieves. *But he did something even worse*, she said in her mind. *He stole my beautiful Nastya's reason.*

"Like some sorcery," the girl said. "Puff! And he's gone. What do you say about that?"

She paused, waiting for an answer.

After a moment, she spoke again, as if she had forgotten to add something earlier. "Don't think I believed what he said... but don't you find his disappearance strange? Or the fact that no one else has seen him? And the toy seller was there, too. I'm sure. He stood only a step higher. It's impossible he didn't see us. What do you think of it, sister?"

Mirna had nothing to say. Since that day, Nastya must have been dreaming of wearing a crown. About riding a horse alongside a prince. There was no need to wake her up from this dream. Let her be the queen of her dreams. What else was left for her beside that...? She was a slave.

"Maybe he's right," Mirna muttered, as she turned her head toward the window so that the girl couldn't tell she lied. "Allah gave some people this ability... Blind men can see, the deaf can hear... Maybe Allah put someone just like this in your path? Who knows?"

"That means... are you suggesting that he predicted my future? God, Mirna, I can't believe you said that. Is something like that possible at all? He's a cheater. He hunts for our money. He lured me with beautiful words... and see what happened? I no longer have the three copper coins you gave me."

Nastya also told everything to the priest when she went to confession before the Christmas Mass.

"That's right," she said. "The man disappeared."

"Is it important that the beggar disappeared, my child?"

"Sorry, I don't understand."

"Are you concerned that he disappeared, or because of what he said?"

She couldn't manage to say that she was more concerned with his words. Mirna might have called her a crazy-woman candidate, but she certainly didn't want the elderly priest in the confessional to think she was losing her mind.

"I know he just wanted to fool me with these words, Father."

"Are you sure?"

"Of course. It's just sweet words that he invented on the spot to make me give him money."

There was silence in the confessional.

"If you think this, then why did you come to me?"

Yes, Anastasia, why have you come? she thought. *Why did you tell the story about how this blind beggar tricked you?*

"I was afraid that I had sinned, even if I believed in that lie for just a moment."

She knew it was a lie. Probably the priest also believed it.

"It is a sin not to believe in the destiny that God has created for us and to oppose it. No one besides Him knows the future."

She thought the same way. *Nobody but God knows the future. The liar beggar also doesn't know it.*

She left the church. She went slowly down the steps and thought she might search for the beggar again. She cast her eyes across the bazaar, where Christians hastily did their last Christmas shopping. Of course, he wasn't anywhere. *A queen, right? Queen... a liar.*

Even though she thought this way, she realized that until now, a deep-buried question had begun to slowly bother her...

Could this beggar be an angel, sent down to tell me that God would come to me?

Maybe it was like that. Even if he wasn't an angel, at least someone noticed her. Apart from him, no one paid any attention to her. He was the only one to see her.

When she reached the last steps, she threw all those questions out of her head. Christmas was now. It would be a sin to sit at the table with such black thoughts. Then the whole coming year would be like that. In her mind, she repeated the prayers she had said in the church. Suddenly she whispered, "Go, Queen of Servants. Toward the estate. The Prince of Grooms, Slobodan, waits for you."

Chapter Seven

New Palace, Chamber of Safiye Sultan
December 21, 1603

Shortly after the afternoon ezan, the Valide Sultan was informed that the sultan's chief physician would soon arrive.

Safiye felt that the machine she'd been preparing for the past days would suddenly start moving.

Finally, she thought. The fate that made her the strongest queen in the world played the last game very unfairly. *Damn it!* She cursed in her thoughts. *Damn both me and fate*. There was an angry voice of protest in her head. *Do not say that, don't curse yourself, Safiye! You were forced to do it.*

"I was forced," she mumbled quietly.

It happened just like the man said it would – three or four days – it was the fourth day. Azrael finally knocked on the door. At least... at least he didn't hesitate.

And if it wasn't so?

She got everything messed up. Exactly... maybe the doctor came to make sure he could announce the good news: "Our ruler is healthy and fit, lady. Allah saved him."

Fools and hypocrites, she growled to herself. *Do they think I don't realize that the whole country hates the Sultan, my son? Don't they understand that it would be good news for them to get rid of him? Can't they hear what the word is in the streets?*

They heard. But hypocrisy, like bribery, got into their blood. Taking on a false smile or a sad expression on their faces, they would walk down those streets.

Let them get lucky, let them catch the opportunity.

It was already almost twenty-four hours that she had been waiting for the doctor to come, praying. She begged Allah not to make him suffer. Let Allah take him to himself. Let him send the doctor when a statement needs to be issued. Let him bring the news that her son was rid of the empire, and the empire was rid of her son.

It was time to play the last scene of the show, whose every minute and every second had been planned for almost a year. Her heart started to pound with excitement.

Ah, empire. How many victims have I sacrificed for you? What else, except my son, could have been taken away from me?

Suddenly, she froze. What if the doctor realized that the death of the Sultan wasn't caused by illness at all?

The man had promised to Allah that there would be no trace. But what if? If the doctor whispers in her ear that the sultan was murdered, that he had been poisoned?

Kill this fear within yourself, her reason suggested. *Didn't you ask how many victims had been sacrificed by you for the good of the empire? Safiye can also be a victim.*

When she glanced up from the needlework held on her knees to look at the maid waiting in the doorway for the news, she saw darkness in front of her eyes. When she tried to pull the thread, the needle accidentally struck her finger.

"Why are you standing like that?" Safiye Valide exclaimed, irritated by the excitement and the pain of her finger. "Instead of hanging out here, go find out if there is any news."

The girl ran out.

Other servants, working on the lace, cast a glance amongst themselves. They were accustomed to the Valide Sultan's anger, but for the past week, she had been even more irritated. She was constantly asking, "Who's that? Has someone come to the door? Go see." Or she constantly chastised everyone, "Why are you looking at me? What a lack of discipline that the servants began to look at their ladies." One of the girls, who slept in the Valide Sultan's chamber, told the others about a strange event.

The servants had never heard of anything like it. Allegedly, one night the Valide Sultan got up from the bed, shouting, "They are coming! They're coming!"

It was obvious that she was restless – fearful.

The Grand Vizier Yemişçi Hasan Pasha had left almost no living soul in the city. In fact, it was the Valide Sultan herself that suggested the pasha to the Sultan, but he also didn't hesitate in realizing his cruel plans. He even succeeded in persuading the Sultan to order the strangulation of Şehzade Mahmud. He was so greedy that there was probably nothing he wouldn't have done. Everyone was a potential enemy. Fortunately, Safiye had finally managed to scare the Sultan with a soldiers' uprising; she ordered him to abduct Hasan Pasha from a palace near the Hippodrome and transport him straight to the executioners at Sütlüka.

"When misfortune comes to the palace once..." the servants secretly whispered amongst themselves. "Yemişçi is dead, but his curse is still over us. Same as Şehzade

Mahmud's curse. The Shah recaptured Tabriz, so I've heard. The soldiers run away."

Another girl gave a shrug in excitement and said, "Oh, dear… those who go to war are fleeing. Those who stay here plunder their homes; rob the craftsmen's workshops. You can't trust anyone. Poverty is knocking on the door. We will see what else the subjects will have to suffer."

Death walked throughout the city – and the Sultan also ailed. The disease had caught him quickly and took over his whole body. He wasn't even thirty-nine years old. He should be strong, but just like his father, he wasn't able to stay away from women. However, he wasn't the type of man who'd visit seven women in a harem in a single night. Despite this, he was still afflicted by illness. "If the doctor doesn't leave him for a moment, it means that his condition is really serious," the girls said. "Doctors have been called even from the lands of the infidels."

Safiye Valide touched her lips with the tip of her finger, where a drop of blood appeared. Then she set aside the needlecraft. All the servants realized that the Valide Sultan was about to get up, so they all rushed to help.

"Leave me alone!" She pushed away the helping hands that reached out toward her. "Do you think I've grown so old that I can't get up?"

Safiye Valide was still beautiful. But when she walked to meet the doctor, her face was completely white. "He's as strong as a mountain. Everything is fine. May Allah give us patience."

While Safiye Valide walked to the meeting, she quietly considered all the news she might hear there. She had an idea to solve every situation.

She sat on a chair on the women's side of the meeting room, separated from the men as was custom, by a latticework screen. Women from the harem could not meet men from the outside, face-to-face. So, she looked through the holes in the grate and noticed the doctor's face.

"Tell me," she said in a frightened voice. "I hope you bring good news. Say that the sultan's condition is stable, and I will fulfill all your wishes."

The man coughed and cleared his throat. "What else can I want besides the health of our people, My Lady? It is sad that I do not bring the news you are waiting for. Seeing joy on your face would be the biggest reward for me..."

That means the end... Safiye thought and sighed.

The doctor hesitated, "But..." He paused again.

"But what?"

"We have no influence on the divine judgments. We must obey, Valide. His Highness..."

It happened exactly as she expected. The man's voice trembled. "The soul left our Sultan."

Safiye moaned with pain. Showing sadness was part of the plan, but she didn't think it would really affect her so much. Her sobs were real! *If such a fate hadn't been written for me... If instead of becoming Valide Sultan, I had remained in Venice as Sofia Baffo, I wouldn't be the victim of my own destiny. I wouldn't be forced to do all that...* She hadn't predicted that her own soul would burn with such fire, that her heart would hurt so much.

"Let him rest in peace..." she whispered. She wiped the tears gathering in the corner of her eyes with the edge of a handkerchief. "How did this happen? Did he...?"

She wasn't able to finish, but the man understood.

"I can promise you, Majesty, that he didn't suffer at all. He raised his head from the pillow... We thought he wanted to drink, so we passed him water immediately. He took a few sips. Then he whispered, 'Light. Show me the light of day.' One of the young doctors immediately took our Lord Sultan into his arms..."

Allah," she moaned. *My son carried in his arms?* For the first time in her life, she felt the burning fire of never-expressed regret. *Was it worth it?* Safiye asked herself. *Should I have sacrificed my son for the good of the empire?*

If it wasn't worth it, why would you do it? The voice of reason questioned.

Safiye didn't know the answer. *What if you didn't do it... if everything depended on the rebellious population? Would it be better if they cut his head, impaled it, and carried it around the whole city?*

Was the situation so bad?

"Majesty..." The doctor's voice snatched her from her reverie and dispersed all her thoughts.

"You're right," she muttered. "It's time to step firmly on the ground and not be sorry. The country needs us. May Allah have pity on our son."

"Amen," said the man. "Amen."

"Has the message been conveyed to the Grand Vizier?" Safiye asked gloomily.

"No, Majesty. We did not want to make any decisions without consulting you. The news of the death of the Sultan has not yet moved beyond the threshold of his chamber."

"You did well. Let's not do anything in a hurry. First, we must prepare; take preventive measures. Only later can we announce that His Highness the Sultan left to be at Allah's side."

She paused. She had to resolve the doubts that tormented her. "Is the reason why my son left us certain?"

The silhouette of the man visible behind the bars didn't even flinch.

"We're not sure," he said. "If you look at the spots on the Sultan's body... I don't know how to say it. I don't think I dare to say it."

"Please tell me. Whatever is done is done. Why don't you dare?"

"I mean... if you look at them..."

"I'll believe your word," Safiye whispered, agitated.

"The plague isn't able to take a life in such a short time, in only three days..."

"Then what?"

"Other doctors believe it is a plague. But I, your humble servant, am not sure. I wonder if..."

She sensed danger.

"If?"

"I wonder if something else caused the spots."

What she'd feared the most had just happened. The doctor had found out. She tried to see his mouth through the bars. She felt the breath of danger on her face, crawling through the grate and trying to reach her.

"What could be the other cause of these spots?" She prayed to control her voice so that it wouldn't tremble.

"There are some possible assumptions," the man said. "For example, a poison."

"Oh, Allah!" She put her hands to her heart in despair and stood up. She was really distraught. *It was supposed to leave no trace behind!* But huge blue spots had appeared on her son's stomach. What's more... yesterday morning she saw with her own eyes, a green spot was visible on Mehmed's lips. She thought it could be from the medicines the doctors gave him. But it turned out otherwise. The man had betrayed her. A crisis awaited them – a crisis that could see heads roll, that would eat the dynasty from inside, that would be able to change the empire, its history, and the ruling families.

"Are you sure of that?"

The lips behind the grate moved. "No, Valide."

But his voice sounded decisive. Or rather, suggested that his sense of certainty depended on certain conditions. Safiye repeated with hatred in her head: *Hypocrite, traitor!*

"Allah," she moaned. "This will lead to the end of the Ottoman Empire..."

The doctor was a wise man. He received the Valide Sultan's message and understood what she wanted to say.

"I thought about it, too, Majesty," he whispered. "If I have to, I will take the secret with me to the grave. This is just my hypothesis. Most likely, we have lost your son because of infection with a very rapidly spreading plague."

She turned her head so that she could see the man from the other side.

"It surely was like that," she muttered. "Besides, who might want to take the life of my son, the Sultan of the empire?"

The doctor laughed ominously in his thoughts. *Oh, you Satan. You are trying to also fool me now? I can give you an entire list of names of people who would wish for the death of the Sultan in a heartbeat. And your name would be at the top of it. But what good would that do to me? None.*

In the end, Sultan Mehmed had died in his arms; he was unable to find an antidote to the poison. Even if he weren't executed, he would have to say goodbye to the position of the Sultan's chief physician. Meanwhile, biting his tongue, the new order could open new possibilities for him. Without even thinking twice, he replied, "No one."

There was a silence that seemed too long for both of them. They'd made a deal. The doctor thought so, at least.

"Your service is very valuable," Safiye broke the silence. "You didn't leave my son alone in his most difficult of days. You tried to snatch him from the hands of the disease and save him. Your merit won't be left unrewarded. I'll call the treasurer. You know that the empire cannot stand the situation when it owes its faithful servant."

The heart of the doctor jumped with joy. *Right. What do I have to do with this? Whichever way it happened, he died. But I am alive. I will now live, surrounded by sable furs, and precious stones and jewels...* He already began to plan. He decided to seal their contract.

"May Allah give our Valide Sultan a long life. Please do not worry. The secret, or rather suspicion, will be taken with me to the grave."

If he could have seen the expression on the Mother Sultan's face at that moment, he would immediately realize that a decision was made about his death. *I don't have any doubts about it – you will take the secret with you to the grave*, thought Safiye.

"You can leave now," she said in a muffled voice. "Until I come to my son's room, let no one know of his death."

The shadow visible through the gratings moved. The man nodded to Safiye, of whom he was sure would shower him with gold for his merit. The woman heard the crack of the closing door. She should start working right away.

When Mehmed's death is announced, everyone will want to win as much as possible. Mustafa's mother certainly isn't idle. Even if she couldn't ensure the throne for her insane son, the capital still swarmed with people who wanted to gain power in the empire by putting a madman on the throne.

She clapped her hands.

"Let the Kaymakam be informed. We expect Kasim Pasha. Even if he has his hands dirty with blood, let him come to me. Also, let somebody go to Handan, the mother of my grandson Ahmed, and tell her I'm waiting for her."

The excitement worked like an ointment for the wound in the heart of Safiye Valide. *My beloved son!* She sighed in her thoughts. *It was written in your destiny that the one who gave you life, was also Azrael... I hope Allah will take you to heaven.*

Kasim Pasha was restless as if flames were burning him.

From that very morning, when he left the council, he couldn't find a place for himself. According to what Valide Sultan had said, the Sultan was about to leave to join Allah soon. Three days. Four. Maybe five.

No news came yesterday, either. Nor today, even though the afternoon ezan neared.

He waited for the servants to spread the prayer rug. He started the prayer. But he couldn't focus. He made a mistake reciting the prayer and was forced to start from the beginning. As he knelt, a thought appeared in his head: *And if it doesn't work?* When he touched the carpet with his forehead, he thought of another question. *And if he is saved?*

When Kasim turned his head to the right, it seemed to him that Sultan Mehmed was sitting right next to him – in one piece. He grew frightened. He turned to the left. The

Sultan sat there, too, reaching out his hand toward him and wagging his finger.

He was on the verge of panic. *People like him have seven lives,* he thought and stood up. If there was no news today, he should think of a solution. If Sultan Mehmed got up from the bed healthy, they would be in serious trouble. Their enemies were ready, just like the ambush set by them. He began to regret that he had allied himself with Safiye; but it was too late, the arrow had been shot.

Use your mind! He reproached himself in thought. *The fact that the arrow has been fired doesn't mean you have to lose hope. If no news comes tomorrow or the day after, you should think about how to save your head.*

He drowned in black and bloodstained thoughts and didn't notice the door to the room open. Nor did he hear the servant address him.

"Pasha." He noticed him only when the man grunted.

"What is it?"

"A message has arrived from Safiye Valide."

Kasim Pasha jumped to his feet. In nervousness, he couldn't find one of his slippers. The servant ran immediately and put it on the pasha's foot.

"Safiye Valide said, 'Let him come, even if he has hands dirty with blood.'"

Well, well!

Or rather... Oh no!

When the Kaymakam approached the room with the grate, he noticed the white figure and realized the Valide Sultan had arrived and already waited for him.

"Is it done?" he asked, catching his breath.

She answered him with an ice-cold voice, "It is done."

Kasim Pasha felt the cold soak into him to the bone.

"It's over," Safiye said. "The empire has lost its Sultan. It is time to put the new sultan on the throne, Pasha. Have precautions been taken, as you ensured?"

Happy, he repeated in his mind, *Praise Allah, praise Allah, praise Allah,* and again he was greatly impressed by the coldness of the Sultan Mother. It wasn't without reason that even the most senior of the viziers and intrepid commanders were afraid of her. She had made the decision that her son had to die and executed the sentence. Such a pain would melt even steel, but here was Safiye – sitting straight, showing no emotion.

"Didn't you hear what I asked, Pasha?" Safiye Valide said when she didn't receive a response from the man. "Have precautions been taken, as you said?"

"Excuse your humble servant, Majesty," said Kasim Pasha. He felt he had to utter these words. Was it possible to do something like this only because of the lust for power?

He had doubts. It seemed that Safiye was one of those who believed that serving the empire was a kind of prayer and a confession of faith.

How was she different from war heroes – martyrs – who sacrifice their lives, and those who took life? The Empire demanded the sacrifice, and Safiye, without even blinking, did what she believed was right. What else could he do, other than say to the woman a few words through which he showed her his respect?

"The pain you feel right now must be huge," he whispered. "Your sacrifice will be blessed. I'm sure the Sultan went to paradise."

I hope, thought Safiye, *that Allah will be treating his faithful servant to a sorbet.*

"The entire empire regrets its loss," Kasim Pasha continued.

"Is everything ready to the last button, Pasha?"

"Of course."

"Send guards to the door of Şehzade Mustafa's room."

"They have already been sent."

"Increase the number of guards. No one will enter his room, and no one will come out of it. This also applies to his mother."

The Kaymakam nodded.

"Regarding Ahmed's enthronement –"

"It will be held in the morning at Eyüp Sultan," the Pasha said enthusiastically.

"Too late. We have to do it today, right now."

"What about custom and tradition?" He was surprised.

"They pertain to ordinary cases. Are we dealing with such a situation now? The city is burning. Do you intend to stick to convention when the empire is digested by flames? He will take the throne here in the palace. He will be taken to Eyüp Sultan later."

"Whatever your orders are, it will be. I will take further action according to them."

"Is the palace protected well enough?"

"The number of guards has been increased."

"Protection must be strengthened even more. Let one spahis unit be transferred to the Hippodrome. Let the Janissaries be on watch. Is everything in order?"

"All preventive measures have been taken. Spahis dressed in civilian clothes have been placed in various neighborhoods and in the vicinities of the hans. Don't worry about it."

"Then don't give me reasons to worry," Safiye suddenly appeared upset. "Is there any news from the Grand Vizier Malkoçoğlu Yavuz Ali Pasha?"

"He's on his way."

"And the commander, Ciğalazade Sinan Pasha? Are you sure of his fidelity? You are responsible for that."

Kasim Pasha nodded, but in the depths of his mind, he began to worry. What he was afraid of had happened. She was trying to consolidate all the power into her hands. She'd put an end to her son's governance and made her word the new law. The child who was to take the throne would be a puppet in her hands.

"Well, then..." Suddenly, she fell silent. "Something else. Let my son's harem be transferred to the Old Palace tomorrow morning."

And you? Kasim thought. *And you? You will not move? Your son is dead. Somebody else will be Valide Sultan now. The last word in the New Palace will belong to Handan. When are you going to move to the Old Palace?*

Something frightening happened as if Safiye Valide read the Pasha's mind.

In a deep voice, she said, "I have decided I will stay here. The new Sultan is still very young, and his mother is callow and inexperienced. Until she officially becomes the new Valide Sultan, she must gain some experience. My task is to stay here and help my grandson and his mother while not showing grief. Isn't that so, Pasha?"

"Of course, Majesty." The Pasha was desperate.

"If so, then go and put my orders into effect. Everything has to go according to the plan."

After Kaymakam Kasim Pasha left the room, a strange expression appeared on his face.

Good that I thought about talking to Handan first, he thought. *At least she won't fall into Safiye's trap.*

When they told her that Handan had arrived, Safiye quickly turned to the door. She opened it and hugged her grandson's mother.

"Handan."

The woman was surprised. Until now, she had never seen her mother-in-law embrace anybody like this.

"I must go to the Sultan immediately, my daughter," she whispered to her ear. "Wait here until my return."

"Yes, my mother."

"The condition of my son has deteriorated, Handan. What I just heard from his doctor doesn't make me optimistic. I want to go and see him with my own eyes. You wait here. We need to talk." Then, without waiting for an answer, Safiye left the room.

There was silence everywhere. The guards stood with their pikes crossed, in front of the Sultan's room, blocking the door. She stopped in front of them and ordered, "Open."

The chamber was dark. The chief physician was talking to two other doctors. Another man sat at her son's head, softly reading the Qur'an.

Shivering, she approached the bed. Her son, to whom she gave life to, now lay dead in front of her.

They'd placed his hands on his chest. Afraid that she would see suffering on his face, she looked at him slowly. But on the contrary, he was in peace as if he were asleep.

With which face do you look at him now? her inner voice asked her. Her conscience was right. Which face should she put on?

She lowered her head, then dropped into a chair brought by one of the doctors.

"Leave," she said. "Wait outside, but do not talk."

They left. Safiye was alone with her already dead son.

"Mehmed..." she whispered. "Look what they forced me to do."

Suddenly, tears began to flow down her cheeks. Then she couldn't think of anything; words couldn't come out of her mouth. She lifted Mehmed's hand, kissed it, and pressed it against her cheek.

"Forgive me, son. If I hadn't done it, they wouldn't spare you."

She sat like this until the evening ezan. Then she got up and opened the door.

She looked at the guards with eyes red from crying.

"Sultan..." she moaned. "Sultan Mehmed Khan has left us." Then she rushed back to her room as fast as the wind, ignoring the uproar she'd caused.

Handan waited for her. When she saw her mother-in-law's face, she ran to her and grabbed her hand.

"Valide..." she muttered. "Does it mean...?"

Safiye nodded. "May Allah bless your son and make his reign last forever, Handan. I lost my son. The country belongs to your son now."

Before the evening ezan, everything was set.

Ahmed was surprised to see his grandmother, who came with his mother.

"Ahmed..." said Handan.

"Sultan Ahmed," Safiye corrected her.

"Your father has left us. The throne is now yours."

Ahmed panicked. "But I have not yet been sent to rule in any of the provinces," he objected. "Without that, nobody can become the Sultan."

Safiye tried to smile. "You will be the first one."

"I'm still young. I just turned fourteen."

"That is no obstacle to be the Sultan."

"I am not circumcised."

"Is it something bad?" Safiye Valide asked in a quiet voice. "We'll get it done right after you take the throne. We will have another reason for joy."

But Ahmed didn't look as if it convinced him. "How can a child of my age govern a large empire, manage viziers, pashas, agas, the whole treasury, and the army?"

Safiye smiled. Just when she was about to say, "I am with you, grandson," something that she did not expect happened. Handan stood in front of her son, raised his hand to her lips, and kissed it.

"Let the person executing the first order of the new Sultan be his Valide. Don't worry about anything, My Lord. Your mother, as Handan Valide, will always be standing by your side and support you."

Safiye felt as if she'd been hit in the face. *Well, well,* she thought.

But this was not the moment to argue with Handan. First, she should prepare for it.

All that Safiye Valide asked to be done according to the plan was done much better.

Ahmed was led to the safe part of the palace in a hurry. In the presence of Shaykh al-Islām Ebulmeyamin

Mustafa Efendi, he was put on the throne. He was amazed that everything was done so quickly. An ermine coat was placed on his shoulders, and since no Sultan headgear that would fit him was found, he was given the headgear of one of the viziers. As it covered almost his whole head, falling all the way down on his brows, he could see only half of what happened later.

Shaykh al-Islām prayed for the life and rule of the Sultan to be fortunate, and the whole Osman family to be eternal. Plenty of people he had never seen before screamed, "Amen!" and then they'd kneel before him, and kiss his hands and robes.

The people learned that Sultan Mehmed had left them, and his uncircumcised son Ahmed had come to the throne, as they came out of the morning ezan for the streets and the drummers, striking the drums, proclaimed the news.

"Long live Sultan Ahmed, son of Sultan Mehmed Khan!"

At the council held that morning, Kaymakam Kasim Pasha held the first personal order of the new Sultan in his hand. The Pasha laughed almost as hard as when he read its working version, written by Safiye.

"You are Kasim Pasha," the order of Sultan Ahmed began. *"My father has left this world by the command of Allah, and I took the throne after him. May the unshakeable city be taken back. If there is any treason in all this, I'll order to behead you."*

Late in the morning, the throne was set up in front of the Babüssaade Palace gate, which provided access to the third courtyard that was between the Sultan's chambers, Enderûn, and the hall in which the council was held. Sultan

Ahmed put on black robes to express the pain of losing his – yet unburied – father. Shaykh al-Islām, the viziers, the Janissaries' commander, the commander of the guard, and the commanders of all the other formations came to kiss the Sultan's hand and show him their obedience.

Handan watched her son enthroned from behind the barred window that overlooked Babüssaade, with tears in her eyes. One of the servants asked, "Where is the Valide Sultan?"

When the servants, surprised by the absence of Safiye, looked at each other quizzically, her inner voice reminded Handan: *Hey! What are you doing? You are now the Sultan Mother. Don't you see? Your son is taking the throne. The whole country pays homage to him. May the luck be with you, too, Handan Valide.*

She looked at the girls and laughed, "It's just a habit. Immediately after arriving at the palace, I will order all to call me Valide Sultan."

The servants ran to her and kissed her hand. They congratulated the new Sultan Mother.

When the official ceremony was over, Handan Valide turned to her room. The servants followed her. One of the girls, who walked at the back, pulled one of her colleagues by the sleeve and whispered, "Well, what's going to happen now?"

The girl was surprised. "What do you mean, dear? We will serve the Sultan Mother."

"But which one? There are now two Valides in the palace. Do you think Safiye will give Handan free rein?"

Handan thought about the same thing. She still heard the voice of Kasim Pasha: 'As soon as the ceremony is over, you must send your mother-in-law to the Old Palace.'

In the evening, after the emotions of the ceremony had subsided, she stood before her son.

"Let your rule last forever, my son."

"You know what, mother?" said the little Sultan. He sat on a beautiful, wide ottoman, and in Handan's eyes, he looked as if he'd gotten even smaller. "Today, when we were burying my father, I thought to myself, 'If only you had lived longer, Daddy. I would have been circumcised. I would mature. I would learn even more.' How do I issue orders for white-bearded viziers, pashas, and scholars? How am I supposed to deal with ruling the empire?"

"Do not worry and do not think about it, My Lord. Everything has its solution. First, you will go to Eyüp Sultan, then you will be circumcised. The viziers will be standing by your side." Handan paused and stared at her son's anxious eyes. "And, of course, Valide will also stand by your side."

"I find comfort in this, too. If not for my grandmother, I don't know what I would do."

What? Does he only think of Safiye as Valide? She grew angry. Although her son did not show her where she could sit, she proudly moved toward the seat next to the ottoman.

"I," she said in a voice so cold, she surprised even herself. "When I said 'Valide,' I meant myself, not your grandmother."

The Sultan was surprised and hesitated for a moment. Then a flash of excitement appeared in his eyes.

"Really?" he said. "I'm really lucky. I have two Sultan Mothers."

Handan bit her lips in anger. If she didn't fight it, she would start crying. Was there no rescue from that woman? Wasn't it enough that she was a puppet in her hands and she was always in her shadow? Even her own son called that woman Valide.

She remembered the warning of Kasim Pasha: "From the first day, you have to control the situation. Start influencing the Sultan. She should leave. Otherwise, the people will recognize her as the ruler instead of Sultan Ahmed. He will be the Sultan only for the title, just as you will be the Sultan Mother only formally."

"That's exactly what I came to talk to you about," she said, and she struggled to keep her voice quiet. "The custom and the law say that the Valide for the Sultan is also Valide for the whole empire."

The Sultan twitched. He felt he had to make his first very important decision. His mother asked a lot from him.

"In this situation," she continued, "I am the Valide."

She paused for a moment. She was waiting for her son to react. The boy did not say anything. His little black eyes stared at his mother. He listened to her without showing any emotion.

"I, myself, have great respect and boundless sympathy for her, but this is what the good of the empire requires. Safiye is no longer the Sultan Mother. The parent of the acting Sultan is the new Valide. That means me. Custom says Safiye should leave here and move to the Old Palace—"

"But..." the Sultan objected. Handan raised her hand and silenced her son. It crossed her mind that she used the same gesture as Safiye. When she wanted to silence somebody, she cut the air with her hand like with a sword.

"This is not my idea, son, to dictate the tradition, customs, good manners, decency, and law. There can't be two Valides, neither in the palace nor in the harem."

Chapter Eight

Kumanovo, the Estate of Ibrahim Karayelzade
January 11, 1604

Frightened, Nastya suddenly jumped out of bed. "God, what's going on?"

The sounds from outside were so loud that it could've indicated the end of the world. The drummers hit the drums, someone announced some news, people shouted.

Brum, brum, brum!

Master Ibrahim also woke up. Nastya realized that when she heard his footsteps on the stairs outside. He'd thrown on some clothes, left the room and ran to see what was going on. All the servants taking care of the wife of the lord had also been on their feet for some time already. The elderly woman lifted her shoulders and kept touching her face, as though she was trying to wipe something off it.

Nastya didn't understand anything of it and whispered to the girl standing next to her, "What is she doing?"

All of the other girls had started to treat her like an enemy, because on Christmas Night, Slobodan only danced with her and no one else.

"Are you blind?" the girl snapped. "Can't you see – she shows gratitude."

"Why?"

The girl left without responding. Nastya opened the window. The courtyard was full of people. The gate facing the street was wide open, and amongst the crowd, she saw Slobodan.

"Hi!" she called. "Look here."

Slobodan heard her calling and turned around. As soon as he saw her looking out the window, his hand went to his head. He took off his cap and smiled.

"Let your day be cheerful, Nastya."

"What is this noise, Slobodan? Why is everyone shouting? Why are they drumming?"

"Sultan Mehmed died!" he shouted, his hands cupped around his mouth so that she could hear him better.

"What? People are happy that the Sultan died?"

"His son Ahmed has become the new sultan. They announce the news of the new ruler on the throne."

In that case, instead of grieving, they are happy to have the new sultan. The previous died, so they have high hopes with the new one.

"Sultan Mehmed... is dead," she repeated to herself. "Another sultan took his place on the throne. His name is Ahmed... Sultan Ahmed."

Suddenly she recalled Master Ibrahim's conversation with Beylerbey Çivici Pasha, which she had overheard one night. 'The Sultan is in very bad condition, Ibrahim. I fear that if the empire isn't free from him, we will not see the sun in the sky anymore. Even his mother is of the same opinion.'

Nastya chuckled. That means that in the end, the sun will rise.

Çivici Mehmed Pasha arrived at Karayelzade's estate four days later, raising tons of dust behind, just as before. However, this time the Pasha arrived without the soldiers.

Master Ibrahim greeted him respectfully and bent down to kiss his hand, but the Pasha hit his hand away, not allowing him to.

Nastya noticed that this time, they both laughed.

Çivici Pasha, all dust-covered, said in a loud voice when he walked up the stairs, "I told you so, Karayel, didn't I? Didn't I tell you to be patient?"

Nastya nodded, just like Master Ibrahim. *He did*, she thought.

The door to the room closed and the men were alone. Her thoughts were with them. She wondered what they talked about.

For a moment, she wondered if she approached the door and pretended to clean it, whether she would manage to hear their conversation. But she found it strange. *Don't think about such foolish stuff. What's up with you, Nastya?* she reproached herself. *What business of yours is it what they are talking about? Should a woman eavesdrop on conversations conducted by men? Especially a maid?*

Still, she was curious.

They are certainly talking about some empire affair, she continued to ponder. She tried to satisfy her curiosity. *The sultan died, another ascended on the throne... surely this is the subject of conversation. The Pasha seems to have brought news again. It looks like he has arrived from afar.*

Suddenly, she realized that she was attracted to the life in the palace that they had talked about that night and that it was like a fairy tale for her – full of secrets, intrigues, ruses. In her dreams, she could open the door to a new world.

She ran downstairs. She poured the brewed leaves and flowers of linden that had been steeping on the stove into a jug and ran back upstairs as fast as she could. She knocked. Without waiting for an answer, she opened the door.

"And that's how it is, Ibrahim. Grand Vizier Malkoçoğlu Yavuz Ali Pasha, as soon as he learned of the Sultan's death, ordered, 'Let the Beylerbey of Rumelia come to see me.' The messenger rode to Üsküp. Oh, you can't get angry with him. Didn't the previous sultan remove me from the post and nominate that savage, Deli Hasan, the leader of the uprising, to be the Rumelia Beylerbey?"

Despite Nastya noticing how Master Ibrahim looked at her from the corner of his eye, she slowly poured linden tea into the cup she put in front of Çivici Pasha.

"Deli Hasan thought the Grand Vizier had called him and hurried to Belgrade. When Malkoçoğlu Pasha saw him, he almost burst out in anger, Ibrahim. It is enough for me. 'Who are you?!' he yelled. 'The man I call Beylerbey fights all his life at the borders of the Empire for its safety. He is not someone who raises his hand at the Empire in its most difficult times!' And he sent him away."

Nastya imagined all this. She felt enthralled and excited. When she placed the börek, a deliciously stuffed filo pastry, in front of the Pasha, she noticed that tears flowed from his eyes.

"This is enough, Karayel. I heard enough. 'Go, find Çivici Pasha," the Grand Vizier ordered. 'I'm going to the capital. Let him catch me on the way.' He later rode a horse from Belgrade to Istanbul. I set off as soon as I received the order, but Malkoçoğlu is exactly as described by his nickname, Ibrahim – sinister. He reached the capital in six days. I managed to reach it two days after him. But everything had already been done. Too bad."

"Nothing happened, Pasha," Ibrahim said. He still looked at Nastya.

Meanwhile, Nastya performed all duties with her head lowered so that their eyes did not meet. A long time ago, she understood that as soon as they looked at each other, he would order her to leave with a wag of one finger.

She set the second cup before him. Next, she walked slowly to the table where she placed the jug.

"Ciğalazade Sinan Pasha," the man continued, "arrived one day before Malkoçoğlu Pasha, but waited for him. The next day, the new sultan was taken to Eyüp Sultan, where he was sworn in, on the sword of the Prophet. Ciğalazade laughed when he was telling this. It turns out that the length of the sword was larger than the height of the Sultan! The sword scabbard reached almost up to his chest."

Nastya imagined a boy and a giant sword. In her mind, as he walked the end of the sword was dragged on the ground.

"Put the jug and the plate here."

The image of the Sultan pulling the sword on the ground disappeared when Master Ibrahim's voice snatched Nastya out of her thoughts. Finally, she decided to listen to the voice of reason.

It's time for me to go, thought the girl. *At the best moment of the story*. She reluctantly walked to the table, took the jug and the plate, and set them before Master Ibrahim.

"If you need anything," she whispered, "I'll be waiting outside."

Çivici Pasha took a sip of linden tea. "I missed the ceremony, Ibrahim, but I witnessed an even bigger event."

Nastya, turning to the door, wanted to turn around and ask, "What event? What happened?" Fortunately, Ibrahim asked that.

"You won't believe it. You really won't believe it."

Ohh! Nastya thought as she reached out to the door handle. *What could be so unbelievable?* To delay her exit, she pressed the knob very slowly.

Master Ibrahim said, "When you leave, carefully close the door behind you."

Now she had no choice but to finally open the door. As she crossed the doorway, she heard Çivici Pasha say, "We thought that both the mother and son were still immature, but they say that still waters run deep for a good reason. Do you know what the mother and son did?"

"You've made me curious, Pasha."

Nastya left, muttering under her breath. Even as she closed the door, she still kept trying to hear everything.

"They chased Safiye away. They kicked her out of the New Palace."

As the girl closed the door, a picture of a sad, depressed woman stood before her eyes. She was adorned with jewels, but she didn't look happy. Tears ran down her cheeks. A woman sent away from home by her grandson and daughter-in-law would probably cry. In that case, the woman they called Safiye must be in despair.

"I don't believe it, Pasha."

"I tell you, I saw it with my own eyes. Handan turned out to be a woman worth respecting. You remember the beautiful carriage that Safiye Valide got from Elizabeth, the English Queen? They parked it by the harem. Safiye got inside, the servants holding her robe. And then she left the palace."

"An era has ended, hasn't it?"

Nastya couldn't force herself to close the door all the way.

"Exactly... Ahmed Sultan's time has begun. Handan Valide's time."

"Do you mean, Pasha, that fate is going to favor the Ottoman Empire again?"

"Let's pray that's what will happen. Malkoçoğlu Pasha immediately began to convey to the Sultan all the knowledge that he must possess, starting with the required greeting of his subjects on Fridays, when he goes to the mosque for prayer. Then, after the first Friday greeting, they took him to the chamber of the Grand Vizier. There he was circumcised. People waiting outside cheered. And those of us inside."

Ibrahim's face lit up. "Did he cry?"

"Only the Chief Sultan's Doctor and the surgeon performing the procedure were allowed in. All the doors were carefully closed, so we did not hear anything. But still, we praised him, as it was customary. I'm not sure we've done the right thing. There hasn't been such a situation ever before. It is the first time that the throne has been taken by an uncircumcised prince. For the first time, a ceremony of circumcision was held for the incumbent Sultan. There were parties all over the city. Malkoçoğlu Pasha also wants the Sultan to start visiting the harem as soon as possible. When I spoke with him the last time, before leaving Istanbul, he laughed that no one could follow a sultan, who has never been with a woman."

"Anastasia!"

Nastya understood why Master Ibrahim had shouted, but she'd kept the door slightly ajar in the hope that she would hear another sentence or two.

"Yes, My Lord?"

"Close the door!"

She blushed. Driven out of her own palace, she tried to put herself in Safiye Valide's place.

Once again, she'd managed to find out quite a lot of new things. Most of them she tried to reproduce in her imagination, like on the stage.

The sword, larger than the sultan.

A new young queen...

The English queen... *What did he say her name was? Eliz... never mind,* she thought.

A carriage gifted to the Valide...

A dress that was so heavy it had to be held by servants.

And the word, the meaning of which she did not know.

"What does it mean to be circumcised, sister?"

Mirna blushed. "Girls don't talk about such things."

"Why? Is it inappropriate? I heard the Pasha talk about it to Master Ibrahim. Sultan Ahmed was circumcised. Is it something good?"

The woman could not refrain from giggling. Still, it was hard for her to explain it openly, so she whispered it into the girl's ear.

Nastya shouted, then covered her mouth with her hands, "What? I don't believe. My God, doesn't it hurt?"

"I don't know," Mirna replied with a shrug.

"Okay, then what's a harem? I thought I knew, but now I'm not sure."

The woman pretended to get angry. "There we go again. Instead of working, you eavesdrop."

On the fourth day after the Pasha's arrival at the property, something happened again. The cavalry squad drove into the courtyard, accompanied by another cloud of dust.

"We are looking for Çivici Pasha," the riders said.

It became immediately clear why they were looking for him.

"From the capital," said the man in front, relaying a message to Çivici Pasha.

Fleeing from the curious gazes of the people gathered in the courtyard, the Pasha went aside and read the message.

Nastya was on the verge of madness from curiosity.

Master Ibrahim muttered, "Allah, let it be some good news."

Çivici Pasha was looking thoughtful. "Good, good," he said. "The Sultan ordered the Grand Vizier to release Deli Hasan from the office of Beylerbey of Rumelia, and restore me to the position. Malkoçoğlu Yavuz Ali Pasha sent a message informing me of this order."

"What about the rebel cutthroat?"

Who? Nastya wondered. Then she remembered. The man, whom the deceased sultan made a Beylerbey in place of Mehmed Pasha – Deli Hasan.

"He got what he deserved."

Nastya was surprised when she realized that she had difficulty breathing from excitement. Everything that happened in that world was breathtaking. Well, but it probably didn't concern her at all, did it? She couldn't find the answer to that question.

After Çivici Mehmed Pasha left, life at the estate returned to normal. Master Ibrahim disappeared somewhere again, and then came back after a month.

After many attempts, Nastya finally achieved her goal and managed to convince Mirna to reveal the secret to her.

"A harem," said the woman with her cheeks flushing, "that's where they find a woman for a man."

"Oh..." Nastya sighed in her mind. "So, they're looking for a queen for the sultan."

But isn't it too early? she wondered later. *He is only as old as me, after all.*

That night, she realized for the first time that she was no longer a child. They wanted to marry the sultan, who was her age. She felt that jealousy, so far hidden deep down somewhere, was beginning to emerge in her – she envied the girl who wasn't even chosen yet. Because, by marrying Ahmed, she was to become a queen.

She wondered if this unknown girl had ever thought she would be a queen in the Ottoman Empire. Didn't that beggar come to her, too, and call her queen? Did he continue to try to convince her when she opposed him, saying, 'But you will become one?'

That was the destiny, which both Mirna and the priest, to which she went to confess, had talked of. It wasn't certain what God had planned for each one of us. God intended for some girl living in the same world as her, who had no idea about anything, to be the Queen of the Empire. And this girl, of whom nothing was known yet, was soon to be Ahmed's queen.

That girl didn't know her destiny yet, but Nastya knew what awaited her. "One word," she murmured. "My destiny is just that. To be a servant. That's it."

She felt something crack in her.

Pull yourself together! She reprimanded herself. *Don't let your dreams, and all the things you stuffed in your head, hurt you. If God had given everybody the same destiny, being a queen would be of no use to you. Be the queen of your heart. That's enough.*

She didn't know why she reasoned that way. Did that mean she believed in the beggar's words? *Seems that way...* she thought and nodded. *Otherwise, why would I bother with such fantasies? I behave as if I could be queen, but if I just didn't want it myself... Rubbish!*

She got up and sat down on the mattress. It was cold in the room. She got cold. She put her hands between the pillows to try to warm up a little.

I wonder what he is like. The question suddenly appeared in her head.

Who? asked her inner voice. *What who is like?*

Well, him. Ahmed. The Sultan.

She was scared she would burst out laughing.

What is he like, right?

Exactly. She knew he was young. According to what Mirna said – when she remembered her words, she took a crucifix in hand – the young Sultan had just been circumcised, and they were looking for a girl for him. She knew nothing more about him. Was he blind or had a squint? Was he handsome?

For a moment, she did not think of anything, she just sat there in the dark. Later, she began to imagine his face. *Let him have such eyes and such hair...* she dreamed.

She surprised herself. *Why am I doing this? Why am I so interested in Sultan Ahmed? How is any of this my business? Get a grip, Nastya!* she scolded herself. *Isn't it enough that you are the slave of Master Ibrahim? Do you want to set a trap for yourself? After all, being a queen is not something one should strive for. You heard it... Safiye Valide, of whom all were afraid, was kicked out from the palace. Who knows what awaits her now? What future is there for the girl they will find for the sultan? Did you forget what your father said in that sermon?*

She heard her father's voice: '*The wind that blows in the valleys, becomes a storm in the mountains.*'

When she imagined her father standing in front of her, tears came to her eyes. "You're right, Dad," she muttered.

She was the Queen of Servants. Only the Duke of Stable Grooms could become her king. She decided to reward Slobodan with her most beautiful smile.

Everything happened quickly.

That day, around noon, Master Ibrahim returned home. As soon as he got off his horse, he quickly went inside. He headed for the stairs and rushed to the second floor. Nastya and Mirna were upstairs.

He looked nervous. He walked toward his wife's room. Passing them, he said, "Mirna, wait for me. We need to talk."

Mirna and Nastya looked at each other. The girl spoke first, "What might he want to talk about?"

The woman shrugged. She tried to hide it, but she was worried. Panicked. She repeated in her mind the question posed by Nastya: *What might he want to talk about? May Allah protect them, let it be nothing bad.*

Master Ibrahim wasn't in the room for too long.

"Come," he said to Mirna. Nastya followed them. The woman opened the door and moved to the side so he could enter.

"Come in," he said.

The woman threw Nastya a look from behind Master Ibrahim's back. Next, she crossed the doorway and disappeared into the room.

"And you, Anastasia, downstairs," said Master Ibrahim to the girl before closing the door. "I'll call you if I need anything."

Right, but in the meantime, the impatience will drive me mad, she thought.

Nastya stood in the kitchen, in front of the stove where flames crackled. She could not sit still. Every now and then, she got up. *They have been talking for so long*, she thought. *What could he want to talk to Mirna about?*

She tried to come up with something, but it was all in vain. Suddenly, something came to her mind. Why did Master Ibrahim send her away? 'And you, Anastasia, downstairs. I'll call you if I need anything.'

The other night, he got angry at her because she did her job so slowly to overhear his conversation with Çivici Pasha. Surely this time he dismissed her for the same reason – not to let her eavesdrop.

Her heart started beating stronger. "Did you eavesdrop? There you go, you got what you deserved. He dismissed you so that you couldn't hear anything," she murmured to herself.

How long has it been? A quarter of an hour? No, more than that. It might have even been half an hour. What was giant Ibrahim Karayelzade talking about with his maid for so long?

It was probably something bad. Or something bad was yet to happen. Finally, she heard footsteps on the stairs. She ran out of the kitchen and almost collided with Mirna.

"What happened? What did he say?"

The woman turned away, but Nastya noticed it all the same.

"You cried, sister."

Mirna passed her. The girl followed her.

"Don't scare me... What happened? Please don't cry, because I'll also cry."

"Shhh..." Mirna silenced her. "Don't shout. You'll bring everybody running. Come with me."

She thought they were going to the kitchen, but the woman didn't turn there. She opened the door to the garden. The wind forced itself inside.

"Come."

They walked for a moment without speaking. The woman leaned against the trunk of a broad tree so that no one could see them. Nastya stared at her. Mirna's facial expression made her shiver.

"I will miss..." she whispered suddenly. "I got so used to... I will miss terribly."

She tried to refrain from crying, but despite her efforts, tears began to flow down her cheeks.

"You will miss? Who?"

"You."

Nastya didn't understand. She had an emptiness in her head. Complete emptiness.

"Me? Why?"

Mirna embraced her neck. "You are going away, Nastya."

She felt her legs bend under her. Her head spun. If Mirna didn't hold her in her arms, she would fall to the ground. *What?!* she thought frantically. *I'm going away? Where? Why?*

Despite her panic, she found the answer to the last question. *Why? The lord is chasing you away. You dared to listen to his conversations. You lost his trust.* Nastya didn't realize that streams of tears also flowed down her own cheeks. All the while, she thought she could feel Mirna's tears on her face, as they hugged. It turned out that their tears of despair mingled together.

I got what I was afraid of, she mused, trying to find an explanation for her exile. *What business of yours is that? Why do you have to know about the goings on in the palace? Why do you dare to eavesdrop on the big Pasha? Can you answer me? Why do you need knowledge of the bloody deceptions and intrigues of sultans and princes? Because some beggar said that you would become a queen? Because when you opposed him, he insisted you would become one? Ah, right, after all, the queen is interested in the affairs of the palace. She should know how other queens behave. Will they take the crown belonging to Safiye and put it on your head? Why do you care about Safiye? Why are you eavesdropping? Go on, answer.*

The more she thought about it, the closer she was to madness. She became overwhelmed with sadness. Just when she was happy that spring was coming and that the flowers would grow... Now she felt that it was, for her anyway, the beginning of a dark winter that would never end. Who knew who bought her? And where would she go now?

"Don't cry dear, don't cry, pretty Nastya. Don't cry, my queen without a crown."

Queen? Nastya's body began to protest. *Damn that word,* she cursed in her mind. *Damn also the day when the beggar called me a queen.*

That day everything changed – her way of thinking, her soul, her feelings. She realized that even the way she walked changed, too. And how she sat down.

"Where?" she finally managed to utter. "Sister, where? Where is our Lord sending me away to?"

In one second, the expression on the woman's face changed. It even seemed to Nastya that she smiled lightly.

"Sending you away? Nothing like that, darling. He's sending you to the capital."

Despite the paralyzing panic, the girl opened her eyes wide. Even her tears stopped flowing out of surprise.

"Where? To the capital? What is the capital?"

"The capital means the place where the Sultan of the Ottoman Empire lives, beautiful Nastya. You know Çivici Pasha. He is Rumelia's Beylerbey again. He will soon leave for Istanbul. That is the custom. A Beylerbey cannot go to the capital with empty hands. And now, there is also a new sultan on the throne. Gold, jewels, fur, silk, ser..."

Suddenly, Mirna stopped and felt awkward. She was about to say 'servants, maids, and slaves.' Fortunately, the girl didn't pay attention to the last syllable that came out of her mouth.

"Everything that would come to your mind," she continued. "Gifts are brought for the Sultan and his mother. If the Sultan has women, then also for them, and for the Grand Vizier. Çivici Pasha saw you here. He liked you; he was pleased with the way you served him. He asked Master Ibrahim if he could have you."

"Why?"

"He will give you to the Sultan's Mother, the new Valide Sultan."

A gift! That was exactly what she was. Something that is bought and sold. Something that can be given as a gift, just like a ring, a necklace, or some precious material. A slave; a maid.

She started crying with streams of tears again. Even though she knew it was stupid, she mumbled, "I won't go. Don't let me go, sister. Don't leave me."

The woman hugged her again. As she stroked Nastya's hair, she said, "I don't want you to leave, either. But Nastya, it will be better for you. You are going to the palace. To Handan Valide."

The storm of emotions that raged in her suddenly stopped. She realized that all the words she had heard so far had been erased. Except one – the palace. "You are going to the palace..."

Didn't the Queen live in the palace? She was just about to go to the palace... She was going to serve the Queen.

She was to see the Sultan of the Ottoman Empire. And, of course, he would see her, too. Didn't these types of things happen in the palace?

Was it good or bad, she didn't know? But she felt a kind of satisfaction that she could not identify at that present moment. *To the palace, right? To the palace? Mother of God, I'm going to the palace?*

Mirna understood that the expression on the girl's face indicated that she had hesitations. She touched the girl's chin with her palm, raised her head, and looked her in the eye. She smiled warmly to cheer her up. "You see?

He didn't lie. The prophecy of a blind beggar is fulfilled... You're going to the palace."

Nastya felt her face twitch in a painful smile. "Yes," she sighed, lowering her head. "I'm going to the palace to be the Queen's servant."

The woman didn't react to this reproach. She stroked her head, touched her cheek with hers, and, taking a breath, inhaled her scent.

"Your destiny awaits you, Nastya. Go out to meet it. We don't know what Allah has planned for you."

"When?" she asked calmly. "When am I leaving?"

"You set off in the morning."

CHAPTER NINE

Skopje - Thessaloniki
March 1604

"Damn it, again?"

The wagon suddenly jumped on the stone and fell into a hole on the road, with Nastya sitting inside. It rolled over onto its side with a thud. She realized that the two wagons following them stopped. The screams and curses of the horsemen and coachmen mingled together.

She moved her hand, then her leg. She was all right. When the wagon rolled over, she only got hit in the head – and yes, her forehead hurt. She touched it with her hand and noticed that her fingers were covered with blood.

"My God... blood." In fear – and to make sure – she also touched her forehead with the other hand.

Yes, she was bleeding. She pulled out a handkerchief out of her vest pocket and pressed it against the cut. She grimaced in pain. "Damn it!" she grunted.

This should all be some kind of a dream – no, rather, a nightmare – and she wasn't sure of that. But she sure expected one thing – that she'd break all her bones soon. If the road continued to be like this, and if the coachman tried to ride over every single stone that's on the road, it would surely happen.

She heard Slobodan, "Hey, Nastya. Are you all right?"

"If you don't count my forehead, then yes," she muttered, trying to straighten up. "What happened?"

"The wheel broke."

"For God's sake," she said angrily. "How many times already?"

She noticed Slobodan's head where the coachman should be sitting. He looked worried.

"I've counted three so far." He smiled, trying to calm her. "Don't move. Let me look at your forehead."

There were still shouts coming from the outside. With great effort into every movement, the groom's son crawled to Nastya, who still lay in the overturned wagon. He slowly pulled her hand away from her forehead so as not to hurt her. "It's cut," he said.

"Damn, there will be a scar."

"Don't worry. It will bleed for a moment, then it will dry up. In a few days, there will be no trace left. And besides..."

"Besides what?"

Slobodan looked deeply into her eyes. "You're so beautiful," he muttered. He smiled and lowered his head shyly. "Even if there is a scar, it won't do anything to your beauty."

Don't be so happy with yourself. I suffer sufficiently, Nastya wanted to answer him, but at that moment, someone started shaking the wagon.

"What's going on?"

"They're trying to put the wagon upright."

It seemed to them that the wagon was slowly returning to its upright position. As Nastya tried to pull herself together, Slobodan jumped out.

"Here's my arm," came the voice from outside. "Come on, hurry."

"Pull!" someone else shouted.

"Careful! Easy, easy."

At some point, they fell silent.

"Hey!" This time, Slobodan shouted. "Slowly, you will break his arm. If he is still alive, he will die from your hands."

"Die? Who is dying?" Nastya moved in a hurry toward the coachman's seat. She looked out from the wagon in the direction from which the voices came. In the place where a broken wheel should be, she noticed Slobodan, along with another man whom she didn't know. All the weight of the wagon rested on their backs. The others tried to pull out something that was squeezed between the ground and the wagon.

"What is it?"

Nobody turned toward her. Slobodan wouldn't be able to answer her anyway; his face was covered with sweat droplets from the effort he put into supporting the wagon.

"Come on, one more time," he said. "Gently, gently, one more time."

So, they did. They pulled slowly. One more time.

When the wheel broke, the man fell, and the metal shaft that connected the wheels pierced his chest like a lance.

"He died?" she whispered with fear. "My God, did he die?"

Nobody answered.

"Come on, jump off!" Slobodan shouted to her. "Down, quickly. I can't hold it like this for long."

Nastya did not jump to the side where the body was, but to the opposite one. At the same moment, Slobodan moved, and the wagon rolled over onto its side again.

"We are staying here tonight," said the mustached cavalryman assigned to Master Ibrahim for protection. "But first, let's bury him. Later, we will take care of the wheel."

They ate, sitting by a fire made by the soldiers. Nobody spoke. Nobody smiled, not even Slobodan. Everyone raised their head from time to time and with a sigh, looked at the mound between the trees. That was where the driver had been buried.

Nastya could still hear the sound of his breaking bones as the men had tried to pull out the metal shaft stuck into his chest. *Damn it*, she thought. *Never again should I get into a wagon. Because every time I did, someone died.*

She was surprised by what came to her mind at that moment. She wondered what the carriage given to Safiye by the English queen looked like, whatever her name was... she couldn't remember her name in any way... something beginning with an 'E.' The carriage in which Safiye Valide got into when she was chased away from the palace. Surely it didn't overturn like theirs; its wheels certainly wouldn't break so easily.

I can't believe it, Nastya! She got angry at herself. *How can you think about that at such a moment?*

Really, how could she?

Later, when the other three women who rode with them saw what had happened to the coachman, they fainted. One of them vomited for a few minutes. Meanwhile, Nastya, despite the whole scene being really horrifying, looked at the bloody event calmly. Slobodan tried to protest, but she watched as three men struggled to get the metal shaft out of the man.

What kind of a person have you become? she asked herself. *You have a heart of stone.*

She spent the night with the three women in the wagon. The wagons were full of gifts from Master Ibrahim. When the women lay down to sleep, there was so little space that they were forced to squeeze next to each other.

Slobodan ordered Nastya to sit in the corner of the wagon. Thanks to that, she could sleep a little further away from the snoring and sweaty women. She leaned against the two corner walls and this way, she was much more comfortable. She stared at the quilt of stars covering them through the crack in the canvas roof of the wagon.

If my mother raised her head, would she see the same stars I'm looking at now? This thought made her miss home, and she felt a great pain in her heart, but it also allowed her to feel closer to her mother. After all, they were under the same roof. When they lifted their heads, they saw the same stars, the same moon.

She felt pain in her heart. Her mother's soul was near her, but her face... She could not recall her face. The face of her parent was blurred as if covered by a thin veil-like fog. God, how could this happen? All that was left of her mother was a song she used to sing in her sweet voice, wishing her a good night:

Mother Mary, look at this angel in my arms.
Tell me the truth: who is more beautiful,
My Nastya or beautiful goddesses?
Give this baby, with cheeks red like a rose,
a happy and joyful life.

Tears flowed into her eyes. She heard her mother's voice as if she was as close as she was sitting by her side.

Nastya knew that even if her mother's face disappeared, covered with a fog of suffering, she would always be with her. She whispered the lullaby softly:

Mother Mary don't let the sky thunder;
say that the angel of Eftalia is asleep.
Don't let the birds chirp, don't let the wolves howl.
Look, God smiles at my Nastya.

The next evening, they reached Skopje. The wagons were immediately directed to the courtyard of Çivici Mehmed Pasha's estate.

Slobodan quietly made his way through the crowd and approached Nastya. "Tomorrow," he whispered, "we leave early in the morning. Please go out into the yard so I can see you one last time."

She didn't have a chance to answer, because the head maid of Çivici Pasha's estate immediately separated her from the others. She showed her where to wash and where to sleep. Then the head maid pointed at a trunk that stood in the middle of the room. "Tomorrow, when you leave, take this trunk with you. This is a gift from the Beylerbey," she said.

"A gift?" Nastya muttered.

"Yes," answered the woman with confidence in her voice. "After all, the Beylerbey can't send the Sultan Mother a naked gift."

Nastya wanted to laugh when she thought of the gift for the 'gift,' but she managed to hold it back. Instead, she just said, "Thank you."

Nastya couldn't sleep all night. From Skopje, they were going to set out, in carriages, to some other city whose name was mentioned by a maid, but she did not remember. But this time, Slobodan would not be there with her. In the morning, she would part from him, too. Goodbyes made her soul burn. She felt that she lost a piece of herself with each parting.

She remembered how Mirna hugged her, saying, "Good luck to you, my queen."

"Sister."

"Just do not cry, please."

She hugged her tightly. "Don't call me a queen."

"Why shouldn't I call you that?"

"Because I'm not one, that's why. I'm a maid."

"Not at all. You are my queen. I don't care what others say."

Later, she stepped away slightly and looked deeply into her eyes. She had a forced smile on her face. "What I'm going to say now, please remember forever. Make an 'earring' out of this, you madwoman candidate. Queens do not cry. Queens do not give in. Step firmly on the ground. Be so dignified that anyone who passes you will think you are a true queen. Everyone is a king in his own kingdom, my beauty. The same way you should be the queen in your own. Okay?"

What could she answer? "Okay." She said it so quietly that she couldn't hear it herself.

"What did you say? Okay?"

"Okay."

It's time to get into the wagons," Slobodan's father, a stableman, then said.

So, it's over.

Nastya understood at that moment the difference between being separated from her beloved by force and her heart burning with regret when she had to say goodbye to them. When everything happens quickly, suddenly, sadness comes later. This time, when she bade farewell to everyone before her departure, she felt the pain right away.

I will never go through another parting, Nastya promised herself. *Never. I will leave. I'll leave and run away. I'll turn around and start walking. I will not look back. Without saying goodbye, without saying goodbye...*

But that day, they had to part. They wiped their tears every now and then, shook, and crumpled with sorrow. They weren't going to see each other again.

"Sister..." she whispered. "Don't forget about me."

"Candidate for a madwoman."

It wasn't clear whether Mirna was crying or laughing. She escorted Nastya to the wagon she was about to board and held her hand as she helped her up. When the coachman snapped a leather whip, she took the girl's hand and kissed her fingertips.

"God, Mirna."

"I was the first one to kiss your hand, my queen."

The wagon began to move away, and Mirna waved to her. When she noticed that Nastya cried, she touched her earlobe, which was supposed to remind the girl: 'Make an earring.'

'Queens do not cry. Be the queen in your own kingdom.'

So, it was supposed to be. The decision she'd made at night, she put into effect in the morning.

She went out to the courtyard to peep at Slobodan. The boy, full of hope that the girl would come, did everything to delay the departure – but it was all in vain –

Nastya did not come. He looked at the windows, but couldn't see her. Finally, he jumped on the scary wagon they had come here in. He sat down on the seat of the driver, who had died two days earlier. Nastya, seeing the disappointment on his face and the sadness in his eyes, jumped out of the place where she had been observing him and shouted, "Slobodan! I am here."

"Oh no!" Slobodan shouted, laughing aloud. He didn't say anything, but in his voice, she felt a reproach as if he wanted to say, "Where have you been? We're already leaving."

I wish you all the luck, she thought. She bit her lips. Something squeezed her throat so that she couldn't get out a word. She opened her eyes wide so that tears wouldn't start flowing from them. *Never!* She repeated the oath in her mind: *I will never again say goodbye. Never. I will leave. I'll leave and run away. I'll turn around and start walking. I won't even look back. Without farewell, without saying goodbye.*

It was around noon when they left the property. This time, the group consisted of eight carriages loaded to the limits of capacity and a unit of soldiers, and it seemed to her that the carriage she traveled in this time, was more comfortable. She had also been given a girl to help her.

"Her name is Sofia. She will help you," said the principal maid.

How will she be able to help me? Nastya wanted to protest. The girl was no more than ten and had curly hair.

The next day, at sunset, a city appeared before them. Located in the valley, it seemed to open its arms to the sea. On the left side, she saw a castle.

"What is this city?" she asked the coachman.

"Thessaloniki."

They descended the hill. The voice in her head repeatedly told her: *Run. Find a ship. Cry. Beg them to take you home. Do something. Run, run!*

Was she really capable of doing that? Could she escape from the whole horsemen division and save herself? If you caught a slave who escaped, despite the money paid for them, would they still be killed? Even if she escaped and wasn't caught, would she be able to find a ship that would take her to Milos? Even if she found it, would the wind be strong enough to take her home?

She didn't know the answer to any of those questions.

The big black ship with a wide deck, which they boarded in the harbor, struggling with sea waves and winds, was about to take her to the capital.

That night, for the first time in many days, she managed to fall asleep. Also, the next night. In her dreams, she saw Mirna. Her hand was touching her ear. 'Make an earring. Queens do not cry.'

She stirred. Someone stroked her cheek.

My God... she thought in panic.

She tried not to move. Maybe she should scream and call for help? What if he had a knife in his hand? As her mind slowly woke up, she heard voices from up on the deck. Screams, footsteps. Something had to be going on up there. The hand touched her cheek again. Then it moved to her hair. If she didn't react and kept silent, would he think she likes it? She jumped up in anger. She saw dark eyes wide open with fear.

"My God, Sofia, what are you doing? I almost died of fear. I thought that..."

It was evident that the girl was terribly scared, too. "We have arrived," she whispered.

"What?"

"The ship came to shore. We've arrived at the place they were talking about."

Nastya stood up. She put on the cape she had taken out of the trunk given to her by the Beylerbey.

"Come on," she said to the little girl. "Let's go on deck. Let's see at what hell we have arrived."

As she climbed the stairs, a fresh morning breeze hit her face. She ran the last four steps, taking a deep breath of the sea air into her lungs.

The sun shone straight into her eyes, and the sun's rays dazzled her. Her eyes closed under the strong light. She heard Sofia say quietly, "Oh dear..."

"What happened?" She opened her eyelids slowly. The only thing she saw through her squinted eyes was the blue sky mixed with the turquoise sea...

Then suddenly, she noticed the little green hills on both sides of the coast that stretched between them like a river. When she turned her head to the left, she noticed the sun, which was enchanting the area with its rays. She lost her breath.

"Great Father..." she sighed and took out her crucifix. She couldn't even imagine such a beautiful city in her dreams. This had to be the Golden City that she knew of from her Grandma's stories. The city of kings and queens!

We must have gone off course, crossed her mind. Otherwise, how would it be possible? The storm raging at night had to have taken the ship in its arms, moved it over the Kaf Mountain, and brought here, into a beautiful fairytale land.

"Hey!" she shouted at one of the sailors who ran past them.

The man started climbing one of the huge masts.

"What is this city?" Nastya shouted after him.

The seaman paused for a moment. He gave a puzzled look at the girl who looked up at him.

"What do you mean, what is this city? You don't know? The heart of the Ottoman Empire, Istanbul."

"Istanbul..."

Nastya once again took out her crucifix. She touched her breast. Her heart pounded loudly.

She took Sophia's delicate wrist in her hand and pulled her toward the railing. She tried to take in the view of the whole golden silhouette of the city. A strong wind blew the hood of her cape off her head. It scattered her hair. She squeezed the little girl's wrist harder. The wind was so strong that Sofia's tiny, light body could barely stay upright.

"What is this place, sister?" The girl was just as enchanted with the view.

"The place to which destiny has led us." She surprised herself at how mysteriously her voice sounded.

Mother Mary... She thought. *Tell our father. May he forgive me for having opposed him so many times. Thinking that I was going to hell, I found myself in heaven.*

Chapter Ten

New Palace, Harem Chambers
April 1604

"What will they do to us, sister?" Sofia stared at her with dark eyes that she had kept on her for some time.

I do not know, either... crossed her mind. After they left the ship, they spent the remainder of their journey in a closed carriage.

Although they were both dying of curiosity, they couldn't see anything. They could hear the passersby's voices, but could not see them. The wheels of the carriage jumped on the rocks, but they didn't make any sounds as frightening as the wheels of the wagon in which Nastya traveled from Kumanovo to Skopje. Something must have been put on the metal shaft that connected the wheels to stop them from creaking. Also, people could sit in this carriage on both sides.

To keep from getting bored while traveling in the dark interior of the carriage, she imagined that the carriage, pulled by horses, was the carriage given by the English Queen to Safiye Valide. "Just look, the seats are so soft!" She laughed under her breath. This pastime went on for the whole journey.

As she sat, she assumed a majestic pose. She straightened her back and raised her head.

I am Safiye Valide, she thought. *No, no.* She shrugged. *I am Queen Anastasia. And Sofia is my Chief Servant. When I climbed into the carriage, she held my clothes. When I get out, she will do the same. My dress has a very long train. I will instruct my tailors not to make any more like this. If they don't listen to me, I'll order my guards to stick needles in their hands.*

In her fantasies, she had a crown on her head and a necklace of giant pearls and rubies around her neck. She looked at her hands. Rings, decorated with diamonds and emeralds, immediately appeared on her fingers. The material of the cape only looks thick... but it's really silk. Later, she changed her mind. She would be cold in silk. Velvet would be better. Velvet, with a color reminiscent of the darkness of the night... She ordered her tailors to decorate it with silver, which would look like the stars.

Her eyes stopped at the tips of her ugly boots, made from thick leather. She quickly hid them under the robe. Now she had shoes decorated with silver on her legs. At their tips, there were two tiny gold balls!

After she had dressed herself in her mind, it was the turn of the surprised Sophia, as it was customary for the Queen's First Servant. She dressed her in an ankle-length dress with a flower motif. To this, she added a beautiful vest and a decorative apron that reached to the knees. She gently combed Sofia's hair, which was tousled by the wind. *Yes, that's enough*, she thought. *Servants cannot be dressed better than Queens.*

When the carriage stopped, Nastya ordered in her head the words she was going to tell the king, who waited for her in the throne room.

Slobodan sat on the throne with a huge crown on his head. Ibrahim, whom she thought was the master of Karayelzade's estate in Kuman, stood near the throne. He was the King's Adviser.

Queen Anastasia slowly bowed to King Slobodan. "Your Highness..."

The King's eyes gleamed. "My Queen... The light shines from you. Today, you are even more beautiful."

At that moment, the carriage door opened and when the interior filled with light, nothing remained of the king nor the queen. There was nothing left but two frightened girls.

She'd expected a palace. But what they saw after leaving the carriage did not resemble a palace. They stood in a courtyard surrounded by tall walls. The coachman brought Nastya's trunk and set it on the ground. He turned and walked away.

Opposite them was a two-story wooden house, painted green. Several people with swarthy skin entered and exited through the door of the house that overlooked the courtyard. They were people with skin so dark that at first glance, she could not recognize whether it was a man or a woman. This was the only reason she thought the place they had come to, was the palace. If there are dark-skinned servants here, it means they are in the palace. Was it not so in the stories?

Of course, the dark-skinned servants were not the only people who were there. There were also light-skinned people like Nastya and Sofia amongst the bustle of people. Men and women with flawless, fair skin. Some were dressed in similar clothes that indicated what kind of work they were doing. For example, the girls who brought in trays and later carried them out, emptied, wore blue galligaskins, white shirts with wide sleeves, and tight, short, red vests. Muslin scarves, covering their hair, fluttered in the wind.

Nobody asked them who they were, where they'd come from, or why they waited there. None of the passing people asked them to leave or move aside. No one asked if they were thirsty. Everyone passed them as if they weren't there at all, or as if by some spell, they were invisible.

Nastya began to feel scared. At first, she couldn't understand why, but later she realized the reason – even though there were so many people here, there was silence. Everyone was quiet as if they were not there. Their connection to reality was composed only by the rustling made by their galligaskins and vests as they passed through the courtyard in a hurry.

She didn't remember how long they waited.

Eventually, a plump, dark-skinned woman came up to them. "Are you the girl who's come from Skopje?" she asked in such a quiet voice that Nastya wondered for a moment whether the woman really had said anything, or if she'd just imagined it.

This was the first time she'd ever met or talked to someone with dark skin. The woman had very thick lips, just like she'd heard in stories – but she was beautiful, lovely; her teeth were like pearls and her eyes... like two dark circles that constantly moved.

Nastya nodded.

"How are we to call you?"

"Nastya."

"No, you guessed wrong. From now on, we will call you Hatice. Remember your new name."

What? What new name, what does it mean? She wanted to protest. She would never accept it. She was Nastya. Anastasia Vasiliades – the name given to her in honor of her ancestors. She couldn't give it up. "I already have a name, I don't need a new one."

"Who is that, Hatice?" The mysterious woman looked with fear at Sofia, whose eyes pierced her.

"Listen, I will repeat myself again. My name is Nastya. I don't need another name. And this is my helper. Her name is S—"

"Your helper?"

"What is so strange about that?"

"Huh, since when does a maid have a maid?"

Nastya didn't even notice when her hand went to her ear. She heard Mirna's voice: 'Be so dignified that everyone would think you are a real queen.' She raised her head. She straightened and pushed her chest forward. The best thing to do was not to answer the question.

"She cannot stay with you."

Sofia quickly grasped Nastya's dress and hid behind her back.

"I don't know who you are," she said to the woman, putting on a gentle smile. "It's not important. But know that Sofia is with me, and she will stay here."

The woman shuddered. She stared in Nastya's eyes for a moment. *I've had a thousand problems on my head; and now I got the thousand and first one*, she thought.

"My name is Dilşad," the black woman said. "Girls call me Sister Dilşad. I am a helper of Babüssaade Aga..."

Babüs what? Nastya thought. *She said Babüs what?* To hide her surprise, she gave the woman a broad smile.

"Listen. I don't know why, but I feel that I like you. Otherwise, I would have wrenched that tongue out from that foul mouth of yours long ago, Hatice."

"My name is Anastasia," she insisted. "Or you can also call me Nastya. But if anybody calls me Hatice, I will not react. The name given to me by my parents is enough for me. Additionally, Sofia is with me, and it will stay this way. I will not leave her anywhere."

The woman narrowed her eyes and stared at her from under long eyelashes for some time. Next, she glanced at Sofia, who looked out fearfully from behind Nastya's back.

"Well, let it be like this for now. Come with me."

Sofia immediately grabbed Nastya's trunk. When she grabbed the handle and tried to move it, the courtyard filled with the terrible sound of metal as she dragged it – with which the corners of the trunk were covered – shattering the silence in the courtyard.

"Allah!" Dilşad jumped. "Shh! Damn you, girl! You'll put the whole harem on their feet! Leave this –"

"The trunk is mine," Nastya interrupted. "Where Anastasia is, the girl and the trunk follow."

The woman's eyes pierced her.

"I said I'll only accept the girl for the time being. If you also want to have your trunk, take it in your hand. Or leave it. And do not worry, they will bring it. Who would want to take your shabby clothes?"

"They are not shabby at all," she said and motioned for Sofia to let go of the trunk.

They followed the woman and entered the building. Ahead of them, they saw a corridor that was so long that they couldn't even see its end. Or maybe it was just dark there. There were rows of doors on both sides.

"What's this place?"

"The harem."

"The harem? It's here?"

"You don't like it?" The woman laughed. "You really don't know anything. This is the back part of the harem. All servants, stable boys and others working in the palace live here. The proper harem is at the end of the courtyard. You didn't think you would be living there?"

"Why wouldn't I think that?" she replied. "My master offered me to the harem."

The woman suddenly stopped. She turned back. This time, the looks she gave them both were not that friendly anymore.

"Okay," she said dryly. "This place also belongs to the harem."

She took them to a small courtyard with five corners. Buildings surrounded it on all sides. When Nastya raised her head, she saw two floors upstairs, and she noticed wooden railings. It was a dark, cold, and terrifying place, that stank from dampness and moisture.

She thought she had made a big mistake. She'd thought that God would reward her by sending her to paradise. Even if the city looked like heaven, this place resembled a dungeon. It seemed that God, sending her to a prison in the middle of paradise, wanted to punish her disobedience.

Sofia was also scared. She looked at everything with frightened eyes. If Nastya let go of her wrist, she would've probably run away.

"People call this place the Novice Courtyard," the plump woman explained to them. "Service in the harem begins here. If you learn everything well, you will serve well.

If you do not stand up to anyone as you did to me today, and if you are lucky, you will not stay here longer than a year or two, and you will get a place in the dormitory."

"Dormitory?"

"Yes. That is where the girls serving in the harem sleep and live." The woman looked around. "I'm afraid all rooms are occupied. Find something to sleep on and find yourselves some free corner somewhere. Then take care of yourselves... Well, that is enough information for today. I'm gonna go have somebody bring your trunk."

The woman turned away, to leave them alone. As she moved away, swaying her hips, Nastya called, "Hey! Does Handan Valide live here?"

The woman stopped. She turned her head slowly.

"What did you say?"

"Handan—"

The plump woman approached her so fast, she barely had time to see her move. "Shhh..." Dilşad caught Nastya, shook her, and showed her a fist almost as big as Sofia's head. "The holy name of the Valide can never come out of a maid's mouth." She looked into girl's eyes with anger. "I will have a lot of work with you. Nobody has taught you manners or how to behave. But never mind. I will teach you everything..."

Nastya's hand went back to her ear again. She remembered the earring given to her by Mirna. 'Stand straight. Do not bend.'

"I want to see her. Beylerbey sent me to serve the Sultan other Handan, and..."

Dilşad let her go. Nodding, she muttered something under her breath. Next, she began to mock Nastya, "Oh really? I'm sure she's worried about you. She wonders what happened to this girl who was supposed to come here. She should be here now."

The woman changed her voice and facial expression. "Now find a corner and stay there. And don't try to protest, Hatice," she said flatly, then she turned and walked away again, swaying her hips. "I'm not so understanding to everyone," she said at last. "But as I said, I like you. You're new here. Be yourself, but talk to no one in the way you did today with me... If you do so and you play a great lady, you will face glory."

"Glory?" The girl was surprised. "Who is that?"

The woman stopped at the door.

"Hold on. You two will definitely meet."

Several times, she tried to enter a room whose windows faced the courtyard, but each time she was sent away. The rooms were small. Three or four girls slept in each of them, crowded together. And none of them wanted to accept two more. Finally, one took out a thin mattress and said, "Take it. Lay it by the door and curl up on it."

"But there are two of us."

The girl stared at her blankly.

Nastya realized they were all in a hopeless situation, so she laid out the mattress given to her by the girl. She placed the trunk by her side. They tried to put it on the mattress, but it wasn't possible – one of them would have to sleep on the stone floor.

"Let's sleep in turns, holding watch," Nastya said to Sofia, while she tried to smile despite the tears that gathered at the corners of her eyes. "First, you go to sleep. I will hold watch first."

Sofia did not think twice. She lay down immediately and closed her eyes. Nastya looked at her for a while. In her mind, she repeated the words of the lullaby that her mother used to sing. Later, she imagined she saw a prince. He took out his sword and walked toward the small courtyard. The maid of Babüs-something tried to stop him. When the prince struggled with the woman, she saw his face. Slobodan! Prince Slobodan!

"Nastya!" the prince shouted. "Where are you?"

"Here I am, my prince, here!"

Slobodan ran, but he could not get closer to her in any way.

Suddenly she jumped in fear.

"Get out of my way, stupid!"

She opened her eyes. God, she was so tired that she'd fallen asleep sitting on the stone floor. The woman who came back after finishing work jumped over them while trying to get into the room.

"I'm talking to you, stupid girl. Get out of the way!"

At the same time, she kicked Nastya, who rolled over in pain.

She saw a face bending over her, eyes burning with anger. "Who are you? It's the first time I've seen you here. And the last time. If I see you sleeping in front of the door of my room again, I'll scratch out your eyes."

She tried to get up. Everything hurt.

"Take this youngster away, too!"

The angry servant who'd pushed Nastya began to kick Sofia, who had been sleepily looking at her.

At that moment, something snapped in Nastya. "Don't touch her!"

The woman left the girl alone and immediately turned to face Nastya.

"What did you say?"

"Don't touch her," she repeated. Even Nastya was afraid of her own voice. The woman remained impassive, though.

"What will happen if I do?"

"I'll kill you." She didn't even take a second to be surprised that she'd said it so easily. Then she caught the hair of the maid, who'd tried to strike Sofia. The woman cried out in pain and anger. When she looked at her hand, she noticed the bunch of hair she had gripped in her fist.

"Hit her," one of the other girls said.

"Scratch out her eyes!" another shouted.

"Hit, break, tear!" There were voices from all over the room.

They began to laugh.

The woman howled. When she prepared to jump on her and scratch her, Nastya noticed that other women had surrounded them. The doors of all the rooms around the courtyard opened, and servants from the harem formed a circle around them. They'd all forgotten about their fatigue – watching an argument stirred emotions in them and brought entertainment to their monotonous life.

"Tear her apart, Mürüvvet!" Apparently, that was her name.

"Kill her!"

"Give her a lesson!"

Mürüvvet grabbed Nastya's hair with her hands, and Nastya reciprocated.

At that moment she heard Sofia's tearful voice, "Sister..."

She wanted to shout at her, “Don’t be afraid!” But at that moment, a roar of pain came out of her throat. Nastya jerked the woman with all her strength. But she was taller and more strongly built than Nastya. And strong. Nastya was in a hopeless situation. It was clear how this fight would end – Mürüvvet would tear her apart – she was going to scratch her eyes out and disfigure her face.

Suddenly, Nastya sensed that the woman’s ear was under the hair she was holding. She remembered how she bit Cyprian. She grabbed her ear and dug her nails into it with all her strength.

“Let go!” Mürüvvet shouted with a groan.

She didn’t listen. On the contrary, she dug her nails in even harder. She turned the woman’s head and tried to reach the ear with her lips.

Mürüvvet lost strength in the hand with which she had been trying to reach the girl’s face.

In only a few seconds, she could scratch Nastya, who tried to catch the woman’s ear with all her strength... She caught it. Her teeth tightened on the woman’s body.

A shrill cry pierced the air. The woman lost all her strength. The fingers, with which she held tight to the girl’s hair, slowly opened.

Nastya, let the ear out of her mouth and pushed the servant with all her might.

Mürüvvet, whose one hand involuntarily caught her bleeding ear, lost her balance and fell to the floor.

Silence fell on the courtyard.

She noticed heads leaning out from behind the wooden balustrades; everyone watched her.

"Sister Nastya." Sofia ran up and hugged her. Two women hurriedly approached Mürüvvet, who now lay on the ground, writhing in pain.

"You almost bit her ear off!" one of the women said.

"Then she should thank God I haven't done that," Nastya said boldly. "I warned her not to touch Sofia."

Somebody brought a piece of cloth. Someone else bent over Mürüvvet and examined her ear.

"Eh, the wound is not deep. There will be no trace in a week."

A cloth was pressed to the bleeding ear, and they helped her up. Mürüvvet rested on the shoulders of two women, and as she passed in front of Nastya, she shot her a killing look. "Just don't turn your back on me," she hissed. "And don't think that I will leave it like that."

Nastya was silent. *You've made enemies already on the first day in the palace, queen...* She sighed inwardly.

That night, Nastya met with glory. She tried to protect her face when the stick fell on her shoulders, head, and back, in the middle of the yard.

"What is your name?" someone snarled, lashing down another hit with the stick.

"Nastya."

"I did not hear that, repeat!"

"Nastya, Nastya!"

Every time she said 'Nastya,' the blows fell on her back again.

"They said your name is Hatice. Are you a liar, or are they?"

"My name is Nastya."

The blows fell again.

"What? What did you say?"

Reason whispered in her ear that she should finally give up. Otherwise, she would die.

"What?" A scream could be heard again. "What's your name?"

From where she fell, Nastya whispered, 'Hatice.' It hurt her just as much as those blows. And maybe even more.

"What? I could not hear! Repeat. What is your name?"

"Hatice, Hatice. My name is Hatice."

"Well done. We have reached an understanding. Welcome among us, Hatice."

They must have expected her to cry and beg, but she did not even argue. In her mind, she still shouted: *My name is Nastya! Nastya. Daughter of Kostas Vasiliadis and Eftalia. Anastasia Vasilides.*

Sadly, however, she began to understand that it wasn't like that anymore.

She was one big pain. She could not move, she couldn't even lean her back against anything. She just sat cross-legged on the mattress and stayed like that.

Some queen, she thought despite the pain.

More than by the blows themselves, she was hurt by the fact that she let herself be broken and, under the beatings, she'd agreed to accept the new name. And the fact that she was beaten in front of so many servants and farmhands... *Before you were the queen of servants. Well done, you've been promoted. Now you are the queen of whips!*

Sofia didn't know what to do. She struggled to help her, but she couldn't do anything. This powerlessness led her to tears.

"Get up – let's go to my place."

Nastya raised her head and saw the woman the voice belonged to. It was the same woman who gave them one free mattress.

She tried to get up, but it wasn't easy. She only managed to get up with the help of a stranger and Sofia.

"Come on, let's see what's up with your back."

They went into a room. There were three mattresses on the ground: one opposite the entrance and two more along the wall arranged one next to the other. It seemed that the girls who slept on them had to touch each other's legs at night. There was a small table against the wall to the right where two lit torches stood, two glasses, and a clay jug. In the back of the room, at head height, there was a door, most likely into the closet. There was no other furniture here.

"My trunk!" Nastya groaned.

"Lie down, I'll take care of it," the woman said.

Nastya, feeling very sore, lay down on her stomach. It seemed to her that she would never be able to get up again. It was true that she'd defeated that woman, but in exchange, she'd lost her life. The palace turned out to be not her hope, but a trap. *I'm stuck here forever*, she thought. *Nothing else awaits me here. The only thing I can count on in the future is a room like this one. Some paradise. You have your paradise!*

The woman returned quickly. Sofia helped her place the trunk next to the small table. Nastya heard the door to the closet in the wall open.

"It's good that it's over," said the woman.

She moaned something in reply, not understanding herself what she was saying.

"Help your sister uncover her back, baby." She turned to Sofia. "Just be careful not to cause her any pain."

The girl ripped the clothes off Nastya's back with her small hands.

"We'll see how it is," the woman said as she knelt beside her.

Sofia started to cry again. "My dear sister... my beautiful sister!"

"Calm down," the woman reminded her gently. "It's not as bad as I thought. There's no reason to cry."

She put an open jar next to Nastya.

"This ointment helps with every wound. Except for those in the heart..." She smiled, then fell silent, seeing that the girls were not in the mood for jokes. Suddenly, Nastya felt something soft and cold on her back. It was the woman, who'd started to run her hands over the bloody wounds and bruises that had already begun to turn blue.

"At first, it will burn a bit, but you have to endure it. It will pass quickly. This ointment will prevent the wound from becoming suppurated. It will bring relief and speed up the healing."

"Don't move," she said after she had covered Nastya's back with the ointment. She stood up and went to the closet again. Nastya heard cloth being torn. The woman came back and put some fabric on her back.

"Help me now," she said to Sofia. "We will put an undershirt on your sister so as not to move the dressing... Well, it worked. You can get up already if you want. Or continue to lie down if you prefer. We will wait. When they come back, we'll think about what to do next."

Nastya got up and sat on the bed. "Thank you. Thank you for everything! May God reward you for your kindness!"

"Would you like some water?" Without waiting for an answer, she filled the glass. "Here, drink."

"I didn't want it to turn out like that..."

The woman nodded.

"It had to happen someday. Mürüvvet got what she deserved. But you were hurt too..."

Nastya nodded.

"My name is Düriye," the woman said with a smile. "Or rather, they call me that."

"What is your real name?"

"Şarazad."

"And mine is Anastasia... But you can call me Nastya. They want to change my name, too –"

"They don't just want to," the woman said sternly. "They have already changed it. You are Hatice from now on."

"I will never agree to it!"

The woman looked at her meaningfully. "You just agreed, didn't you?"

Nastya bowed her head.

"Do not stand up to them," Düriye said. "Let them call you anything they like. The most important thing is that they cannot erase from your heart the real you – Nastya, whom you still are!"

She was right.

"Where are you from?"

The woman's gaze grew misty. "Cartagena. It's a place on the other side of the Great Water. Very hot."

So that's why she has such a dark complexion.

"And you?"

"From the island of Milos, maybe you've heard of it? From the village of Hagia Eirene."

"That's where they brought you from?"

"No, I was brought from Kumanovo. I have no idea where it is. Some place in this world. Bandits kidnapped –"

Düriye laughed bitterly. "You don't have to finish. Two people out of every three that you'll meet here have lived through exactly the same stuff as you. And the others were brought here and offered as a gift."

As a gift? Just like me... she thought. So, there were many more like her here. They did not matter to anyone. They were whipped. With a beating, their old name was taken away from them, and a new one was given.

"You too?"

"Of course. One day a Genoese ship moored near our village. Everybody ran to the seashore. We were glad that there would be an opportunity to sell our goods and dates to merchants. However, it did not happen. We didn't even realize when the men who landed in three big boats set fire to our village. They kidnapped me. Even as the ship left, my village was still in flames. At sea, we met with a merchant ship from Venice. I was sold to one of them for three bales of silk. The man rubbed his hands, pleased with his good deal. 'At the Venice market, she will go for no less than ten ducats. Venetian gentlemen like such dark-skinned, fiery girls from Africa,' he'd said..."

"Oh my God!"

"But the fates wanted things to happen differently. Ottoman pirates attacked the ship and took everything they could from it. Me, too. They cut the sails and left the ship on the high seas. And then, we all know... And what is your story?"

Nastya told her everything.

"That was it," she said at the end. "The Beylerbey of Rumelia sent me here as a present for the Sultan Mother Handan. We came here together with a whole lot of carts, crates, baskets, rugs, silks, and God knows what other treasures. I've been here for so many days, and I still haven't been introduced to the Sultan Mother..."

Düriye laughed. "What, you still haven't been done what?"

"I wasn't presented to the Sultan Mother..." It seemed that she said the most ordinary thing in the world, but the woman laughed even harder.

"Allah..." she said after a long moment. "You were not presented, right?"

"Well, what else was supposed to happen? Since I have already been given as a gift, shouldn't the gift from the Beylerbey be transferred to the hands of the new owner?"

"It's not that simple. The Valide Sultan now has a million other things on her mind... the circumcision of the Sultan... Soon after that, the wedding..."

"So, the king got married?"

"Padishah," she corrected her. "It's Persian for Sultan or Emperor. They married him to some girl. I haven't seen her, but they say she is beautiful."

Nastya felt something break inside her. *The king had his queen already.*

"What is her name?"

"Mahfiruz."

The woman saw tiredness and sadness in the girl's eyes. "Well, enough of these fairy tales for today," she said. "Now you should lie down. You need to rest."

Mahfiruz, she repeated in her mind. *Queen Mahfiruz. Queen Anastasia. Which of these names is nicer and more pleasant to the ear? Of course – Anastasia! Queen Anastasia. And Queen Hatice?* She smiled. *Queen Hatice... Queen of the Servants, Hatice.*

Suddenly she felt sad. She suffered.

The prince became the king, and he had already found himself a queen.

And she still did not have her king. The prince of the kingdom of the stable – Slobodan – was already very far away.

She took the woman's hands in hers. "God bless you for everything, Şarazad."

The woman looked at her as if she had spoken a magical word. Tears came to her eyes.

"Say it one more time. I haven't heard anyone call me that for years..."

"Şarazad... Şarazad... Şarazad."

"Allah bless you, too, Nastya!" She helped her to lie down. "I'm afraid that after all this, you will not have an easy life here. Watch out for the viper, Mürüvvet. Not only for her but also for other odalisques. Do not argue with anyone anymore; do not quarrel. Never. In the harem, such undisciplined servants are not needed by anybody for anything. Either they are shown the door, or one day they disappear into thin air."

"Odalisques...? And disappear – how?"

"Odalisques, they're a female slave or concubine in the Sultan's harem. And undisciplined servants simply disappear. Just like that! Now you are here and now you are gone..."

Şarazad was right. Tough days began for Nastya.

She was assigned the hardest work that had to be done in the Novice Courtyard. She swept, scrubbed, then swept again, and scrubbed again. Other odalisques, whenever they passed her, spilled – as if by accident – dirty water, only to be able to call, 'Hey, girl. Clean it up, and fast!'

She cleaned, scrubbed, and swept. Nobody heard a word of complaint from her lips.

And there was also Mürüvvet. Nastya knew very well that the woman was just looking for the right opportunity for revenge. For now, the woman didn't stand in her way, and just limited herself to mean remarks spoken at her loudly from afar when talking with other servants:

"Don't think I forgot. My hatred is too great to forget about her!"

"Ah, girls, you don't even know how much I am in the mood for Greek blood... You don't happen to know of any Greek woman who could satisfy my thirst?"

The women gathered around her would giggle, holding their sides.

"Where is that girl they brought from Skopje?"

As soon as she heard the unpleasant, thin voice that resounded across the courtyard, she threw herself at the door.

A man stood next to Dilşad. He was as chubby as she was but twice as big, and twice as dark as his assistant. Nastya thought that if she ever met him at night in a dark corridor, she would surely bump into him. He reminded her of a millstone. A huge head, a pair of black bulging eyes, and a large, wide nose that looked as if it had been flattened with something. His lips were a little fuller than Dilşad's lips. He didn't have a neck at all, and his head seemed to be seated directly on his shoulders. He wore wide, blue galligaskins breeches, boots with upturned tips on his feet and from the waist up, he was almost naked except for a waistcoat on his hairless dark skin. Although the millstone noticed her, she did not say a word to him.

"Where is that girl from Skopje?" he squeaked again. She could not stop wondering how such a huge man could have such a high voice. *Do all the giants talk like this?* she wondered.

"Here," Nastya finally said, and she stepped out into the courtyard. "I came from Skopje."

He pointed a finger at her. "Come over here. From the Beylerbey of Rumelia, right?"

"Yes."

"What's your name?"

She bit her tongue so as not to shout in his face, "Anastasia Vasilides!"

"Hatice..."

The man looked her up and down. *He can't even see his feet past his belly,* she thought, and she had to purse her lips so that she wouldn't burst out laughing.

"Do you know who I am?"

She didn't. *Maybe the king of giants?* She shrugged. "I don't know."

"I am the Aga of the Gate of Bliss. Aga of the Gate of Bliss, Mestan." He said it in his thin voice so boastfully and with such seriousness that she had to tighten her lips even more. She'd never heard anything so comical. "Do you already know what the Aga of the Gate of Bliss is?"

She shrugged again. The millstone immediately drew his eyebrows together and looked at her as if he wanted to warn her not to do that anymore. "I don't know."

"It's time to find out then! Up – Allah," he said, looking up at the sky, "and in the harem – Aga of the Gate of Bliss. You understand now?"

She looked at him and smiled charmingly, but she didn't like the audacity of such a comparison. "I understand."

"If so, do not dare to disturb the peace of the Sultan's harem again. Last time, you got away easily with the whips. You can be sure, however, that the next time I will skin you alive and then sprinkle you with salt..."

He paused for a moment, rolled his eyes, and then opened them wide. He probably thought he would terrify everybody doing that.

"Do you understand that, too?" he shouted suddenly, with all the strength in his chest. It must have seemed to him that his thin voice sounded scary, but instead he was even funnier.

"Understood."

"Well... Now tell me, Hatice. Do you know why I came here?"

Her answer was limited to a look that meant: 'How should I know?' She realized that she didn't want to watch him anymore. She hated him. *I would love to bite off these big ears of yours, without a moment's thought*, she thought.

"I came here because" – in one moment, he narrowed his eyes and raised his head – "Her Majesty Handan Valide Sultan calls you before her noble face!"

Her knees buckled under her where she stood, and she dropped to her knees. *The Holiest Miss! You have breathed hope into the heart of your daughter again!*

They passed through corridors that stretched on forever. Mestan Aga and Dilşad Kalfa walked first. *Just look at them*, thought Nastya. *One would think they were the king and the queen.* They were so haughty, with their heads high and their noses up, they walked as if all the world belonged to them.

As Nastya followed them, she decided to throw the questions that tormented her out of her head. She would probably get to know all the answers soon enough anyway; she will read what her destiny has prepared for her, line after line. She straightened up. She raised her head high and stared at the ceiling. She walked in this pose, enriching it with an additional element of dignity: she slightly lifted her skirt as if it were too long, and she did not want it to drag on the floor. *Oh, yes*, she thought contently. *Life like this is good.* Even though her awful leather boots could now be seen from under her dress, she was ready to pay this price. From the ankles up, she believed she looked like a queen.

Suddenly, a huge door opened before them. Stepping through, they found themselves in a sunny courtyard – or rather a stone corridor in the arcades of the palace. On the left was a string of windows with iron bars; the right opened into a large green space. Her gaze was attracted by a feast of colors at its very center – lots of people in multicolored dresses gathered in groups and waited in front of one of the most splendid pavilions of the palace. At least, it seemed so to her; she had never seen an equally beautiful and refined building before. She saw some strange hats on the heads of the waiting people. They did not resemble the turbans she saw in Kumanovo or in the Beylerbey's palace in Skopje. Some of them were so high that it was amazing how they could stay on the wearers' heads. They resembled towers wrapped in white nainsook. Others were almost as big as the round tray on which Mirna used to prepare börek.

Some men were dressed in black gowns, others in white or red ones. She saw two or three of them wearing jackets lined with fur, and green robes that drooped down to their ankles were visible from under the outer covers.

Suddenly a flash of light blinded her. Instinctively, she covered her eyes with her hand to protect herself from it – surrounding the pavilion from under the arcades, shone ornaments as the sun fell on them. *Did they tile the ceiling with gold and diamonds?* she wondered, delighted with the very assumption.

It all finally began to resemble the palace of her dreams.

And, the whole time, she tried to walk like a queen. At the same time, she tried to get used to all the magnificence that was being revealed to her eyes. *I wonder what these beautiful, filigree columns are made of? Maybe marble? No, probably not, there's no pink marble... Or maybe there is? How can I know that?*

Nastya couldn't help herself. "Who are these people?" she asked.

Mestan and Dilşad kept walking ahead. The woman turned to her for a moment and put her finger to her lips.

"Be quiet."

Just when she began to think that this corridor would never end, they came to a tall, double-leafed, green door. There were four black eunuchs, two standing on each side. Their stature was nowhere near that of Mestan Aga, but similarly to him, they were dressed in waistcoats worn on naked torsos. They immediately opened the door for them. King Mestan with Queen Dilşad passed first, and she followed them.

They were at the beginning of another long corridor. Nastya, however, did not seem to see it. What she had just seen, all the splendor and richness, took her breath away for a good moment. *The palace...* she thought, excited. *This is the real palace! I managed to get all the way here. Nastya, the daughter of a priest from Hagia Eirene, in the Ottoman palace!*

She felt strange in her heart. She felt like crying from the emotions but obediently followed the 'royal' couple in front.

Everything was so wonderful here, she didn't know what to look at. They were constantly passed by servants, hurrying to their own destinations. At the sight of Mestan, they bent their heads slightly in greeting. The girls working here were more beautiful and much more nicely dressed. It struck her that there were so many black children here. She could not even tell if they were boys or girls.

It was much quieter here than in other parts of the palace. She tried to catch the smallest sound but did not even hear the rustle of fabric or the sound of footsteps. Only now did she understand why the impression that she walked on the clouds had not left her since she had entered the corridor – her feet almost drowned in a thick carpet that was spread along the entire corridor. *Hey,* her mind said suddenly. *What's up with you, Nastya? Pull yourself together. How can the queen be such a scatterbrain?*

It was a palace from her dreams and fantasies. She pinched herself secretly so that no one would notice. No, this time it was not a dream.

She was also part of this magnificence, and thus she should behave with dignity, too.

So, she did. She raised her head and stretched out her neck like a swan. She stared at the ceiling. She straightened up. She lifted the folds of her dress again, which she had released from her hands unconsciously in her daze.

She walked ahead like that.

And then she noticed it.

Her heart began to beat like crazy. The servants that passed them sent her furtive glances. Everybody. They probably took her for a queen. She saw admiration in the eyes of some. Envy lurked in others.

And that meant she was beautiful.

She pretended not to care. She did not let them know that she also watched them out of the corner of her eye. She kept walking, with her head high.

The Queen of the Ottomans awaited her.

She had neither the time nor the inclination to bother herself with jealousy or even with the delight of servants, farmhands, odalisques, and pages.

Mestan stopped abruptly. Dilşad turned left and kept walking forward. Nastya was hesitant about what to do, but the man gestured that she was to follow the Kalfa. After a few steps, the woman turned left again. They were in a blind, narrow corridor.

They stopped at the door on the right.

"Here."

She was surprised. How was the room of the mighty Queen of Ottomans here, in this narrow and dark corridor?

Suddenly, fear began to grow in her. Or maybe... *Did they tell me that Handan Sultan was waiting for me, just to lure me into a trap? Maybe Mürüvvet is already here with a big knife in her hand?*

The woman opened the door and stepped aside, opening the way for her. "Come in."

She was struck by the chill that came from inside. The marble floor was damp. She noticed a large, wooden, arch-shaped door exactly opposite the entrance.

"What is this place, Dilşad Kalfa?"

"The hamam."

"Hamam? Baths? But... but I was supposed to go to Handan Sultan."

"Once again, I tell you to keep quiet," Dilşad said in a trembling voice. "How many times can I repeat to you that you cannot speak the name of Her Majesty aloud?"

"Was I not supposed to visit Her Majesty?"

The woman pushed her inside. "First you have to wash."

"Wash?"

"Oh, Allah!" Dilşad said, nodding her head in pity. "Hello! You didn't possibly think that you would appear before the mighty Sultan Mother without any preparation, in the rags that you are wearing?"

"I have another dress, a nice and clean one, in the –"

"Hey there! It's us!"

A small door opened. Three women appeared in it, naked except for the towel each of them wore.

"Come," said one of them. "Undress and come in here; wash yourself well."

She did not know why, but the woman's look frightened her. "With you here?"

"Why not?" asked the other one. "We will not eat you, stupid. We have exactly the same stuff as you," she added and dropped the towel with a quick motion. "Look and get used to it."

Laughter spread throughout the room. The woman stood completely naked before her. Embarrassed, Nastya closed her eyes.

"You see?" she went on cheerfully. "Everything is as it should be, right? Not too much of anything, not too little."

"Look at me," Dilşad hissed among the laughter. "If you want to get out of here in one piece, I advise you to undress and wash immediately. And then put on what has been prepared for you. It is not nice to make Her Majesty wait too long..."

Nastya decided to submit to everything without thinking about it anymore. "I will undress myself," she said, "but turn around!"

The hamam, in which she entered in shame and in fear, resembled hell. She thought that her body would burn in a moment. Her fears, however, were not confirmed. The bath even did her good. When she poured water on her head, she thought that she was washing away all bad things, worries, and fears from it. This purge calmed her soul.

After entering inside, she took a seat by the marble trough opposite the massive wooden door. When they opened the door after a while, she panicked. She grabbed a heavy basin that stood next to her.

"Don't touch me!" she cried and raised it up threateningly. "I'll kill you!" Her voice bounced off the dome of the bathhouse so loudly that she scared herself.

The woman stopped. She looked at her for some time with a strange smile. The door then opened again, and the shoulders of another woman slipped in through the gap. *Two against one* thought Nastya. *I stand no chance!*

The other woman, however, did not enter. She only gave her friend what she'd brought and left immediately.

"Your clothes," hissed the one who was with her inside. "Don't waste time here for too long. Put this on. If you can't figure it out – call me, I will help you." Then she turned and left.

Nastya breathed a sigh of relief.

She poured two more basins over her head and dried herself with a towel that the woman left on top of the bundle of clothes. She began to dress.

Everything she took into her hands was amazing to her. The touch of the fabric made her tremble each time, especially when she put on the wide, silk galligaskins. Suddenly, she noticed that she was not given her shoes. Was she supposed to go on barefoot?

The door opened slowly. She felt a breath of icy air that suddenly fell into the hot hamam.

"I didn't get my shoes."

"Get out of here first," one of the women said without going inside. "You'll put them on later, so they don't get wet. Now, come out; let's see what you look like."

She left the bathhouse and saw the same three women as before. She understood that she'd managed to make some impression on them. She took a few steps, dignified, with her head up, though barefooted. The chill of water spilled on the floor touched her. Along with Dilşad, they headed toward the exit. The woman who had previously taken her clothes off in front of her now held a pair of red slippers with upturned toes in her hands, also adorned with red tassels. She followed the women. When Nastya was on the step, in front of the door, the woman untied the towel and began to dry her feet with it. Nastya only protested when the towel began to move upward, toward the calves.

"What are you doing?"

The bath lady lowered her hands, resigned.

"Eh, it's a tough job with this girl," muttered one of the women standing behind. "You start again? You will see that one day, you will go too far. Put those shoes on her and let her go away finally."

Muttering under her breath, she put the slippers on her damp feet.

Nastya opened the door and stepped out into the hall. She decided to not even ask what had happened to the clothes she had come here in.

When she raised her head, she saw three beauties in front of her. Three angels who watched her as if they wanted to give an evaluation.

She did exactly the same, wanting to compare herself to them. *I'm prettier than them*, she decided after a moment. But she had to admit that the girls could not be denied their beauty, either.

How do these new clothes fit me? I wonder how I look. If only I could see myself in the mirror...

There was no such need, however. She read from the eyes of the three girls that she looked great, although they didn't tell her anything.

They didn't even ask if she was the one they had been waiting for.

All three of them turned away, as if on cue, and walked forward. Nastya rushed after them, with the white tulle that was put on her head fluttering behind her.

Everyone was watching her again.

Out of the way! Bow to Hagia Eirene, the great, the mightiest lady – Her Majesty Anastasia Vasilides!

They arrived at a great door, where they found a crowd of girls in front of it, to the right pages stood in a row, and to the left there were odalisques.

A woman already waited for her right next to the door. They passed the line of servants and headed straight for her.

"Who is she?"

"Nevcihan, the chief lady of the court of Her Majesty Handan Valide Sultan. She will introduce you to the Sultana," said one of the girls leading her.

Nastya nodded.

"When you get inside, watch everything she does. You behave exactly the same. Stand in place until Her Majesty orders you to come closer. Under no circumstances should you speak up without being asked. Give short answers to the questions. After each sentence –"

"This I know," Nastya said. "After each sentence, I have to add: 'Serene Lady, Your Highness Handan Valide Sultan.'"

The girl's eyes first widened in fear. After a moment, however, her eyes softened, and a soft smile appeared on her lips.

"No..." It was obvious that she could barely restrain herself from laughing. "All you need to do is say 'My Lady.'"

They approached the chief lady of the court. The three angels handed her over to her and disappeared into the crowd.

Nastya suddenly lost her head.

Her eyes met the woman's gaze. Apparently, she had to check if everything was all right and if she looked as she should. The court woman adjusted the scarf on her head and looked again. She did not like something. She pulled the hairpin out of her hair and pulled the scarf back slightly. She took a step back and looked at her again. This time, she had no more objections. She clipped the hairpin back into Nastya's hair. After this change, she was more exposed than before. She adjusted the scarf that fell over her shoulders.

Finally, she stood in front of her and took one last look at her. "We can go in," she said shortly, her voice resonant and calm. Meanwhile, drums tumbled in the heart of Nastya, and trumpets buzzed in her head. "Do what I do. Keep a half step behind me at all times."

She turned her back to her.

"Open."

When the girls in the pink galligaskins standing at the door opened it slowly, Nastya felt her head spin. She saw darkness in front of her eyes.

Holy Mother, she prayed. *Help your daughter, do not let her bring shame in front of the Ottoman Queen! I know this... My fate will be decided behind that door. If a failure is written for me, plead for me with Your Son; ask him to change his plans for me. But if happiness is written for me, I am begging you, do not let him take it away from me because of my sins!*

"We're entering," the woman whispered almost inaudibly in front of her.

Nastya lowered her head. Her legs trembled. She moved ahead. She saw a step. *How high*, went through her mind. She noticed that the court lady walking in front of her had crossed it without stepping on it. She was supposed to do the same. She got scared. *What if I stumble over it and fall?* She did not fall over.

The Queen was somewhere in the room she had just entered. She couldn't see her yet. *Oh well,* she thought. *She must see me already.* Her ears started ringing. *Pull yourself together, Nastya,* she ordered herself in her mind. *What's going on with you? If you don't calm down immediately, your nerves will either finish you up or make you a fool in front of everyone!*

She tried to calm down, to think about something else. But what could a person think of at such a moment?

She saw Nevcihan kneel down. She did the same. The woman put her hands on the ground and leaned forward, then sat back on her feet. She sat but wasn't sitting, at the same time.

Nastya tried to repeat everything exactly. Her legs hurt, even though the carpet was very soft. *I wonder how long we have to stay in this position,* she worried. Her legs suffered more and more.

She waited for the Queen to say something, but she remained silent.

Slowly, rebellion began to build up in her. *If she doesn't want to talk, maybe I could at least look her in the face...? Do I have to stare at the ground like this the whole time? I am in the palace, in front of the Queen of the Ottomans, and I cannot even look at her?*

She had only a silk carpet with stunning colors before her eyes. But even it slowly began to hurt her legs.

She glanced at the court lady out of the corner of her eye. She did not want to miss any of her movements. But she saw nothing but the heels of her shoes.

For a time, there was complete silence, but she guessed that there must be a lot of people in the chamber. After all, the Queen certainly did not sit here alone like a finger. She only heard the girls nearest to her trying to hold their breath. It bothered her. *So, it is not possible to even breathe loudly in this palace?* Someone had to sneeze. She heard a short, muffled, achoo! *Poor girl, they will probably punish her for it!*

And what if I sneeze like that in a moment?

Her throat went dry. She grew scared. *Why did you do it?* she asked the person who had just sneezed, whoever she was, in her thoughts. *Such things are contagious. What will happen if it will be my turn now?*

Nothing, she would just sneeze.

After a long moment, she sensed a movement, exactly opposite herself.

"Is that you, Nevcihan?"

The Queen!

Finally! Nastya's heart began to hammer again. The woman's voice was warm and gentle, but rather than sympathy and tenderness, she sensed in it something that demanded respect and humiliation in front of Her Majesty.

She listened carefully. In a moment, she'd probably see her. First, she would probably order them to get up... But no – she said something completely different.

"With the embroidery hoop, we forget about the whole world. What can we do...? We cannot pull ourselves away from it. We put all our heart into this purple hyacinth. Unfortunately, it does not go too well for us today. See for yourselves."

She guessed that the Queen was now showing her handwork to everybody. From all sides, there were voices of denying and admiration.

"You are too tough on yourself, Lady," the girls chattered.

"Ah, how beautiful!"

"Ah, if only I could do something similar. Unfortunately, my fingers are nowhere near as skillful as the fingers of the Valide Sultan!"

"Congratulations, Your Majesty. Knock on wood..."

"This hyacinth looks so real, My Lady. It makes you want to reach for it and put it in the water."

Ah, you hypocritical liars, thought Nastya, who, fortunately, managed to refrain from laughter. Anyway, their fresh, joyous voices set her in a better mood.

"Oh, I wish..." the Queen continued to complain.

Of course, she did not believe their flattery.

"Look, don't you see it? What is it supposed to be? It doesn't ever look like the one in the picture. Always too small or too big. Have you ever seen such a hyacinth?"

The girls tried to protest shyly, but no one dared to say anything flattering anymore.

"Never mind," Handan Sultan said finally. "It absorbed us so much that we didn't even notice how much time passed. We didn't notice your coming, either."

Hey, I'm here, too. You haven't seen me yet! Nastya thought with a slight reproach.

Nevcihan knelt on the ground the whole time, as did she, and she'd completely lost feeling in her legs. She would have fallen if she was told to get up. The pain was becoming more and more unbearable. She was not used to it. Her right hand, which she kept in front of her all the time, also became numb. She looked at the rug to distract herself from the pain. Her hand rested on a large red rose. It had green, frayed leaves, and spikes. *How beautiful,* she thought. *Almost like a real one. Makes you want to pick it...*

"Is this the girl?"

Thank God, finally. She focused on what was about to happen next.

The Valide Sultan had finally noticed her.

"Yes, My Lady."

The chamber went silent again. This time, it seemed to her that it went on forever. The woman said something to one of the girls in a quiet voice. Nastya, however, couldn't hear it – she was so nervous, her heart almost popped out of her chest.

"Yes..." said the Queen suddenly. "We want to see your face. Raise your head."

She was surprised. *Who is supposed to raise their head...me? Or maybe she said it to one of the court girls? God, what to do? And if it really wasn't to me, will she be very angry if I look at her?*

Suddenly, she felt she had had enough.

Come on! said the little voice in her head angrily. *Lift that head, show yourself to the serene lady, Her Majesty Handan Valide Sultan!*

She finally brought herself to do it.

She wanted to cry out 'All Saints!' out of emotion.

The Queen sat opposite, separated by a space of about ten paces in front of her, by a window, on a large sofa set on a platform, among silk and satin pillows. At least ten beautiful girls sat around her.

When Nastya realized that the eyes of all the women in the room – including the Queen! – were on her, she suddenly wanted to escape from there. There was nothing for her here, after all.

She was a pureblood servant. A peasant woman who, under the influence of a beggar's prediction, self-styled herself as a queen! Nobody would like her here probably, and they would start mocking her. She should escape from here. And as soon as possible. As far as she could go.

What is this nonsense? her reason interjected. *And whom do you think she was before she became a queen? Maybe even a peasant woman just like you, who knows?*

Even if so, now she sat in front of her as a Sultan Mother. Nastya wondered what fate had prepared for her. Meanwhile, following the path it had set, she'd arrived here. Whatever is to be next, will be. She must submit to and accept what has been written for her. She dismissed the thoughts of escape and focused her whole attention on the woman in front of her.

How about the crown? Where's the crown?

The Queen was without a crown. *How is this possible?*

Instead, she saw a strange hat on her head. It was round above the forehead. It widened and flattened upward as if something had been pressed on it. Two long, sharp spikes protruded from it, from which hung a belt of four rows of chickpea-sized pearls. Under it, one could see an emerald; big like an open hand.

The Queen was pretty. Very pretty. *Like a picture,* thought Nastya. Although her son had already become a king, she was still very young. *I wonder how much older she can be than me? Five, ten years?* she wondered, trying to determine her age. *No, definitely not ten*, she decided. *At what age did she become a mother?*

The robes she wore were wonderful, decorated with small diamonds and brilliants. Suddenly she felt uneasy. *I wonder how I look. Damn, I haven't even had time to look at myself in the mirror or even in a tray. Who knows if these weird Ottoman clothes fit me at all?*

"Indeed, she is just as he wrote," Handan muttered. "Get up, child. We want to see you in all your glory."

Finally!

She wanted to get up, but suddenly she felt a sharp pain. She thought that if she stood on her feet now, she would fall to the ground like a log. She'd lost the feeling in her legs from the knees down. She slowly straightened up, all the time praying in spirit. The blood began to flow rapidly to the part of the legs she'd been sitting on. At first, she felt a painful numbness, then a pleasant lethargy spread over her body.

Stand before the Queen like a queen! she ordered herself. *Clench your teeth and throw away this weakness, immediately!*

She turned slightly to the side. She turned her face toward the light entering the room through the window behind the Sultan Mother, which occupied the whole height of the wall. She raised her head and straightened, dignified. *What about my hands?* she thought in panic. *What to do with my hands?*

She had not practiced this at all. Out of the corner of her eye, she looked at Nevcihan, who got up from the floor with her. She decided to behave like her – she joined her hands and rested them under her belly.

Now she focused all of her attention on Handan Sultan's face, trying to read her thoughts from it. She immediately knew what the flash of her black eyes meant.

She likes me, she likes me! Mother of God, the Serene Lady, Her Majesty Handan Valide Sultan likes me!

At least half of the girls surrounding the Sultan Mother also looked at her approvingly. The others also accepted her, but in their eyes, Nastya noticed admiration as well as jealousy.

"Last week," Handan Sultan began, "the Beylerbey of Rumelia, Çivici Mehmed Pasha, was received by His Majesty. Earlier, in a letter to us, he mentioned you, but we had so many things on our heads that we could not take care of you. It was not easy for us... First, our son's Coronation, right after that, the ceremony of circumcision. Then the Padishah suddenly fell ill... Fortunately, Allah has kept our son for us as well as for the entire Sublime Porte. He quickly recovered, thanks to the medics. And almost immediately, the obligation to organize another ceremony fell on us. We didn't even notice when the days and weeks spent on the wedding preparations passed..." She fell silent and returned to the needlework she'd kept in her hands all the time. Her fingers kept running around the embroidery hoop.

Nastya did not see anything but those fingers. One word kept circling around in her head: 'Wedding.'

As soon as it fell from the mouth of Handan Valide Sultan, she felt her body begin to tremble, her cheeks flush.

She already knew that the King had married. Yet to hear it again, and personally from the Mother Sultan, was a severe blow to her. She was afraid that the scream growing in her mind would break out of her mouth, but after a moment, she began to think more reasonably. *What's going on with you? What did you expect, that the King would be waiting for you?*

Nastya expected Handan Sultan to resume the conversation. She still watched only her fingers, sticking the needle in the fabric and pulling it out again, and again.

Go on! Nastya grew impatient. *And then? What happened next? Speak already!*

The Valide Sultan was silent. There was such a silence that Nastya was not entirely sure if the other girls even breathed. All you could hear was the needle sinking into the fabric stretched on the hoop.

After a long moment, Handan Sultan looked away from her needlework and looked at her.

"What were we talking about...? Çivici Mehmed Pasha, during an audience with the Sultan, began to talk about you. He expressed the hope that we were satisfied with the services of the girl he had sent as a gift from Skopje. When Ahmed told me about it, we remembered the last letter from the Pasha. It made us very embarrassed. So today, I ordered Nevcihan to bring you in right away. It's time."

She lowered her head again and threaded the needle through the fabric a couple of times.

"The great Pasha could not praise you enough in his letter. He wrote that you are beautiful, and at the same time very talented."

Nastya looked at the girls discreetly. Those who had just looked at her with kindly admiration now joined those who were jealous of her. Of course, they'd heard so much praise for her, after all... It could not have ended otherwise. Not only was she beautiful – she was also talented. What could they do other than to envy a girl whose name, beauty and ability were praised before the Padishah?

"Who has taught you to serve? The Pasha was really very pleased with you."

She opened her mouth, but no sound came out. She panicked. She tried once again: "Mo..." She did not have enough air to say more than one syllable.

She felt that the Valide Sultan's maids could barely resist laughing.

"Mom and Mirna Abla," she finally said in one breath. *Damn it!* She forgot the title she was supposed to add after each sentence. She wanted to make up for it quickly, but instead of 'My Lady' she said, "Honorable Mother."

Where did this 'Honorable Mother' come to her mind from? One of the girls giggled, indignant. Handan Sultan, however, instead of being angry with the stranger, scowled at her maid. The girl did not expect such a reaction from the Sultan Mother. When, after a while, the Valide Sultan looked again at Nastya, her gaze was kind and gentle. Apparently, she did not take offense.

"Pasha wrote us your name, but we cannot remember it now. What's your name?"

Nastya swallowed. She remembered perfectly well the whipping that she had already been given for her stubbornness in this matter. "Hatice," she said quietly.

"Hatice?" Handan Sultan looked at her as if she were surprised.

What was so strange about it? Just Hatice. Hatice. That terrible name – Hatice.

"But of course, that is not my real name," she added.

"I guessed not. So, what is your real name?"

"Anastasia Vasilides."

"Really, Vasilides?" Handan Sultan asked.

Nastya understood that this question was not addressed to her. "Anastasia is a very popular name... I bet we could find three to five slaves with that name in the harem at the moment." The Valide Sultan paused to stick the needle into the fabric a few more times. She quickly gave up, however, and left the needlework, bored.

"Do you know?" she started in such a tone as if she was about to gossip with an old friend. "One of the women of our son's great-great-grandparents also wore that name in childhood. His great-great-grandmother came from Lehistan... Here, the great-great-grandfather of our son gave her the name Hürrem..."

From Lehistan? I wonder where that is, Nastya thought.

"And you, where are you from, Anastasia?"

She really liked the fact that the woman addressed her with that name. There was something strange about the tone of her voice and her look as if encouraging her to give the answers she expected from her.

"From over the sea," she replied. "From an island in the Aeg–"

"From an island in the Aegean Sea?"

It was weird, but the eyes of the Valide Sultan shone this time. Nastya could not understand the reason for her sudden interest.

"Yes," she said, bowing her head. "Our island is called Milos. I'm from Hagia –"

Again, Handan Sultan did not let her finish. "Hagia? Ah, so you are Roman!" she joked.

A Roman? But why? She raised her head. "Greek. I'm Greek."

"That's what the Ottomans call Greeks. So, we said right, you are a Roman," she chirped happily.

Nastya did not understand anything. Where did this outburst of joy come from? Why was the Sultan Mother so glad to learn that she was Greek? And why did the Ottomans call the Greeks Romans? She tried to read from her eyes what the woman was thinking, but she did not succeed. She only saw indescribable happiness in them.

"From now on, you will live with us. We want to have you in service."

Her reaction to the unexpected words surprised her. Shouldn't she be happy, even jumping with joy? Meanwhile, she took it quite calmly as if it didn't make any impression on her. She did not even think about the prophecy of the beggar she had seen on the steps of the church in Kumanovo.

"What we have seen only confirms what the Pasha wrote in his letter. Your culture and good manners are evident," Handan continued. "But the palace is something completely different, Anastasia. And especially the Sultan's harem. You will have to learn a lot, adapt to certain things..."

Emotions, which she had not experienced a moment ago, only now, slowly began to manifest.

So, from the beginning, my destiny was just that, she thought. *To live in the palace.* What was to happen next was still hidden from her.

The voice of the beggar sounded once again in her ears: 'Beautiful queen!'

I'm not a queen.

'But you will become one!'

Could the prophecy be fulfilled? This thought made her shiver. So far, every time she thought about it, she pushed it away with laughter and derision – maybe the queen of servants! – But now... now for the first time, she began to think about it seriously. For the first time, she said to herself, *Maybe indeed?*

"That's why," Handan resumed, "one of our court maids will take care of you and teach you everything you need to know about the life in the palace. What talents do you have, Anastasia?"

What else was she able to do? She dealt with practically everything here. What more was expected from her? She could cook, make sweets, she sewed, threaded beads... Besides, she could fish... In Hagia Eirene, she could use a fishing rod as well as any boys. She rowed... What else... But all this was not enough?

"Can you read and write? Do you play any instruments? What is your voice like? Can you tell long, breathtaking stories to entertain us on the long winter evenings? Can you tell the future from tea leaves?"

"Of course, I can read and write," she replied haughtily. Who did she think she, the daughter of Kostas Vasiliadis, was?

A grimace crossed the face of the Valide Sultan.

"But, of course, in Greek, right? Anyway, it does not matter, my dear... I'll assign to you..." She paused and took a moment to glance around at her beautiful court maids scattered throughout the room. "The best one will be..." She seemed to look for someone specific. "Oh yes... I'm giving you Eftalya!"

"Eftalya?" Her hair stood on end. *Ah, dear mommy*, she thought. *You found me!* Nastya looked in the direction the Valide Sultan looked and saw a girl. It was one of the maids that took her from the hamam and brought her here. The same one with which she'd exchanged a few whispered words in front of the entrance. She was happy about the choice. She had felt sympathy for her already at that moment. So Eftalya, right? She probably also comes from...

"Eftalya comes from a Greek island, too," Handan said. "She came here straight from Rhodes. She will be both a friend and a teacher to you."

The girl immediately bowed to her. "I follow your order, My Lady."

"Try to teach her everything she needs to know about life in the palace and the harem as quickly as possible. And then we'll see."

The Valide Sultan suddenly clapped her hands.

"Well, good luck... It's enough for today," she said and got up from the sofa. Following her lead, the other girls also got up from their seats. Two of them ran to the Sultan Mother and brushed the lap of her caftan. The main lady of the court, Nevcihan, adjusted her headgear, moving it a little more toward the forehead. This time, the Sultan Mother's cap did not seem as funny to Nastya as it did the first time.

The Valide Sultan stopped in front of her. Nastya immediately lowered her head. A small white hand touched her chin.

"Look at me."

She slowly carried out her order. They now stood eye to eye. A strange light still shone in the eyes of the woman. Nastya saw it. Her look was warm. Friendly.

"Yes," Handan Sultan said in a voice that seemed to be heard only by her. "Your eyes are as blue as the Aegean Sea."

She noticed that the eyes of the Sultan Mother were the same.

"Eftalya will prepare you. In the evening, we will see each other in the Rosarium." She gave her a goodbye smile.

And then, Nastya did something unbelievable.

"Are you leaving already, My Lady?"

Amazement took the breath away from all those present at the scene. It was improper to ask the powerful Valide Sultan about such things. Nevcihan looked at her with reproach.

"I want to rest a bit. Did you want something else from me?"

As she spoke, vanity, haughtiness, and pride emanated from her again. It scared Nastya a bit, but she could not forget about the crying Sofia. She'd promised she would never leave her, after all.

"I..." she whispered. "I'm not alone here."

A wave of astonished whispers swept through the Mother Sultan's chamber. What was that supposed to mean: 'I'm not alone here?' The faces of the ladies of the court now also showed happiness, as well as surprise. This would be the end of this girl, who had just been complimented by the Valide Sultan. She would fall out of grace as soon as she crept in.

Handan did not react at all as they expected of her. "You're not alone?"

"Yes, Honorable Mother."

She allowed herself to say it for the second time, and for the second time, it caused a growl of indignation.

"I mean, in the courtyard..." she added. "There is with me..." In no way was she able to collect her thoughts and find further words. The stir around her, the jealousy of the Valide Sultan's courtiers, and the scornful looks effectively distracted her. She noticed Eftalya standing close to her. She looked at her desperately, as if she wanted to ask her for help. Eftalya bowed her head slightly and closed her eyes. What did she want to tell her this way? That she should continue saying what she'd started? And anyway, what else could she do now?

"There is by my side," she picked up from where she got stuck, "a girl that the Beylerbey in Skopje gave me, My Lady. Her name is Sofia. She's still a child. She says she is ten years old already, but I do not believe it. If you ask me, I would say that she can be no more than nine. When I was separated from her to be brought here, she cried a lot... And I..." Her eyes stopped again on Eftalya. She saw a smile on her face, which she could not explain. Without a trace of envy, an honest and warm, heartfelt smile. "And I gave her my word that I would never leave her alone. Can I keep her with me...? My Lady."

If a tiny pin holding the headscarf fell out of her hair at that moment, it would certainly be heard falling to the ground. Handan Sultan did not take her eyes off Nastya during her speech, not even for a moment. Neither did the court girls. Their eyes seemed to say: 'You are finished already. You're dead. You have just signed a death sentence on yourself.'

"What if you cannot?"

The Queen's voice was dry. She still stared into her eyes.

What does she want to read from them? Nastya was alarmed.

"What if you cannot, Hatice?"

For the first time, instead of Anastasia, the Valide Sultan called her Hatice. It meant that she was finally angry. So, apparently, the so-called decisive moment had arrived. Everything now depended on how Nastya would answer. It would decide her end – or the beginning.

"If I cannot keep her with me," – she looked the Sultana boldly in the eye – "I'm afraid I will not be able to stay here, either."

"Allah! forbid!"

"Well, well."

"Big mouth!"

All this was in conflict with etiquette, but the girls could not keep silent anymore. Something like this was unheard of! The maid, who was honored with compliments by the Great Valide, dared to ask her questions. And as if that were not enough, she now rejected the Sultana's grace, paying with ingratitude for the kindness she had received.

"What?!" The room brimmed with indignation.

"Foul language!"

"Shame!"

"Who talks like this to the Valide Sultan?"

Only Eftalya's eyes expressed sadness. Her gaze seemed to ask: 'What have you done?'

But there was no turning back. She gave her word to Sofia. She'd promised that she would either come back to her or send someone for her.

Handan Sultan suddenly raised her hand. The room went quiet instantly. Now she would probably tell Nastya to get out of there. And probably not just from there, but from the palace, too.

"Never mind," she said. There was no anger in her voice. "We've given you Eftalya. Let her take care of everything." She then turned and gracefully withdrew to her bedroom, located in the adjoining chamber.

Nevcihan looked at her for a moment, dazed, then started after her mistress.

"One more thing..." Handan unexpectedly turned around in the door. "You have to be ready for the evening. As I said, we will meet in the rose garden. I have a surprise for you. I want to introduce someone to you, my child."

She felt the irritated, hostile looks of the court ladies on her. They probably wondered if she was a witch, by any chance. If any of them had committed even a thousandth part of her insolence, the Sultan Mother would immediately and without hesitation drive them out of there to the four winds. Nastya sensed the tense atmosphere perfectly. It seemed to her that she was sitting on a powder keg – and all it needed was a small spark... She prepared for this blast.

"Let's go already." That voice belonged to Eftalya. "First, we need to find you a place to sleep."

"And Sofia?"

"We'll send for her."

The girl pulled her by the hand out of the room into the hallway.

"You drove our girls crazy. They are bursting with jealousy. Do not forget that in this place, envy is the greatest danger that can threaten you. It is much more dangerous than snakes or scorpions!"

"Here, you probably do not run out of it..."

"Indeed. Always keep an eye on those who are jealous of you. And if you are jealous of somebody – don't let it be noticed."

"I will do that, hodja." Nastya chuckled.

Eftalya frowned. "Do not fool around."

"I swear, I'm serious."

"The palace will teach you everything, you'll see. And if you are not a good student, you will never get used to it or even..."

"Or even what?"

The girl's hands went to her throat. "You will die."

It shook her deeply.

"How do you want me to call you? Hatice or Anastasia?" Eftalya asked suddenly.

"Nastya would be best."

"And you can call me Talya... That's what my mom called me when I was a child."

"You have another name? I mean, one that you've been given here?"

"No. That is because I never had to go to the Novice Courtyard. It was purely by accident. I was brought to the palace on the day Her Majesty became Haseki Sultan, the Sultan's favorite, and chief consort. I caught her eye, so she took me in. I lived right away in the harem, by her. But if you first went there, it's no wonder they changed your name."

Nastya was envious of her. *What can I do, such is my fate?* she thought sadly. *I wonder if it will smile at me, too.*

"And for Allah's sake, who gave you that name?"

"There is a woman named Dilşad Kalfa there. It was her. I told her I didn't want it; I cried. It didn't help me in any way..." She stopped as if hesitating on whether to continue. In the end, she brought herself to say it. "And when I opposed her, I was whipped. Under the blows of the whip, I pretended that I agreed to the name. But I'm still Nastya."

"There is no room for opposition here, Nastya, don't forget about that. Whatever they say, just nod. Let them think that you agree with them in everything, that's enough. Meanwhile, in your head, keep thinking what you think."

She opened the door and let her through. "This is my room. It is rare that the Valide Sultan's courtiers live separately. Only Nevcihan has her own room, besides me!"

Suddenly, Nastya decided to ask her a question that had bothered her for some time. "Talya, can I ask you something?"

"Of course, ask."

"The Queen, just now..."

The girl laughed. Her laughter was soothing, like the sound of water being poured into a glass. "Do not call her that," she said. "If someone hears it, you may get in trouble. There are no queens here, just Sultanas. And she is a Sultana and even a Sultan Mother. Handan Valide Sultan!"

"I know, I know," Nastya chuckled. "A noble, generous, serene lady, Her Majesty Handan Valide Sultaaaaan!"

"Be quiet." Eftalya put her hand on her lips. "Someone might hear. They'll think you're making fun, and then –"

"But I don't have anything bad in mind, really! It's strange, but I even liked her. Very much. But I have heard this long title so many times, and still every time it makes me laugh the same... Just look, Honorable –"

"I told you to be quiet! That's how it is with the Ottomans. They love to exaggerate everything. You're going to get used to it. Now give it a rest; you were going to ask me something. Ask, then."

"I noticed that the Sultan Mother changed as soon as I said that I came from an island in the Aegean Sea. Before, she had talked to me as if out of duty, and then..."

Eftalya listened to her, confirming her words with a nod of her head.

"She said I was a Roman. Why Roman? I'm Greek. From that moment on, she began to look at me completely differently. She even seemed to be happy."

"She was very happy."

"But why?"

"Because she is the same type of 'Roman' as you or me."

Nastya held her breath. Her eyes were big with surprise.

"Okay, okay." Eftalya smiled. "Don't be angry, Greek woman. But she doesn't come from the islands like we do. I heard she is from Thessaly. Her real name is Helena. She came to the palace as a child. And you worry that they changed your name! They also changed hers... and look where she is now."

Nastya sat back in response to her words. "So... you said that she was also once... Holy Mother... I can't express myself... My tongue refuses to obey me, Talya. So, she too, just like us... Do you understand me?"

"Sure," she said, nodding sagaciously. She sat next to her. "It's called luck, my dear. I do not know what she did, but in any case, she managed to sneak into the good graces of Safiye Sultan..." She broke off abruptly, giving up the story. "But this is not the time for that story. What would you know about Safiye Sultan? You couldn't –"

"I heard about her a little," she protested. "She was kicked out of here –"

Eftalya did not let her finish. Her hand, as fast as lightning, rested on her lips again. This time, however, she also warned her with a look. She slowly moved her hand away.

"You are supposed to teach me everything, right? What happened next?"

"Nothing," Eftalya said abruptly. "If I start telling the story, I will not be able to prepare you for the evening. And let's not forget about Sofia – you don't want her to stay in the courtyard forever, do you?"

Nastya crossed herself, scared.

"Either we take her from there today, or you may not see her again. Later, it will be difficult for us to determine where she ended up."

"Then I will go for her quickly... But I'm afraid that I will not find the way on my own. We made so many turns on the way here..."

"Under no circumstances should you leave from here," said Eftalya as she stood up. "Wait here for us. Sit down, take a rest, sleep, or think, do what you want. But do not move one step from here. If, in the meantime, someone comes and asks what you are doing here, say that the Valide Sultan has assigned you to Eftalya. Nobody will check it out anyway. Mestan Aga..."

"Aga of some gate..."

Eftalya looked at her as if to tell her, 'Don't do it!'

"In his own person. He usually doesn't appear here. But if he comes, then don't be afraid, do not even get up from your place. If he asks anything, say that you are now in the Valide Sultan's service, that's all." She moved to the door. "And I'm going to look for your protégée."

"Talya?"

The girl turned to her.

"Please... Bring her to me, please."

Eftalya smiled.

What a beautiful smile this girl has, Nastya thought. When she was about to leave the room, she called again: "Talya?"

"Yes?"

"I haven't told you... Do you know my mom's name is the same as yours?"

Eftalya grew embarrassed, rolled her eyes, and smiled again. "I'm glad," she whispered and turned to the door with mixed feelings.

"Talya?"

"Now what, again? If you keep stopping me like this, this girl will never get here. Keep that in mind."

"The Sultan Mother... who does she want to introduce me to?"

"What?"

"She said she wants me to meet somebody. Do you know who she was talking about? Maybe the Sultan?"

Eftalya left her question unanswered. She went into the corridor and walked away as if fleeing from Nastya and her questions.

It seemed to her that time stood still. *What if Eftalya doesn't find her there?* Doubts drove into her brain like a knife blade. *Damn it! I forgot to tell her that Sofia is with Şarazad!*

She knelt as if she were in church in front of the altar. She crossed herself. Then she folded her hands to pray and put them next to her lips. She raised her eyes.

"Holy Virgin," she began quietly. "I am begging you, have Sofia in your care. Don't let anything bad happen to her. It's the only thing I'm asking you for. I give up even on all the beautiful things that God has written for me... It's enough that Eftalya finds her and brings her to me!"

Suddenly, she felt the second blade piercing her brain. *Mürüvvet!* Panic overcame her. *I hope she won't take advantage of my absence and try to get revenge on Sofia!* There was no doubt she would be able to do that.

She couldn't sit still like this. She should immediately catch up with Eftalya and find the girl together with her.

But how would I find her? I don't know the way... I'd get lost before the first corner. And how would I explain it? Who would believe me, even if I said that the Valide Sultan has taken me into her service? They'll laugh at me, yell at me, and eventually, it would end up with the whips again and the cry, 'You are a liar!'

'So, you say that the noble, generous, serene lady, Her Highness Handan Valide Sultan has accepted you in her service, right? We will see if after a visit with the whips again, you will still want to lie like that!'

You have no other choice, you have to wait! Nastya told herself. *Pray and wait patiently.*

And so, she did, reluctantly. She prayed and waited. But the time dragged on mercilessly. Nothing was happening. Nobody opened the door. Or maybe it was locked? She approached it, and it opened as soon as she pushed it lightly. She hesitated for a moment. She wondered whether to look outside. *What if somebody noticed me? Grabbed my arm and walked me out of there? Yes, it's best to close it and wait.*

But curiosity took over. She opened the door just enough to stick her head out.

She looked out into the corridor. Now it was much more crowded than before. Two women passed right by the door behind which she stood. She heard one of them say, "I'm telling you, this girl must be a witch. Everything will probably come to light soon."

"What witch, what are you talking about? How can such a child be a witch?"

"A child? You call such a shapely girl a child? Didn't you see how that coquette was standing, how she was looking, how...?"

Nastya didn't hear the rest. Together with the girls, their voices also went away.

Don't leave the room, her mind advised her again. *You heard with your own ears how hostile they are to you, how they talk about you behind your back. Who knows how they will behave if they see you alone outside?*

She closed the door. She approached a small window in the opposite wall. It opened onto a courtyard, surrounded on four sides by walls the height of an adult man.

A huge tree grew in the center of the courtyard. Its trunk looked gray. Each of its frightening branches looked almost like a separate plant, and they were hardly seen from under the big green leaves. She had never seen such a tree before.

I wonder what it's called, she thought. But she quickly shrugged. *You need to know that now, really...?*

She had to occupy herself with something, though, so as not to go mad with curiosity.

Where are they, for God's sake?

Suddenly she remembered the words of Eftalya, which had completely confused her. 'I don't know what she did, but in any case, she managed to sneak into the good graces of Safiye Sultan...'

That's exactly what she said when she was telling her about the beginnings of Handan Sultan's stay in this palace. Then she didn't want to continue the topic anymore.

'Sneak into good graces...' What did she do...?

Safiye Sultan.

These words contained the key to success. It is thanks to them that Helena had turned into the powerful Sultana, Handan Valide Sultan.

Eftalia didn't bring herself to say it directly, but everything could be understood all the same. Helena was brought here in exactly the same way as she was – as a slave girl – a maid... Maybe even a concubine.

Safiye Sultan... The same woman who was recently banished from the palace showed kindness to her. Then Helena also managed to earn the heart of Safiye's son... That is, the King... the Padishah. The servant or concubine, Helena, at some point became a noble, serene lady – Her Majesty Handan Valide Sultan. After the death of the Sultan, the fates smiled at her once again, and as her son was practically a child, the reins of power passed in fact, into her hands. It was something indisputable.

And it all started with 'sneaking into her good graces.'

A servant concubine had succeeded. Now she was the most powerful woman in the world. She was strong enough to get rid of the woman who once stood in the place where she was now, the woman thanks to whom her whole life had changed for the better.

Everything else is empty words, she thought as she looked thoughtfully through the window. *There is only one way to the top: you must get into the Sultana's good graces. That's all.*

It's easy to say, but how is it done? She didn't know.

Wooden benches were set around a tree whose name she did not know. She thought the tree was like a woman who sat on the bench, spreading the folds of her dress. A woman who was a prisoner in these walls.

Just like me, she thought. *Oh, if only these walls did not restrict the tree so much, if only it could look at the sea instead of looking at us. If only it were able to stretch its branches to the endless blue of the sea. In the fall, the wind would take its leaves straight to the seawater... And maybe the waves would carry one of those leaves to the island of Milos and wash it up ashore there. And it would stick to my mother's barefoot?*

She sniffled. She thought her mother might not remember her face anymore. She was certain, however, that as soon as her mother bent over for this leaf lying on the sand, she would know that it had come to her straight from her little Nastya.

"Sis..."

At first, she took it for a voice coming from the dream world she sunk herself into for some time.

"Dear sister..."

Nastya shuddered suddenly. *Jesus is that...? Is that her voice, or am I imagining this? Maybe my fear is playing with me like that?*

This time, it seemed to her that some strange patter came from the corridor. It resembled the sound of tiny feet running on the carpet.

"Nastya, dear sister!"

"Quiet," another voice reprimanded her.

That's her! Oh God, it's her!

Suddenly, the door opened wide, and the girl rushed through like a hurricane, her arms opening wide.

"Sisteeeeeer! Dear Sis..."

"Sofia! My little one... Sweetheart."

They embraced each other as after a long separation.

The time that had dragged on so much while Nastya waited for Sofia, now accelerated rapidly.

Sofia sat on the sofa under the window and watched them. She still sniffled every now and then.

Eftalya took a step back and looked at Nastya. She must have liked what she saw because the smile on her face turned into an expression of sincere admiration. The girl was breathless from the bustle that accompanied the preparations for the meeting with the Valide Sultan. She left and entered the room maybe a thousand times, bringing and taking back more and more new clothes. Nastya tried on everything. The ones she did not like, Eftalya immediately took back, only to bring others in their place. Galligaskins, shirts, short kaftans, knee-length outerwear... A belt with a copper buckle, shoes, tulles... Literally everything.

The girl from Rhodes did not forget about Sofia, either. She looked like a little angel now. The only thing she lacked was wings, but in the end, one could think that they hid under her long hair that tumbled down to her waist in soft waves.

Eftalya fixed something and took a few steps back again to look at the result of her work. She nodded appreciatively. Her lips twitched.

"Did you say something?" Nastya asked. "Something wrong?"

"No, I'm just praying. May Allah protect you from an evil eye, Nastya. Before you were just beautiful, now you are a stunning beauty! Come on, come on," she said after a moment, and hurriedly turned to the door. "We have to go now."

When they reached the stairs leading down to the garden, Nastya suddenly grabbed Eftalya's hand.

"Talya," she said in a voice breaking nervously. "Who does the Mother Sultan want to introduce me to? Please, tell me."

The girl just shrugged. "I really don't know."

Nastya held her wrist for some time, while she questioningly searched her eyes. She didn't believe her words. She did not believe her one bit. Talya was hiding something from her.

"Oh, God!" A soft exclamation escaped Nastya's lips.

When she saw Istanbul for the first time – while still on the deck of the ship which she was convinced would take her to hell – she thought to herself that she'd arrived at paradise, after all. The garden, in which she found herself now, only confirmed that first impression.

The Garden of Eden! It was the first thought that appeared in her mind as soon as they stepped out into the courtyard. As she passed through the door, she found herself in the embrace of the blue sea, that stretched out before her eyes. She spread her arms as if in flight and breathed in the well-known scent which she had already missed so much. She felt her blood circulate faster in her veins – every part of her body felt ecstatic from joy.

The courtyard ended with a green meadow. The flowerbeds – with red, yellow, white, and pink roses – seemed to greet her happily. A path ran through the middle of this sea of roses, shaded by two rows of Babylonian willows growing along it. It led to a gazebo with a golden roof. Some other flowers grew behind it, that looked like tiny cups hanging on thin, green stems – the likes of which she'd never seen before. Behind patches of red flowers were patches of white ones, and then also yellow and pink. Among them were also multicolored specimens – red with yellow spots, yellow with red ones... She also noticed a row of purple ones, almost black. These were by far the least numerous, and they were even surrounded by a low, iron fence.

"All Saints... wonderful... amazing..." Nastya didn't have enough words for her delight. "Talya, what are these flowers? I have never seen them before."

"They call them tulips."

"Tulips? I never heard of them."

"They're very popular here. Beautiful, aren't they?"

"Wonderful, amazing!"

Suddenly she remembered something. "And that tree that can be seen from your window? Do you know what it's called?"

"Magnolia."

"My God, it's magnificent..."

"Just wait till it blooms, then you'll see."

Eftalya entered a stony path. "The Valide Sultan should appear soon. We'll wait for her in front of the gazebo. You will be able to look around for a bit."

The gazebo was being prepared for the arrival of the Sultana. A wonderful sofa was set up in it, which almost pleaded to be sat upon. A row of soft pillows had already been laid on it. A table made of silver and mother-of-pearl stood in front of it, at arm's reach. On the ground, she noticed a beautiful rug, with several cushions for sitting scattered on it. Small tables were placed between them.

There was a nervous hustle and bustle here – when one servant left, a few more came in his place, constantly bringing something. Some brought carafes and jugs, others glass goblets decorated with golden leaves. There were mountains of fruit on the two crystal plates. Various kinds of snacks were prepared on the other dishes.

Suddenly the black servant brought something carefully on the silver tray. That was too much for Sofia. "Look at this!"

A fluffy bird with a golden head, golden back, and greenish-purple wings sat on the tray.

"It's a pheasant," Eftalya explained.

"Is it alive?" Sofia widened her eyes in terror when Eftalya's gaze told her that it was not.

"Will they eat it?"

"Of course."

"But how can they, it has eyes... It will look at them..." The girl was on the verge of crying.

Meanwhile, Nastya was taken by all the unspeakable beauty that stretched before her eyes. *So that's what it was to be a queen – dressing in silks and satin, embellished with diamonds, emeralds, and rubies, looking at this earthly paradise, sitting comfortably on a magnificent sofa, eating a pheasant...*

Looking from the gazebo toward the sea, in a place where the tulip beds ended, one could notice a gentle decline. Hundreds of trees in spring robes – white and pink – stretched their branches to the sea, as if wanting to throw themselves into its arms. Far to the left, a dark shadow heralded the presence of the pine forest.

One could live here, whispered her heart.

One could even die here, added her mind.

She wondered how it felt, to close your eyes forever when you look at paradise. To die with the knowledge that the last thing you saw in your life was a paradise? The grumble of reason interrupted her blissful mood. *Ask them*, it said mockingly. *Ask those who live here: kings and princes, queens and princesses... I wonder if they would agree with you that they live in paradise. Or maybe what you think is a paradise, they change by their passions into hell on earth?*

It had always been like that. Even in the moments of her greatest happiness, her mind knew how to invent and to whisper something that raised doubts in her. *I am so happy,* Nastya responded to herself, *that even your philosophical pessimism will not spoil it for me now!*

"They're coming!"

Nastya turned toward the palace. At the gate of the harem that overlooked the courtyard with roses, appeared a real army. With its chief at the head, of course, Her Majesty Handan Valide.

Her heart, so far peaceful and happy, suddenly began to beat faster. Everything was going to become clear now. *Who will you introduce me to?* Nastya asked Handan Sultan in her thoughts. *The Sultan? Do you really bring my Ahmed to me?*

"Look and learn how a Queen should move," Nastya muttered to herself.

The Valide Sultan looked dazzling. She was magnificent. She was the embodiment of majesty and dignity.

This time, Handan Valide Sultan wore a hat that looked a bit like those worn by men, but much more sophisticated. It was lilac in color, crossed by lines of a thin, golden chain that divided it into small squares. Miniature gold balls were pinned in places where they came in contact. A ruby in the shape of a drop of water rested on her forehead and sparkled in the sun.

Handan Sultan now resembled a swan gliding on the water.

One of the courtiers held a canopy on a long bar above her. *Nonsense,* she thought to herself. *I would leave it in her palace. It's funny. It casts a shadow over the majesty of the Sultana. And besides, the spring sun doesn't burn that much, especially at this hour.*

What business is it of yours? Nastya's logic responded immediately. *Don't worry, you surely won't face similar dilemmas: to use a canopy or not. So, no need to think about it in vain...*

She remembered the alabaster complexion of the Mother Sultan. She thought that her skin might just be very sensitive to the sun. Handan Sultan was almost transparent – it seemed to be almost possible to see people behind her.

Then Nastya noticed a second canopy, following the first one. *Who is that? The Sultan? Really, is Sultan Ahmed coming here to meet me? Oh God... Lord Jesus, Blessed Lady, and All Saints! Padishah...*

Cut that nonsense, her mind interrupted again. *Can't you see, these are all women.*

Indeed. A group made of only women approached them. The few men who accompanied them were not real men. Like that aga of some gate, Mestan with the squeaky voice.

She wondered who walked under the second canopy. Would that be Nevcihan? She remembered how she'd behaved before the Valide Sultan and immediately ruled out such a possibility. After all, a gold canopy would not be carried over someone who was obliged to fall to the ground before Her Majesty. The tassels of the canopy shaded the face of the woman who walked beneath it so that she could not see anything. But even from a distance, the glare from the golden ornaments on her satin jacket blinded Nastya's eyes.

The Sultan Mother walked slowly to the end of the stony path, along with the retinue of the courtiers. Before she could set foot on the lawn, in the middle of which there was a gazebo, a black page appeared before her out of nowhere and unfolded a roll of red silk in front of her. This way, a silk road was created that allowed the Sultana to pass through the damp grass with dry feet. Handan Valide now walked on it, taking small footsteps with her small feet, on which she had slippers embroidered with gold. The woman under the second canopy waited for the Sultana to get to the gazebo, and then she also stepped on the silk. Apart from them, no one walked on it, not even the girls who held the canopy over them.

Handan Sultan noticed them when she was in front of the four steps leading up into the gazebo.

Nastya immediately greeted her with a bow. The woman passed them, throwing only a passing glimpse at her and Sophia.

She doesn't like something? It was the first question that came to her mind. After this, many others appeared. *Maybe she doesn't like Sofia? Why hasn't she paid attention to us at all? Earlier, she was much more cordial. Maybe she was offended when I said that I couldn't stay with her without Sofia? Or maybe someone told her something bad about me?*

The girl from under the other canopy now came up to the stairs.

She was very young – young, pale, and haughty. *Maybe I would look like that, too, in that red jacket, embroidered with gold*, Nastya thought. *The scarlet of the satin and the warm yellow of the gold could overshadow the natural color of her complexion.*

But who is she?

She poked Eftalya so that no one would notice. Instead of answering, she twisted her lips, ordering her to be quiet.

A few more girls entered the gazebo behind them. The others waited outside. She could not even turn her head to check what was going on inside. The pillows on the ground that they had seen earlier had apparently been prepared for those court girls that accompanied Handan Sultan to the gazebo.

She could not see anything, but she could guess a bit from their movements. Inside there was a bustle. She heard the clink of glass. One of the courtiers probably poured a cold sorbet for the Sultana.

The women sat in the gazebo without exchanging a word. She could only hear the rattling of the plates and glasses.

Finally, after a long time, she heard the muffled words, "Let her come in."

Another voice immediately picked it up and repeated like an echo, "Let her come in."

After a moment, one of the ladies of the court appeared at the stairs. "You. Come here."

Nastya could hear the jealousy in her voice, but now was not the right time to think about it. She stood behind Sophia and, slightly pushing her in front, stood with her on the first step of the stairs.

"Only you. She must stay."

She looked at the girl, who, standing at the top of the stairs, looked down at her blocking the entrance to the gazebo.

"The Sultan Mother will definitely want to see her, too."

An unfriendly smile crossed the courtier's face. "If it were really like that, Her Majesty would have said, 'Let them come in.' However, she clearly stated, 'Let her come in.' So, you come in, she has to stay here."

Nastya ignored her words. They went up two more steps. The courtier blocked their way. Nastya now felt like an acrobat on a rope suspended above the fire. Either it would burn and break, and she would fall into the fire, or she would fall by herself, losing her balance. Either way, the same finale was waiting for her – she was supposed to burn.

What she was about to do – that is, to go on with the game, 'if she doesn't stay, neither do I' – really wasn't any different. But she had no choice. Suddenly, completely unconsciously, her hand went to her ear. Mirna's earring!

Be so dignified that anyone who passes you will think you are a real queen.

She raised her head and looked at the court lady, who was giving her a triumphant and contemptuous look. Nastya stared at her threateningly. *I hope she sees the lightning that falls from my eyes*, she thought. She did not move one eyelash. She immediately noticed that the girl's contemptuous smile was slowly beginning to fade. *I won*, she thought happily. *I defeated her.*

"Stand back," she hissed through her teeth. "If Handan Valide Sultan does not want to see her, Eftalya will just take her out."

She did not give the courtier an opportunity to answer. She pushed Sophia forward lightly and walked past her. She immediately fell to the ground before the Valide Sultan. The awkward movement by her side told her that Sofia followed in her footsteps, even if she was a little late.

"There we are," Handan Valide Sultan said. "This is the girl I was telling you about, Mahfiruz."

Mahfiruz? For God's sake, who's that?

"Get up, get up."

Nastya had waited only for that. She was eager to have a look at the woman Handan had just called Mahfiruz.

She straightened up. She lowered her arms along her body, joining her hands below her waist. She stood sideways, assuming a majestic pose. She noticed that Sofia faithfully tried to imitate her.

Mahfiruz... So, she was the pale and haughty girl under the other canopy. *Young,* remarked her inner voice. *It's possible that she is even younger than you.*

I can see for myself, Nastya replied to her inner voice. *But it is much more important who she is. Would Handan have a daughter, too? Look, they sit side by side on the same sofa.*

It's definitely her daughter, she decided. *Who else could sit so close to her?* The Valide Sultan sat back, leaning against the pillows. She bent her leg in at the knee and pulled it to her chin. Mahfiruz sat next to her, almost on the edge of the sofa.

Nastya felt anxious. *Who are you?* she demanded in her mind. *What are you doing on the sofa next to the Mother Sultan?*

Despite Handan's words, Mahfiruz still stared at the ground. She didn't even look at Nastya.

Look at her, how proud she is. Whoever you are, raise your head and look at me. What is it on this floor? Did you drop something or what?

She sensed that all the court ladies waited vigilantly for what would happen next. Handan seemed not to remember the reserve with which she had greeted them in front of the gazebo.

Handan Sultan looked at them with a kind smile again. After a moment, she focused her eyes on Sofia.

"That's her?"

"Yes, Honorable Mother."

As soon as she spoke those words, a murmur of indignation passed through the gazebo. Even Mahfiruz was surprised enough to move her head.

Come on, Nastya was persuading her in her mind. *Come on... raise your head. I am here – look. It was I who made all the pretty court ladies, who sit at your feet, jealous. Raise your head and see what it means to be really beautiful.*

The thoughts that now rolled through her head, and the anger that had suddenly overwhelmed her, amazed her. *Are these really my thoughts? Why is this so important to me? What do I care who she is? Let her do what she wants – she doesn't need to look if she doesn't want to. The most important thing for me now should be the Valide Sultan sitting behind her.*

"Most charming."

That's all? Was that all Handan Valide Sultan had to say about Sofia? 'Most charming?'

"Yes, My Lady. She is a beautiful child."

It seemed that the Mother Sultan did not want to pay any more attention to her.

"Yes," she said, then turned to the girl sitting next to her. "As I told you... she said she was not alone here and she asked us if she could keep the girl with her. I asked her what she would do if we did not agree. And she said, in that case, she would not be able to stay with us! Can you imagine such a thing? Nevertheless, we liked her courage and loyalty. Faithfulness is so rare today that when you come across its specimen, it makes you so astounded that you are even able to forgive any lapses in etiquette... That's what we did. So, what do you think about her?"

Mahfiruz had no choice but to finally tear her eyes away from her hands. She looked at Nastya reluctantly. They looked at each other for a while, judging each other.

A block of ice, thought Nastya. *I have no idea who you are, but looking at you, one can't help but shiver from cold.*

But it was something else that repelled her and caused anxiety. Suddenly, she found herself feeling hostile to this girl. *But why?* She tried to find out. *You don't even know her.*

The first thing Mahfiruz thought about Nastya was that the girl was pretty. *Well, let's say she's not that bad.* Inside her, something moved uneasily, however. When Mahfiruz understood that it was jealousy, she smiled to herself. *How could you possibly be jealous of such a servant?* Still, she was jealous. *I don't like you, servant*, she thought, sending her a searching look. *Not at all.*

This look made Nastya shudder. *The eyes, God, her eyes!*

Indeed, they looked like something from some other world. First of all, she was unable to determine their color. It was as if they did not have any color at all – they were neither black nor green, neither brown nor blue... Rather something between blue and gray, like icicles that hang from the edges of the roofs in the winter, and change color depending on the light. In the sun, they resemble a light blue, and as soon as it got dark, they turned cold gray, like the steel of a sword.

"Oh..." Handan Sultan interrupted their silent exchange of glances. "How absentminded we've gotten. Sometimes it's hard to keep up with all this..." She looked at Nastya. "We forgot to introduce to you. This is Mahfiruz, our daughter-in-law."

Our daughter-in-law" The King's wife... So, the Queen?

Nastya heard the ringing in her ears. What the Sultana said next, echoed in her brain as if they were talked under a huge dome.

"Mahfiruz Sultan is the legitimate wife of our son, His Majesty Ahmed Khan."

Ah! she thought mockingly. *The real Ice Queen! The Ugly Queen! A conceited, cold, nasty Sultana! A stone!*

But could the Queen be ugly? The Queen should be beautiful. Even in fairy tales, it was like that. And this one was ugly. *Ugly, but she's the Queen,* she thought bitterly. *And I? So, what if I'm beautiful when I'm an ordinary servant? And she might be ugly, but she's still a queen...*

Mahfiruz looked away and looked at Handan again.

"There is one more surprise," Handan told her daughter-in-law. "You share the same name!"

Mahfiruz was surprised. "Share the same name? How come?"

"In the Novice Courtyard, she was given your first name, Hatice. Can you imagine?"

What? Hatice? So, it's her name, too? I was given the name of this stone?

"I cannot imagine." That was Mahfiruz.

Nastya was surprised. She heard her voice for the first time. The proud stone had spoken and with a voice as cold as itself. *How cold it is, here with her... She cannot imagine, look at that. As if I could imagine it. Go ahead, take this name. Choke on it.*

"To give a servant the name of a Sultana..." Mahfiruz hissed through her teeth. Her voice was as sharp as the blade of a knife.

"But my real name is Anastasia," Nastya blurted out. "They call me Nastya."

"Ah, right," Handan chirped. "I will call her that, too."

The Valide Sultan did not seem to understand how much Mahfiruz resented this situation with the name. She joyfully continued, "Two Hatices. Also, you are peers."

"How old is she?" Mahfiruz did not even look at her when she asked. The question was addressed to Handan, anyway.

But it was Nastya who answered it. "Fourteen."

She noticed that her voice was now as cold as the voice of the Sultan's wife. It pleased her.

"We will be fourteen in a month."

This time, Nastya left it unanswered. Suddenly, she grew scared. She could very easily read the envy in the eyes of the court ladies looking at her. Could Handan and Mahfiruz see jealousy and anger in her eyes equally easily?

Change the topic, prompted her worried inner reason. *You must stop this conversation immediately. Otherwise...*

She lowered her head immediately.

"With permission, Honorable Mother," she said softly. "I would like to tell you something."

"Do you have somebody else with whom you cannot possibly part?" Handan liked her own joke very much; she laughed. The ladies of the court also covered their mouths with their hands, as if refraining from an explosion of laughter with difficulty.

Nastya did not take offense. She just made a sad face. The Valide Sultan noticed.

"Here, here," she said. "We like your honesty very much. Especially in a place like this, it is worth its weight in gold. Speak up; we'll see what you have to say."

"I am extremely grateful to you, My Lady. I thank you very, very much. With all... with all my heart. Also, on behalf of Sofia."

She hoped that it would be enough to direct the conversation to other tracks.

"But for what?"

"For not separating us."

"If we decided otherwise, you really would not stay at our side?"

If you like my honesty so much... here you go. "I would not stay," she answered without blinking.

"But it would not depend on you. If we told you to stay, it would be your duty to submit to it. Anybody who does not follow orders must face severe punishment."

"I would subject myself to it."

"Even if it was death?"

Nastya now tried to put her whole soul into her look. "Yes," she said firmly. "Even the death penalty, because isn't parting worse than death?"

It was impossible to read the praise or disapproval of her words in the face of the Valide Sultan. She just nodded slightly. And that could mean anything, either 'You're right,' or 'Just wait, I'll show you.'

"But, it is impossible to avoid separation," Mahfiruz said suddenly.

Nastya felt like she was freezing. She felt anger rising in her. *You heartless boulder... icy witch. What nonsense are you talking about?*

"One day, you will eventually have to part," continued the daughter-in-law of the Sultan Mother. "That's life. Parting is a natural part of it, isn't it?"

Of course, she did not expect an answer.

"We have already gone through many separations as well. With our mother and father, with our brothers, home, and homeland," Mahfiruz continued.

Eftalya sensed that a storm was slowly forming in Nastya. She walked aside, unnoticed, and began sending her desperate, silent signs. Her eyes seemed to cry, "Don't do it! Do not answer her! Be quiet!"

Nastya decided to apply the tactics of Handan Sultan. She nodded slightly. *Let her explain it any way she wants,* she thought. But her rebellious heart did not want to give up so easily.

"It looks like the separations served you well. They brought you both a crown and happiness..."

Silence. She felt Handan Valide Sultan's look on her.

"It was worth it to go through such separations to be the wife of His Majesty, wasn't it? If someone asked me..." Nastya broke off for a moment. Nobody asked her anything, did they? Her mind continued to appeal to her reason: *Do not go any further with this!* Still, she continued.

"If someone asked me... but then, I'm just an ordinary servant. Girls like me have nothing to lose but friendship and love..." She remembered that she should show her some respect in the end. She swallowed. It cost her a lot, but eventually, she managed to say it, "Mahfiruz Hanim."

As she said it, the eyes of the young Sultana suddenly became steel gray. She caught this moment. She read the death sentence in these eyes.

Idiot, her mind chided her. *Well done. You just earned yourself a new enemy and a much more dangerous one than Mürüvvet!*

The steel-blue eyes of Mahfiruz suddenly wavered. She tried to say something but didn't succeed. She hastily covered her mouth with her hands and jumped to her feet.

Seeing her condition, the courtiers wanted to get up to help her, but Mahfiruz quickly walked past them and leaned over the fence at the back.

What happened to her so suddenly? Nastya wondered. *Is she dying or what?* She caught herself not being moved by that at all. She only repeated to herself: *Is she really dying?*

After a long moment, the Sultan's wife returned to her place, supported by the ladies of the court. And then Nastya understood. *Oh, God, she's pregnant! The Ice Queen is pregnant!*

"I can't believe that. I can't!"

They were returning to the palace along the rocky path.

Enraged, Eftalya kicked pebbles in front of her as she walked. Sofia trotted in silence a few steps behind Nastya.

Eftalya stopped abruptly. "I really congratulate you," she muttered. "You managed to get an enemy in the person of the Padishah's wife. Bravo."

"I didn't want it at all... But I can't sit quietly all the time, afraid that someone will think something bad about me. I am a slave, a servant... well, so what? Am I supposed to let people ill-treat and humiliate me at every step?"

"Yes."

"What?!"

The girl started walking again. "Ah, Anastasia, you don't understand anything... Servants should not look or talk in this way, even among themselves, let alone toward the woman of the Padishah..."

"What way? How did I look at her?"

Eftalya laughed. "As if you wanted to drown her in a spoon of water, I swear. I wonder why. What did Mahfiruz Sultan do to you?"

"She didn't even look me in the face. Didn't you hear what she said? 'To give a servant the name of a Sultana...' What rubbish. Let her choke on her name; I didn't want it from the beginning. I didn't ask for it."

"What you said wasn't any better. Every word of yours was saturated with venom. Especially when you said to her, 'Mahfiruz Hanim.' Allah protect me... Just to remember your voice..."

"Why, did I say something wrong?"

"You spoke to her as if she were your friend or relative. Meanwhile... Do not forget that she is the rightful wife of His Majesty. The Sultana. Mahfiruz Hatice Sultan is –"

"Hatice, right... There's still that great name of hers, Hatice. A name just for her. Hatice Sultan... Ha!" She laughed.

"Nastya, don't talk like this!"

"Pregnant."

Eftalya was surprised by the word. "What? What are you talking about?"

"She is pregnant. She will have a child."

Eftalya nodded. "Yes..." She looked into Nastya's eyes to better understand what she had heard. "Pregnant. Even if so, what business is it of yours? Her importance will increase, even more, you need to understand that. Now they will really treat her like a princess –"

"Why? Because of the pregnancy?"

"Of course. They will satisfy her every whim. If she wants them to bend mountains down for her, they will bend them down."

"I understand, but why to such a degree?"

This time Eftalya looked at her with pity. "If she gives birth to a son... a successor to the throne. Understand that at least – it is possible that she carries a future Padishah... And if so, then in the future, she will be Valide Sultan!"

The girl fell silent, panting.

"Eh," she said, seeing Nastya staring ahead thoughtlessly. "You still don't get it? Your beautiful head doesn't want to accept it, does it? In that case, I will say it as simply as possible – she is the King's wife, Nastya. The Queen. The Queen of the Ottomans."

"A pregnant queen," Nastya hissed. "The Ice Queen will bring an ice block to the world."

Eftalya didn't understand what she meant at all. "Excuse me?"

"Well, what can we do? If she is the Queen of the Ottomans, I am at least the Queen of my own heart."

"Cut it already, will you?" Eftalya said, stomping her feet with anger. "She will not forget the things you told her today so easily. I would not be surprised if she complains about you to His Highness tonight."

"She will tell Ahmed about me?"

"Allah! forbid!" Terrified, Eftalya looked around and put her index finger to her lips, ordering Nastya to be quiet.

"For Allah's sake, what are you doing, Nastya?! You are asking for death. You must not talk about the Padishah by his name!" She suddenly saw that she was talking into emptiness. Nastya was not next to her. Worried, she turned around and saw her a few steps behind. The girl stood like a column of salt in the middle of the path.

"I'm asking seriously: will she tell him about me? That is, the Sultan?"

"You can be sure. The Sultan Mother liked you... This shield will protect you for some time. But in the palace, everything changes very quickly, also sympathies. Tomorrow, there may no longer be a trace of her. Well, let's go."

Nastya looked at her absently. Eftalya was not entirely sure if the girl heard what she had just said. She started walking, pulling her arm.

"For example, see for yourself... Let's take Safiye Sultan. Just a few months ago, she adored her daughter-in-law. With reciprocity... Handan Sultan was almost crazy about her. As soon as her mother-in-law sat down, she immediately put a pillow behind her back. When she was about to get up, she was the first one to jump up from her place to help her. Everyone talked about this extraordinary sympathy between them, between mother-in-law and daughter-in-law. And now what? It's over. After the death of His Majesty – that is, our previous Sultan – Safiye Sultan thought that her influence on the ruler would be even greater than before. After all, her grandson, who is now on the throne, is in fact still a child. She made a mistake, however, to believe that her daughter-in-law would still humbly fulfill all her desires. Are you listening to me at all?"

She listened, and very carefully. Nastya did not know why, but she swallowed almost her every word. It seemed to her that there were valuable clues in this story, the keys to her future. She did not fully realize why she was so intrigued by it. What she heard was like a fairy tale, with an end that she was eager to find out. She nodded.

Eftalya, who had already been whispering, now lowered her lips toward Nastya's ear even more.

"And meanwhile, guess what happened? Just ten days after her son's coronation, Handan Sultan showed her mother-in-law the door. The mighty Safiye Valide Sultan, the same one of which it has been said, until recently, that no force would be able to move from this palace, so deep were her roots in it. She didn't expect her inexperienced daughter-in-law, whom she expected to control at her own discretion, to be able to throw her into the Old Palace. Where were those recent sympathies and respect now? In the palace, nothing is what it seems to be. Don't trust anyone. Besides..."

"Talya?"

The girl turned to her, nervous. "What is it?"

"When will I see him?"

"Who?"

"You know... him. Ahmed... Padishah. Sultan Ahmed."

"Nooo! Leave me alone, monsters!"

She was dreaming about Hatice – the Ice Queen, who had the same name as was given to her in the Novice Courtyard. She was terribly white... No, no, she was rather ice-blue, just like her eyes. She wore clothes made of ice. Icicles hung from everything on her. Sharp like daggers. Nastya was there, too. She did not see herself, but she knew she was there. On the ground, she saw a pair of bare feet moving forward in tiny steps.

Those were her feet. She walked toward Hatice. She approached her... nearer... As she got closer, the icy eyes of the girl opened to devour her. They were now a bottomless, icy depth. Nastya suddenly realized that she was wrong. It was not her walking, it was those eyes that drew her toward the Ice Queen. She saw that her bare feet were already at the very edge of the abyss. She would fall into it in a moment. She fell. There was laughter somewhere. Was it Hatice laughing like that? She turned around, but could not see anything. Where was Hatice, anyway? A moment ago, she wanted to devour her with her icy eyes... And now she was not there. Lost somewhere.

When Nastya looked around for her, there was the sound of an explosion. The earth shook under her feet. Everything became red. The maddening cold blue of Hatice's ice world poured with bloody red in an instant. Blood dripped even from the icicles. Nastya screamed. She wanted to escape, and then she saw her. Hatice! Oh, Jesus... She laid with her legs apart in the middle of this icy world flooded with blood. And her eyes... her eyes... They were not there! Blood spurted from empty eye sockets. Her arms were spread wide. She looked as if she was stretched out on the cross. She tilted her head and looked down... she looked at her lap. She was stunned. Terrified. No, rather, she laughed madly. Her belly was open. Something dripped from it. Something liquid, jelly-like. Falling to the ground, it thickened, and slowly took shape... A child!

Nastya ran away, screaming. A baby born of blood chased her... She kept looking back. One after another, bloody newborns came out from the womb of Hatice, and immediately ran in pursuit of her – waving their little bloody hands and leaving bloody marks on the ground. They threw themselves at her. And she screamed at the top of her lungs, 'Noooo! Leave me, monsters!'

And then she woke up, drenched in sweat. Breathing was difficult. She pressed her hands to her heart and sat like that for some time.

The oil lamp had long since gone out. The room was dark. In the light that fell through the window facing the backyard, formed shadows that looked like scary creatures. Eftalya slept on her bed and Sofia lay curled up in the corner. Nastya leaned over her, listening to her breath. The blissful calmness on the girl's face made her feel warmer in her heart.

Trying not to make noise, she crawled on all fours to the window. She raised herself on her knees and looked out. The powerful trunk and the branches of the magnolia growing in the middle of the courtyard now reminded her of a thousand-head dragon from fairy tales. She wasn't scared of it, though.

Why should she be afraid of a shadow that would dissipate as the day comes? There were real monsters in her life, after all – one with icy eyes.

God, how am I to understand this? Nastya wondered. *What did you want to say to me? Was it just an ordinary dream? Or maybe the future?*

"Nastya?" Eftalya had woken up and now looked at her.

"Go back to sleep," Nastya whispered to her. "I cannot fall asleep."

"Did something happen?" Nastya heard a clear worry in Eftalya's voice.

"I had a strange dream."

Something moved in the darkness. It was Eftalya, who raised herself up on her elbow.

"A dream?"

"Yes," she whispered. She knew that it sounded very childish, but what she'd dreamed was not an ordinary dream. She was sure about that. She had to share it with someone.

"Go back to bed," said Eftalya. "We'll have to get up soon. Let's sleep for at least half an hour more. Come on."

Nastya turned toward her. She didn't realize that against the background of the window, lit with this mysterious nighttime light, to Eftalya eyes, she looked like a black witch.

"Talya..." she hissed. "I saw the future."

"What?" Her surprise was reflected in her voice.

The black witch nodded. "I saw the future."

"You are crazy."

"Talya, Mahfiruz Hatice Sultan will give birth to blood!"

It was still dark when Eftalya woke her up. "Time to get up!"

"Talya... But it's still night."

"Yes. Just like when you did not let me sleep, saying that you supposedly saw the future... Come on... get up. It's already after the morning ezan."

"But I don't say the prayers five times a day, the namaz."

"It doesn't matter... In the harem, life begins with the morning prayer. Afterward, you can tell me more about your dream."

"Can Sofia sleep some more?"

"Let her sleep. And get up, I'm telling you. We must show up in the courtyard; everyone is probably waiting in the rows already. Let's go."

Outside the door, two pages were waiting for them.

"What is going on?" Eftalya asked. Her voice was tough, but Nastya sensed a note of anxiety in it.

"You're moving to another place," drawled one of them.

"We are moving?"

Nastya suddenly panicked. Had what Eftalya feared happened? Had Hatice complained about her to the Sultan, and he ordered the pages to chase them both away? So, was this what life here was supposed to look like? Living in constant uncertainty?

"Yes," the other one answered. He watched Nastya through his eyelashes, thinking she could not see it. "By order of the Mother Sultan. Her Majesty said that two other girls live with you here. As this room is too small for three people, she recommended that we find a more suitable place for you."

A triumph of victory flashed in Nastya's eyes.

"We've been looking all night."

"Finally, we found one room," added the other. "We came to help you with your things."

She was surprised that Eftalya accepted it so calmly. Shouldn't she be happy instead? Or maybe she felt embarrassed that she was so wrong? She'd expected Hatice to make some hostile move against Nastya, and meanwhile her mother-in-law – the Mother Sultan herself – had personally ordered the pages to find another room for them, and as soon as possible, during the night.

"We don't have too much stuff. Some clothes, a few towels, underwear..."

"And a tiny trunk," Nastya cut in.

As the pages were about to come in for the stuff, Sofia appeared at the door.

"What's going on, sister?" she asked, rubbing her sleepy eyes and shaking with fear.

"Nothing," said Nastya in a soothing tone. "We're moving to a better place, that's all."

Eftalya, however, still felt uneasy about something. "Wait a moment," she said, stepping in behind the pages. "Where is the room that you found?"

"Opposite the big granary."

Eftalya's face grew red. "You mean the room in the dead-end corridor, down there?"

"Yes. It is much larger than this one."

"But it has four bare walls. No window. It's dark there, like in a dungeon. There was no other place in the whole huge harem?"

"But this is the room that was indicated to us..."

"Who indicated it to you?"

Nastya wanted to ask what was going on, but Eftalya pushed her aside. "You keep out of it for now," she said angrily. She turned back to the pages, who did not know how to get out of this situation.

"Who?" she repeated her question. This time, her voice was already much sharper. "Who put us in that dungeon, tell me!"

"Well, who else could it be...?" the older of the pages blurted out finally. "Mahfiruz Sultan."

The girls exchanged glances.

It turned out Eftalya was right! And sooner than she expected.

Without saying anything, Eftalya started collecting her things. Nastya did the same. She decided not to say a word until she saw the room assigned to them. *It will be better this way*, she thought. Both girls were sad and nervous now. It would not be difficult for them to say a few words too many in this situation. Or perhaps Talya was exaggerating a bit, and this room was not that bad at all? This one was indeed too small for three people... But for Talya, it was probably like a real apartment. With a window; bright. Without bars. And with the great magnolia in the courtyard. Eftalya mentioned that she should see it blossom. She wondered what its flowers were like – what color. *This summer, she will not see them*, crossed her mind. *It's because of me that she has to leave her apartment...*

Not ten minutes later, they found themselves in front of their new room.

"Everyone has already found out," Eftalya muttered.

Nastya looked around with unseeing eyes. She did not even see the servants that passed by them. Only that glacial look of Hatice occupied her mind. And one question: *Why did she do this to me?*

The honorable, serene lady, Her Majesty Handan Valide Sultan... why did she do it to me? And Nastya had liked her so much.

"I said, everyone, has already learned about it," Eftalya repeated, seeing that Nastya was silent.

"What?"

"They've already heard!" She pointed her finger at the court girls that giggled as they passed by them. "Don't you see how happy they are with your exile?"

"Exile? So, I have been exiled?" she asked as the pages parted, letting them enter. Sofia walked in first. Eftalya followed her. Nastya passed through the door as the last one.

"Yes," she answered herself. "It's really an exile."

Chapter Eleven

New Palace, Harem
July 1604

They spent the first night in the windowless room sitting on their beds and talking. Sofia fell asleep with her head rested on Nastya's knees.

"She's sleeping."

Eftalya stroked her head. "What else can you do in this darkness?"

The room was lit by only two oil lamps. The friends could not see each other's faces, even though they sat very close together.

"Forgive me, Talya. It's all because of me."

The girl waved her hand dismissively. "Come on. Apparently, it was supposed to be this way. All in all, we should even be happy."

"Why?"

"You found out for yourself that you can't show emotions here. This lesson has cost you relatively little, believe me..."

"I will complain to the Valide Sultan first thing in the morning. I will tell her everything, I will say how sorry I am –"

"Don't you dare do that, Nastya. Look where your big mouth has already taken you. Is it still not enough for you?

Give it a rest. We will not be here most of the day anyway; we are always on the run here and there. We will only be back here for the nights. It's even better – we will not have problems falling asleep in this darkness."

"Oh no," Nastya protested. "I still want to be able to look at that tree. I want to see it bloom. I'll talk to the Valide Sultan about it as soon as I see her."

Eftalya tried to dissuade her from that dangerous idea. "Last night, you couldn't sleep. You woke me up. Tell me about that dream at last." She tried to change the subject.

"It was not a dream," Nastya said mysteriously. "I saw the future!"

"You've really gone crazy... No one can see the future."

"But I did. I swear to you that I did, Talya. Hatice will give birth to blood!"

Talya became scared. *I hope no one heard that,* she thought. It was a blessing in disguise that their new room was in one of the most secluded corridors of the harem. And besides, they were whispering. *At least she has already learned that much*, Talya consoled herself in her mind.

"Okay, but tell me in detail what you dreamed about?"

"Listen... Everything was white. I..." And then she recounted the shocking dream to Eftalya, scene by scene, without leaving anything out. "And then I woke up," she finished.

Just then, one of the torches burned out and filled the room with an unpleasant smell, and it got even darker than before. Horrified, Eftalya hugged her hands to her chest, with her wide eyes now the brightest points in the darkness, as she peered at Nastya. She couldn't catch her breath from emotion.

"You will see," said Nastya. "The Ice Queen will give birth to a bloody baby."

After a long moment, Eftalya stretched out on her bed. "I was joking that 'you might be crazy' and so on... And meanwhile... Allah, you really are crazy!" she said, laying her head on the pillow.

Nastya smiled. "Think what you want. If only the mighty, the serene..."

"Nastya!" Talya shouted so loudly that she was afraid for a moment that she would wake Sofia up. She immediately put her hands on her lips.

"You understood whom I mean," Nastya whispered. "Let the day come at last, and you will see what else your crazy companion will do and say. If only I could find myself in front of her..."

In the morning, however, it was not given to her. Neither in the afternoon. She did not receive an invitation to the rosarium for the evening, either.

It was the same the next day. And for many more days...

And weeks. Nastya only saw Handan once, and it was through the window that she was told to make squeaky-clean.

They forgot about me, she thought, in pain. *They threw me into this dungeon and completely forgot about me.*

It took another ten days to convince her that she was still remembered, after all. On the tenth day, the chief court lady, Nevcihan, told her that Handan Valide Sultan was expecting her in her apartments.

"I knew it, I knew it!" Everything inside her was mad with happiness. "I expected this. I knew destiny would not leave me halfway!"

Handan Valide Sultan's chamber was crowded to the limits. Nevcihan sat on the sofa, letting the persons whom the Sultana wanted to see into the small room next door, one at a time. There were a lot of women of all ages there. Nastya noticed a lot of ladies of the Valide Sultan's court among them. They all talked to each other in a whisper.

"Who are these women?" she asked Eftalya.

The girl just shrugged. "I have no idea. This is the first time I've seen most of them. Today is the first Thursday of the month."

"Well, so what?"

"It's the day the Mother Sultan sees her people. She always invites everyone she wants to see on this day. She listens if someone has any problem..."

"Very good," said Nastya happily. "She will finally hear the complaint of your 'crazy' companion today!"

However, everything went differently to what she'd expected.

The one who listened was not the Valide Sultan, but herself.

"Oh, it's you?" Handan Sultan said as she reached for a glass of sorbet standing in front of her on a small table.

"Honorable Mother..."

The woman silenced her with a gesture of her hand. "I have two messages for you. From now on, no one will call you 'Hatice' anymore. We have decided that this is not the right name. You can keep your old one. At least for now."

Nobody talked to me like that anyway, I never got used to that name, either, she thought. They always called her, 'Hey, you,' 'Hey, girl,' or 'Hey, you there, come on here.' She wanted to say something about it, but she gave up. Something told her that the second message would be much more important for her.

"You're moving to the Old Palace tomorrow."

Nastya felt as though fire burst in her face.

"To the Old Palace?"

"To tell you the truth, you would be very useful to us here right now; Mahfiruz doesn't feel well, and she will soon go into labor. You would have things to do. But, apparently, it wasn't written for you. From now on, you will serve our mother-in-law, Safiye Sultan. You can take that child with you. Eftalya will stay here.

She tried to say something, but she failed. So, another exile awaited her.

"The praise about you reached even our mother-in-law. She personally asked His Majesty to send you to her service."

A lie, her inner reason rebelled. *And as plain as a pikestaff. How could Safiye possibly hear about me? What have I done, that my fame would reach her ears, that she would bother to ask the Sultan himself for me?*

"We did not want to offend our mother-in-law with our refusal. And, in the future, we will see..."

Then she turned to Nevcihan, who waited at the door. "Who is next?"

And that was it – the end. Eftalya was right from the beginning to the end. In a place like the palace, even if one managed to sow the seeds of sympathy, it was rare that their fruits were collected. There was no place for attachment, loyalty, or similar sentiments here.

She left the room.

Eftalya guessed everything from the expression on her face.

"You are not going to ask what she told me?"

The girl only shook her head sadly. "I don't have to. An exiled servant will probably join the exiled Sultana."

Chapter Twelve

Old Palace
August 1604

You lost, you lost! The Ice Queen defeated you!

This voice ate at her brain from the inside. Whenever it fell silent for a moment, her heart immediately resounded in its place: *You lost!*

Nastya no longer knew what to think. The feeling of failure, which she could not admit even to herself, was as painful as the inevitability of parting with Eftalya.

Not true! She tried to close her eyes to the reality. *I have not lost! She has not beaten me yet. And she won't! You will see. I swear to you! I will defeat the Ice Queen in the end!*

As she made this oath, she wet her index finger with saliva and dragged it down the wall. She did the same thing last night in the windowless room – the place of her first exile.

"I swear to you, Talya," she told her, spitting on her finger, "you will see that I will come back here again!"

Tears poured from the girl's eyes. She just nodded without looking her in the face. "Of course, you'll definitely be back, Nastya."

Her voice, however, told something entirely different. She did not believe that her friend would ever come back to the New Palace. It was impossible. There was no coming back here from the Old Palace. Most likely, they would never see each other again. Well, unless someday they sent her there for something; or sent Nastya here. If they were lucky and fate put them in each other's way, they would have the opportunity to exchange a few words and hug each other. But that was all they could count on in the future.

Nastya put her hands on Eftalya's shoulders in a comforting gesture and looked deep into her eyes. "What's my name?"

"Nastya."

"So, you can trust me. Nastya keeps her word. If she says that she will come back, she will be back!"

"I hope so..."

"Believe it, Talya. Look at me. I am also very, very sad. But I still don't cry. Why?"

"Well, why?"

"Because I made a promise to myself... I gave my word that I would never say goodbye to anyone anymore. That's why. No more farewells, never, ever. And I'm not saying goodbye to you now, either. Because I know I will come back here. We'll meet again. Besides, I need you here. You'll be telling me what the Ice Queen is up to."

"But..." Talya said with another sniff, "you know we won't be able to do that, right? I mean, talk to each other."

Nastya knew that. "I don't know how yet, but we will be able to keep in touch. I will come up with something."

So far, however, she had not succeeded.

It had been more than a month since her exile, and she had not received even the smallest bit of information about what was happening in the New Palace.

Her suspicions were also confirmed quickly – Handan had lied to her.

Apparently, Safiye Sultan heard so many good things about her. Supposedly, she personally asked the Padishah to send Nastya to her service.

One big lie, she thought with irritation. *So where has Safiye Sultan been for the past month? Supposedly she wanted to have me by her side so badly. And now what? Why hasn't she called for me yet? Of course, she has no clue that I am here. She doesn't even know of my existence, so how could she call for me?*

Was it proper for a queen to lie like that? Apparently, yes. She decided to remember this, too – even queens lie.

Nastya had another worry.

Would what she saw in her dream come true? Would Mahfiruz Hatice actually give birth to blood?

After a day's work, when she had nothing else to do, she immediately returned to the servants' room. She lay on her bed and thought about various issues, seeking answers to the questions nagging her. One of them was just that.

Would the Ice Queen, the wife of Sultan Ahmed, really give birth to blood?

She didn't know why this issue bothered her so much. Was it just because she hated the girl? Why was she so interested in what she would give birth to? *She may give birth to whatever she wants*, she thought during the sleepless nights. *Even if she gave birth to a stone, it's none of your business.*

Also, she transferred the jealousy and hostility that she had for his mother to an innocent child. Wasn't it a sin, in any case?

She didn't know that.

She also thought about the beggar every night. She wanted to curse him, but she couldn't bring herself to do it. If not for his stupid lie, she might not suffer so much now. *If only I never met him*, she thought with regret. *It was he who messed with my head, just a peasant girl, and woke up the dream of a crown in me.*

Sometimes she felt like she was tortured. Her thoughts kept circling around the beggar, the Valide Sultan, and the Ice Queen. They did not lead anywhere, however. She felt suffocated. As soon as she was happy that everything was beginning to look well, she'd suddenly been thrown out of the palace. Did she really deserve such a punishment?

For some time after moving to the Old Palace, she derided herself. *The Queen of the servants has been taken prisoner!* But this prisoner was to escape one day. Who knows, maybe even one day a prince would appear, who would take her out of this prison and put a crown on her head. And then grandmothers would tell their grandchildren the story about Nastya from Milos, ending with the words: 'And they lived happily ever after.'

With time, when the illusion that Safiye Sultan was aware of her existence had left her, she even gave up on those hopes and dreams. *You're not a prisoner at all*, she told herself one night, her face pressed against the pillow. *This is your true kingdom – the room of servants. Only here you can reign as you please. Enough with these dreams about the future already. Your path ends here. Nothing else awaits you in your life anymore!*

The pillow muffled her quiet sobs.

If it were not for Sofia, she would have probably gone completely crazy. The girl distracted her from unpleasant thoughts. Nastya was happy that the rules of the Old Palace are not as strict as in the New Palace.

Now she was the subordinate of a certain Fitnat Kalfa, a woman with abundant breasts. On the third day after her arrival, Kalfa called 'the new one' over to her.

"Are you assigned any responsibilities yet?"

"Not yet." So far, she had only been shown the rooms for the servants.

"Well. In that case, we'll make up for it. Every morning, you have to show up in the stable yard. You will be responsible for the carriage of the Distinguished Lady. It has to shine like the sun, do you understand? No mud, nay, if I see as much as a grain of dust, I will make you lick it off with your tongue, understood?"

A distinguished lady's carriage? The one Safiye Sultan got as a gift from the English Queen Eli – something? She was happy. It wasn't that bad; at least every day she got the opportunity to go outside into the fresh air.

"That's all?"

"Not enough for you?" Fitnat asked. "First, deal with that. If you still have too much free time left, I will make sure to find you extra work to do, don't you worry about that!"

The woman looked carefully at Sofia, who clung to Nastya's dress.

"And you will go to the rooms of the noble lady," she said. "You will wipe the oil lamps, refill the oil, clean the wicks, and polish the windows. From now on, these are your new responsibilities. In the evenings, after work, you will be able to cling back again to this one."

She smiled and left. She had a sharp tongue and looked scary, but she was not a bad woman.

Both were satisfied with the tasks entrusted to them.

Sofia could not get enough of it. "I've grown up, I've grown up. Now I am also a maid; I will work in the palace!" She even began to walk differently.

Every day, Nastya went to the stable yard with real pleasure.

The moment she saw the carriage for the first time was engrained forever in her memory.

The Queen's carriage stood exactly opposite her. A gift from a real queen to a real queen. It charmed her. It glowed in the middle of the courtyard like the sun, blinding the eyes of the viewers. It was not harnessed, so its shaft rested on the ground. She almost ran to the carriage. She wanted to caress the gold handle at the door and get to work immediately.

"Hey, you there! What are you doing?"

She became scared. Her hand stopped frozen in the air, halfway to the door handle. A man stood in front of the annex of the stable in which the carriages were kept, and glowered at her.

"This carriage was entrusted to my care. That's the command I received. I have to clean it from dust –"

"She will clean it from the dust, well, well." The man walked straight toward her. He stumbled on one leg.

"Just look!" he yelled when he was halfway. "Does this carriage remind you of any of these dilapidated junks you used to ride in so far?"

Of course, it didn't! It didn't look like any of them. But, she'd not said anything about that. Nastya could not help herself and looked angrily at the man.

"How do you know what wagons I used to ride in earlier, huh?"

The groom finally limped to her and looked down at her. "Right, after all, no one knows about royal carriages like you do! You also got one as a gift, right? Perhaps from the queen of the Spanish infidels, Isabella?

"What?"

"Quiet!" he shouted. "You will not touch it with the tip of your finger, do you understand? As soon as I see that your dirty, greasy fingers as much as rub against it, I will tear them out together with your whole hand, right here on the spot. Don't say that I didn't warn you!"

Actually, there's not much to clean here, she thought. The whole magnificent vehicle shone with cleanness in the rays of the sun.

"You must not approach the carriage before you take linen and suede cloths from me. You will need them for work. Do you see these ornaments? You need to clean them too, thoroughly, and carefully. They have to shine like everything else."

She saw them perfectly well. They were wonderful and extremely elaborate. Each side of the carriage was adorned with a slender gold column. Connecting at the top, they formed a huge crown with a red stone the size of a fist on the top. *Oh*, thought Nastya with delight. *Is it a ruby?*

"Don't touch anything with your bare hands. You can pull the handle only with a cloth. Before you get inside, spread a piece of cloth in front of yourself. But don't think you can get in there like that, in your dirty boots. You have to leave your shoes outside; you can only walk barefoot on the cloth. Cover the seats with a clean cloth as well. Don't you dare start before you cover everything like I said! I don't need to add that there is no sitting inside, do I? Did you understand everything?"

She nodded affirmatively.

"You will clean the glass with a different cloth. You will get a separate cloth for everything, anyway. Don't even think to touch the windows with the same cloth you used earlier to wipe the door. You can't imagine how precious these windows are. If something happens to them... I wouldn't like to be in your place. You must be careful. This is the most important thing that you should remember in every second of this work: attention, attention, and once again – attention!"

And the heart, Nastya added in her mind. She wanted to put all her heart into this job, so that Safiye Sultan would say at the earliest opportunity, "I have never seen it so clean and shiny!"

They both quickly grew used to their new duties. Fitnat was right. The cleaning of Safiye's royal carriage did take her all day. Washing, rinsing, wiping, and the arduous cleaning of each ornament... Neither did Sofia finish her work before the evening, when all the torches and lamps were already lit.

When the girl returned to the servants' room after the first day of work, Nastya immediately rushed to her.

"So, how was it? Have you seen her?"

"Who, sister?" Sofia's voice was tired, but even now filled with love.

"Her. The Honorable Lady..."

"I have."

"And what is she like?"

"Beautiful. She has golden hair."

"Did she tell you anything?" She immediately regretted this question. What could Safiye Sultan have to say to the oil lamp girl?

Sofia shrugged. "Nothing, dear sister."

The Sultana did not say a word to her. And she probably never would.

And Sofia? Would she have the courage to tell her something?

From that day on, Nastya continued to think about it.

What if Sofia whispered a word to her in the appropriate moment? Something like, "My sister, Anastasia, works downstairs. She cleans your carriage every day. She would really like to say something to you."

Sofia could do it.

And Safiye? She would call her to her presence afterward and say: 'Tell me what you have to say to us, child.' She would... She felt she would go crazy if it didn't happen.

Chapter Thirteen

Old Palace
September 1604

"Who is that girl, Raziye?"

"Which one, My Lady?"

"That one, down there."

Raziye Kalfa slowly approached the Sultana and looked out through the window. There were at least fifty girls in the courtyard – which one did she mean? She couldn't ask Safiye, 'Which one do you ask about, My Lady?' That would be unthinkable.

The Sultana grew angry, not hearing an answer.

"That's the one I'm talking about, woman," she hissed. "The one who stands under the pine tree. Just look at her; how dignified she looks. One could think she was not a maid, but a Sultana. Do you see her already?"

Of course, after she'd mentioned the tree, Raziye immediately fished her out of the crowd. "I see her, My Lady."

"Who is she, and what's she doing here? What's her name? Do you know anything about her?"

How could she know that? "I will find out everything you are interested in from Fitnat tomorrow, My Lady."

Safiye smiled, her eyes still locked onto the girl below.

"Oh really?" There was a hint of anger and ridicule in her voice. "I wonder what you'll say? Maybe you will ask her: 'What is the name of the girl who stood there, under the pine tree yesterday?' She will surely know who you mean..."

Raziye panicked. She'd made a stupid mistake, suggesting such nonsense in the presence of the Sultana. Praise Allah, Safiye was not as ruthless as before – sending her to the Old Palace knocked the sword out of her hand. Were it not for that, Raziye would pay for her moment of distraction by being punished with a falaka and suffer the torment of having her feet whipped.

"Take a good look at her," Safiye ordered dryly. "And now run!"

Raziye immediately rushed to the door.

"The girl must not be made aware that we are asking about her. Show her to Fitnat from a distance. If she leaves by then, and you do not see her anywhere, tell Fitnat to gather all the girls in the front yard tomorrow at noon. Then you will show the girl to her discreetly."

Raziye Kalfa ran out of the room.

Safiye continued to look at the girl from behind the curtain. She'd been watching her for four days. She noticed her for the first time when she went toward the carriage in the stable yard. At that time, she only saw her back, but nevertheless, what caught her eye was the way she moved. She'd even thought, *What a rogue. Like she was going to the palace, not to the stable*.

She'd stood by the window until the girl left the stable with a bundle of cloths. Then she saw her face. *She's beautiful. I wonder where she's from, and where she learned such a step. Even I've never walked so proudly and majestically. But why is she behaving like that?* she'd pondered.

This girl – her behavior, posture, looks, and the movements of her head, strongly reminded her of somebody – even though she couldn't specify precisely of whom – the mere fact of the similarity was doubtless.

When she came downstairs the next day, she'd immediately searched for her. A group of girls gathered at a distance from her, and she'd picked her out among them right away. She wouldn't have a problem with that, even if she stood there surrounded by not a dozen but a thousand other girls; everything in this girl seemed to shout, 'Here I am!'

"The girl is there all the time, good," she muttered under her breath. "I hope Raziye will quickly find Fitnat Kalfa."

Why did she stand under that tree? Did she wait for someone? If so, then for whom? Certainly not for any farmhand. Even the neutered pages were forbidden to appear in this part of the palace.

She heard Raziye's footsteps outside.

"Your Highness!" Having barely stepped into the room, she fell to the ground. For a moment, Safiye was not sure whether she'd be able to get up. She was as pale as a cloth and breathless from the run.

"My... My... My Lady," she stammered, barely able to catch her breath. "I... found... found out..."

"Wait. Take a rest."

Then she saw someone approach the girl. It was a child who ran towards her with open arms. From her place, she couldn't see the child's face, but for a moment it seemed to her that she was the new oil lamp girl. But Safiye wasn't sure. The girl under the tree also opened her arms and rushed to meet her.

She's beautiful, Safiye said to herself. *An unspeakable beauty.* She didn't like dark hair, but the girl was different from other brunettes. As soon as she saw the little girl, her face shone like the sun. She had never seen a smile fit somebody so much.

Except you, added her inner voice. *Well, except me,* she agreed with it in spirit. *She smiles at least as beautifully as me. Just look at her, even as she runs, she doesn't lose anything of her charm and grace. Allah, who is this girl?*

She turned to Raziye. The woman had recovered somewhat. "Who is it?"

"They sent her here from the New Palace, two months ago."

Suddenly, Safiye started listening intently. *They sent her,* she thought. *So, she'd been expelled. Like me.*

"What is her name?"

"Fitnat could not tell me off of the top of her head. Anas... or something like that. She will ask her and immediately give me –"

"Tell her not to dare!" Safiye yelled suddenly. "Under no circumstances! Get back to her immediately; tell her not to ask her anything. She might accidentally blurt out that someone was asking about her."

The woman rose from the floor on trembling legs. Safiye Sultan noticed.

"What can I do?" She turned toward her. "That's how it ends when you start doing something on your own."

When Raziye was already in the doorway, Safiye suddenly asked her, "Did you at least find out where she came from?"

"She is Greek, My Lady. A gift from the Beylerbey of Rumelia for the Sultan Mo..." The woman caught herself and didn't finish. She shivered with fear. She'd almost called Handan the Sultan Mother. And then, of course, Safiye would get furious. She still considered herself the only Sultan Mother of the Ottomans, the Great Sultan Mother Safiye.

"For Handan Sultan," she corrected herself quickly.

"Well, well," Safiye muttered as the woman left the room. She approached the window again and looked outside. They were not there anymore. *Strange*, she thought. *Why did Handan send a girl here whom she got as a gift from the Beylerbey?*

Did she really kick her out of there? Or maybe she sent her as a spy? Until now, intuition had failed her only once – Handan was not as naive and did not let herself be controlled as easily as her feelings had told her.

But she'd sensed something intriguing in this girl, at first sight.

You should become aware of the situation as soon as possible, Safiye, she told herself. *You must determine what to expect from this girl*.

She was going to do it. But first, she had to take care of something else.

She clapped her hands. "Semiha, my cape, fast!"

She tapped at the door cautiously.

Knock!

Something moved inside. In the candlelight that burned in the hollow of the wall, a dark silhouette that laid on the bed looked like a bale of material.

She tapped the door a second time.

Knock!

The shadow started to listen. In the flickering yellow candlelight, its eyes glowed under the hood like two glowing embers.

The third rap to the door was much stronger, followed immediately after by a fourth one.

Tap-knock!

The mysterious figure stood on all fours. Its shadow now fell on the wall, which had long since lost its color under a layer of dirt and soot. It conjured up images of a terrifying creature. The figure struggled to her feet.

"Eh," she moaned involuntarily. "This leg will refuse to obey me completely one day."

She shivered at the sound of her own voice and staggered as she moved to the door that led to a small courtyard. While she'd waited in this cubicle for more than two hours, her nose got used to the smell of tallow, mold, and dirt. But she wasn't sure whether this time if she'd be able to withstand the foul odor she would smell when she opened the door. Disgusted, she put her hand on the bolt. She barely opened the door when the odor from the yard burst into her face.

"Damn it." Grimacing, she walked quickly to the door that led to the street. "Is that you, Rachel?"

It was difficult to say whether the voice that answered her question belonged to a woman or a man. "I'm back already."

She didn't want to stay in this stench one more second. *I hope you brought good news*, she thought, as she struggled to move the heavy iron bolt. She pulled it, but the slider refused to move.

"Damn it," she cursed under her breath again. She didn't have enough strength to move it. "I can't open it."

She tried again. This time, she pulled with all her strength. She struggled with it until she lost her breath. Again, it did not work. *Well done, you should have locked it even harder*, she thought, angry with herself. *I wonder how you will open it now.*

Suddenly, panic overtook her. *What if I'm not able to open it?* She felt that she would give up her spirit if she stayed here any longer. Dampness had already penetrated her to the bone. She was convinced that she had been breathing the vapors of poison all the time. *Who knows what nasty stuff it is that stinks like this*, she thought. She shivered with fear. Somewhere in this darkness, death already waited for her with a scythe in her hand. Safiye, who just a year ago shook the world as Valide Sultan, now was to die in this hideous mouse burrow among the filth and squalor.

What sent you here, woman? Her mind would not leave her alone. *What do you mean, what? How can you even ask that? You know all too well this is the only way...*

Ever since her grandson, incited by his mother, had banished her from the New Palace, she could only keep in touch with her people this way.

No one could come to her, to the Old Palace, openly. Even if she called someone, they would not come, out of fear. Viziers and Pashas, who had previously considered the new Valide to be completely harmless, were convinced by the expulsion of Safiye that there was nothing that she would not be able to enforce on her son, who in truth was still a child.

That Greek vixen hasn't just outmaneuvered me. She tricked the entire Sublime Porte! Safiye thought bitterly.

The fact that Handan was really a still water only hit her when her grandson's Firman, his official ordinance, was read to her. But by then, it was already too late. She couldn't protest with a single word, for everything was in favor of this order – there could not be two Valide Sultans in the harem. With the advent of the new Valide Sultan, the old one could only retreat to the Old Palace to wait for death within its walls.

But she did not wait idly. As soon as the carriage brought her to the place of exile, she'd barely put her foot on the stairs that led into the Old Palace before she took action.

"Find Rachel for me!" she ordered.

Rachel was one of the ladies of the court, whom she gave freedom to back in the days of her glory. The woman was eternally grateful to her for this.

She kissed the edge of her Lady's dress as soon as she was brought before her presence. Without wasting time, Safiye went straight to the point.

"The time has come for you to show us your gratitude, Rachel," she said. "It's time to test your faithfulness in practice."

Rachel, with a purse full of gold in one hand and of silver in the other, very quickly agreed to become a liaison between the Sultana and those state dignitaries who still remained loyal to her.

Handan Valide Sultan soon learned, however, that Rachel regularly went to the Old Palace. She immediately sent her spies, who told her about every step of the woman.

Safiye found a way out of this situation. She told Rachel to find some inconspicuous place where they could meet secretly every Tuesday night. Safiye was going to appear there incognito. Once she said what she had to say, gave what she had to give, took what she had to take, and heard what she had to hear, she'd return before dawn to the place of her lifetime imprisonment.

And the whole system worked like a charm. Until that night. She sent Rachel with the message, and this time she decided to wait for the response. After the woman left, she closed the door behind her.

And now she waited for her on the other side of the door, and she could not handle this damned bolt in any possible way.

"It got stuck," she said. "Do you know if there's anything here that I can use to pry it open?"

"There is..."

Safiye immediately heard the anxiety in her voice. She was afraid she might be followed.

Someone might be interested why a woman, after leaving the palace of Davud Pasha, went straight to such a lousy place and waited at the door on a dingy street in front of a shack. Especially someone who would recognize her as a former lady of Safiye Sultan's court.

"You'll find an ax leaned against the door of the outhouse," Rachel whispered. "I placed it next to this so that it wouldn't open on its own."

As soon as Rachel said, "next to this..." Safiye's stomach immediately rose to her throat. She thought that there was no way she would go there. It was probably where all those disgusting smells came from. Besides, Allah only knew what could hide behind the doors in the darkness of the yard.

This thought caused her panic to turn into fear. Right away, it seemed to her that something brushed across her feet. She thrust the bolt again, this time with all her might, and she even tried to force it with her shoulder. Eventually, something budged.

"Praise Allah, I think I did it!"

She clenched her teeth and tried again. This time there was no doubt – the bolt moved.

"I did it!" The joyful sound of salvation could be heard in her voice.

At the next attempt, the gate went down with a creak. She opened the door, and Rachel immediately slipped inside.

Safiye did not want to stay there any longer. She walked quickly through the yard and led the way into the room.

"So, what did he say?"

Silence. Safiye turned and looked into the face of the woman, who only just now entered the room.

"What did he say, Rachel?"

"He agreed. Except... the mighty Pasha suggests that we should wait a little longer."

"Wait? But until when?"

"At least till the Sultana gives birth. He said, 'We will see what will be born.'"

Safiye quickly turned her back to Rachel. She didn't want the woman to notice the look on her face. *Damn it. What an idea. Wait! Doesn't Davud understand that I'm in a hurry? After the delivery, it may be too late. Or maybe... he betrayed me, too? He pretended to agree only to buy time... Maybe he reports about everything to Handan?*

There was no other way, however.

Now Nasuha Pasha had to be probed.

"And the other one?"

"Pasha tells you to leave it to him. He said it would be better if he took care of it himself... when the time comes."

Immediately, she thought only one thing: *He's dodging! He's evasive. Why should I leave it to him? Until now, I did everything myself... why should it be different now?*

"Before our next meeting," she again turned to the girl and looked her straight in the eyes, "you will go to Nasuha Pasha. We'll see what he says. Ask also the wife of Sunullah Hodja Efendi if she would support us with the right fatwa, if necessary."

She put her hand in her bosom pocket. Even before she took it out, Rachel heard the clink of coins. Her eyes flashed.

"I will do everything the way you want, My Lady!"

After she left and made her way out into the street, Safiye stopped under a tree for a moment to take a deep breath of clean air. She felt dizzy and her eyes still burned from the poisonous fumes in that room.

As soon as she recovered a bit, she got up and went to the appointed place to meet Semiha. She moved silently, hiding in the shadows just below the walls.

She thought about Davud Pasha's answer to her message. From the very beginning, she'd fed his pride, referring to him as her 'fearless Pasha.'

'We have heard here that while Celali rebels like Kalenderoğlu, Black Said, and Tavil Halil send blusterous letters to our grandson the Sultan – 'Let the capital and Rumelia stay with you. Know, however, that Anatolia is ours from now on' – you are forced to sit back and do nothing,' she remembered.

Then she tossed him the bait: *'On the day when His Highness Sultan and the Sublime Porte need support from their faithful servants, shouldn't you lead the army and strike the troops of the rebels as the commander-in-chief?'*

She also didn't forget to clearly outline her goal to him: *'How long can you delude yourself, wasting valuable time, that the Valide Sultan will be able to show her son the right way? There is no time to lose; we cannot hesitate a second longer. The time of action has arrived, fearless commander Davud Pasha. Allah grant that the time will come when we can enjoy hearing the news of your victories!'*

Davud Pasha was an experienced man, and he had enough wisdom in his years to understand the main message of this letter: *'Let's handle the issue of Handan as soon as possible. Our grandson's wife is still very young. There will be no obstacle for us to return to the palace as Valide Sultan. If you give us your support now, we will appoint you the commander-in-chief on the day of our return.'*

Rachel also whispered to him the way Safiye wanted to achieve her goal – poison!

Anger overcame Safiye when she remembered the response she had just received. *And this laggard advises us to hold back! Until when? What do I care what Mahfiruz will give birth to?* she quietly fumed. *Doesn't he see what Handan's politics has led to? What did Ahmed do to those guilty of the whole bunch of mistakes that were made in Austria? Have we not bowed to the Safavids? And the rebellions? Didn't all the decisions made from her inspiration only bring bad luck to the Sublime Porte? What does Pasha want to keep waiting for? For this woman to bring the country down? For the rebels to stand at the gates of Istanbul? What does he mean: 'Let's wait until the Sultana gives birth?!' Or perhaps he thinks that if Mahfiruz gives birth to a son, she will take over the control of the state? Doesn't he see that if we return, we will have the greatest influence on the Sultan as his grandmother?"*

She did not stop thinking about it even when she met Semiha. A vague suspicion began to germinate in her. *Maybe you made a mistake, Safiye? Maybe you shouldn't have revealed your goals to Davud. What if Handan had bought him even before you?*

If so, her days were already numbered. Maybe right now, the door to her chamber was opening with a bang? Perhaps the hangmen were already walking around it, looking for her?

She sat in front of the window until dawn and pondered on all these doubts. She had a plan, but she couldn't make it happen. Finally, her mind suggested the right solution: *Wait all you want, Pasha, but the fates will not wait."*

She looked at her reflection in the glass. She flinched, seeing the gleam in her eye. "Neither will death," she said quietly. "Azrael is impatient. Since you are afraid, we will take his role upon ourselves. We'll put death on her finger!"

Chapter Fourteen

Old Palace
November 1604

The air smelled like winter. The sun looked out less and less from behind the clouds. A gusty wind appeared from out of nowhere and played among the clumps of fallen yellow and red leaves, lifting them into the air. While blowing, it carried away the remaining leaves, which bravely hung on to the branches.

On the way out to the courtyard, Nastya felt it again. A strange impression had bothered her for some time. It was always signaled by a tremor that scared her.

As soon as she opened the door, the wind carried away her headscarf. She managed to catch it. She headed for the carriage which waited for her in the middle of the yard as usual. *I wonder if he's there again*, she thought.

She couldn't just turn around and check.

It had been more than ten days since she had felt it for the first time. She felt it at every step. In the yard, in the garden, and even in the courtyard of the servants' hall. It seemed to her that someone watched her – a spy!

Could the Ice Queen be behind it? But why? She'd thought that more than once. *Was I so important to her that she ordered others to follow my every step… even here? Hadn't she already taken her revenge? She'd got rid of me from the New Palace. It was because of her that I'd had to vanish from everyone's eyes; because of her, I was completely forgotten. What else could she want?*

She took a few more steps. *Was he up there today? Behind the window in that corridor?* She waited for her brain to send her a warning signal. But nothing happened.

Ever since this feeling started to follow her, she'd tried to calm herself down many times. *Maybe you are wrong? Maybe it's just an ordinary illusion?*

However, this caused her to think up further questions, because what was better: to be followed, or to succumb to such illusions? If someone was actually watching her, it meant that she was in danger. But what could be behind the illusion? Could the blow that Hatice had inflicted on her by sending her to the Old Palace have caused more dangerous consequences than she'd thought? Maybe she was starting to lose her mind?

She took two more uncertain steps, waiting for the moment when she would feel the strange trembling. If that person is out there somewhere, her brain should warn her about it, as usual – *He's here. He's watching you.*

She had heard that voice for ten days. Who knows, maybe even longer.

Today, however, the warning did not come.

She headed straight to the stable. She picked up the bunch of cloth rags and returned to the carriage as usual. She hung them over the carriage wheel and ran for the bucket.

"Just make it fast today!" the main coachman yelled after her. "It's going to rain. When you're done, we'll put it inside."

If only I could stay in it when it starts to rain, she dreamed. *Sit comfortably on the soft velvet seats and listen to the rain drumming on the roof...*

She looked at the sky. The coachman was right. A huge cloud spilled across the sky, blocking all the sunlight. She smelled the earth; somewhere nearby, it must have started raining already.

"It's starting to rain!" she shouted in the direction of the stable. "You can get it in straight away if you'd like. I'll wait for the rain to pass and deal with it later."

The man appeared in the doorway. He also looked up at the sky. "In that case, don't waste time and at least take care of the interior."

Nastya felt great gratitude for him. Inside, the carriage was as delightful as from the outside. Carved columns, decorated with leaves of gold, climbed up on both sides of the seats. The vaulted ceiling was lined with polished stones. When the sunlight fell inside, millions of sparks had to float over the travelers' heads. The door on the left probably didn't open, because if you pulled the handle in the inner compartment, a small, low table appeared. There were glasses and carafes with sorbet – worthy of a queen – on it. Cleaning them, Nastya would shake with fear. They were so intricate and delicate that she was always afraid they would fall apart in her hands.

She carefully polished the gold door handle. Then she wiped the glass. She left cleaning the ornaments for last. Experience had taught her that once she started to wipe them, it could take at least half a day.

Now, she took to the step. She wanted to wash it with soap and water. According to her, there was no such need – since she had started to work here, she had never seen nor even heard of Safiye Sultan using this carriage. From the moment the coachman warned her about it, she'd never stood on the step. To get inside, she hovered on her fingers and supported herself on her knee.

She soaked the rag well and leaned over the step to wipe it.

"What is this?" Nastya was suddenly surprised. She took the rag in her left hand and gently touched the trace visible on the step. Someone had stood on it! She was sure she'd left it impeccable yesterday. She wiped it – even though it was always clean – and checked carefully before calling the driver to pass the carriage to him. The man also looked at everything once again.

If he had noticed something like that, he would have admonished me a thousand times already for it, she thought. Perhaps one of the grooms entered the carriage during the night? But nobody would dare to do that. It was strictly forbidden – not even a fly had access to Safiye Sultan's carriage. Apart from Safiye, only two people could enter it: the chief lady of the court and herself – the cleaner of the Sultana's carriage – Anastasia!

Where did the shoe print come from then? There was no other explanation other than someone had to have stood on it and...

Nastya shuddered at the very thought of it. *If someone comes inside and damages something, you are finished, girl! All the blame will fall on you...* Panicked, she put her hand on the door handle. She pulled at it and opened the door hurriedly.

"Holy Miss!"

Even though she had never seen her, even from afar, she recognized the Sultana immediately. It could not be anyone else. No one but she could be that beautiful. No one else could sit like that and look like that. It was the Sultana, Safiye!

"Get in here with me quickly," said the woman sitting inside. "Come in and shut the door behind you."

Nastya carried out her order with her heart beating loudly. She almost collapsed on the seat. She sat, embarrassed, trying to take up as little space as possible so that she would not accidentally poke the Sultana's knee with hers.

"Do you know who I am?" Although the woman spoke in a whisper, the strength of her voice made an impression on her. "Answer me. Do you know who I am?"

"I... I know, My... My Lady."

"So, who am I?"

"Ma... Magnificent Lady." She swallowed. "The Great Sultan Mother."

"Now only Safiye Sultan."

She sensed a slight tone of complaint in the woman's voice.

"What's your name?"

"Anas..." She lost her breath so much that she could not finish. She raised her eyes slightly and met Safiye's gaze. *All Saints,* she moaned inwardly. *Why does she look at me so strangely?*

"A... nas..."

"Oh, for Allah's sake... Stop stammering, I wouldn't like to be disappointed with you. What are you scared of here? I just asked for your name."

Nastya realized that it was high time to get a grip. One of the Sultana's sentences sounded in her head particularly loudly: *'I wouldn't like to be disappointed with you...'* What disappointment did she talk about? Did Safiye Sultan have any previous thoughts or ideas of her?

She slowly raised her head and looked at the Sultana. The first thing she thought was that she was still beautiful. She had never seen such golden hair before. The golden curls dropped from under the scarf to her shoulders. Her complexion was almost snow-white; her eyes like the ocean.

Nastya immediately sensed that she hid some mystery.

"My name," she started with a strong but gentle voice, "is Anastasia Vasilides, My Lady. That is, in the New Palace, they called me Hatice... but I did not want to agree to it. Then they gave it up themselves. I am... Anastasia. Where I came from, I was called Nastya."

The woman watched her closely. "Just as I thought..." she blurted out.

"Pardon? Did you say something, My Lady?"

"I said you are exactly what I thought, Anastasia."

"I hope you thought well about me, My Lady." *Bravo, Nastya! How did you come up with that answer?*

Safiye could not help smiling. "Well, well."

She caught Nastya's chin and turned the girl's head to the right and left, down and up.

"Well, well," she repeated. "Just as I thought. You are what you look like."

Why won't she tell me straight away what she wants to say?" Nastya wondered. *What does it mean that I am just as she thought? And that I am what I look like? What was it all about?*

Suddenly, everything slowly began to fall into place in her head. *I am what I look like. Meaning I am what she saw... Mother of God! Was she the one who had been watching me? That was her gaze I felt all the time? Safiye Sultan watched me secretly? But why?*

In her words, there were so many puzzles and ambiguities. Now, however, everything became clear.

"Do you know why I came here, Anastasia?"

"I don't know, My Lady."

"To ask you something."

Was it necessary to secretly sneak into her own carriage and scare her just to ask her something? She could just order her to appear... wouldn't it be simpler? Nastya waited impatiently for the question.

"Why are you here, Anastasia?"

What? Why am I here? She wanted to cry out, but she managed to restrain from it. A smile appeared on her face.

"Because I was sent here," she answered quietly.

"I heard that you arrived here from the New Palace. But why?"

She nodded. The Ice Queen stood in front of her eyes right away. Safiye immediately caught the fleeting expression of hatred that appeared in her gaze.

"Did they banish you from there, too, Anastasia? Just like me..."

Nastya was surprised by the mocking tone of her voice. It must be some kind of code. With the comment, 'just like me,' Safiye had given her a sign. But what did she mean?

Once again, she limited herself to nodding her head.

"Who?"

Nastya was silent. She wondered how Safiye would react if she told her in response: *Hatice. The Queen of Ice*.

"Tell me. Who drove you out?"

"I don't really know for sure, but..." she whispered, not feeling it necessary to hide her sadness. "Hatice. Mahfiruz Hatice Sultan..."

I thought so! Safiye thought triumphantly. *That lump of ice must have gone mad, having such a fiery girl in front of herself. As soon as she saw her, she understood that she must keep her far away from Ahmed. A cunning little highlander. She did not show her feelings, though.*

"Oh..." Safiye interrupted. "You're wrong, child. Haven't you found yourself here because of the same person as me?"

Their eyes met. Safiye pierced her with her gaze as if she wanted to see what was happening in her head. Nastya held the Sultana's gaze calmly. What's more, she looked at her in a similar way. What was she supposed to be afraid of, after all?

"Can I ask you whom you mean, My Lady? Who... who could have done such a thing?"

"Our son's spouse," Safiye hissed. Her voice cut through the air like a whip. "She was the one that sent you here."

"Sultan Mother Handan?"

Safiye summoned a bitter smile on her face. *I want you to think that way*, she added in her mind.

"None other."

"It's impossible; she was very kind to me. Especially when she found out that we are compatriots –"

Are you Greek, too?" Safiye laughed strangely. "There you go. And yet you're pretty. And even more than pretty... a real goblet of fire. That woman doesn't want beautiful girls like you to be too close to the Sultan. She was the one who sought out the cold highlander for our grandson. What did you call her?"

"Hatice..."

"Exactly... a block of ice!" Safiye leaned into her ear as if gossiping with her friend. "My grandson must be terribly cold by her side..."

"The Padishah..." She bowed her head as if she were very embarrassed. In spirit, however, she admitted that the Sultana was right. *I'm sure he's cold. He's freezing. How could you not get cold, sharing a bed with ice?*

"So, Handan decided to chase you away as soon as she saw you."

"But it was as I said, My Lady. She showed me a lot of kindness. She even allowed me to keep Sofia with me."

"Sofia? And who is that?"

"The little girl who came here with me. The Beylerbey of Rumelia assigned her to my service."

To her service? These words surprised Nastya almost as much as they did Safiye.

A servant of a servant, she thought feverishly. *How could I say that? What if she doesn't want me now?*

"The girl Çivici Mehmed Pasha gave to your service, right?" Safiye asked. There was no trace of ridicule or anger in her voice. In fact, it was not even a question. At the same time, she thought, *Well, very well. That's what I expected. Intelligent, sharp, rebellious, and ambitious. This attitude, this look... You might think that she is the Sultana, and I am the nanny who spent her whole life in her service.*

Nastya tried to cover her blunder at all costs. She didn't want to let go of the Hatice issue, either.

"But it wasn't the Valide Sultan who got upset with me," she insisted. "It was Hatice..."

Safiye couldn't care less, but still, she asked, "Interesting. For what reason?"

Suddenly, something tapped over their heads. First a single drop.

Pitter-patter

Then a few more.

Pitter-patter, pitter-patter, pitter-patter.

A moment later, the rain began to hit the carriage with increasing ferocity.

Pitter-patter -pitter-patter, pitter-patter-pitter-patter-pitter-patter.

Damn it! Safiye swore in spirit. It was not the right time for rain. The coachman would probably appear in a moment. He should not see her sitting there, knee-to-knee and having a chat with the maid. That could provoke suspicion that would be disastrous for her.

She had left the New Palace only recently, after all these years. Her influence was still feared, and it was suspected that she secretly kept in touch with state dignitaries, plotting a conspiracy with them. What would Handan think if she found out about this conversation – in such strange circumstances – with a beautiful maid who had just been sent here by her? What's more, she would not be able to explain it in any way. It would take just one question – 'Why did you talk in the carriage, not in a chamber' – and she wouldn't know what to say.

And nobody would even ask her that, anyway. The information – already strange in itself – would probably reach Handan's ears so embellished that the Valide Sultan, even if she had to go out of her way, would do anything to force her son to give her a death sentence...

Nastya noticed that something bothered the Sultana. However, she couldn't lose this opportunity. She had to keep talking to show the Ice Queen in the worst possible light.

"I answered her questions too boldly. And then..."

"Anastasia." The woman put a finger to her lips, ordering her silence. "I have to go now. But at night," she grabbed the handle of the door on the other side – the one that Nastya thought could not be opened – "they will bring you to me. Then we will finish our conversation in peace."

She opened the door. A few drops of rain fell inside, wetting the golden curls of her hair that peeked out on her forehead from under the scarf. Tossing the hood over her head, she looked both directions. She stood on the step. "You will tell me about everything..." And then she disappeared into the rain in the blink of an eye.

Nastya still sat in her place, dumbfounded. She didn't even close the door. After a while, she saw with horror that the big drops of rain wetted the beautiful rug and the place where the Sultana had sat a moment earlier.

She threw herself toward the door and slammed it shut. At the same moment, another sound reached her from the opposite side. Someone ran towards the carriage. The door suddenly opened.

"Are you crazy?" the coachman shouted. "What are you looking for in there? Get out of there right away, out, now! How dare you trample this carpet with your dirty legs!"

She was grateful to him nonetheless. She jumped outside hurriedly.

"Don't think this is the end!" the driver shouted after her. "Let it just stop raining, you'll see then! You will lick out all this dirt that you carried inside with your own tongue... you'll see!"

She didn't care. Something had finally moved in her life. Raindrops hit her like a whip as she ran to the entrance for the servants.

What actually happened? Nastya wondered. *Why did she run away so suddenly? Did the driver scare her? But why? Does she not want to be seen with me?*

As she sat in the kitchen in front of the fire, trying to dry her hair, she felt a strange feeling overwhelm her. Was it not the same thing that she felt when she stepped down from the carriage in front of the palace in Kumanovo? And when she met that beggar on the stairs of the church? And that night, when Ibrahim Karayelzade talked secretly with Çivici Mehmed Pasha? Each time it appeared, it announced some dangerous turn in her life.

Everything indicated that black clouds were gathering over her once again.

From the beginning of her stay in the Old Palace, the servants' room had never seemed as depressing to her as it was now. For the first time, she felt disgust for all the girls who snored on their beddings, exhausted after a day's work.

God, she prayed as she waited for the person sent by Safiye. *What am I still doing here? What am I looking for here amongst them? Do you expect me to accept such a life? Please, give me a sign. If this is really all I deserve, I will surrender to it with humility.*

Nastya believed, however, that she deserved a lot more. No doubt she was worthy of a different fate. Probably there was a reason why she had to be here right now, in misery and hopelessness. It was God who probably wanted her to experience it in this way. If she came out of this trial victorious, she would get what she really deserved.

She waited patiently until the call for prayer after sunset. Sofia had already been asleep for a long time. She watched her, while among all these thoughts, anxieties, and fears, she tried to find a way for herself. She wanted to understand what had happened to her today. She was right. Someone really had been watching her.

What's more, it turned out it was Safiye Sultan herself. Something absolutely unbelievable. The words kept rattling in her mind: *'You know why I came here? To ask you something.'*

I must have gone completely crazy... How could this happen? This is Safiye Sultan, after all. The Golden Queen, whose power and beauty are legendary... And she has been watching me from behind the curtain. She snuck into her own carriage and waited for me, only to ask how I got here... And when it started raining, she ran in panic through the other door...

It all resembled a madman's dream.

'But at night, they will bring you to me.'

It was also very strange. If Safiye Sultan wanted to talk to her about her life so much, why not just invite her?

She stroked Sofia's hair, trying to distract herself from her thoughts. Out of the corner of her eye, she also observed the other girls. They were all so pale and exhausted, depressed...

She couldn't stand it anymore in the room. Thousands of smells filled the air. She felt it was too stuffy. She put on her shoes and went out into the yard. The cold, damp air hit her in the face. She stood by the door until the dry frost penetrated through her entire body. She started toward the water tank, located nearby. She noticed that someone had followed her through the kitchen door.

"You," whispered the woman, passing by. "Follow me."

So, she'd been waiting for her. For this dark shadow. Following, she noticed this stranger's back. *Dark, hunchbacked shadow*, she thought.

"Where are we going?"

"Where necessary."

The shadow did not say anything else. It stopped at the wall covered with ivy, looked around discreetly, and then suddenly disappeared. From the sounds that reached her, Nastya guessed that a passage was hidden behind the ivy.

"Come," the woman said hurriedly. "Move it."

She did. A narrow corridor stretched before her.

"Come on, go ahead."

There were stairs at the end of the corridor.

"Go upstairs," said the voice behind her.

She climbed a few steps and turned back. She saw that the shadow remained at the bottom of the stairs.

"You're not coming?"

"Go on," replied the shadow. And that was all.

Nastya went up the stairs and stood in front of the door. She wanted to open it. The door, however, did not give way.

"It's closed," she said, turning back toward the shadow below.

But nobody was there anymore.

Nastya tried to push the door again. This time, it gave way. She peeked inside timidly. She was already there – right opposite her.

"Come in, my child," said the Sultana. Her voice was friendly and gentle. "Here, we can talk freely."

She came in and closed the door behind her.

Was that supposed to be her room? A closet without windows? There was an old chest against the wall. On the other side, there was a small sofa lined with a rug, on which Safiye now sat, tapping her feet on the ground. A small table was in front of her, a lectern on the side. On the ground in front of the table sat a thick cushion for sitting. There was no other furniture here, not counting the two big oil lamps burning on the wall.

Safiye was aware of her surprise. "Come, sit down here," she said and pointed to a place for her. "You have already shown your respect enough," she said, seeing Nastya's embarrassment. "We have a lot to say to each other, and this might take a long time. That's why I will let you sit. Sit down."

Nastya had no choice. She sat on her knees, just as she had learned from Eftalya. She knew that her legs would start to get numb soon.

"So..." Safiye smiled. "First, we will explain what probably interests you most. You wonder why we are constantly meeting in such strange conditions and why you were brought here in secret, right? You'd love to know that..."

Nastya only smiled in response.

Oh, Safiye thought with admiration. *What heart won't she conquer with this smile? What knees won't bend before it?*

"It's for our good," she continued. "For ours and your security. For some time, nobody should know about our meeting."

I wonder why? Nastya thought.

The woman smiled as if she had heard the question. "You'll find that out later... Now it's your turn. Tell me, Anastasia. Why do you think Mahfiruz is hostile to you?"

Nastya found herself easily charmed by the tone of Safiye's voice. Handan's voice was also so cordial, at first, that it warmed her heart. But then later... later. *Don't be fooled this time! They are all the same. First, they make a good effort and get your heart, and then they drive you away from themselves. Don't let them fool you again. On the contrary, play the same game with her.*

"I talked to her too boldly," she began. She tried to make her voice as mild and sweet as possible, and the smile on her face engaging and honest. Her eyes, however, did not cease to study the woman sitting in front of her. "I couldn't help myself. I objected to her. I think she felt offended. When I said to her 'Hanim,' her face became green right away. And... she began to vomit."

Safiye listened to her in silence, only nodding her head. It was difficult to say what it was supposed to express. 'Go on,' perhaps? Or maybe: 'Well done; you did very well.' Nastya hoped that it was the latter.

"I even got a reprimand for it from Talya," she continued, opening her eyes wide. "She was sure that Mahfiruz would complain about me to the Sultan, but I didn't believe it. And yet, it turned out that Talya was right –"

"Talya? Allah! How many friends do you have, Anastasia? You throw these names at us as if we should know them. Who is this Talya?"

Safiye deliberately modulated her voice. She forced herself to make it sound friendly and kind, sometimes even tender. She was not used to showing those kinds of emotion. *I hope I am doing a good job.* She was aware that the girl watched her every move and listened carefully to her every word. She no longer had any doubt that she had come across a worthy opponent. *If Handan sent her here to spy on me, I must admit that she chose her well.* The girl was great in the role of an innocent. But there was something that she missed in her calculations. It did not occur to her that it takes one to know one.

"Oh, I beg your pardon, My Lady," Nastya chuckled. Suddenly, she realized that she was fraternizing a bit too much with Safiye Sultan – she had been acting as if she were talking to a good friend. She immediately stopped laughing. "I should have mentioned her earlier, My Lady. Talya... I mean Eftalya, but I call her Talya... and she calls me Nastya... Handan Valide Sultan gave her to me as a guide and a teacher of life in the harem. But we quickly became friends."

Stupid! Safiye thought. *As a guide and teacher... right! I don't understand how you could not see that Handan placed a guard by your side who would tell her every step you made. Where did your acumen suddenly disappear, eh?*

"She came here with you, too?" If so, it meant that she now had two spies on her head. *You can send even two hundred, Handan,* she thought vindictively. *You will not stop me anyway. Azrael's scythe is already in my hands!*

"No," Nastya replied. As expected, her legs began to grow numb. She moved restlessly. "The Valide Sultan did not allow it. Talya stayed with her. I suffered because of this parting very much, My Lady. Really, I..." she was not able to finish. Her eyes misted.

"You love her so much?"

"Of course, I love her. Can you not love your sister?"

"So, you trust her so much, this Talya?"

"Completely."

"I see." Safiye felt something vaguely begin to bloom in her head. This something was slowly taking shape. She still didn't know what it was going to be when completed, but she had no doubt that a plan was beginning to form in her brain. She knew herself well. Whenever this happened, a voice said to her: *I see.* Like it did right now... *I see.*

"She took action right away..." The girl's voice snapped her out of her reverie.

"What does that mean, Anastasia? That 'she took action right away'?"

Nastya told Safiye how the next day after talking to Mahfiruz, they were thrown out of Eftalya's room. She described the dungeon to which they were sent so colorfully, that Safiye could have sworn that the girl was sent to a real torture chamber. Then Nastya lamented that Handan did not call on her any more... not counting the last meeting, when she informed her of the deportation to the Old Palace.

"Talya was absolutely right," Nastya finished her story. "Who knows what Mahfiruz told the Valide Sultan and the Padishah about me, only to incite them against me..." She paused for a moment and looked at Safiye, watching her carefully. "I didn't stand a chance. On the one hand, a Sultan's wife... on the other, an ordinary maid. It is only natural that they were in favor of her. I don't have any ill feelings about it toward them..."

I give up, thought Safiye. *If this girl is a spy sent by Handan, it will be a really hard time for me. If all she told me, her facial expressions, and tone of voice is really just a game... But if she's telling the truth, you are finished, Handan! With this girl on my side, I can do everything I want with you!*

She noticed that she was slowly beginning to lose the suspicions she'd had about Anastasia. *I fell into her snare... Maybe believing her words will be the biggest mistake I will make in my life, but there is something about her that intrigues me...*

Everything she had just heard was very likely. The girl was fierce, just as she thought. Well, and her beauty. No wonder she made Mahfiruz worry. If she'd stayed in the New Palace, Ahmed would have to see her somewhere sooner or later. Mahfiruz herself was pregnant, so the Sultan probably did not approach her now. Mahfiruz noticed that Anastasia stood out against the other slaves in the harem, and quickly sensed the danger. She was afraid the maid might threaten her position. She insisted, therefore, that she did not want to see her in the harem, and the Sultan gave in to her... In this way, she got rid of the danger threatening her in advance. She had planned it well.

This whole story held water. Perhaps, at some moments, Anastasia got carried away and exaggerated certain things, but it was clear that Mahfiruz was behind her exile. *But the girl should be convinced that it was different.*

Anastasia could hate Mahfiruz at will. For Safiye's plans, however, it was necessary that she should start to feel a similar hostility toward Handan.

It was the time to grab the weapon. She decided to attack from all sides. That mysterious, mocking expression appeared on her face again. She looked Nastya in the eyes with a meaningful smile.

"So, according to you, Handan did not put her hand to it at all, right? Do you really want to tell us that you believe that?"

"Yes, My Lady. She was forced to get rid of me from there."

Safiye sighed as if she was greatly disappointed. "And I took you for a smart girl."

Nastya looked at her with anger. "Because I really am! But the Valide Sultan could not go against her daughter-in-law. Who am I, that she would defend me?"

Here is the right moment to release the arrow, Safiye. Shoot!

The Sultana jumped up from her place, enraged. "I don't want to ever hear that again, do you understand? Don't you dare to talk this way about yourself! What does it mean, 'Who am I?' Never again feel sorry for yourself in this way, never!"

The rainy clouds that had been gathering in Nastya's eyes for some time suddenly broke open.

It didn't make the slightest impression on Safiye. She went over to the wall covered with a rug. "If you don't know who you are, I'm afraid we can't do anything for you." She caught the carpet's fringes and said without looking back, "Wait here." Her voice was sharp as a knife. "Someone will come for you soon."

She lifted the rug slightly. Nastya saw through the tears as the wall behind it slowly moved away to the side. She stood up and walked quickly to the woman.

"I..." she called after her. "I know very well who I am!"

The game is won! Safiye thought happily. She stood still for a moment, staring at the wall. If she turned to her at once, Nastya would see a smile on her face. "Really? In that case, tell us: who is it that you are?"

Nastya came closer. She raised her head and looked at her with tearful eyes. "The Queen," she said quietly. "I'm the queen. Queen Anastasia."

Safiye Sultan gave her a quick look. She didn't look surprised. She nodded and approached her. She smiled sweetly now. "Oh, no," she said. "The Ottomans have neither queens nor sultanas named Anastasia. So, you are Hatice Sultan, my child."

Nastya laughed delightfully. Safiye sure acted crazy today. In general, everything that had happened to Nastya today was like that. Now she had also heard something like that, and from the queen in exile.

"Hatice Sultan..." Safiye repeated under her breath.

"But..." Nastya began timidly. She felt that for the second time, she was experiencing a scene that had already happened in Kumanovo, on the stairs of the church. "Can a maid become a queen?"

In response, she heard exactly the same thing as then. The only difference was that this time it wasn't the beggar who gave it, but Safiye Sultan.

"You will become one!"

Chapter Fifteen

The New Palace
November 1604

Sultan Ahmed had walked around his apartment deep in thought, for some time, while the Viziers waited patiently in a line, with their heads bowed and hands folded in their lapels. Nothing was heard in the room but the Sultan's footsteps. This grave silence was disturbed by an ugly, unpleasant scream that suddenly sounded outside.

The Padishah walked to the window, where he saw a peacock, strutting around the garden in full display, with its tail spread wide. A turkey also walked nearby, but with her head bowed as if aware of her ugliness, especially compared to such a majestic and stunningly colorful male. She pecked intensely at something in the grass, ashamed to peek out.

Ahmed was surprised that such a beautiful bird would make such a sound. *Apparently, this was a divine arrangement, so that in all of creation, virtues would be combined with disadvantages. Look at the beauty of this bird and compare it to the ugliness of its voice! But isn't it the same with me?*

He was always destined to become a Padishah. Allah himself girded him with a saber and sat him on the throne. He lived in a splendor that was hard to imagine, even in one's wildest dreams and fantasies. Heads rolled, and mountains crumbled at his command. He could have everything that his heart desired. If necessary, he had thousands; tens of thousands of servants ready to die at his command – actually, he had some doubts about that, but it had been customary to say so. When the last soldiers of his army reached the Topkapi gate, the other end of the army already stood in the foreground of the Hagia Sophia. All this depressed him immensely. Allah gave him a life that most people could not even dream about, and he was still unhappy and anxious. And what's worse – he was afraid.

He sighed heavily. *Did I ask for all this?* he thought. *No. I never wanted to be on the throne.* If he could direct his life himself, he would've loved to become a shoemaker and work at an indoor bazaar. Or a jeweler, who created beautiful tiaras, rings, and necklaces from gold, diamonds, and emeralds.

Who prepared such a fate for you, Ahmed? What a pity you didn't have any influence on it, he thought with regret. *You were born to become a Padishah. For the weight of the whole world to be placed on your shoulders.*

In the harem, slave women fought wars amongst themselves. Each of them dreamed of giving birth to a son and securing her future that way. Besides, he had crowds of agas, beys, and viziers on his head, each of them eager to earn some wealth and power, either counting on the current ruler, or on one of his sons – whoever, in his opinion, would have the greatest chance of taking the throne in the future.

There were many contenders and only one throne. Whoever would take it, would not be able to please everyone. There was always a group of disappointed people who had counted on the coronation of another prince. So, they'd keep waiting for the throne to finally go to their favorite. Backstage power games involving dignitaries and princes were only a matter of time.

According to the law, the throne went to the eldest son of the ruler. Okay, but what if something happened to the heir to the throne? And then to the next heir, in order? And the next one? No prince, as he went to sleep each night, could be sure he would see another sunrise again. He could not take a deep breath of relief, even when his older brother would become Padishah. Because it meant that he might now bloodily deal with his younger siblings, who could endanger his power in the future.

But, it was not just the brothers who were a deadly threat. It could also be the father...

Sultan Ahmed nodded sadly at the memory of his own father, who gave an order to strangle every one of his nineteen brothers immediately after taking the throne. His childhood passed in the same chambers that witnessed their deaths. He laughed and played between the walls that saw their struggle with an executioner, that heard their pleas for mercy.

When he later found out what events of the past hid behind the splendor of the palace, the hair bristled on his head. It seemed to him that a ghost of one of his murdered uncles waited for him at each corner.

With time, he began to fear his own father, too. *And if I fall victim to a libel? If one day, somebody 'well-meaning' whispers to him: 'I would rather have my tongue cut out than to have to tell you this, but...' And if the Sultan decided that, for the sake of Sublime Porte, he could sacrifice not one, but even a thousand sons?*

How many times had he jumped up from his bed at night, terrified, at the sound of footsteps? A hundred? Five hundred? Or a thousand?

A son was afraid of his own father, a father of his son, the eldest brother of a younger one, and a younger brother of the aga who took care of him. How could anyone want such a life? No wonder he had always been more attracted by the friendly and calm disposition of the turtledove, than by the majesty of a peacock.

That's why he'd wanted to give up the throne when his grandmother came to his chamber to kiss him on the forehead that fateful day. What did he say to her then? 'Don't even take me into account. Our brother, Prince Mustafa, is a lot more suitable for this than us.'

He remembered the impression his words made. Safiye and Handan jumped to their feet, exclaiming, 'What kind of an idea is that? You know Mustafa is crazy!'

To him, however, Mustafa was the wisest of them all. He pretended. He grew up in the same fearful atmosphere as Ahmed, listening for the footsteps of the executioners, trying to understand what was behind an eavesdropped whisper or a captured gaze. He escaped into madness to wriggle away from the crown. All of his antics – conversations with the walls, running up a tree with a scream of 'They follow me!' and many others – they were but a clever game.

Mustafa got away with it. Meanwhile, Ahmed was left at the mercy of his grandmother, mother, and the man whom they were about to bring to him: the deputy of the Grand Vizier, Kasim Pasha.

He'd tried hard to avoid it, crying out, 'I am still a child!' Then he tried, 'I haven't been to a sanjak yet!' where, as a son of a Sultan he should have worked as an administrator and learned how to rule the country, to be prepared for rulership by the military and court administrators, but no one listened. Finally, he used the last argument: 'I have not even been circumcised!'

'You will be,' his grandmother had replied to him. 'Allah will grant that very soon, we will have this ceremony as well. But first, there is the coronation awaiting us. First and foremost, you must take the throne!'

He took it, and what happened? Nothing. The power fell on him and crushed him with its weight. Just a short time ago, he was only afraid for his own life – now he was responsible for the lives of millions. Before he took the throne, the borders of his world were marked by the walls of his chamber, now he didn't even know where his domain began and where it ended. He sent troops to places he'd never heard of before.

And even greater darkness enveloped him. He fell into the clutches of even greater fears.

He tried to not look in the eyes of the people who knelt before him to kiss the hem of his cloak. He was afraid that he would see their thoughts in them. He'd paid a high price for being a son of a Padishah. Now he paid a similar fee for sitting on a throne that he took by the will of fate.

He thought about the circumcision ceremony, and his cheeks burned. Allah only knew how much he was ashamed then. Indeed, it was an unusual sight – an almighty Padishah walking to his own circumcision! As he walked to the Hall of Circumcision, dressed in a large gabardine, he noticed mockery on the faces of the dignitaries he passed by, carefully concealed under the mask of faked respect. The pain their insincerity had caused him was much larger than the pain inflicted by the blade of the knife.

He'd wanted to sink through the earth whenever he heard reports of the voices in the street: 'Well, well, we've got ourselves a Sultan who has not even tasted a woman yet.' As he'd walked into the room where the newly married Mahfiruz Hatice waited for him, his heart almost stopped beating. He had no idea what he should do or how to do it. Another thought was equally terrifying: *What if I fail?*

He tried to comfort himself. *Every man has gone through this, now it's your turn!* A man who failed with a woman could be at most laughed at... but for him, the Padishah, he would have suffered a loss of respect in the eyes of his subjects. Even if after that, if on the third, fifth, or fiftieth night he would be the most successful, it would not matter anymore. Someone who is a Padishah should always be like a sword – unfailing and decisive.

Thank Allah he didn't fail, and all eyes immediately turned to the belly of Mahfiruz. Fortunately, the girl quickly became pregnant and did not give the opportunity for more gossip and speculations. Instead, people wondered who she would give birth to:

'I wonder if the Sultan managed to beget a son?'

'And even if it will be a daughter, then what? In any case, it's life coming from Allah!'

'True, Sublime Porte expects, however, that the Padishah will give it the future heir to the throne...'

How many things the Sublime Porte expected from him!

Khe, Kheit! he wanted to shout, like the bird he observed. *Don't swagger like this, peacock,* he thought. *The Great Sultan Ahmed stands before you, who in the past three months gave the Sublime Porte three occasions to celebrate. Which Padishah before me took the throne even without being trained in sanjak? Or wore the saber before he was even circumcised? Or took a wife only a month after circumcision, and almost immediately fathered a descendant? Praise Allah, we've done it all, one by one, in such a short time. Who before us brought so much joy to the people?*

He was far from being able to respond with laughter – or even with a smile – to what was being said about him. Despite so many sacrifices, bad news came recently, one after another. In Hungary, the situation did not look good. Three more fortresses had fallen into the enemy's hands. He was about to cry when he learned about the loss of Yanikkale. And right after that, Estergon...

"Oh no, not Estergon!"

People started to talk amongst themselves. Viziers saw the opportunity for themselves and sprang into action. His mother reopened the subject of Safiye Sultan from time to time: 'She is behind all this, son. She prepares a coup that will put an end to your rule!'

But why would she do it? She'd insisted on him taking the throne much more than his own mother did. Handan did not let anything show. She began to mention the crown only when his father fell ill. Why would the same grandmother, who'd immediately appeared to greet him as the new Padishah after his father's death, now plot against him? *And for whose benefit? Mustafa's?* he wondered. Wasn't it Safiye Sultan who said with indignation, 'He is crazy!' when he told them that he wasn't interested in ruling; that he wanted to yield the throne to his brother? Why would she now suddenly want to bring him to power?

He remembered how severely his mother looked at him when he shared his doubts with her. He remembered what she said to him then. *'You've already forgotten, son. As soon as you took the throne, everyone agreed that it was customary to kill Prince Mustafa so that he would not bring a claim to the throne in the future, and would not involve the country in a devastating dispute. Only your grandmother stood up for him. Don't you remember how she took him under her wings, how she begged you to spare his life? Apparently, she had an interest in this. Now everything has slowly begun to come to light!'*

Nothing started coming out! Ahmed had thought then. His mother, however, was convinced that Safiye was behind all the rumors. She also believed it was Safiye that spread the seed of discord. Ahmed tried to intercede for his grandmother every time.

'Mother... On your word, we sent her to the Old Palace. What more can we do? From there, she can't contact anyone after all... And even if she succeeded to somehow, who will still listen to her?'

So, he was stuck like this, suspended between two women. *What two? Three!* he thought bitterly. As if it were not enough, they threw this Mahfiruz Hatice into the mix. And now another worry was already on its way. *We'll see what will happen when the baby is born...*

He didn't know who really *was* the Sultan here. Of course, he was the one officially crowned, and he sat on the throne in the Audience Hall. For the first fifteen days of his rule, however, Safiye Sultan was the real ruler. It was she who suggested to him to appoint Kasim Pasha as the governor of Baghdad. He'd obeyed her, despite his mother's objection.

Look, Safiye Sultan, what misery this Pasha of yours has brought upon us!

With her departure to the Old Palace, Handan took over the reins of power. He personally admitted the Viziers were right when they said that he should personally take command and lead the army against the Hungarian giaours. He did it, not because he wanted to go down in history as a hero, like his ancestors, but only because of fear of possible rumors.

The Valide Sultan, however, unleashed all hell, objecting to this decision. 'What will the boy, who doesn't even have a mustache yet, look for in the battlefield? If you want to go to war personally, why do you need your agas, Viziers, and Pashas? They will sit comfortably in the capital, and the Sultan will wander around the border, right?'

So, what was he supposed to do?

His mother prompted him, 'Isn't it time to make use of Malkoçoğlu Yavuz Ali Pasha, My Lord?'

'But we made him the Great Vizier, according to grandmother's wishes.'

How could Ahmed – who'd stayed away from any intrigue – know that his mother strongly disliked it? Why would one of Safiye's people be the second person in the state? Lala Mehmed Pasha was ideally suited to this position; he'd once been Ahmed's educator, and more importantly, he hated Safiye Sultan like a sin.

'It's in your power to put him at the head of the troops now, as your deputy... That would work well. The order is yours, My Lord.'

Is it? he thought bitterly. *I wonder if I will be able to stop the rumors that this decision will cause.*

Indeed. Both the people and the soldiers valued Ali Pasha very much. However, it was hard to find someone who would appreciate the fact that the Padishah remained in the harem instead of taking command in person. The same things could be heard everywhere:

'Infidels have gone mad. So many of our boys were killed again...'

'These fortresses were inherited from our ancestors, weren't they?'

'The souls of those who once died there will not be able to have peace now.'

'Certainly not. After all, the land in which they now rest is now trampled by the feet of the giaours.'

'It looks like the time for a holy war has come, so why wait?'

'Malkoçoğlu Yavuz Ali Pasha is already marching to the front,' someone cut in, and words of dissatisfaction came out of a thousand lips.

'Why isn't the Sultan going to stick his head out of the harem? Why won't he take command himself to avenge our fallen?'

'What does he need that saber for, if he doesn't make use of it?'

The spies reported to Ahmed about such conversations and even tougher ones. The hungry people whispered. Prices were rising like crazy, and thieves and robbers harassed everybody. So, the people tried at least to make up for their wrongs by spreading rumors and ridiculing the sultan:

'Padishah should mount a horse and set out against infidels himself.'

'But he can't mount one!'

'Why is that?'

'You don't know? They've just circumcised him. If his noble jewels experienced any damage on the back of a horse, who would give the country an heir to the throne?'

'He has just had his first taste of a woman, why would he trade her for a horse?'

'Would you be happy to mount a horse instead of a woman? Why would he do that?'

The spies did not talk about it, and he did not dare ask questions – but he was sure, however, that conversations like those would be followed by the terrifying peals of a disgusting cackle.

He remembered the anger with which his mother had exploded when she found out about everything. Her voice still sounded in his ears: 'Fools! Ingrates.' Then he thought about the words his grandmother had told him on the day of the coronation: 'Simple people think with a purse. When you fill it for them, you will be the best ruler in the world for them. But if it gets empty, it's hard to find a worse one than you...'

Thus, at the cafes and wine bars, people must have started talking that the Sublime Porte had never had a worse Padishah than him...

Everything that was going on in his soul was reflected on his face.

He sat down on the throne with a grim expression. He put one leg under himself, bending the other one at the knee.

I will show them they are wrong! Ahmed thought. *They will see who sits on the throne, to whom the power and command in this country belongs...*

He clapped his hands.

"Bring in the traitor!"

Chapter Sixteen

Old Palace
November 1604

'You will become one!'

Holy Mother! Nastya thought feverishly. *What game is my destiny playing with me? The blind beggar I met years ago turned my whole world upside down...*

To get a few cents of alms, he'd thrown three words at her: 'My beautiful queen!' That was enough for her to become the hostage of her dreams. When she tried to protest and told him that she was just a simple maid, he told her that she would become a queen. And now fate made her experience it for the second time – only this time, the fates used this powerful woman.

'Hatice Sultan. The most beautiful Sultana in the world.'

'But I'm only a servant, not a Sultan!'

'You will become one!'

What was she supposed to say when someone asked her? Who was she really? – Anastasia or Hatice? A servant, or maybe a Sultana with a contaminated mind, who gave her soul to the slavery of dreams? And she believed, like an idiot, that one day they would come true.

Ever since that night meeting with Safiye Sultan, it seemed to her that she had completely lost contact with reality. She saw herself as a Sultana who, like Handan or the Ice Queen, wore a crown on her head and dressed in silks, satins, velvets, and expensive gems.

She had to finally admit it. One night, she concluded she had indeed gone crazy. If she were normal, would she believe that she would one day become an Ottoman Sultana?

But if that's the case, then Safiye is even crazier than I am, she told herself as she lay in her bed.

'There are neither queens nor Sultanas named Anastasia among the Ottomans. You are Hatice Sultan.'

'No. I'm just a simple maid, not a Sultana...'

'But you will become one!'

She said those words with such certainty, it burned like embers: "You will become one!" Then Safiye sat down on the sofa again and told her to go back to the place opposite her.

"I want to know everything about you, Hatice," she said.

And so, Nastya told her about everything, one thing after another. When her story came to an end, she experienced another surprise.

"Oh God, and that's it?" It had taken her only fifteen minutes to tell everything about her fifteen years of life, most of which was the period after her abduction. The beggar on the stairs of the church. The prophecy, Mirna, the arrival in the capital, and a blood-chilling look of the Ice Queen... That was all. She looked sadly at the woman who'd listened to her attentively.

"So, the beggar told you the same thing: 'You will become one!'"

"Yes, My Lady..."

"And you didn't believe it, of course?"

"I don't know, whichever way I would answer you, it would be a lie. But everything else is true. I became her, at least in my fantasies and dreams. At night, I am the queen, and I welcome the new day again as a maid, who wakes up to the sound of her name when they call her to work: 'At your service!' If I only knew that mixing dreams with reality was so painful, I would have ridiculed that beggar."

"What about my words, Hatice? Don't you find it strange that, without knowing your story, I repeated to you exactly the same thing as him, telling you exactly the same future as he did?"

It did seem strange to her, even very strange.

"Don't you see that all this cannot be a coincidence? Don't you see that something very clearly pushes you in one direction? And now it has also put me in your path. You really do not see the finger of divine providence in all this?"

I don't know, she thought then. "Perhaps..."

"Our stories are more or less the same. A beautiful girl is kidnapped and falls into the hands of pirates. She ends up in a slave market. She is bought and given as a gift to the palace. One day, by accident, she meets a young, handsome Padishah, whose heart begins to beat faster at the sight of the slave. He sings her songs, writes poems for her. And with time, he takes her as his wife. Their children are born... Who would believe that such a life could really happen? But don't even fairy tales contain a grain of truth? My life was exactly as I just described to you a moment ago. And yours will be exactly the same!"

"What should I do then, My Lady?"

"Submit yourself!"

She shuddered at the tone of the Sultana's voice. "Submit? To whom?"

"Your destiny. Me."

"You are my destiny, My Lady?"

Safiye laughed heartily. "Of course not, Hatice. I... I am only the person who will change it completely for you!"

Nastya felt shivers run up her spine again. "I am a poor girl, My Lady," she said slowly, with the last pieces of resistance that remained in her. "I am aware that my dreams are impossible to fulfill. I have a rich imagination, I'm ambitious, rebellious... But that's all. I am begging you, My Lady. Please don't play with my head like that liar beggar, not you too. Don't awaken unattainable desires in me. The Sultanate is not something from my world..."

"Hatice! Stop pitying yourself immediately!"

She stopped in an instant.

"Just tell me one thing. Are you on my side or not?"

What did it matter? "Of course, My Lady."

"I..." Safiye began, straightening proudly, "I want to go back to where my place is. To the New Palace. And you?"

Is my place there as well? Nastya wondered. With the divine will, she only stayed there for a short time... it was just an episode in her life. *Maybe you don't want to admit it to yourself, but... didn't you accept that palace as your home?"*

"Me too," she said after a moment. "I'd like to go back there, too, My Lady."

"But as who, Hatice? As a maid who sees herself as a queen only in her dreams, or maybe as a true Sultana of the Ottomans?"

Eh, all this madness will finally bring misfortune down on me, she moaned inwardly. *This woman is messing with my head as if she wanted to arrange everything in it anew. How can I continue to live with the demons that she let into my soul, how to tolerate their intrusive whispers: 'You will become a Sultana! You will become a Sultana!' How can I accept that I will not achieve what cannot be achieved?*

"Think about it well," Safiye said, leaning toward her. "Once you have it answered for yourself, there will be no turning back from the path you've chosen, my child!"

What else was she to wonder about? About the thing, she wanted with all her heart?

"I..." she hesitated. She was well aware herself that there would be no turning back... If she chose to enter the path, she could only step down as a madwoman – to an asylum – or as a corpse, thrown into icy water or a burning fire. "I..." she resumed with difficulty, "I want to go back there as a Sultana!"

Safiye got up from her place, extend her hand to Nastya, and helped her up.

"Well then. If you do everything I tell you, that's what will happen. You will become a Sultana, and you will even give the Ottomans more Padishahs."

After these words, there was a long silence.

"Hatice?" Something glittered in Safiye's eyes like millions of fireflies. "We have a lot of things to do. It's time to roll up your sleeves. We must plan the fate of Hatice Sultana!"

Then she turned her back to her and headed for the rug that covered the secret passage. "Now we have to part. Remember... No one should know our secret until the time comes."

"When will it be?"

"Soon, Hatice. Very soon..."

Suddenly she disappeared behind the carpet, and Nastya was left alone in the room.

She only remembered being stunned, not thinking about anything until she heard footsteps at the door. She didn't know if she would be able to come back to her senses after everything.

When she heard the crack behind the door, she went over and opened it. There was no one outside. She returned to the courtyard alone. It was empty, too. There was still some time until dawn. Her heart jumped to her throat at the hoot of an owl, which stared at her with its bulging eyes somewhere in the distance.

"Onwards," she said, laughing to herself like crazy. "Go ahead, Hatice Sultan. A pile of pots is already waiting for you to wash."

From that day, it was as if she was absent, to the extent that she didn't even respond to her name. She left callings of 'Nastya, Nastya!' without any reaction. *Safiye killed Nastya that night,* she answered to them in her mind. From now on, she was the Sultana, Hatice. Or maybe just Crazy Hatice.

Yes... she thought as soon as she put her head on the pillow after a day's work. *I'm just Crazy Hatice, no one else.*

But as soon as she fell asleep, Hatice, the Sultana, surfaced from the depths of her mind. She strode dignifiedly and gave orders:

'Drive that girl out of the palace. Let her go wherever she pleases!'

'What girl, Hatice Sultan?'

'That one... The highlander Mahfiruz, with the icy eyes.'

'But she is the wife of the Padishah, after all. And besides, where would she go from here?'

Her eyes threw lightning. 'To hell!'

Chapter Seventeen

New Palace, Rumelian Garden
November 1604

At the order of the Padishah, the massive gates slowly opened. Outside, a shuffling of a chain could be heard. A man appeared at the entrance, supported by two guardsmen.

The Viziers trembled with fear and only looked at him out of the corners of their eyes. Some thought: *Well... Kasim Pasha, everything has its price in this world. If we'd let you get away with it, we would probably be in your place now. Thanks to you. Well, let's see what will happen next with you...*

Two guardsmen led the prisoner before Sultan Ahmed. Kasim Pasha had been tortured with the falaka, so he was unable to stand up on his own. When he was let go, he slumped at the Sultan's feet like an empty sack, with a frightening clatter of the chains that bound his legs and arms.

Ahmed looked at the man lying on the ground. *And he is the one who passed the throne to me that night when our father died?* he thought.

Kasim Pasha's hair had been shaved with a dull razor that left bloody marks on his head. The man's eyes now looked like two bloody cavities. Half of his beard was shaved while the other half was left intact. There were signs of burns on his bare chest. He wore knee-long galligaskins, so big that they almost slid off his legs. They were only supported by a rope, which was tightened around his waist.

Oh, Pasha! thought the Sultan with compassion. And at the same moment, he grew angry. *There can be no mercy, no mercy! Ahmed, you are a Sultan. And he is the culprit. You're mad at him. There's no mercy!*

"Get up, cursed man!" he roared. He did everything in his power so that his voice would not sound like a boy's squeak. "Aren't you ashamed to lie down in our presence?"

The man at the Sultan's feet twitched and crawled closer. The Viziers were horrified at the sight of the soles of his feet. After the whipping, they had been covered with salt. He tried to get up, but he collapsed again.

"Lord..." he made a loud groan. "I can't do it... My legs...

"Quiet, traitor!" the Sultan shouted. "You deserve it."

One of Kasim Pasha's eyes was covered with a terrifying scar, while it was difficult to tell if the second was still in the eye socket – only a bloody cavity could be seen in the place where it should be.

Be strong! A warning voice echoed in Ahmed's head. *There's no mercy. Be determined and tough. Show them all that Sultan Ahmed is a real sultan!*

"You, insolent cur!" he shouted again. "You treacherous, hungry dog! A thief without mercy! You are not ashamed of your servants, you are not afraid of our anger, you must have Allah to thank for nothing, too! Is this why we took you on duty? We have appointed you the Governor of Baghdad in recognition of your merits.

Weren't the people and property that we entrusted to your custody enough, that you still reached out for food, property, money, and the virtue of widows, orphans... of all the Baghdad's poor?"

Kasim Pasha tried to stay on all fours. "Slander!" he moaned. "Allah is my witness that it's all lies..."

"Silence, you reprobate! Did we allow you to speak, that you let your evil tongue loose? Not only do you disturb my peace with your presence here, but you also sully our palace with your abominable voice!"

"Slander, insults!" the Pasha groaned. He burst into tears. His lamentations intensified in the sobbing. "Slander, it's all lies!" Suddenly, he raised one hand and began to nibble on the beard he still had. He lost his balance and fell to the ground again with the clash of chains.

"Silence, you profligate! Slander, you say? You are innocent? You have only been a victim of slander, have you? Raise your head and look around, show me the father of this lie. Who is it? Davud Pasha, Nasuh Pasha, or perhaps Sarikçi Mustafa Pasha? Who? The Supreme Commander Malkoçoğlu, who is at the head of our troops marching on infidels? Ciğalazade, who set out for a campaign in the East? Who threw this slander at you? Say it – he'll pay with his head for it!"

Kasim Pasha tried to answer something, but the blood that flowed from his swollen lips did not allow the Sultan to understand his words.

"If not them, then maybe the poor, whom you fleeced in Baghdad? Was it the poor who defamed you in this way, sending one petition after another, one complaint after another? From a villager who had two sheep... didn't you take one of them? And that woman who had only ten coins as her whole fortune? Didn't you take eight coins from her? At night, drunk, didn't you break into one of the houses? Didn't you hurt the host, humiliating his wife and daughter?"

The Padishah, without getting up, picked up a handful of scrolls lying next to him. "You say it's all lies, all slander... Is it? In that case, what is this?" He threw the complaints at the Pasha lying in front of him. "Is this also the work of your enemies? So how do you explain the gold that was found in your residence in Baghdad?"

"It's taxes I was supposed to bring to Your Highness..."

"Since when do simple people pay taxes in gold? And the diamonds, emeralds, turquoises, and sapphires? Are they also from taxes?"

The cries of Kasim Pasha changed into a howl.

"Suppose you convinced us and we believed that all of this was going to go to our treasury... I wonder, wicked man, how do you explain the gold hidden in the walls of your residence and in the wells in the garden?"

"Lord... Lord... Lord..."

Despite the nervousness, no other words came out of his mouth.

Ahmed suddenly bent over him. "Lord, Lord... What?!"

The man crawled to the feet of the Sultan and began kissing his shoes. Two guardsmen ran up and dragged him away by the chain. The Pasha kept repeating just two words:

"Have mercy... have mercy, have mercy, have mercy..."

He didn't notice Ahmed giving a signal to someone at the gate. He only heard a sound – the sound of bare feet approaching him. A scream escaped from his throat. "Nooo!" Fear for his own life gave him such strength that he shook off two guardsmen in a single move. "Noooo... I'm begging you! Save me... It's slander... Slan..."

At that moment, the first of the executioners put a noose around his neck. When the other did the same, it seemed to Ahmed that his heart would stop beating. His head spun. He had to say something to give vent to his fear, compassion, and disgust.

"If you had robbed me, I might have had mercy on you, Kasim. But for the tormenting of the people, mercy may not be shown by the Sultan, but only by Allah himself. So, go and settle your bills with your Creator."

Although Kasim Pasha tossed around, screamed, and begged, the third rope was also wrapped around his neck.

The gathered Viziers watched the scene in horror.

This is when you should really keep cool, Ahmed, the Padishah thought. It was a test for him. Either he passed it and proved that he really is the Sultan, or he would fail, and provide further reasons for mockery. *Look!* Sultan Ahmed ordered himself. *Whatever happens, look at all this calmly, Ahmed!*

Kasim Pasha stood in the middle, surrounded by three executioners pulling ropes in three different directions.

"Nooo, noooo!" he grunted, while he still could shout. At the same time, he tried to break the oiled ropes with his nails, which were pulled tighter around his throat with every second.

Then the fourth of the executioners entered the stage – in black galligaskins and a black kaftan, his head covered with a long red cap – to finish what his assistants had started. Kasim saw a terrifying yatagan in his hands – the feared and famous single-edged Ottoman knife with the double curvature blade. Foam began to roll from his mouth. He howled.

"Silence, traitor!" Ahmed shouted once more. "You should have thought about the consequences beforehand. You better pray now that you do not stand before Allah like a giaour."

But Kasim did not see or hear anything anymore. His senses left him; all ties that connected him with the world were broken. Driven by animal instinct, he did his best to stay alive for as long as possible. He wrapped the chains that hung from his arms around his neck as if that would be able to stop the blade which was about to shorten him by the head in just a moment.

The executioner raised the yatagan over the left shoulder of the convict. The forked steel glowed in the air for a moment, and then like lightning, hit Kasim Pasha's shoulder, and fell on his neck. It was impossible not to hear the crack of the bones breaking. His head, separated from his body, rolled on the ground. Everyone watched the blood squirting from the neck that had carried the governor's head just a moment before. The four executioners now dragged a shrunken body, still shaking in convulsions, in the direction of the gate, leaving behind bloody stains.

"Throw his carcass into the moat behind Edirnekapi," ordered the Sultan, before he headed towards the exit on the left. "Let it be a warning to everyone," he said and walked away, his Viziers left in the state of the highest terror.

From today on, you really are a Sultan, said the voice in his head.

I could do perfectly well without it, Ahmed snapped in response.

The bustle in front of her room told her about her son's arrival.

"Your Highness!" Handan Sultan bowed before Ahmed. "You have done a real honor to your mother."

She raised her head and looked into his eyes. She grew scared.

"Allah!" she shouted, gasping. The Sultan's face showed an array of colors, from white to green and from yellow to purple. Suddenly, a terrible thought appeared in her head. *Or maybe this is...* She panicked. *Or maybe Safiye ordered someone to poison my son?*

"My Lord, are you sick? What's wrong with you?" she asked anxiously.

Sultan Ahmed looked at his mother as if he looked at a wall. "Everything is fine," he whispered. There was something strange in his voice. "Before we came to you, we witnessed the execution –"

Handan stirred. "Whose?"

Ahmed looked at his mother as if he had only just now noticed her presence. "You knew him, too, mother," he hissed.

The woman seemed to hear the tone of revenge in his voice. But on whom? On her or on this convict? "Can I ask who you are talking about?"

"Of course. About the one who passed us the throne on the day of our father's death, the former deputy—"

"Kasim Pasha? Son, did you give an order to behead Kasim Pasha?"

Suddenly, Ahmed noticed a flash of triumph in his mother's eyes. It was as if she was happy because of what he had just gone through.

"It might have shaken you a little, but do not torment yourself about it, son," she said in the sweetest voice she could assume. "Kasim Pasha was her man. Who knows what Safiye plotted together with him?"

Naive, thought the Sultan. *She still thinks that grandmother wanted to reward Kasim Pasha by nominating him as the Governor of Baghdad. It wouldn't even occur to her that it could be completely different, that her mother-in-law had sent him to Baghdad as an exile, to keep him as far from the capital as possible. And this narrow mind tells me what to do...*

"I'm leaving, Mother," he said and turned to the door.

"Where, Your Highness?"

"To the Rumelian Garden."

"To the Rumelian Garden?!"

Even the beheading of Kasim Pasha did not surprise her as much, he thought. It improved his mood.

"Do not neglect the Sultana Mahfiruz, My Lord. Her condition..."

Ahmed did not want to see anyone. Neither the Viziers, nor the Pashas, nor even the flirtatious concubines of his harem, whose charms he was slowly getting used to. Most of all, however, he did not want to see Mahfiruz right now.

"Mother!" he said in a raised voice. It was his first serious reprimand aimed at her, his first opposition. It struck him that he did not care at all. He was a Sultan, after all. Today, he'd proved that he deserved this title. Someone, whose one nod takes another man's Allah-granted life, could not be afraid of his own mother.

"We're organizing a hunt, Mother." His voice was strong, his expression firm. His Highness Sultan Ahmed was to celebrate his first execution.

For the next three days, the entire capital talked only of the execution of Kasim Pasha.

"Look at that!" the drunkards said in wineries. "We misjudged him badly. Way to go, Padishah!"

On the fourth day, a grey dog with a black head jumped out of the moat behind Edirnekapi. It held a big human head in its mouth. It didn't even occur to anybody that it belonged to Kasim Pasha, once a powerful and well-liked man.

"Go away!" they shouted, throwing stones at it. The dog tucked his tail and moved away, not letting go of the prize from its mouth. One could see the impatience in its movements... it wanted to start its feast as soon as possible. Kasim Pasha and his mutilated body went into oblivion on the heap of rubbish.

On the fifth day, a cavalryman entered the Rumelian Garden, raising clouds of dust behind him.

"Sir, sir! Great news!" he shouted, even before he got off the horse. His exultation caused quite a stir.

He was brought before the Sultan.

"What is going on?" Ahmed asked in a cold tone. "What is the good news – has our army defeated the Hungarians?"

"Congratulations, My Lord! Your son is born."

Chapter Eighteen

Old Palace
November 1604

Semiha stopped briefly in the doorway and looked timidly inside. The Sultana's head drooped to her chest. She was sleeping. She had fallen asleep in a sitting position, resting back on soft pillows.

But was she for sure asleep? Many years had passed since Semiha learned that in the palace, this kind of nap usually did not mean anything good. She tiptoed to the sofa.

"Lady?" she whispered.

No reaction. Semiha felt panic overwhelm her. *Easy,* she told herself. *You must stay calm. First, make sure...*

She looked at the Sultana's chest. It slowly rose and fell, but not enough to calm her fears. She put her finger to the sleeping woman's nose and waited to feel her hot breath. *Thanks be to Allah, she's alive! At least for now.*

"Your Highness... My Lady... Please wake up. News!"

"News? Couldn't it wait until we wake up, Semiha?" Safiye Sultan did not even open her eyes.

She'd been feeling very old for some time now, especially since she'd been sent here. She didn't even want to look in the mirror anymore, so she'd given that up completely. She didn't want anything to overshadow what she'd seen in it last time – the reflection of a smiling, golden-haired woman. She wanted the face of that Venetian beauty Sofia Baffo only, or the golden Mother Sultana of the Ottoman Empire, Safiye, to be the last vision of herself she kept in her memory. Even at her moment of death, she wanted to be convinced that she still looked the same.

It seemed that nowadays, whenever she sat down somewhere, even for a moment, her head would immediately fall on her chest. It even aroused her suspicions. *Are they poisoning me?* Handan would be able to do that, she had no doubt about it. Besides, she was cursed... The Sultana Nurbanu never showed her feelings to her; she never made it obvious what she thought of her to her face. She even forgave her on her deathbed... But was it possible that she didn't wish her the same in her mind? Could the victim not curse her torturer, knowing who it was? Did Nurbanu also take such naps?

She couldn't remember it now.

She even forgot how much time had already passed. When she recalled it in her memory, it seemed to have happened only yesterday, but, after some thinking, she concluded that it was the distant past. The only thing she remembered exactly was the man's whisper: 'It will be painless. As if she fell asleep. It will take her without leaving any trace.'

Now maybe it was Handan who was listening to similar assurances from the death dealer...

'Your majesty doesn't need to worry,' he praised the bottle, turning it around in his fingers. 'It will be painless. It will not leave the slightest trace. Nobody will suspect anything.'

"This cannot wait, My Lady."

The determined tone of the courtier made Safiye give up thinking about the past. She opened her eyes slightly.

What a relief, she thought, when she noticed the malicious, almost joyful expression on Semiha's face. *So, it's nothing bad.* She sat up straight and waited for the girl to adjust the pillows behind her back.

"Well, tell me. What is this news that is so urgent that it couldn't wait until we woke up?"

"Allah give you a long life, Lady. Not only has he already given you a son and a grandson, but now you have also his descendant!"

Safiye did not understand at first; she was still drowsy from sleep.

"Wait, wait," she said. "What are you talking about, for Allah's sake? Just say what happened?"

"Mahfiruz Sultan gave birth."

Safiye looked at her and froze for a moment. "She gave birth?"

The girl confirmed this with a nod of her head, smiling.

"What is it? A girl?"

Semiha sensed from the voice of her Lady that she would very much like to hear such an answer. Without a word, she shook her head.

"A boy, then?"

"Yes, My Lady."

The courtier started talking, but Safiye did not hear anything more. Her thoughts were occupied by Handan Valide Sultan. *How the pig must be happy now! A prince was born, the heir to the Ottoman throne. And this from the concubine she had personally chosen for her son. Could she want anything more?*

Her position had been strong earlier, but now she'd established herself a thousand times more. The same applied to Mahfiruz. Until recently, Handan was the mother of a ruler widely regarded as a kid, without experience in a sanjak, who was circumcised only after taking the throne. And now today, her son was a strong young man who begot a male descendant. *And that icy wife of his*, she thought. *It was not enough for her to be a married wife of the Padishah, she also gave him the heir to the throne. And that means that in the future, Mahfiruz will be the next Valide.*

Suddenly she moved. "Where's Hatice?" she said feverishly. "Let Raziye know; let her find her immediately and bring her to me. And then summon to here, all the seamstresses from this city for me!"

Raziye knew exactly where to look for Hatice. She could be in only one of three places: in the servants' room, at the magnificent carriage of Safiye Sultan, or with a hodja who – on the orders of the Sultana – was teaching her to read and write in Ottoman Turkish.

She found her in the courtyard by the carriage. She was busy polishing the handles at its door.

"Hatice!"

Nastya turned and saw Raziye. She was the hunchback shadow that had led her through a secret passage to meet Safiye. So now she was going to go to her again, and in broad daylight too. She looked around.

A few girls were busy with their work. Instinctively, she headed for the wall covered with ivy. However, something totally unexpected happened. Raziye stopped her.

"He, he, he, not that way, dear!" she said with a grin, and she pulled Nastya toward the magnificent gate that led to the part of the palace where the apartments of Safiye Sultan were located. Apparently, the time had come to step onto the stage!

Raziye Kalfa, swaying from side to side, led her all the way to the sumptuous stairs. There she handed her over to Semiha, the main lady of the court of Safiye Sultan.

Nastya's heart began to hammer out of nervousness and at the sight of the splendor she had in front of her eyes. The balustrades of the stairs winding on the upper floors were made of burgundy crystal. They looked like wide-open arms that embraced the floor above the courtyard, lined with red-and-black-veined marble.

The look of surprise on Semiha's face made Nastya feel happy on top of her nervousness; the reason of which she was not able to realize at that moment.

"Are you sure this is Hatice?"

"Yes."

Semiha, who due to her position was used to looking down on everyone, showed both surprise and now also worry on her face. Needless to say, it was inconceivable that on the orders of the Sultana herself, a common maid would enter the rooms through the entrance intended for guests.

"Hey, aren't you the servant they call Nastya?"

The girl raised her head and looked boldly into the woman's eyes. "Not anymore!"

Semiha opened the door and stepped aside. "Hatice is awaiting to bow down before you, Lady."

Hatice entered, and her mouth dropped open, and her head tilted. She was awestruck in admiration of the wonderful decorations on the ceiling. The spacious room took her breath away. *Mother of God!* she thought dazed. It seemed to her that she was suddenly surrounded by a sea of colors. Everything was completely green. Ah no, rather in a shade of gold. And this red, navy, blue, white, turquoise... What could she say about them? And this carved ceiling... how high! If it were not for that, the vault of the room would probably all be in the clouds. The green upholstery of the walls was decorated with winding roads, flowers, and branches made of gold flakes. Here and there, one could also see red and white, but Safiye's apartment was definitely dominated by shades of green and warm yellows – the colors of paradise and power.

This whole paradise was bathed in light. The entire length of the opposite wall, from the ground to the ceiling, was occupied by a magnificent window made of cut glass. The upper part was decorated with leaves, roses, and tulips, arranged from yellow, red, blue, and green glass. The sun rays that passed through it poured into the chamber in beams of multicolored light.

The outer side of the window was covered with a magnificent pentagonal grate. Farther beyond it was a calm sea.

In the past, whenever the sea loomed unexpectedly from somewhere in the distance, her heart immediately began to break free from her breast. *Carry me away, waves; carry me to my beloved island!* Hatice had thought in such moments. However, today she noticed that for the first time, she was not overcome by an intense longing. Strange, but with this view in sight, not even one tear stood in her eye, even though it reminded her of the hills fragrant with thyme on her family island of Milos.

She'd been gradually getting rid of everything that had any connection with her old life – which started with her name and memories... In their place, a new person had been born, someone with a completely different body and soul. Someone who felt at home here.

The only thing she remembered, and which she did not abandon, were her dreams; and the only sound she kept in her mind was the voice of the blind beggar on the stairs of the church.

"Come closer, my child."

Safiye's voice snatched her from the sea of colors in which she was immersed, and brought her back to the real world before she could sink into her dreams. The Sultana sat on a sofa covered with golden silk this time. The sunlight from the window behind her seemed to envelop her fair hair in heavenly light. Just as this place was different from the hidden room where she'd been taken that night, and in which there was not a single decent thing, Safiye Sultan also looked different and wonderful today. She was more beautiful than she was then, but also paler... Much paler.

Suddenly, Hatice understood why she had the impression that she had found herself in a kingdom of colors after entering the building. There were a number of women were seated on low, soft benches set beneath the walls. She tried to count them, but unsuccessfully... she only counted to twelve before she gave up. Apart from them, the room was filled with at least as many ladies of the court. Every woman held bales of cloth in her arms; they even lay on the sofa on which the Sultana sat. Bright shades of silk dominated – pink, white, purple, and sapphire. Velvet cloth ornamented in gold-embroidered patterns also dazzled – purple, maroon, and the color of pine green. There were also pleasantly scented flax and shiny satin, which seemed to ask to be caressed. She even noticed fabrics whose names she did not even know, and which she had never seen before. Some lay in bales, while others, slightly unwound, just waited for words of admiration.

"Come on," Safiye said. She gestured at a place next to her, inviting her to sit down. "We have no time to lose. I have called the fabric sellers and seamstresses from every corner of the capital here. You only need to choose, and they will do the rest. They will sew all you need at one go. We are really in a hurry..."

The Sultana turned to the seamstresses and said something to them, but Hatice let it go.

Choose? Me? So, these great fabrics and all these people... are they for me? But why? For God's sake, what's going on here?

It seemed like she was too quick to be happy she no longer had to hide her familiarity with Safiye Sultan. In the palace, an aura of mystery hovered over everything. How could one live like that?

"Why are we in a hurry, My Lady?"

The Sultana pressed a hand to her chest with a sigh. "Ahh, right... You do not know anything yet. Because how would you know...? In all this confusion, we forgot about it altogether, and nobody thought of telling you."

What did they forget about? Telling me what?

"Great joy happened to us, my child," Safiye chirped cheerfully. She opened her eyes wide. "Mahfiruz Sultan gave birth to a child!"

"What?!" Hatice felt as if boiling water had been poured over her. Or rather, as if she'd stepped on incandescent coals.

The Ice Queen had given birth! Her heart flooded with a wave of bitterness, so much so, that she didn't pay attention to the tone in which the Sultana had spoken the last words.

All the prayers that she had brought to God at night to try to prevent this birth had not been heard. She gave birth. The Ice Queen gave birth... She was not even curious about the sex of the child because what could possibly be born? Obviously, ice would not give birth to a fire!

She realized that her furious anger had started to grow stronger. Thank God she saw the look on the Sultana's face in time. She'd already wanted to snap, 'What's so unusual about it to enjoy and celebrate? How many women give birth each day...?' From Safiye's look, however, she understood that the joy she had just expressed was only a show.

"You will need to have several outfits made immediately."

"Several sets... for me?" *All the seamstresses and silk sellers in Istanbul were brought running just to sew a few outfits for me? It was so hard to understand all this...* "For me? I think I have another two sets of clean clothes. I really do not need –"

Safiye and the seamstresses laughed at the same time.

She was hurt by this spontaneous reaction, but even more so, however, she was hurt by the behavior of the court ladies, who tried to mask their laughter, covering their faces with their hands.

"Oh, child, child..." A plump woman chuckled, jealously stroking the silk roll she held in her embrace. "How do you imagine it? That the court lady of Her Majesty, sent to visit the newborn descendant of our Sultan and present him the gifts from his great-grandmother on her behalf, will go to the New Palace in old rags?"

To the New Palace?

Again, an impression came over her – boiling water, hot coals... She didn't know what to think about it. She should probably be happy to go to the New Palace, even if only because she would see Eftalya there. However, knowing that she would also encounter Mahfiruz caused her pain. Damn it, she'd have to bow to her. Bend her neck in front of her. And maybe the Ice Queen would not even honor her with one word. She could imagine the pride and contempt with which the Sultana would look at her...

One of the women rose from the bench and deftly unwound a scroll of fabric onto Safiye's knees.

"What do you think about it, My Lady? Straight from China. Pure silk. I think it will also be good for our little prince, right?"

Little Prince! Oh! she moaned in her mind. A boy! Just the last thing she needed. The Ice Queen gave the Sultan a son!

My dream has not come true, she thought with disappointment. *After all, the Ice Queen was supposed to give birth to blood. The red liquid dripping from her gaping womb would turn into a bloody baby on the ground... Meanwhile, a boy was born.*

The position of Mahfiruz was strengthened even more. The Sultan had already been fulfilling all her whims, including Hatice's exile to the Old Palace. So, what will it be like now?

And they want her to drop to at the feet of the Sultana and celebrate the birth of her son; to look at her, compliment her, and pray for her health; to show her respect without showing her jealousy, hatred, and anger.

Hatice Sultan, pfft, she sneered in thoughts. She was supposed to become a Sultana, and instead...

"Hatice, why haven't you chosen anything yet?" There was more encouragement than anger in Safiye Sultan's voice. "Go on, don't be shy. Let's close the issue of garments as soon as possible so that we can send our gifts to Prince Osman."

Osman! Ice son of the Ice Queen... So, his name is Osman. Hatice thought.

"Prepare for her also a few pieces of underwear, nightgowns, and everything she will need there. Our Hatice will stay four or five days in the New Palace. Keep this in mind!"

Four or five days in the New Palace!

Hatice leaned over Safiye's knees to the plump seamstress. "Can I see this black silk?"

Chapter Nineteen

Old Palace
December 1604

The preparations, which, according to Safiye Sultan, were to end as soon as possible, lasted a month.

Hatice forgot what sleep was. She spent all day long with seamstresses now. They kept telling her to turn left, turn right, bend, and get up, and when it turned out that there was something wrong with the finished kaftan, everything had to be started over, right from the beginning.

Although it all tired her terribly, she couldn't sleep at night, so she spent the nights thinking.

She thought about how she'd behave in front of Mahfiruz. Each time, however, a detail appeared that she'd overlooked earlier, and the whole plan had to be put together again. How should she enter Mahfiruz's chamber? How would she pretend to greet her, while at the same time not bowing before her? What should she tell her? How should she look at her?

She replayed all this in her mind hundreds of times. And then the child... How was she to look at him? What to say and what to leave out? What will the Ice Queen think when she sees her in all these new outfits? Will it ever pass through her mind: 'How beautiful she is?' What did it matter anyway? She probably wouldn't even look at her face from behind those icy eyelashes...

And why did she need so many kaftans? One kaftan would be enough for this visit, no more. *Mahfiruz will not call for me all the time*, she thought. *Well, maybe I will meet her again when visiting Handan Sultan. That would make two kaftans in total...*

"Let's make it three, that's enough," she kept repeating to the seamstresses. "Why do I need so many shirts, corsets, jackets, and headgear, for God's sake?" Besides, among the things that were being prepared for her, there were ones she knew she would never put on. For example, the underskirts, which emphasized the shape of her body, or the galligaskins made of silk tulle. During the fittings, she even blushed out of shame.

"What is it supposed to be?" she complained. "It is completely see-through! I will not wear this!" she protested, cocking her head up.

The seamstresses were not too concerned about it, though. Although they worked all the time, the end of their efforts was still not in sight. *Oh God...* she thought. *They dawdle so much!* She would like to snatch all the threads and ivory needles from their hands and sew these kaftans she will never wear, herself.

And the cap... when she first saw it on Mahfiruz's head, she'd made a promise to herself that she'd never wear something like that. But no, one just like it was being prepared for her now!

"It's a waste of the work, Kalfa, I will not even touch it. What is it supposed to be? The acrobats at our fairs wear something similar. I don't want to be laughed at, you understand? Nobody will make me wear it!"

"Her Majesty..."

It did not convince her. "You can tell her this... Let her know that I don't want this something, not even she can force me to do it!"

She would never have thought that this pointed 'something' required such a workload. First, they had to prepare a stable base, and then roll it up into a cone and stretch the fabric over it.

Once they had dealt with all this, it was time for a try. Despite all Hatice's resistance, with the help of a few court girls, the cap was finally on her head. The court ladies, jealously watching the effects of these efforts, pinched her as if wanting to calm her down. She kept quiet out of pure contrariness, without even making the slightest squeak, even though her arms became covered with bruises.

She also still awaited the torturous 'put on – take off.' The girls held, and the seamstress stood in front of her and gazed at her carefully.

"Take it off, take it off! Too wide on the right!"

Damn it! When the right side was corrected, some flaw was revealed on the left...

Safiye Sultan had not seen her since their last meeting. She did not even appear once to ask her how she was doing.

Hatice knew, however, that every evening the main seamstress, Hayganoş Kalfa, gave the Sultana a detailed account of the work progress.

When the whole procedure began to drag on, she'd repeatedly command herself each day: *Have patience!*

Don't complain... after all, you will go to the New Palace. What else do you want? Who knows, maybe the Padishah will see you this time?

And even if he saw her, so what? She had no answer to that question. She didn't know.

The only sure thing was that she should be patient...

Finally, the day came when the results of the work of the seamstresses were carefully laid out in front of her on the sofa. They were all present, together with Hayganoş Kalfa.

"Help her put on this white chemise. Not that one, child, I said this, with thin straps!"

She loved the way Hayganoş spoke – the regional dialect she spoke with was so unique to her. The woman couldn't help it; she did not know otherwise.

The girls pulled a thick shirt off her. When they wanted to do the same with the underskirt, they met Hatice's resistance: "Let me do it!"

She had already got used to undressing in the presence of other women, and she no longer blushed with shame. In the beginning, however, she objected very much. "No way!" she repeated.

Hayganoş then called her to order. "I say, undress. What did you imagine, that you have something that we do not have?"

She was right. After all, what was she supposed to hide, and from whom? The protests and screams would not work at all, anyway. She slowly adapted to the rules governing the palatial life: some people command, and the others follow orders. There was nothing intermediate.

You could either order or be a subject to those orders. Since the former was unattainable for her, she would always be the one who carried out the orders.

She slipped off her chemise. She now stood naked from the waist up in front of a multitude of women. One of the seamstresses gave her a thin silk chemise with straps. Hatice hurriedly put it on over her head. The touch of the fabric on her skin made her shiver.

Oh no, not again... she moaned in her mind. Whenever the silk touched her bare breasts, her nipples immediately hardened. She was ashamed. She looked away to avoid the eyes of the women who all watched her closely. It was difficult to escape them though. They were everywhere. They surrounded her.

"That is what I said, let's also try this one," murmured Hayganoş. "The canary one."

She took off the white chemise and put on the yellow one.

Then she took it off and tried on also a pink one, then a black one...

She liked the black one most. Hayganoş, however, insisted on the white one. One by one, she tried on everything sewn for her. She dressed and undressed, dressed and undressed.

It will never end, she thought grimly. *You will see. After all, it will be Safiye Sultan who will ultimately decide what you wear for the road, and what you will wear in front of the Ice Queen and the Valide Sultan. You will have to put all of it on, again and again..."*

However, that didn't happen.

The door suddenly opened.

"Thank Allah, you've finally finished!" Safiye Sultan stood in the doorway. "We were already afraid that this day would never happen, Hayganoş!" She lifted the edges of her kaftan and settled down on the sofa.

Everyone respectfully bowed to her, almost to the ground. As the seamstresses had not yet managed to remove all the pins from the kaftan, Hatice could only greet her with a slight nod of her head. But even that was painful.

"Forgive me, My Lady," she whispered. "But the pins..."

"I understand, I understand... Hayganoş?"

The main seamstress immediately came over and knelt before the Sultana.

"Hatice is leaving tomorrow. I think she should dress in black... what do you think?"

Hurray! Hatice was happy in her heart. *So, she, too, liked the black the most.*

Hayganoş nodded without saying a word.

"You selected a red silk sash for the black kaftan..."

Hatice was surprised. *You weren't here at all,* she thought. *How do you know about it?*

"We do not like it," the Sultana continued. "These two colors smother each other."

Hatice suddenly understood. Safiye Sultan had to have watched them! She saw everything.

She knew everything. She also knew about her minor rebellions and the scenes she'd made to the seamstresses. Maybe she even heard with her own ears how she had complained that even Safiye Sultan would not force her to put 'this pointed something' on her head?

"For the journey, dress her in black. The only lighter element will be a silk sash embroidered with gold. It will match the black outfit. I have not seen a girl who could look so well in black."

"It will be as you wish, My Lady."

"Let her wear red for Mahfiruz. And as for this cap..."

So, she heard... Hatice grew nervous.

"It's probably not a good idea, I do not want it," Safiye finished. "That other one will be better. Just add a piece of black tulle to this carmine chiffon; it should be visible from the top. And a small diadem over all this... Ha! What do you say, Hayganoş?"

The woman rubbed her hands. "It will be beautiful, My Lady."

"Pink will be the best for a visit to Handan. I do not want any other color that day. And especially not that green tulle you attached to her hair... Allah, how tasteless one has to be to combine pink with green!"

The seamstresses lowered their heads.

"You will go with her. You're responsible for her wardrobe from now on. Choose two girls to help. If something goes wrong, you are responsible for it, Hayganoş. Hatice should look like a fairy when giving gifts to our great-grandson!"

"But I've always called her that, My..." Hayganoş blurted out with a grin.

"So, don't talk so much, and make her that fairy!" Safiye interrupted her sharply.

The authority in her voice made an impression on Hatice. *You should try it out*, she thought. *Sharp, but not coarse. Free, even with humor, but without fraternizing. Here's how orders should be given.*

"After her departure," the Sultana continued, "the New Palace should only talk about her. And so loudly that we can hear it even here." She waved her hand suddenly. "You can leave. Everybody. Hatice, you stay."

The seamstresses and courtiers immediately left the room.

"Come here," said Safiye, indicating the place beside her.

Hatice quickly read what lay behind her expression and tone of voice. Safiye wanted to say to her, 'I kept my word. You wanted to go back to the New Palace, and you are going back. Now it is your turn to keep your promise!'

Except she did not promise the Sultana anything...

"You will take Sofia with you, my dear," Safiye said, smiling sweetly. "You will go there together. Pass my gifts, say everything exactly as I taught you. And then come back."

They sat in silence for a moment, studying each other. Safiye Sultan perfectly understood what the expression that appeared on Hatice's face meant.

"Here is our plan," she began in a whisper. "Tomorrow is Thursday. When you arrive, you will have some rest. They will have prepared a separate room for the courtier who comes on behalf of Safiye Sultan. If they want to put you together with other girls, even with two or three, do not agree to it under any circumstances. Put your foot down and say, in that case, you will not move from that place, do you understand? My messenger will not share a room with anyone. Do you understand? Will you be able to oppose them and get your way?"

Hatice nodded. *Oh yes, I will!* She thought in exultation, *This woman reads my mind. Maybe she is a witch?*

"That inaccessible girl informed us that she will wait for you on Friday. Handan, in turn, should see you on Saturday. You will also spend the Sunday in the palace... What was your friend's name? We always forget."

"Eftalya."

"Right. You will talk to her. Tell her we have a couple of words for her. You will come back on Monday. Do not ask anyone for permission to leave! The coachman and your escort will know already. They'll take you on Monday morning and bring here." She slowly put her hand on the girl's knee. "Be that as it may, soon you'll be back there permanently." She smiled and patted her on the knee.

"Well, now go to bed! You have hardly slept in the past month. At least get a good sleep tonight. And do not think about anything anymore. I want you to look dazzling tomorrow. They will pack everything for you, don't worry about it."

Hatice stood up. Even though she had not had the intention before, she kissed the Sultana's hand and put it to her forehead, as it was customary here.

My God, she thought and shuddered from the excitement. *It's tomorrow... I'm going tomorrow already!*

Before leaving, she turned back to the Sultana. "My lady...?"

"Ask."

She must indeed be a witch. How did she know that I wanted to ask something?

"A moment ago," she began, "you had such a strange expression on your face..."

"I know, Hatice. You understood it as: 'I kept my word. You wanted to go back to the New Palace, and you are going back. Now it's your turn.' Am I right?"

A witch, great God, a witch! Or one of your blessed saints! Because how can you explain it another way?

She nodded. "But... I did not promise you anything, My Lady..."

Safiye's pale face took on color, and her eyes flashed. "You will become a Sultana, Hatice! Remember when you told me you were a queen?"

Chapter Twenty

Old Palace, New Palace, Harem
January 1605

While Hayganoş and her two helpers dressed her, Hatice reached the end of her patience.

First, they put on the black chemise. Then black-and-white satin galligaskins, with buttons of beads at the ankle, and the incredibly captivating kaftan made from black damask on the top, decorated with trimmings in the same color. According to the wishes of Safiye Sultan, Hayganoş tied a gold-threaded sash at her waist.

The nervous Kalfa suddenly chased away the girl who had been arranging Hatice's hair for an hour. "Go away, I told you. Can't you hear?"

She could not have heard it because the main seamstress had not said anything like that to her.

Everyone was tense – both Hayganoş with her two helpers, and Sofia, who stood next to her.

As for herself... she was perhaps the most nervous of them all. *Come on, let it be over!* She was impatient.

Hayganoş stroked her hair, lifted it a bit, and let it out. It had become as soft as silk from combing for a long time, and now it fell in waves over her shoulders and down to her waist, like a waterfall.

She took out a piece of black tulle from the bundle next to her. She unfolded it and brushed it several times. Hatice had the impression that millions of tiny gold dots rose into the air. She had never seen this fabric before. It was dotted with yellow spots, invisible at first glance, but as soon as the light fell on them, they shone like gold dust.

"That's from Safiye Sultan," Hayganoş said. "She personally asked us to pin it to your hair. It's yours from now on. It belonged to our Lady's mother-in-law, you know who I am talking about?"

She didn't know.

"They called her Nurbanu Sultan. It was difficult to say which one was more beautiful: Nurbanu Valide Sultan or her young daughter-in-law, Safiye..." She stared straight ahead as if she suddenly saw them both in front of her. "Ah, how fast the time flies..." She sighed quietly.

Hayganoş fastened the tulle to her hair with a clasp decorated with a pearl. She ran a hand over it several times. Hatice couldn't see it, but she knew that her hair now shone with gold specks.

"Ah!" Sofia cried out. "My beautiful sister... You're more than beautiful!"

Hayganoş also decided that there was nothing more for her to do here. "All done! Well, are you ready?"

The seamstresses took a few steps back and admired the effects of their work for a long moment.

"So beautiful..." one of them said in an undertone.

"Like a picture," added another.

"What did I tell you...? And you did not believe. One might think that this is not Eve's daughter, but a real fairy. Such a beauty, even in black, let alone purple or pink..."

She smiled viciously. "That's what our mistress meant. In a few days, people will be talking nonstop about you in the New Palace!"

"Who knows? I haven't seen myself yet; I don't even know what I look like. I wonder, how is my hairstyle?"

"I am telling you, don't worry, darling. You look like the fairies have dressed your hair, do you understand?"

Her words pleasantly tickled Hatice's pride, but as for convincing her – they didn't do that.

"I feel somehow strange in these clothes. Tulle... Galligaskins... I cannot imagine how I look in all this. It's all really beautiful, but does it fit me?"

"Oh, it does!" said one of Hayganoş's helpers. "The Kalfa is right. You look like a fairy!"

"If only we had a mirror..."

"A mirror?"

"Yes. If I could see myself in it, maybe it would calm me down a bit, that is of course if I would be happy with what I saw. And if not, then at least I could hide somewhere..."

"In that case, come with me, come on," said Hayganoş suddenly.

"Where?"

"I said, follow me!"

They left the room, Hayganoş leading the way. They took many turns until they suddenly found themselves in a place where four corridors met.

Hatice stopped short. An unspeakably beautiful girl appeared in front of her, behind a huge fireplace in the middle of the room.

She was dazzling. There was no doubt that she had to look quite inconspicuous compared to this girl.

Small butterflies flew over her hair... Or maybe fireflies, who knows? Millions of fireflies. Her eyes were delicately lined with something black. They were large. 'Blue like the Aegean Sea,' she recalled the term used once by Handan Valide Sultan.

Her cheeks were pinkish as if stroked by the wind from the warm seas, and her lips too – fresh and red.

Like her, the mysterious beauty was wrapped in black. The collar of a black, satin chemise revealed a portion of her neck. Black galligaskins, cut on the sides – starting from the knees – fell down to her ankles. She wore a black kaftan embellished with a branch motif that reminded her of the branches of the magnolia tree she had seen from the window in Eftalya's room while she was still in the New Palace. The kaftan was spread to two sides at the waist, revealing a gold-embroidered sash that wrapped her slender waist.

The sleeves of the decorative kaftan were so wide that the pleated sleeves of the chemise she had underneath protruded through them. They were decorated on both sides with five glass buttons. From under the galligaskins, she could see shoes with upturned toes, made of the same material as the kaftan.

It would be hard to find a more beautiful woman in the entire world, she thought jealously. Sofia suddenly appeared just behind her and immediately fell to the feet of this beauty.

"Sister, my beautiful sister!"

"Ah!" Hatice was surprised. "My God! Is this really me?"

After a moment, Hayganoş also showed up.

Only now did she realize that she had been standing in front of a mirror for a few moments. She had never seen such a large mirror before. Although she was dressed the same way as the woman stood before her, she'd thought it was one of Safiye Sultan's courtiers. For a moment, she was even angry that the girl was dressed just like her. It didn't surprise her, however, that she had not guessed the truth... she never knew that she was so very beautiful. She'd never noticed it before. Well... she was aware of her beauty, but this wasn't the beauty typical of every girl her age. The luminous face of Hatice, who looked back at her from the mirror, was now bright like a full moon. She was so much more than beautiful...

It took her breath away.

"Impossible," she whispered. "Is it really me?"

Hayganoş Kalfa's assistant came up from behind and smiled. "What did you think? I told you that you are no less beautiful than the queens... didn't you understand?"

"Queens?"

"Come on, get ready!" insisted Hayganoş. If it weren't for her grumbling, Hatice probably would've not been able to take her eyes off the mirror. "The carriage is waiting!"

Of course, it was nowhere near as elaborate as Safiye Sultan's carriage. Hatice, however, thought it was wonderful. As she sat in the horse-drawn carriage, she imagined she was the queen, and Hayganoş and Sofia – who sat opposite her – were her court ladies.

The assistants of the main seamstress and the wardrobe rode in the second carriage. Safiye Sultan's gifts for her great-grandson were placed in the third one, escorted by six horsemen on each side.

While she looked through the carriage window, screened with tulle, her thoughts drifted far away from her: first to the island of Milos, where she threw stones at the sea;

then in Kumanovo, where she looked at the snowy mountains and forests from the window of her room.

Suddenly, a blind beggar appeared on the edge of the road. He waved at her. "Go!" he shouted after the carriage. "Go straight toward your happiness. A crown already awaits you, beautiful queen!"

When he disappeared, she heard the parting words again, that Safiye Sultan said to her yesterday:

'Ah, Hatice! You will be a Sultana!'

"Stooop!"

The noise that came from outside was like the sound of a storm.

Hayganoş opened the tulle curtains and peeked out the window. "We're here."

This time, other sounds came to their ears. Her heart pounded as if there were thousands of drums in it.

"Do you have permission to enter?!" shouted the sentry to the coachman.

"I have everything necessary."

"Who are you? Who are you bringing?"

"Ahmed, a slave. And I am bringing Hatice, our Lady Safiye Sultan's courtier!"

A Sultana, she thought begrudgingly. *Hatice Sultan!*

"Wait!"

The sentry suddenly disappeared under the conical dome that covered the arcades. He came back a moment later, and shouted to the driver without even going near them, "Go inside! Come on, what are you waiting for?"

The carriage's wheels twitched, then the clatter of horseshoes became more pronounced.

Only then did Hatice glance outside from behind the curtain. She was returning to the New Palace as a messenger of Safiye Sultan – through the very same route she had left it earlier.

I'm back. This time for a short time, but I will soon come here permanently. Wait for me.

The horses stopped. The wheels froze, making the last rasp. She heard the coachman jump to the ground. The carriage door opened. Hatice did as Safiye instructed her. She did not get off at once. Hayganoş moved, though, as if to get to the exit.

"Wait!" Hatice reminded her in a whisper.

So, they waited. The coachman looked at them with urging eyes, but she did not pay any attention to him. They were to wait until she'd decided it would be enough.

"First you," she finally said. The plump Hayganoş struggled to get up and squeeze through the narrow door.

"Now you, honey."

Sofia vigorously jumped outside.

Now everyone had to be waiting impatiently for her. The girls who did not even wave her goodbye when she was driven out of here now probably stood there in line. They waited to greet the courtier of Safiye Sultan, the beautiful Hatice.

She slowly put her leg out, as she had practiced many times before. The crystal button, holding black satin galligaskins to her ankle, spread yellow and green sparks in the sun. She put her leg out, almost to the knee. She focused and slowly looked out of the carriage. Her eyes immediately went to the welcome retinue.

The women who came with her stood in a row. Except for them, in front of the gate stood only ten others: three servants, four pages, one odalisque, and two grooms.

She thought that her eyes would throw thunderbolts. Nobody was there... Not even a single court lady. To welcome her son's great-grandmother's favorite courtier, the Queen of Ice delegated ordinary servants!

Without showing her resentment, she straightened up proudly. She summoned the most wonderful of her smiles on her face. She could swear that sparks flew out of her eyes. She heard one of the servant's sigh deeply.

You're right... she thought. *There is much to sigh about!*

She took the edges of the kaftan at knee height and lifted them up slightly. It was also one of the gestures she had studied. She was supposed to walk first, and Sofia with Hayganoş and her assistants right behind her. And at the end, everyone else would follow. She was about to move toward the palace when confusion arose in the ranks of the servants.

"Nastya!"

She recognized the voice immediately. *Talya!*

The girl pushed herself to the front and hesitated for a moment. Hatice noticed doubt in the eyes of her devoted friend, as she thought: *No, this is not my Nastya.* It was true. She was no longer Nastya, nor Anastasia. Talya took a few timid steps toward her.

She waited. After a while, she let herself be carried away by emotions and opened her longing arms widely. "Eftalya!"

The girl was already about to throw her arms around her, but suddenly she stopped and sighed. "I can't believe my eyes! If I did not see Sofia with you, I would think it is someone else. Nastya, is it really you?"

She understood that her friend did not dare to embrace her, seeing her beauty and all the splendor. On the one hand, she enjoyed it, but on the other hand, she felt her heart tighten. She embraced the girl vividly and inhaled the scent of her hair.

"Nastya is dead," she whispered. "You have Hatice Sultan in front of you!"

"God damn it, damn it!" She paced furiously back and forth in the little room without a window.

She had imagined a spacious apartment with a view of the sea. It was unimaginable, after all, that Safiye Sultan's courtier, sent with the gifts for her great-grandson, would live together with the other girls.

And it indeed did not happen. The party that came to meet them led them through the dark corridors used only by the servants. They went up the stairs, opened the door that appeared in front of them, and Hatice found herself again in front of her former room, the same one that Mahfiruz had given her back before she caused them to be sent to the Old Palace. Along the way, she saw almost no one, and she too remained unnoticed.

"Are you sure it is here? So, we came back to this hole, right?"

"That was the order of our Sultana..." answered the page, dropping his head.

"Which one?"

He was afraid to answer anything.

"The ice witch?"

In one moment, the black face of the young man became pale as a wall.

Suddenly, she caught something terrible in the back of her mind. *Why don't you just die... die... die?*

It was only after a long moment that the meaning of those words reached her; it pierced her brain like a needle. She froze. Even as Anastasia, she knew many people she did not like much. She didn't remember, however, that she would have such hatred for someone, or that she would ever want someone's death. She did not even wish it for Mürüvvet or Mestan, the aga of the Gate of Bliss who – through the whipping – made her acquainted with the glory of this palace.

So, it must have been a feeling that was characteristic of her new identity and her new soul. What's more, she didn't even feel guilty because of it.

Of course not! Hatice told herself. *There was nobody who would hate you as much and be as much your enemy as the Ice Queen. Look where you are now; it is also her doing... Let her die in agony, and as soon as possible!*

Nastya had left behind the life in which she loved people selflessly. No more 'turn the other cheek.' Now, reborn as Hatice, it was better to return to the principle: 'An eye for an eye, tooth for a tooth.' Nobody gave anything in life for free; you always had to fight for yours – she'd already learned this. Hatice would get what she deserved, even if she had to tear the heart out and pick the eyes of anyone who would stand in her way. Even if it was Mahfiruz in her way. Even if she were to cause death...

They will say that you have no heart, her conscience protested in a weak voice.

Let them say it. Better that than 'poor girl' or 'silly maid.'

For a moment, she thought about starting an argument – 'This is not the right place for the courtier of Safiye Sultan!' – but she quickly gave up on the idea. Was her purpose not to stand before the Ice Queen and to dazzle her with her beauty and splendor, to make her go mad with jealousy? Didn't she want to see the Padishah? If she got angry now, she would not achieve any of it. Like hatred, anger should also be used only at the right time.

She nodded unconsciously. *Remember that, too,* she ordered herself. *Do not let your anger, hatred, or pride ever take precedence over reason. Never lose sight of the real goal. To achieve it, and when it is necessary, pretend that you put it all aside. And when it's the right hour, without mercy, without even a moment of hesitation, strike the enemy in the heart like an arrow sent from a bow.*

A page opened the door. Eftalya, who had been standing in the doorway fearing her reaction, timidly raised her gaze to her.

"Two extra beds were added here," she said. There was a sense of relief on her face.

Hatice was surprised. *How little it takes to make a man happy,* she thought. Eftalya seemed to her now like a tiny sparrow looking for crumbs to feed on. *It is the only thing she expects of life. A few crumbles of food and a place for a shelter."*

When evening came, the friends sat opposite each other. There were many topics to discuss since their last meeting.

"Go ahead, tell me!" Eftalya encouraged her. "What's going on? What does all this mean? You didn't like the name 'Hatice' before. You hated it, especially after you learned that it was the given name of the Sultana Mahfiruz. And now I see that you have already become accustomed to it..."

"I thought more about it." She smiled. "All in all, it is more suitable for a Sultana than Nastya. Nastya Sultan," she said in a changed voice, carefully listening to it. "Now listen to this – Hatice Sultan. Did you hear how it sounds? It grows in the mouth – Hatice Sultan!"

"You will never give up, will you?"

"Give up what?"

"The pursuit of your dream..."

"A dream?" she said sharply. "This is no longer just a dream... it's a foregone conclusion, Talya. It's just a matter of time. This day is fast approaching, I feel it."

"You were already crazy when you were here, and there you probably went out of your mind completely... Anyway, it doesn't matter, you will do everything in your own way. I'm just afraid that this ridiculous dream will bring misery upon you."

"Look into my eyes!" Her voice cut through the air like a knife.

Eftalya shuddered. She was afraid to look at her.

"I'm telling you, look..."

She raised her head uncertainly. Their eyes met. Eftalya already knew that it was hard to resist Nastya's look – her tongue, just like herself, could not get used to 'Hatice' yet – but this time, there was something completely different in it. Fire.

"What do you see?"

She could not answer that she saw nothing. And she couldn't bring herself to tell the truth, either. She just shook her head to show that she did not know.

"Look at them well. You see? She walks with a crown on her head. The new Queen of the Ottomans. Beautiful Hatice Sultan. Don't you see it?"

Eftalya swallowed. How could she tell her friend that in the fire that burned in her eyes, she only saw the Angel of Death with a scythe in his hand, who spread his black wings? She no longer had any doubts that the girl was crazy. Something stung her in her heart. *My poor, little Nastya,* she groaned inwardly. *I have heard that such obsessive ambition can make someone lose their mind. The same has apparently happened to my beautiful Nastya. Ambition banished her reason.*

"What do you think about her?" She tried to change the subject.

"Who?"

"About Safiye Sultan. What is she like?"

"Terrifying!"

The girl laughed. "You're right. You know, I probably wouldn't be able to look her in the eyes."

"Why?"

"I would be afraid. I'm surprised you could get used to her. She sent you here on her own behalf, so things must be well between you. Somehow, I could never like that woman..."

And I? Do I like her? Hatice asked herself this question for the first time. She couldn't answer 'yes' or 'no.' She no longer knew how she really felt about her. If she had any feelings for her at all, it was probably only because of the help that Safiye had provided her. And if so, it was supposed to last only for as long as Hatice could somehow serve her purpose. She was convinced that little would remain of them after reaching it. She doubted that Safiye would treat her exactly the same. So, was it sympathy? Today, it is here, and tomorrow there is no trace of it? Just an ordinary transaction. It was only in the palace that she'd discovered that what she once took for love was, in fact, pure madness. Or maybe people just deceived themselves? Who knows, maybe there really is no love anywhere in the world, not just here?

Suddenly Hatice remembered the words of Safiye Sultan. "She likes you," she said.

"What? Safiye Sultan... likes me? You've become a liar since the last time I saw you. She doesn't even know me!" She hesitated for a moment. "You say she likes me? Very funny!" Eftalya wanted to laugh, but the look on her friend's face stopped her. *Allah, how her eyes changed,* she thought.

"She likes you," Hatice repeated with conviction. "And she thinks about you. I heard her say that she would like to see you at her side. She even plans to have you married!"

"What? Married?"

"Yes... You don't even know how many times she said it. She also told me to give you a message from her."

"A me-me-message?" she started to stutter from astonishment. "For me?"

"If you do what she wants, she will give you back your freedom. She said, 'Let Talya know that her liberation lies solely in her hands.'"

Liberation!

Freedom!

It took her breath away. It was something so abstract to her that it even went beyond her dreams. But she didn't want her dreams to take away her common sense like they did to Nastya. Instead of asking what the Sultana wished, she just said, "Come on, let's get some sleep." But she felt that until she found out what the Sultana wanted from her, sleep would be elusive. And the same would be after she found out, anyway.

The preparations were accompanied by an incredible bustle.

The assistants carefully put a red taffeta kaftan, embroidered all over with gold, over her head. It tightly hugged her body from her shoulders and neck to the waist, bulging only over her breasts, and then playfully fell on the stomach. The fabric also embraced her hips, dropping lower in waves down to her calves, and a little below the groin, the edges of the kaftan spread in two directions. To stiffen this large cut, the seamstresses had strengthened it on both sides with a stable ring inside. Hatice now reminded Hayganoş of a scarlet ibis who'd spread its crimson wings. That is why she kept telling her, "Fly already, I say fly! Why aren't you flying?" Hatice also thought she looked like a bird in this creation.

Eftalya watched her, looking enchanted. She had never seen anything so beautiful. Neither such a pretty girl nor an equally wonderful outfit. *She will overshadow both Sultanas*, she thought. *I hope all this will end well!*

Hatice remained standing all the time, as she waited for her retinue accompanying her to be ready to leave – Hayganoş forbade her to sit down until she was in front of Mahfiruz Sultan.

"How do I look?" she asked, her question not directed to anyone specific.

"Like a fairy," one of the girls answered.

"Like an angel," another whispered in delight.

Sofia wanted to embrace the legs of her 'beautiful sister,' but Hayganoş stopped her at the last moment, blocking the way with her large body. "I say... calm down, girl! Don't you understand?"

"More beautiful than beautiful," said Talya.

"And like a queen." Hatice smiled sweetly and winked at her.

The door opened, and she finally went out into the corridor. She walked the way she'd practiced every day at the Old Palace. Her posture and look emanated such dignity that an outsider would think they had a real Sultana before them.

Hayganoş had strictly commanded her to lightly roll her sleeves up to the elbows, so that they would not fall on the wide hip gores of the kaftan, spreading in two directions. She walked, following the instructions she'd received, now more like an eagle who'd spread its wings to dive and strike its chosen victim.

Six girls that Safiye had assigned to assist her waited for her at the front – the most trusted of the Sultana's courtiers. They were dressed in white from head to toe. The only element of the outfit that stood out like a peacock's tail was a motley feather, attached to a headgear above their foreheads.

Behind them, eight odalisques stood in two rows. They held gifts from Safiye Sultan in their hands, each wrapped in a square piece of fabric decorated with pearls. Sofia stood between them, smiling charmingly. The girl looked very pretty in blue. Six other servants stood behind the odalisques. Hayganoş Kalfa and the assistants took their place at the very end of this procession.

Everything was ready. The time had come to create some confusion in this palace. Hatice stepped forward. She glanced over her shoulder. Eftalya stood a step behind her to her right.

"Are we ready?"

The answer given in a whisper was affirmative.

She shook her head ostentatiously and lifted it up. Her hair that cascaded down to her waist, and the carmine tulle attached to it, waved in the air. Both her eyes and soul were now turned toward the highest goals.

"Let's go then," she said quietly.

The retinue moved ahead.

It was accompanied by the rustle of fabrics and the steady sounds of legs stepping on carpets. They were still in the blind corridor, where almost none of the harem residents ever went.

When they reached the corner, Hatice held her breath.

The Sainted lady, she prayed in her mind. *Help me in this!*

They turned the corner and found themselves in the corridor leading to the rooms of the Valide Sultan. It was nothing like that empty, dark corridor – it was full of people and so bright that when they entered it, they all squinted their eyes involuntarily. There they were greeted by the whispers of the servants.

"Look at her..."

"Who can it be?"

There were no court ladies, pages, or servants of Handan Sultan or Mahfiruz among them.

Only ordinary maids stood here. Hatice didn't expect any of them to recognize her. It was obvious, though, that she'd made a great impression on them. Although it was in contradiction with the palace rules, they stopped work and watched her pass. One could read delight and jealousy in their eyes, almost the entire range of feelings.

She imagined how she must look at that moment. When she revived this picture in her imagination, a slight smile crossed her face. *They are right. I look dazzling.*

Wrapped in red, she walked like a lady, surrounded by girls dressed in white. The golden handle of the ivory comb that fixed the carmine tulle to her hair, and the tiny pearls on it, had to look like a real crown in the eyes of simple servants.

"Look how she's showing off, this vamp," one of the servants whispered.

"But how beautiful she is... Very beautiful," her companion did not agree with her.

"A coquette, nothing more," the first one smiled sneeringly. "What's with you; you don't have a husband, so you've started to sigh at women?"

In about ten paces, the corridor was to fork in two directions. *The one to the left leads to the icy one,* she moaned inwardly. Going to the right would lead her to the Valide mother's apartments. Today, she had to turn left, where according to her plan, she would soon live.

She turned left. She held her head high. She walked like a queen, not paying the slightest attention to her subjects and servants as if she did not see them at all. The girls who followed her also behaved impeccably – they walked with dignity as befits a queen's retinue. Safiye Sultan took great care that they'd mastered their role.

The impression they made was staggering. Conversations fell silent as all heads turned toward her.

Mahfiruz's chamber was at the very end of the corridor. As far as she could be from her place; it was also quite crowded in front of the entrance. *Very well,* she thought with satisfaction. *Let the whole harem see me.*

The crowd grew as she approached her destination: maidservants and pages of Mahfiruz Sultan, odalisques, and women from the palace tailor's workshop. Everyone, without exception, froze and watched her slowly pass by.

She passed a group of Mahfiruz's courtiers.

"Ah," someone whispered. "Isn't that one of our girls?"

Suddenly, a wave of joy flooded her. *God, is that him? Aga of the Gate of Bliss – Mestan! That monster that whipped me then!*

"Which one?"

She didn't even have to look where the other voice came from. She recognized her immediately.

Dilşad! That old witch who held me when Mestan ordered to hit my back with a stick, mocking at the same time: 'There you go, find out what the glory in the palace tastes like, you will never forget it!'

"That's her, the same one who bit one of the girls in the ear in the Novice Courtyard!"

"You mean Anastasia? The one whom I gave the name Hatice? What an idea... it's impossible!"

"That's her, I'm telling you."

"Mestan Aga, you've really started having problems with your eyesight. What are you talking about? She was a shameless servant, and this one here, Allah forgive me the name, is a true angel!"

Exactly at that moment, she passed by them, as dignified as a swan. She heard Dilşad whispering, "Incredible... It's really her! Hatice?" Dilşad spoke to her quietly.

Hatice looked at her out of the corner of her eye, in disgust, as if she'd seen a worm. She turned her head away from her immediately, however, and took her previous pose. *Oh, what a delight to see their surprised faces!* she thought joyfully.

As she approached the door, the surprise and envy of people standing in the corridor bothered her more and more. In fact, it was quite scary.

Allah, please save her from the evil eye. I am not asking you for anything else! Hayganoş prayed quietly. The evil eye was something that she feared the most because it was able to overthrow even the largest mountains.

When the retinue stood by the chamber, all the quarreling amongst the guests who'd come with congratulations for the young mother, and the other visitors and courtiers who tried to make some order here, fell silent in an instant. Without losing her dignified poise and maintaining her forward focus, she listened with pleasure to the whispers coming to her from the crowd.

"I wonder who this beauty is?"

"I don't know. Probably the daughter of some Pasha or Vizier."

"Listen, could it by any chance be one of the daughters of the Shah of Persia? Maybe he sent her to congratulate our Sultana? Who knows...?"

"Yes, yes. She must be a Persian princess..."

Hatice felt the light breeze from the south lift her soul into the blue sky. She was unbelievably happy. She felt dizzy. She was a Sultana, a Sultana! And not just in her dreams anymore. Odalisques and servants thought her worthy of the title, and these were people associated with the palace, whose whole life passed in these corridors, who had already seen more than one great lady here.

Suddenly, a mocking voice broke out from the crowd. "Well, then, I am the daughter of a Shah from behind the seventh mountain."

She recognized it immediately. *Taciser.* A lady of Mahfiruz Sultan's court, the one who shouted at her on the day of her exile, 'Come on, coquette, get out of here!'

"Are you all crazy or what?" She sneered further. "Aren't there enough real princesses in the world that you call her that? She is an ordinary servant. Wait, what was she called...? I don't even remember!"

But I remember you. And I will not forget about you!

"His Majesty banished her to the Old Palace. Our Lady did not want her here, that's why. You called an ordinary maid a Sultana! Really, I have no words..."

Oh no! Anger grew in her. *You do not have to listen to it!*

Suddenly, Hatice turned her head toward Taciser. *Here you are; a viper.* She looked at her as if she wanted to burn her with her eyes.

"Open up!" she hissed in her face. "Hatice, lady of Safiye Valide Sultan's court, has come to give the gifts for the Prince, the great-grandson, in the name of her Lady. Open this door!"

Taciser looked away as if she could not withstand the lightning that flowed in her direction. *She twists like a viper in the fire*, thought Hatice.

"What are you waiting for? Open this door!" she repeated her order.

After a moment, the door opened.

She stood in front of the Ice Queen.

I am here, devil. Look at me. See the beauty who came here to beat you down into the ground and take your place!

Mahfiruz Sultan sat on a sofa, looking to the right. Hatice immediately noticed the cradle with three women kneeling around it.

Mahfiruz didn't pay attention to the guests. She was saying something to her son's nannies.

Hatice crossed the doorway of the room and stopped. She curtsied and bowed her head so slightly that it was difficult to tell if she really did so. Seeing this careless greeting, the court ladies who stood on both sides of the room began to whisper to each other, but she did not pay any attention to it. Eftalya and Sofia, who were supposed to bring the gifts, stayed at the doorstep. She took three more steps forward. It was impossible that this hag didn't notice her, even out of the corner of her eye.

She waited.

The Ice Queen did not stop talking to the nannies.

She waited.

The infant's crying sounded from the cradle. Mahfiruz scolded one of the women. She bent over slightly and adjusted something inside the cradle. She was doing everything to avoid looking at Hatice.

Despite the anger rising in her, she waited.

Safiye Sultan had predicted this: 'She will try to provoke you. Do not play her game, under no circumstances. Wait till the end. Let her be the first one to lose her patience!'

It was not Mahfiruz however, who lost patience first, but her most trusted lady of the court. She leaned over and whispered something in the ear of her mistress.

"Who?" Mahfiruz asked, pretending to be surprised. She could have sworn that the girl whispered 'Hatice' in her ear. "What?" asked Mahfiruz. "Her courtier? You let her in?"

"I'm here." She could no longer hold back, seeing the Sultana almost turning her back on her, ostentatiously to prolong the conversation with her courtier. "Court Lady Hatice, sent by her Lady, Safiye Sultan, the grandmother of His Majesty Sultan Ahmed, with affirmations and gifts for her great-grandson.

Each of these words had been thought out and studied many times to give them hidden meaning. The congratulations were from Safiye Sultan, not from her. She came here only following a special order from the Sultana.

And she was no longer the unfortunate servant Mahfiruz had once driven out of here. Now she was the beautiful Hatice, who was about to snatch the Sultan from her hands. Hatice, who swore to make Sultan Ahmed lose his head over her.

Mahfiruz finally had to look at her, but it was hard for her. She straightened very slowly from the cradle.

Turn away, turn away! Look at me! Hatice ordered her in her thoughts.

She turned. She raised her head. She turned her icy eyes toward her.

I can die now! Hatice cried in triumph in her mind. *Finally, I've finally seen it. I saw delight, jealousy, panic, and fear in this block of ice... I can die!*

Her beauty and elegance had indeed dazzled Mahfiruz. Hatice, unmoved, withstood the look of her cold eyes. A prepared smile was ready on her face. It was a smile of a woman aware of her beauty, a bold and haughty smile. Her eyes showed modesty, and even compassion for the woman who stood opposite her, whom she, unwillingly, overshadowed with her beauty.

"It's you..." Mahfiruz's voice was uncertain. She cleared her throat. "Are you the Hatice that the Sultan's grandmother mentioned in her letter?"

These words, together with surprise, contained contempt and conceit.

The devil's recovering, she thought. "Yes, I'm Hatice."

"We remembered you with a different name..."

"Probably as Anastasia."

"Ah yes, that's right. Anastasia."

She had a ready answer for that, too. "My Lady," she said, looking her straight in the eye, "told me to leave Anastasia in the past. She said the future belongs to Hatice. In other words: the servant, whom you knew earlier, died. Hatice was born, and now stands before you."

Look at me, she continued in her mind. *Look at me well. Here is Hatice, who will soon give you sleepless nights... Tremble in front of her beauty and strength!*

"I hope you're comfortable in your room." The devil now made an allusion to her past.

"You showed extraordinary tact, Madam, ordering to prepare my old room for me."

"We could not find another room worthy of you."

Worthy of me... You mean, worthy of a servant! "I assure you, Madam," she said, emphasis on every word, "that I never forgot about it. I do not know why, but I always had beautiful dreams there."

"Dreams?"

"Yes. How to say it... actually, not dreams, but the future. Last night, it happened to me again. I saw the future."

She was under the impression again that there was a spark of fear in the icy stare.

Mahfiruz laughed mockingly. "The future? Do you think one can see the future?"

"Can't one?"

Damn her, Mahfiruz cursed in her head. She was aware that she could not concentrate today, and it irritated her extremely. She could not deny it: the most beautiful woman in the palace stood before her. *What did this old witch do with her? That is not a kaftan suitable for a maid or even a lady of the court. That kaftan is worthy... of a Sultana!*

She looked discreetly at her own kaftan. It was not as rich and impressive as the kaftan of this girl. She especially liked its hip gores, that spread like a bird's wings. It was the first time she'd seen something like that. It was amazing. She thought she needed to have one like that made for herself, but she gave up on the idea quickly. *Me, the mother of the only son of Sultan Ahmed, would look at the clothes of some girl? Did anyone see anything like that?"*

"If you can, tell us about this future. We would also like to know it."

Hatice smiled. *One drop of poison for today is enough,* she thought maliciously. *Now you can wonder at will what kind of future I dreamed for myself...*

"My Lady mentioned that you would visit the Old Palace for the customary celebration of the appearance of the prince's first teeth. If this will be your wish, Madam, then I will tell you everything then. Of course, if it does not bore you. But now, I would like to do what I was sent here for. I would not want to tire you too much... after all, you have recently given birth."

She gestured slightly with her hand. The steps that sounded close behind her told her that Eftalya had started her task. The first odalisque gave her a bundle, which the girl then brought before the Sultana.

"A gift from Her Majesty Safiye Valide Sultan to you," she announced in a raised voice. "A satin quilt embroidered with pearls."

Eftalya laid it in front of the sofa where Mahfiruz continued to sit. Then she stepped back and approached the second odalisque. One of the Sultana's courtiers parted the edge of the package.

Inside was a quilt in the color of ice blue. The Sultana looked at it and nodded without a word.

Eftalya now placed another packet in front of her.

"A gift from Her Majesty Safiye Valide Sultan for you, Madam," Hatice announced again. "A summer kaftan made of Indian silk, decorated with diamonds."

Eftalya stepped back again. Then she brought the third bundle, followed by others.

Hatice announced each of them separately:

"A gift from Her Majesty Safiye Valide Sultan for you, Madam..."

"A gift from Her Majesty Safiye Valide Sultan for you, Madam..."

They contained silk jackets decorated with precious stones, satin coats, and velvet capes.

Everything was blue. Bright, ice blue.

"I see that the Sultan's grandmother has painted us blue," Mahfiruz hissed.

Hatice boldly confirmed it with a nod. "Her Majesty thinks that this color fits you extremely well."

Eftalya brought the last gift. It was at least as big as the one with the quilt.

"A gift from Her Majesty Safiye Valide Sultan for her grandson, His Majesty, Sultan Ahmed," she announced, almost shouting. "A kaftan made with ermine fur, decorated with rubies."

When the courtier wanted to unwrap the fabric to also present this gift to the Sultana, Mahfiruz prevented her with a gesture of her hand.

"There's no need to. We guess that it is blue, too..."

"No. The Valide Sultan had bales of amber velvet brought from Damascus especially for this kaftan. It is decorated –"

"Thank you. Let's hope the Sultan will like it."

"And..." Hatice gestured again.

This time, Sofia came forward. Mahfiruz recognized her at once. "She has grown up, matured," she murmured to herself. There was no sympathy or kindness in her voice – just an icy statement, that's it. A statement deprived of emotions.

"A gift from Her Majesty Safiye Valide Sultan for the firstborn son of her grandson." *Which meant 'not yours'* – "Prince Osman..."

Sofia came over and put the package next to the Sultana.

This time she personally unpacked it.

"White silk rompers. A tiny green kaftan, for when the prince is a bit older... And also, white, black, and blue shirts, galligaskins... Two pairs of Morocco shoes. And... for the first turban..."

She waited for Mahfiruz to take it in her hands.

"...Made of ostrich feathers, a brilliant plume, inlaid with emeralds."

It was the last gift. Icy eyes, full of hatred, followed the slightest movement of Hatice.

And that's when the confusion arose. Crying wailed from the cradle. Mahfiruz got up to take care of her son. She pushed back the nannies who tried to calm the baby, sparing them no reproaches. At the same time, she waved her hand toward her, which probably meant: 'Go now. I can't look at you anymore. Away!'

The child's crying was a true miracle that God had sent for her so that she did not have to bow to her goodbye. She was about to cross the doorway when she heard the voice of Mahfiruz behind her.

"Wait! We have turned a blind eye to your ignorance, but I do not know if you can count on a similar tolerance on the part of our mother-in-law. She will most likely not let you go away with such impertinence. Know that the House of the Ottomans has only one Valide Sultan. And it is Handan Sultan."

She knew that she should let it go, but it was definitely too difficult for her. She stopped in the doorway, even though she knew she shouldn't do it, also because of superstition. She turned back.

"I do not doubt," she said boldly, "that Handan Sultan will not blame me for the fact that I also call her mother-in-law this way. After all, she owes her current position to her..."

Mahfiruz wanted to say something in reply, but Hatice was not in the room anymore. For a moment, she stared at the door behind which she'd just disappeared. If Hatice had looked back now, she might be scared, seeing the icy eyes in flames.

Mahfiruz leaned over the cradle for a long moment. She took Prince Osman in her arms and patted him on the back, trying to calm him down. She kept her eyes on the door. *Mahfiruz!* said the voice in her head. *This girl is very dangerous.*

And beautiful, she added herself.

The more reason for you to do something, hissed the voice, *because that means an even greater danger for you.*

She gave the baby to the nurse. "Where is Taciser?" she asked quietly. "Make her come here immediately."

"We can't do it; it's too dangerous!"

Eftalya knew that all her opposition was in vain, yet she didn't give up. "In the palace, and above all in the harem, the servants cannot walk anywhere they like."

Hatice nodded – she pretended to listen to her, but her thoughts were in some place completely different. Since she'd left Mahfiruz's room, she'd had only one thing on her mind: *Did I defeat her? Destroy her?*

The little voice in her head enthusiastically answered these constantly repeated questions: *You defeated her.*

Did I destroy her?

You destroyed her.

Did I look good?

Yes.

Just good?

You were beautiful. Like a queen.

It is probably time to end with this 'queen' nonsense... It should be: 'like a Sultana.' Did I really look like that?

You were beautiful, like a painting. You shone like the moon, like the day. You were a Sultana of angels, of fairies.

God, I want to dance from happiness!

Eftalya quickly understood that although Hatice looked at her and nodded, she didn't hear her at all, and was in fact, in a completely different world. "Are you listening to me at all?"

"What?"

"I'm asking if you are listening to me. What you are thinking about is very dangerous, Hatice. The places in the harem where servants can enter are strictly defined. You cannot walk around it just like that!"

"But you are a lady of the court of the Valide Sultan..."

"Okay, but think what would a courtier of the Valide Sultan possibly have to do in the Novice Courtyard? If Mestan Aga or that witch Dilşad see me, the first thing they will do is let the headman of the eunuchs know. And then Handan Sultan will chase me away, at best –"

"Talya... I'm not asking you. I want to go there. I want all of them there to see me."

"You shouldn't leave this room."

"Eh, Talya, Talya." Hatice sighed deeply, puffing her cheeks and lips. Stomping loudly, she went to the door, opened it, and peeked out through the gap. The corridor was dark and silent as usual.

"There is no one; we can go. If I could find the way there myself, I really wouldn't drag you with me."

"Don't you understand? You are no longer part of this palace. You're a stranger here. You cannot leave without permission..." Suddenly she stopped, resigned. "But why am I wasting my breath? You won't listen to me anyway."

Hatice ran to her happily. She felt like a bird. She wanted to sing, dance, and laugh.

"My beloved Talya." Hatice stroked her cheeks. Eftalya tried to break free. "My beloved Talya," she repeated, this time stroking her hair.

Eftalya broke away again, but the expression of anger on her face slowly began to turn into a smile.

"Talya, my angel... Lead me there. You must know some secret passages! We will sneak in unnoticed to the Novice Courtyard. I would like to see Şarazad, Talya. Please understand me. That woman was one of the angels that God put in my way, even before you. I don't want to leave here without seeing her first. Take me there, and you can come back. You'll stay here at night; everyone will think we're together. And in the morning, you can come for me, and we'll come back. Nobody will pay attention to us; everyone will be hurrying to their morning duties. Well, what do you say?"

"Do you really just want to talk to Şarazad?" Her face showed that she did not really believe it.

"Not only her," Hatice admitted. "I want everyone there to see me. Those women and girls, charwomen and servants... I want even the stones and walls there to see Hatice Sultan, who was born in the place of Anastasia. I need it, Eftalya. The surprised faces I will see will only give me courage. I need it. Please..."

At least she is honest, thought Eftalya. *She doesn't even try to cheat me. For reasons that she doesn't understand herself – and most likely will never understand – she just wants to get revenge on her past and her former persecutors, showing them what she is like now in the place where she was insulted, tormented, and beaten.*

She remembered how, after leaving Mahfiruz, Hatice threw her arms around her and whispered in her ear, "I defeated her, Talya. I destroyed her. I threw her off balance. I made the devil mad!"

Maybe, after returning from the Novice Courtyard, she will behave similarly. Perhaps she'll whisper to her, 'I have overcome my past, Talya. I crushed it to dust. I destroyed it. I wish you could've seen the astonishment in their eyes... And how they elbowed each other, just to be able to touch my kaftan!"

"And if Şarazad is not there?"

"We'll wait for her for a few minutes and then come back. You have my word. At least she'll find out I was looking for her. And if we find her, Sofia and I will stay with her. And you can come back."

"I love you very much," Eftalya said quietly. "You can be my Nastya, or Hatice, sent from Safiye Sultan... it does not matter. The most important thing is that you are my sister!"

They embraced each other heartily and looked at each other with love.

"Fine," Eftalya smiled, freeing herself from the embrace. "You'll wait there until I come back for you. I'll take you..." She opened the door and peeked out. *Even if death awaits at the end,* she added in her mind as she checked out the corridor.

They did as Hatice said. Eftalya led them through a lot of dark corridors. Finally, they stopped at a wall, which very clearly indicated that there was no further passage.

"That's all I can do for you," said Eftalya. "The Novice Courtyard is behind this wall. If I were seen there with you, the news would immediately reach the head of the eunuchs."

"I understand. But how will we get there? There is no door here."

The girl ran her hand along the wall, as she searched for something. In the end, she found it.

"When I leave, put your hand in this hollow... you will find a handle there. If you press it hard enough, here" – she pointed to the wall on the right – "the wall will part wide enough so that you will be able to get inside. It will be dark, but don't be afraid. Remind yourself what the Novice Courtyard looks like. There are huge carpets hanging on the walls, remember?"

"Yes..."

"You will find yourself exactly behind one of them. You must wait for the right moment and leave. Most likely, nobody will notice that you walked out from there. There is a huge water vessel there, it will cover you. Well, unless one of the girls is getting water from it."

Hatice remembered that it was exactly opposite the small room in which Şarazad lived.

"She should be in her room at this hour."

"And if not?"

"I'll wait a few minutes. In case anything happens, immediately return behind the rug."

Hatice nodded. "Will we do the same in the morning, too?"

"Wait there after the morning ezan, until I open the passage. You understand?"

"Yes."

"In that case, good luck!" Eftalya stepped back a few steps.

Hatice suddenly felt a strange anxiety in her heart. "Talya!" she called after her and threw herself at her. Sofia did the same. They hugged the girl. Talya suddenly opened her arms wide to embrace them both at once. "I will never forget it," Hatice whispered. "I owe you again."

Their eyes grew moist. Eftalya tried to smile.

"Tomorrow, after visiting the Valide Sultan, you will finally tell me what Safiye Sultan wants from me, and we will be even." She took a few steps. "Come on, go. I can't stay with you any longer," she said and walked away.

Hatice's eyes followed her for some time.

"Come!" Sofia called her. "Let's see if we can make it through this passage..."

The wall parted slightly, and they slipped into the darkness through a small crack. Hatice reached out and found the rough back of the carpet. For a time, they listened to the voices coming from the other side. They heard the clatter of clogs. She tried to determine where it came from. She concluded that it was on the left. *Water tank*, she suddenly thought. She remembered that there was a huge stone tank at the entrance to the courtyard. Probably some servants were washing dishes in it after a meal. A pair of clogs knocked very close to them and then quickly moved away. The hubbub here, so well-known to her, was a sign that the women, tired after a long day of work, had already returned 'home' and now exchanged the latest gossip from the past day, sprawled on the beds in their tiny rooms around the courtyard, each of them now in her own world.

"Come on!"

Without letting go of Sofia's hand, she ran her other hand along the carpet to the right. When she reached its edge, she pushed it. It took a lot of effort to pull aside the heavy fabric, but when she saw a ray of light seep into their niche, she understood they'd succeeded. She went through the gap first and helped Sofia leave. As usual, three torches burned in the Novice Courtyard. The flickering light cast by the fire was only strong enough to brighten the nearest surroundings. The remaining parts of the courtyard were covered in darkness, especially shadowed against the wall at which they were located. As it was cold, the doors to most of the servants' rooms were closed. From the few that were open, the light of torches and the whispers of women slipped outside. She looked left and found that she was correct.

Two servants were standing at the water tank. One was washing a cup, and the other was telling her something in a low voice.

Without taking her back from the wall, Hatice looked to the right, where Şarazad's room was. Her door was also ajar, so she was in her room. But to get there, they had to pass two other rooms along the way.

She gestured for Sofia to be quiet. She was not sure if it would be of any use, though. Their hearts pounded so loudly that she was afraid that in a moment, one of the curious women would hear it and peek out to see what the strange noise was.

Tiptoeing, they passed the first door. As they approached the second, it suddenly opened. Light spilled out from inside. They stopped short. The shadow of a woman standing in the doorway fell on them.

"At this hour, I won't bother to go all the way there," the woman said. After a moment, they saw a bucket in the hands of the shadow rising and immediately falling in their direction. Water splashed right next to them.

"May Allah punish you," the grumpy voice of another woman was heard from inside. "You always pour out dirty water there, and then in the morning, Dilşad tells us to clean it up. Move your legs and take it to the tank like a human!"

"I'm tired, like a dog, I really can't. Besides..." The door closed with a bang. The streak of light and the shadow of the woman immediately disappeared. The voice also died down so that they did not hear the rest of her explanation.

They waited a moment and carefully moved on. Damn it! Right opposite a door, the floor creaked under Hatice's foot. Thank God, the sound was lost in the buzz around. At last, they stood at the slightly ajar door of Şarazad's room. Hatice slowly peeked through the crack.

She was there. Hatice felt warmth in her heart. Şarazad sat cross-legged on her bed. She was patching something. Opposite her, in a place where they once crouched, some other unknown girl now sat. *Some other wounded chick*, she thought. She pushed the door slightly.

The woman noticed the movement and raised her head. She saw Hatice and froze. Her first thought was that she was being visited by a Sultana. A beautiful, wonderful Sultana... Allah!

Şarazad could not believe her eyes. It was clear that she wondered if this beautiful girl, wearing a magnificent blue velvet jacket, was really the same girl she'd known. What she saw was hard to believe.

Hatice called Sofia over with a gesture of her hand.

The woman's eyes slowly grew larger, and the expression of lethargic surprise on her face began to give way to joy. Şarazad sprang up with a cry, "Anastasia! Nastya! Praise Allah! Sofia... my little dove!" Her voice rose even above the bustle of the courtyard.

"Şarazad Abla!"

"Hey there! Get up, come here, look who has come! The night is over for us, the sun has risen!" she shouted as she threw herself at Hatice's neck.

While they greeted each other effusively, kissing and hugging, the doors in the courtyard opened one after the other.

Everything is going my way, thought Hatice, once again embracing the woman. Streams of light, in which the silhouettes of women were drawn, fell outside from the opened doors. Some of them had been ripped out of sleep by the shout, others had not even gone to bed yet. What united them was the fact that they were all tired and depressed, deprived of hope and love in their lives.

"My little Nastya!" Şarazad kissed her on the cheeks. "How did you get here, girl? They said you were banished. Meanwhile... Ah, you look so great!" she called out, delighted, without letting Hatice out of her arms and all the while showering her with kisses. At the same time, she didn't stop shouting: "Girls... girls! Get up, come and admire this beauty of all the beauties! Guess who has visited her Şarazad Abla?"

Hatice had been sure that Şarazad would behave exactly like this. The harem saw her in all her glory, now it was the turn for the rest. She wanted the rumors about her beauty, clothes, and hairstyle to reach the furthest corners of the palace. Those who did not see her were to at least hear that the servant, Anastasia, had returned as Hatice Sultan.

"Why are you yelling like mad, you Tunisian witch?" one of the women woken up by her screams growled. "You've put the whole courtyard on their feet. Who came that you're so excited... Mahfiruz herself, or what?"

The women gathered around the wide-open doors of Şarazad's room laughed mockingly. Şarazad didn't care.

"Someone much more beautiful!" she said boldly. "Come on, look at this sun, this moon and star... At my beloved dove, a little angel."

Those who had noticed her now stood as if frozen.

Hatice stood between Sofia on one side and Şarazad, who still embraced her, on the other. She looked so beautiful and impressive that it took the breath away of all those looking at her. At first, none of the women were able to speak a word. After a while, however, nudging began:

"Do you see what I see, Emine?"

The girl, to whom these words were directed, nodded her head.

Another whispered, "Nastya!" There was doubt in her voice, however. Although Hatice did not see the speaker's face, she quickly recognized the voice. Mürüvvet. The same one whose ear she'd bit on the first night after arriving at the palace. She looked at her with a smile. It was the look and the smile of a queen, willing to forgive her servant, gracious and reserved, at the same time warm and haughty.

"Mürüvvet Abla..."

The woman was confused. *Abla? Why is she so friendly to me? Has she forgotten already that I was her enemy?*

Hatice watched the embarrassment on the face of the girl standing in front of her, still keeping her 'royal' smile.

The woman's hand went unconsciously to her ear. Bitterness poisoned her heart; despite all the time that had passed, she still couldn't forget about it. When she realized her gesture, she immediately dropped her hand. She wanted revenge. She even thought about throwing herself at the interloper and tearing her hair out. But something strange happened. The desire for vengeance was suddenly supplanted by amazement and delight. She was unable to move. Was it really her? That other one was a servant and this one...?

"Anastasia?" she asked in a colorless voice. "Is it you?"

"Yes, but not Anastasia anymore. I'm Hatice now."

She imagined this scene thousands of times during the long, sleepless nights. She slowly approached Mürüvvet. "You won't give me a hug?"

The crowd at the door spontaneously parted in front of her. Smiling to the right and left, she walked a few steps along the line of women. She stopped in front of Mürüvvet, who still stared at her with astonishment, and opened her arms wide.

The girl did not do anything that could be expected of her. She did not rush at Hatice like an arrow released from a bow and did not tear apart the woman, so suddenly transformed into a Sultana, on the spot.

"It is you?" she asked with a smile. "You are the Hatice who has been on the lips of everyone in the harem since yesterday?"

Hatice nodded proudly, though timidly.

Mürüvvet rushed to her in one huge leap. They stared into each other's eyes for a moment. Hatice didn't see a hunger for revenge in her anymore; Mürüvvet didn't find secret hatred in her eyes, either.

She extended her arms to her. "Anast... Hatice!"

"Mürüvvet!"

They embraced each other.

Then, one more unthinkable thing happened. The women gathered in the courtyard began to clap their hands happily. This scene – especially in a place like this, usually bereft of kindness or sympathy – squeezed tears from the eyes of all its witnesses. One of the new girls, who did not understand anything that was going on, looked quizzically at her neighbor.

"You don't know anything," she said while she wiped her wet cheeks. "Of course, how could you know? I will tell you everything later... for now, you should know that this girl, who looks like a great lady, was once one of us."

The girl looked at her in disbelief.

"I'm telling you, another Sultana was born among us. Maybe not really a true one, but whatever. She outshines even the real ones... just look at her."

Mürüvvet was still in shock. She moved a few steps away from Hatice, leaned back, and looked at her closely.

"What happened to you?"

Hatice told her story, again and again, the whole night.

She knew that that night, many girls dreamed – closing their eyes – that like her, they made a journey from a servant to a Sultana. Sighing heavily, they imagined they were just as beautiful, that they also dressed in silks and velvets embroidered with gold. *God only knows how many queens will be born here tonight,* Hatice thought. There was not a trace of ridicule in it. She looked at each of these girls, giving them her most beautiful smile. *Poor things... The spell will be broken as soon as the first rays of the sun penetrate the courtyard. They will rise from their beds, on which they have fallen asleep as queens, and will wake up to be servants again...*

Didn't she, too, experience something like this once?

The corridor was dark. There was no one around who could see him standing flat against the wall. Before he left the secret passage, he looked both ways. Once he made sure nobody around, he came out of hiding. He was dressed in black. He made a gesture as if he wanted to summon someone. Indeed, after a moment, a second black, hooded figure appeared. Stepping on their tiptoes, they headed for the door directly opposite them.

While he listened to what was happening behind the door, she kept her eyes on the dark corridor. It was true that anyone rarely traversed it, but they still needed to take precautions.

He slowly pushed the doorknob. He opened the door wide enough so that he could peer inside through the crack. He was still in the corridor. At one point, he waved at his companion. It meant that she should approach. 'We're going in.'

He slipped inside, and she followed him. The door was left ajar. They moved silently like cats. The room was dark. Judging by the smell of smoke, three candles had to have gone out quite recently. They stood still for some time while they waited for their eyes to get used to the darkness.

The figure standing in the front noticed the bulge on the bed on the left. Someone slept there. Without moving, he turned his head the other way. He stared intently into the darkness. The other two beds were empty. He looked over his shoulder at the woman. He held up his index finger. It meant: 'One.' She responded with a shrug -- two were missing.

The second shadow shifted noiselessly and went to the bed, from which came the sound of the sleeping girl's breathing. She leaned over... For a moment it seemed to her that the whiteness of the pillow illuminated the darkness. Hair... The girl's thick hair was scattered all over the pillow.

Here. The coquette is here. Deep asleep. She will not wake up from it. She will not see the sun again.

She moved a little to one side and made a sign with her hand to the person behind her.

The second figure moved forward and bent over the sleeping girl. If she woke up now, the hands raised above her were ready to immediately tighten on her throat.

There should not be the slightest sound in this room. Even their lips and noses were covered so that their breaths could not be heard, and the victim would not feel them on her face. He looked at her as closely as the darkness allowed. *I guess everything is all right; she looks like she was described,* he thought. The sleeping woman couldn't be clearly seen in the dark, but there was no doubt that she was pretty. Fresh.

Young, hissed Satan in him. *Exactly the way you like, nice and fresh...*

He felt a wave of warmth flood him. It occurred to him to lie down next to her. He imagined closing her mouth with one hand and putting the other on her breasts, clearly visible even under the quilt. He would have a little fun with them, and then he would go a little lower. He would touch the place between her legs, caress her hip. Hmm, maybe she would like it, too – who knows? She would give herself to him without resisting. He would slowly take his hand off her lips and suck on her lip and tongue. This way, he would prevent her from calling for help. And with his hands...

However, he felt the presence of his companion, so he reluctantly left the sea of lust in which he had sunk for a moment. *Damn it,* he swore inwardly. *As if I could not taste her first, and then strangle...* He couldn't. That woman next to him kept urging him with her eyes.

Resigned, he nodded. *All right, all right...* He looked at his hands, all this time raised in the air. He straightened his fingers. He felt them becoming as hard as steel. He held his breath and leaned over the pillow... He leaned... He leaned... Finally, the steel fingers clenched on the throat of the sleeping girl. At first, her body stretched like a bowstring and almost lifted in the air over the bed. The woman accompanying him grabbed the pillow and pressed it with all her strength on the victim's face to prevent her from screaming.

She kicked with her legs. The quilt covering her slipped to the ground. The white legs that emerged from under the nightgown, which slid up all the way to the waist, kicked through the air like crazy. She frantically waved her arms over the pillow covering her face, and desperately tried to reach the murderers as if she wanted to tear them apart – if only she could.

"Die, coquette!" the woman holding the pillow hissed through her teeth. "Go parade in front of the devils in hell!"

The girl's body almost slipped off the bed. The murderer released one of the hands clasped at her throat, took it out from under the pillow and grabbed the victim's leg closer to him.

He thought more about penetrating her body into its depths than about the immobilization of her. It was driving him mad.

The fight suddenly came to an end. The girl's arms calmed down and fell. The legs that had been thrashing the air did it slower, slower... until they stopped completely. Even though he knew that ruthless death had already spread throughout her body, he did not think of withdrawing his hand from between her legs. It was still warm there. Nice and warm!

The woman next to him kept pressing the pillow.

"Well, who will you be ordering around now? I'll show you! 'Open this door!' Pfft!" She growled, leaning over the corpse. "Come on, show off again. Say that you are the lady of the court of Safiye Valide Sultan. Go ahead, order me around! Can you hear me? Did you think that the last voice you heard in your life would be mine, coquette?

The warmth under his hand cooled down. The man quickly withdrew his hand, at the same time loosening his grip on the dead woman's neck.

"Hey!" he hissed at the woman, who now pressed the pillow with almost all the weight of her body. "It's done..."

The shadow did not stop smothering the deceased.

"I'm telling you that this is the end, Taciser. Leave her. Take the pillow away and give me the bag."

She did not take it away. She left it on the woman's face, then pulled out a sack from somewhere and handed it to the man.

"Help me. Let's finish it and get out of here as soon as possible."

It took them a lot of effort, but eventually, they managed to push the body into the bag.

The man threw it on his back, and Taciser checked that the corridor was empty. "Let's go," she said after a moment. "Clear."

Despite the burden, the man walked very fast. By the time Taciser closed the bedroom door, he had already reached the secret passage on the opposite side and stood there waiting.

"I will do the rest myself," he muttered to the woman when they were inside. "And go, tell her it's all over."

When the call for the morning ezan was heard, Şarazad approached the sleeping girls.

"Get up, it's time!"

Hatice immediately got up and woke up Sofia.

"They'll soon bring a pot with soup from the kitchen. Have some before you go."

"We cannot stay, abla. We don't want to put Talya in any more danger."

They hastily adjusted their clothes and prepared to leave.

"Don't forget about me," she said, embracing Şarazad. "I'll tell you now... There's no reason to cry. We aren't parting forever, do you understand? So, I'm not saying goodbye. Just don't forget about me. I won't forget you either... And when the time comes, I'll find you, Şarazad Abla."

Hatice opened the door and froze in surprise.

Mürüvvet slept on the doorstep. She woke to the sound of the door opening. "Are you going already?"

"Yes, I have to," answered Hatice. Without wasting time, she embraced her. "One day, I may ask you for something important..."

"Anytime. If only it is in my power, I will help you."

"It will be!" she whispered to her ear, leaving.

Hatice and Sofia quickly turned to the rug at the back. She turned and smiled for the last time. "Greet all the queens for me!" she said under her breath. She pulled back the rug and disappeared into the dark passage.

And then... Then the real nightmare awaited them.

A minute... two... five... ten. The wall did not open. *She's late.* So, they had to wait a little longer.

A minute... two... five...

Already in the second minute of this unexpected delay, she had begun to worry, but now she was really afraid.

Maybe they noticed her coming for us and told her to do something? Very likely. She couldn't say, after all, 'Wait a minute, let me just pick up Hatice and Sofia...' Or maybe they found out she brought me here? Some enemy of Eftalya's saw us and reported her to the head of the eunuchs? That would be a disaster. If that was indeed the case, it was probable that they had thrown poor Talya out of the harem, all because of her. Or maybe even from the palace?

Do not think about it now, she ordered herself silently. *Instead, think of what you can do. You must get back to your place. There is not much time. Did you forget that you are visiting the Valide Sultan today?"*

She did not forget. She grew nervous. Also, this anxiety cast a shadow on her heart.

Why hadn't Eftalya come?

God, how are we going to get back now? Handan Sultan is not going to wait for me. What if I don't have time to pass her the gifts from Safiye?

She should find a solution immediately... But she had a total emptiness in her head.

She held Sofia's hand a little tighter. She knew that she, too, was losing her mind in this dark passage.

"Five minutes more," she whispered. "Five minutes..."

Hayganoş opened the door joyfully.

"Get up, it's already...!"

The room was empty.

"Ah!"

Eftalya's quilt and pillow were on the ground. The beds that Hatice and Sofia had used were completely untouched.

"Where are they, does anybody know?" she growled.

She motioned the assistants to put aside the bundle with the clothes that Hatice was to wear today. Worried, she went to the door. She looked out into the corridor to see if anyone was coming. Not a living soul. All of the servants were busy with their usual morning duties.

"Maybe Talya took them to the garden?" one of the girls said in an undertone.

Kalfa looked at her angrily. She raised her hand and tapped her forehead.

"I keep telling you that this girl is crazy, and you don't believe it," she said to the other assistant. "Dear, does she really think that the palace is her father's house? 'I'm bored, so I'm going to the garden for a moment...' Did anyone see anything like that?" She paced around the room, never stopping to grumble.

"We have less and less time... We should be finished already!"

She did one, two more laps. "And how am I supposed to prepare her?"

She looked threateningly at the girls. She pointed a finger at them as if they were responsible for the absence of the three girls.

"What are you waiting for? Why aren't you looking for them? I'm supposed to do everything, huh? That's what you want?"

The girls rushed out into the corridor like they'd been burned.

"Where are we supposed to look for them?"

"We cannot walk around the palace like this. First, she says that it's not our father's house, and then she tells us to go out and look for them. Only where, in such a huge harem..."

"Don't worry. We'll walk a little bit and look around. Then we'll come back and say we could not find them."

"You're right. After all, it was not us who was to visit the Sultana Mother. She should have stayed in her place..."

Hatice didn't wait another minute. Something soft brushed against her leg.

"Oh Jesus!" she shouted in fear. "What was that? A mouse? Or...? Oh, God... It can be anything in a place like this. I will not stay here one more moment!" She pulled Sofia's hand and hurried to where they had come from. They pushed the edge of the carpet with difficulty and found themselves again in the courtyard.

It was crowded. The rooms around had been empty for a long time. They tried to catch sight of Şarazad or Mürüvvet in this crowd but to no avail. They were probably already in the kitchen. The girls who had dreamed of sharing her fate at night woke up again to the lives of ordinary servants and now they were busy like bees. The pages carried something, and the odalisques and the farm workers walked quickly, but silently, to and fro across the courtyard. Everyone was busy with their own duties.

It was possible that nobody even noticed their return. They were no longer afraid that someone would see and stop them. Now it would even be good for them.

They had to get back to their room as soon as possible.

"Why didn't Eftalya come?" Sofia asked. It was evident from her eyes that she was scared.

"I don't know..." she replied, trying to sound casual. "Maybe she was called to the Valide Sultan?"

Sofia winced. Of course, she didn't believe it. "If so, she would probably send someone else instead. Or she would let us know somehow..."

She didn't have an answer for that. Panic was overcoming her more and more.

"Hatice?!"

They turned toward the entrance to the Novice Courtyard. Mestan Aga's assistant, Dilşad Kalfa, watched them, her hands on her hips.

They approached her, trying to smile. Maybe it was God himself who sent her to them?

"What are you looking for here?"

She grumbled something in reply, but the woman ignored her. She examined her suspiciously with her eyes.

"Shouldn't you be in the harem? What are you doing here this morning?"

So, she doesn't know that we spent the night here. "After the morning ezan, we came to see Şarazad, but –"

"Don't you know it's forbidden? Well, maybe you really didn't know. But the Valide Sultan has given you one of her courtiers as a guide. She didn't know, either?" She looked around the courtyard. "Maybe she is the one who brought you here, huh?"

"Nooo..." Hatice replied hurriedly. "The Valide Sultan called for her, even before the prayer. I took the opportunity and came here –"

"You came here, just like that... Don't tell me stories here. I'm supposed to believe that you found the way from the harem up here by yourself..." She gave her an angry look. "I came here... what nerve!"

Their position was getting more and more complicated. Hatice approached the woman. "Dilşad Kalfa, come on... The good God simply sent us a guiding angel, isn't it enough for you?" she said with an ingratiating smile.

The woman looked at her strangely. *Right, who wouldn't help such a pretty girl? Even the eunuchs would risk the loss of whatever had been left for them there for one of her smiles...* "Thank Allah that the guards did not see you. What did you want from Şarazad?"

"Nothing in particular... You know, she took care of us once. I thought it would be nice to visit her while I am in the palace... But what can I do? Apparently, we were not meant to meet. And now..." she paused as if giving up the rest and looked at the woman.

As she expected, Dilşad did not leave it without asking, "Now, what?!"

She shrugged and smiled like an unruly child. "And now we have to go back to our room. We have a visit to Handan Valide Sultan planned for this afternoon."

"Will you find your way there? Or do you hope that Allah will put an angel on your path again?"

Hatice could not stop her hearty laughter. "Not at all, because God has already done so."

"Well, really?" she blurted without thinking and looked around.

"He sent us an older sister for help... You!"

It was difficult to know what she thought. Dilşad's black, taut skin effectively masked her feelings. Fortunately, there were still her eyes. It was from them that Hatice read that the woman would escort them wherever they wanted.

We made it. We're coming back! Blessed Lady, thank you!

"It's here," Dilşad said half an hour later, as they reached the entrance to the dark corridor that led to their room. "From here, you will need to find the way yourself..." she hesitated for a moment.

"Yes? Do you want to tell us something else?"

"Actually... I wonder. Could you whisper a word to the Valide Sultan about me, once you are there? About moving to some better place?"

Hatice smiled, catching Sofia's hand. "But how could I not whisper! And don't forget to talk to Mestan Aga. Tell him I remember him. Don't let him forget me either..."

"Why? Why should he remember you?"

"Just pass it to him. He will understand."

They ducked hurriedly into the corridor and turned at the corner. The first thing they saw was Hayganoş's two assistants pacing nervously in front of the door.

At the sound of footsteps, the girls looked up. Recognizing them, one of the girls immediately rushed into the room, shouting, "She's here! She's here!" and the other ran up to them.

"Where were you, girl? Hayganoş has almost given up the ghost! And she was close to dragging us into the other world, too!"

Hatice giggled. The worst was over. The trip to the Novice Courtyard had taught her a few things. Neither friendship nor hatred is eternal. And her beloved friend, for some reason, left her at a critical moment.

On the other hand, Mürüvvet, the one she had considered her own mortal enemy, came over to her side because of a few warm words. So, it is true. There is no door that could not be opened with a properly chosen word...

She also learned that one should keep a cool head even in the most dangerous and hopeless situations. Panic is the greatest enemy of reason.

Besides... During this escapade, something happened that she hadn't taken into account before. She'd based everything on the assumption that Eftalya would help them. She was supposed to take them there, and then pick them up and lead them back. But she didn't show... or she couldn't come. And she hadn't thought about that possibility even for a moment. A lesson for the future was that you always had to have an emergency plan up your sleeve. One that she could complete from the beginning to the end by herself, without the help of others. This morning, God sent her an angel in the form of Dilşad. But the Creator had the weight of others on his shoulders, and he might as well have been busy with something else. From now on, she should always devise a rescue plan, and not count on intervention from above.

Hayganoş rushed out of the room, waving her hands. Her rounded body rolled straight on toward Hatice. "Do you want to kill me?" she growled. After three steps, she ran out of breath and stopped in place. She put her hand to her chest.

Hatice came up to her with a giggle.

"And you're laughing?" she gasped with difficulty. "I'm dying here, and you're laughing, yes?" Hayganoş grabbed her hand and tugged toward the room. "Time is running out, and we still have to dress your hair!"

And Eftalya? Why didn't she come out to meet me?

Hatice stopped.

"Eftalya..." she whispered. "Where is Eftalya?"

The woman shrugged in response. "If you don't know, how should I know?" She jerked the girl's hand again. "Come on, I said, we don't have time! And she will surely reappear."

As she entered, Hatice felt an iron vice grip her heart. She didn't know why, but her heart pounded from an unspecified fear. Something must have happened. Something bad.

"Are the gifts for the Sultana ready?"

"Ready."

She looked at them. Four packages wrapped in gold satin lay prepared on the trunk near the door. She put her hand in her bosom pocket. From her inner pocket, she took out a little bag made of golden silk and handed it to one of the helpers.

"Put it on top."

The girl did as she was told, and the other one began to brush her hair. Hatice sat without saying a word.

"I'm afraid..." she whispered after a long moment. "What if something happened to her?"

"Relax, my dear. What could have happened to her? She was probably called to the Valide Sultan... who knows when and what she will want? You'll surely see her there. Maybe she'll even come out to welcome you."

"I hope..." she said as if to herself. Still, fear was slowly taking control of her.

She looked great in pink and pearls. It was more than mere beauty. She looked wonderful as she walked, swaying slightly to the sides.

An army of servants, standing on both sides of the corridor leading to Handan's apartments, watched her as if enchanted. Hatice was, however, indifferent to it. Her thoughts were with Eftalya.

She looked for her out of the corner of her eye amongst those waiting outside the room. *Eftalya, where are you?* she constantly repeated in her mind.

Eftalya was not there.

As she approached the crowd gathered under the huge doors, she did not stop praying: *God, let her be there. Let her be the one who will make them all step aside and make a passage for me. Let me see her when they announce me...*

Someone announced her arrival. Not Eftalya. She was not in the waiting room, either.

In that case, she's there, she told herself. *Where I saw her for the first time. She will be standing with the other court ladies, just behind the Sultana Handan.*

She crossed the doorway and found herself in the Valide Sultan's apartments. Sofia, together with the odalisques carrying the bags with the gifts, and the other members of the retinue, stayed on the other side of the door, as previously.

This time, she greeted the Sultana without failing to follow the etiquette.

"Allah!" the voice in front of her chirped. "It cannot be you!"

It belonged to Handan. "We were told so, but we did not believe," she continued. "Get up, Anastasia. Let us look at you."

Hatice immediately looked around the room. Her friend was not here; neither was her enemy. Mahfiruz was probably singing lullabies to her son in her apartment.

Really? Is it possible for the Ice Queen to produce a voice that can lull an infant? A soft, warm, and sweet mother's voice, full of devotion and love?

Where are you, Eftalya? Hatice thought while she stood upright in front of the Valide Sultan. *God, where is she?*

There was a long silence. All eyes – those of the Sultana Handan, the surrounding courtiers, and the other people in the room – all stared at her like at a picture. When she'd visited Mahfiruz, she had burst with pride and joy. And now she didn't care much about being an object of universal admiration and jealousy. She wasn't even curious what was whispered around her.

Handan was the first to break the silence.

"How beautiful you are, my child. We assessed you similarly last time, but what we see today... You are so..." She moved her hand from the top down, pointing to her. "Pink really suits you very well..."

She turned to the group of girls standing against the wall on the right. "How do you say that?" she began with a smart, joyful tone. "In the hands of the master, even a stone turns into a precious stone. The honorable lady showed her artistry. She made a unique pink diamond from our Nastya."

Hatice thanked her for this compliment with a slight curtsey.

"But she's calling you by some different name, right?"

"Yes, My Lady," she affirmed kindly. "Safiye Valide Sultan decided that the name given to me in the palace – Hatice – is more appropriate."

A shadow passed over Handan's face as she heard her title being used for someone else. However, she had already mastered the art of hiding or quickly controlling her emotions. Her face immediately brightened again with a smile.

"Her Majesty," she began, accentuating every word, "always knows what will be best."

Hatice was struck by the fact that, speaking about her mother-in-law, Handan did not see the need to call her 'Sultana.' She did not even hide the irony with which she spoke about her. Right now, however, Hatice did not dwell on it. She still hoped that the door would open at any moment and Eftalya would enter the room.

"What is the news from Her Majesty?" Handan asked suddenly. "We hope, with Allah's will, that her health is good."

Even though her thoughts were somewhere else, Hatice sensed something – like Handan was expecting bad news – in her tone.

"All is good, My Lady. She does not cease in prayers for the good fortune for our Sultan. She congratulates you warmly for the birth of your grandson, and for the little prince, she sends the wishes of a long, happy life."

Safiye had arranged this speech for her. It contained everything. There was only not enough room for Handan and Mahfiruz.

"Thank you very much," the Valide Sultan replied dryly. "In this case, we have false information. We had heard that she is feeling worse lately; it worried us very much."

In an instant, Hatice decided to lure her into a trap.

"She just got pale," she said quietly. She noticed that the woman's body in one moment stretched like a bowstring. "She is tough on herself," she continued. "She personally looked after all the preparations relating to my visit and the presents. She kept an eye on the smallest of details. No wonder it exhausted her. At least that's how I saw her just before my departure."

"She got pale..." Handan muttered. She bowed her head to hide the joy with which her eyes were shining. She didn't succeed in it, though...

Everything was suddenly clear to Hatice. There was no doubt that Handan was waiting for news about an illness, not the health of her mother-in-law. *Or maybe even death*, the voice in her head whispered. She shuddered all over her body. How often this word – death – popped up in the palace life... It even got inside her head – because this was always the first eventuality that came to her mind.

"She should not overdo it like that. Maybe she does not want to admit it, but she's not that young anymore..." Handan stopped abruptly and looked at the girls behind Hatice. "But, we do not see with you the girl we gave to accompany you," she said suddenly. "What was her name?"

Hatice's heart almost jumped out of her chest. "Eftalya, My Lady..."

"Ah yes, Eftalya. Where is she?"

Hatice lost her head completely. *Oh, God, she's asking me that, she's... She doesn't know anything!*

"Shouldn't she be accompanying you? Or is she sick, perhaps?"

Hatice didn't know what to answer. After all, she could not just say she'd disappeared. Or maybe the Sultana just tried to probe her in this way? Maybe she'd learned that Eftalya, contrary to the rules of the harem, led them to the Novice Courtyard, and maybe even had already punished her? And now only... Such a possibility made Hatice shiver again. She didn't want to think what such a punishment would look like. And yet, she did not do anything bad. Did anything happen, after all? She just led them to another part of the palace so that Hatice could brag a little...

Hatice shrugged imperceptibly. "I don't know," she answered in a whisper.

"I see that you brought someone else in her place."

Oh my God! And that's all? Eftalya is missing. The Sultana does not know anything about it, and she instead asks where she can be. Also, instead of taking care of it and ordering a search, she has moved her attention to Sofia as if nothing happened... So that's what it looks like? This is the Sultana's attachment to her courtiers? A total indifference?

"Come here," said Handan to Sofia. "You've grown up; you got pretty. Your friend took good care of you. Since her companion has got lost, try to replace her. Let's see what the Honorable Lady gave us."

At these words, Hatice finally managed to collect her thoughts.

Sofia brought the bundles with gifts, one by one. Placing them at Handan Valide Sultan's knees, she announced each time in a loud voice: "A gift from Her Majesty Safiye Valide Sultan for the mother of His Majesty the Sultan, the venerable Handan Sultan..."

Handan opened bundle after bundle with great interest.

A wonderful kaftan... Two unbelievably beautiful pieces of headgear, with a completely new design. Short kaftans, galligaskins, chemises, jackets...

You could think that there was a small mound of gold next to Handan – because each and every item was in that color.

"Wonderful, very beautiful," she repeated every time the contents of the bundles appeared before her eyes. After the last of them were emptied, containing two pairs of headscarves with golden fringes, she turned to the ladies of the court.

"The Dignified Lady had a weakness for this color in her youth. Apparently, she was not seen otherwise than dressed in gold. And now she has graced us with gifts of the same color."

She looked at Hatice again and hesitated for a moment.

"You said that she seemed a bit pale to you, didn't you?" she asked the question in such a tone as if she was ordering her to answer: 'Yes, she was pale, even very pale...'

"Yes, My Lady," she replied, keeping her eyes on the Sultana Mother. "That's what she looked like to me."

Pale! Pale... So, she's withering... Handan tried to suppress the joy that filled her. Suddenly, however, she met Hatice's eyes. *Why is this girl looking at me like that?*

She grew irritated. *No one taught her that you should not look at a Valide Sultan like that?* That's why she so vehemently rebuked Eftalya at the first meeting. *As if she wanted to read my thoughts.* She turned her head to the side and pretended to play with the fringe on the headscarf. *She guessed! Is she a witch or what? She guessed my joy... But it's nonsense! How would she do that? I think I've become too suspicious.*

Handan was so happy that she decided not to think about it anymore. Even if the girl indeed saw the sparks of happiness in her eyes, she could not know its reason. *Pale... That was the key word.*

The other man had told her the same: 'Our Lady will wither like a rose. She will become wrinkled, she will get weak, and one day she will eventually... fall off the branch.'

'How long will it take?' Handan had asked.

'If we want, it will be even just an hour, and if we want it differently, it can be a whole day. Or a year...'

'It's too short... And a year, on the other hand, is too long.'

'You're right, My Lady. If we want no trace of the rose left on the branch, then... Let's say a month.'

'Let's say. But are you sure? If it's necessary...'

'Your Highness...' She remembered the venomous smile that appeared on the foxy face of the Italian as if it happened yesterday. 'I'm not doing this for the first time...'

The man was worried that the client would get nervous and leave without buying a potion from him.

'I just...'

'Please do not worry... Nobody will know why our rose wilted and fell down. A rose is a rose... It must wither one day, right? It should start to wilt within a week.'

And it has just started.

Handan's thoughts returned to the present. "Ask the Noble Lady, on our behalf, to not tire herself too much, will you? Do not forget about it."

You don't really care about it at all, thought Hatice. *It's even possible that as soon as I leave, you will begin to pray for her death.*

Handan Valide Sultan moved impatiently in her seat. "If that's all the gifts..."

Hatice became scared for a moment. *God, I almost forgot about it!* Her hand went hurriedly to the sash that was tied at her waist. "Please forgive me, My Lady." She took out a golden silk bag. "It's because I got so nervous... I almost forgot the most important gift, which the Valide Sultan ordered me to give to you personally."

The woman's gaze went immediately to the pouch. "What is this?"

Hatice kissed the item, respectfully touched her forehead with it, and handed it to Sofia. The girl approached the Sultana. After repeating her friend's gesture, she slowly laid it on Handan's hand.

The Sultan lifted it and showed to the courtiers, shaking it.

"Gold?"

No sound. She shook it again.

"Or maybe diamonds, rubies, or emeralds?"

No clang came out of the pouch again.

"So, what do we have here?" she asked. She untied the leather strap and put two fingers inside. A look of relief appeared on her face as she felt what was inside. She took out a big ring.

"A gift from Her Majesty Safiye Valide Sultan for the mother of His Majesty the Sultan, the venerable Handan Sultan – a ring decorated with precious stones," Hatice said in a loud voice.

The woman was surprised. The ring was crowned with a large stone, surrounded by three circles – of turquoises, diamonds, and rubies. This stone did not resemble a rare, precious gem, though.

Handan took the ring and looked at it under the light. The circles of diamonds and rubies immediately sparked, and the stone in the middle did not react in any way. It remained completely expressionless, matte gray. It looked like a regular stone.

Anger filled the Valide Sultan. So, the mother-in-law decided that she deserved only a modest stone?

"What is this?"

'Wait for her to ask,' Sultana Safiye had ordered her before the departure. That was why she was quiet while Handan turned the ring in her fingers.

"That ring once belonged to Hürrem Sultan, My Lady."

In an instant, the expression of disdain on Handan's face disappeared.

"This stone has magical powers. Supposedly, it was washed in the blood of a thousand dragons."

"A thousand dragons?"

"Yes. In the blood of immortal monsters. The great-great-grandfather of our Sultan, Suleiman Han, brought it all the way from the palace of the Emperor of China as a gift to Hürrem Sultan. The one who wears this ring enjoys unlimited power and a very long life. All diseases and evil powers stay away from its owner."

"Well, well..." Handan muttered. She did not take her eyes off the ring.

"Before her death, Hürrem passed it to her daughter-in-law, Nurbanu Sultan. Then it was inherited in turn by Safiye Sultan."

"But we have never seen it on the finger of the Noble Lady..."

Safiye had anticipated this question, too.

"She puts it on only at night. This is precisely its charm, its whole power. For dragons draw strength in the darkness of the night, so that they could use their power in the light of the day."

Handan wanted to say something, but she gave up.

Hatice did not miss the opportunity. "Now the ring wants to go into your hands..."

"What? Into our hands? We've probably never heard bigger nonsense. How can a ring want anything? And even if it did, how did the Honorable Lady understand it? Did it tell her about it?" Handan did not see the need to try to hide the malice in her voice.

Hatice did not pay attention to it, and she even smiled. "Yes," she blurted out suddenly. "It has such power that when the right time comes, it indicates to its owner the next person who has to wear it on her finger."

The woman still looked at the ring. It was as if her gaze were glued to this dull stone.

"It indicates? But how?" Bored, she put the pouch aside. "What nonsense! How can it indicate? What's that supposed to mean?"

"The ring," Hatice began in a mysterious tone, "when it wants to move into another hands, reveals to her owner in a dream the person for whom it wants to ensure power, health, and a long life from now on."

Handan still looked at the ring, even though she didn't hold it in her hand any longer.

"What if the owner doesn't want to give it away to the new one? Who would voluntarily give away such a powerful thing? In truth, this whole story seems to us completely preposterous..."

"Revenge," Hatice whispered. "The ring takes revenge on the owner if she does not want to give it to the next one, My Lady..."

"It takes revenge?"

"In just a few weeks, the owner wastes away, leaving almost only skin and bones. Scary black wounds appear on the body and..." Hatice fell silent as if she could not describe these horrors further. But Handan understood that death would follow the 'and.'

She took the ring again and began to turn it around in her fingers... "So, the Honorable Lady saw us in her dream? The ring pointed to us, did it?"

"She said to me, 'The ring picked my daughter-in-law.' You should thus put it on your finger as soon as possible so that it does not lose its power and can ensure you strength and health."

Hatice paused and looked the Sultana straight in the eye. *Damn it... Come on, put this damn ring on already. Safiye Sultan said maybe a hundred times that I couldn't leave until you do this. Put it on, I want to leave already...*

There was a long silence, or maybe it just seemed so to her. Handan still rotated the ring between her thumb and index finger. She looked at it against the light, from underneath...

"All right," she finally said. "It is not worthy of the hand of the Valide Sultan, but since it was made with such great craftsmanship... Let the wish of the Honorable Lady be fulfilled."

She put the ring on her finger.

Finally! Hatice thought happily. At the same moment, she heard the big door open behind her.

She was so happy that she forgot where she was. *She came, she finally came, my beloved Eftalya!* Overjoyed, she turned back. *Oh my God!*

The Queen of Ice!

At the same time, Mahfiruz noticed her. "A ghost!"

The Sultana's scream echoed off the faience tiles on the wall.

Hatice noticed that the icy blue eyes of the woman grew large with fear. She raised her hands to her head first, then extended them in Hatice's direction and repeated, terrified, "A ghost!"

She staggered and slipped into the arms of one of the courtiers. The girl tried to support her, but Sultana Mahfiruz fell to the ground.

It caused quite a stir. There were shouts from everywhere: "She fainted, fainted, Mahfiruz Sultan fainted!" Everyone, including Handan, gathered around her.

"Doctor!" someone from this crowd shouted. "Call a doctor immediately!"

Hatice stepped back to the door. She didn't even look at Mahfiruz. She had only this scream in her ears: 'A ghost!'

The hiss of a viper, she thought. Going to the waiting room, she turned to Sofia.

"Did you hear? Why did she call me a ghost?"

Hayganoş Kalfa, along with her two assistants, stood curiously in the doorway, trying to see anything in the crowd. Hatice grabbed her hand and pulled her aside.

"Did you hear what she said to me?"

The panicked woman just narrowed her eyes, letting her know that she had heard.

A ghost! The ice queen said to me, 'A ghost.' Why?

And suddenly she understood.

She remembered the words of Hayganoş, who told them that in the morning, after entering the empty room, she had seen Eftalya's pillow and quilt lying on the ground. She did not pay attention to it before. But now, everything formed a logical whole.

The Ice Queen thought she was dead.

Someone had to have told her: 'We've killed her. Hatice is dead.'

And when she saw her in front of herself...

Oh my God! They killed Eftalya instead of me!

Chapter Twenty-One

Old Palace
January 1605

They spent the night all in one room – Hatice, Sofia, Hayganoş Kalfa, and her assistants, the courtiers... The odalisques responsible for the bundles stood in turn by the door.

Nobody closed an eye.

As it had been agreed upon earlier, one of the ladies of the court of Sultan Handan came to show them the way out after the morning ezan. Everyone was in a hurry.

"Have they found her?" Hatice asked suddenly.

"Who?"

"Eftalya."

"No... she's disappeared into thin air," answered the courtier indifferently. Then she came closer to Hatice as if she wanted to reveal a secret. "Such things happen here. Some girls suddenly disappear..."

"How come?" she asked, her hand pressed to her chest. "Are they killed?"

The courtier turned and looked at her strangely without slowing her pace. Certainly, this happened, too. But such things were not talked about aloud.

"No," she giggled. "They simply disappear. That is, they run away to their lovers, outside... You know what I mean."

Hatice was sure, however, that Eftalya could not have escaped.

When they reached the stable yard, everything was already prepared for them.

There was no time to lose.

"Without further ado," she addressed her companions. "Let's get in one carriage and get out of here as soon as possible!"

So, they did. Hayganoş sat next to her.

The wheels began to turn. Her heart pounded. She held her breath until they'd left the palace and found themselves on a tree-lined road toward the Hippodrome. It seemed to her that at any moment, someone would shout after them, 'Stop them, they're running away!'

Nobody shouted, however. Nobody chased them.

She was silent all the way. There was only one question on her mind. *Why? Why did she want to kill me?*

By the time the carriage entered the gateway to the Old Palace, she already had an answer. *She understood that I would take Sultan Ahmed from her!*

Hatice sensed it right away. There was a strange atmosphere in the Old Palace. There were almost no signs of life in the courtyard where they arrived when it should've been crowded with grooms, farmhands, and servants at this hour. Besides, it wasn't there... Safiye Sultan's carriage. She must have gone somewhere.

A young farmhand came out of the stable. Wiping his hands on some rag, he watched as the visitors exited the carriage. More specifically, one of them – Sofia. As soon as Hatice caught the gaze of the young man, she glanced at Sophia from the corner of her eye. The girl's cheeks were flushed. In spite of all the anger and everything she'd gone through, she felt warmth in her heart. *So that's what's going on,* she told herself. *Is my dove already trying her wings out for a flight on her own?*

She suddenly realized that she'd never experienced anything like that before. She couldn't remember ever blushing under the gaze of a boy. The figure of the stable boy from the Karayelzade's estate, Slobodan, appeared in front of her eyes.

She was ashamed when she realized how long it had been since she'd thought of him. Yes, maybe it was only him that she felt a little more sympathy for. But that was all – a little more. Slobodan was not a prince who could make her a queen, after all. But now Ahmed...

Stupid islander! Hatice scolded herself, just like Mirna used to do. *Ahmed who? The one who doesn't even know about your existence... the father of the son of the same Ice Queen who hates you so much that she tried to kill you?*

How could she still imagine a return to the New Palace under similar circumstances?

*The queen of devils must be probably lamenting now that she let me out of her gras*p, she thought. Yes, the New Palace was forever unattainable for her from now on. This time, Azrael missed the target, but next time... But no, there would be no next time. She would grow old and die at the Old Palace, along with Safiye Sultan.

She adjusted her kaftan and headed for the gates that overlooked the stable yard. The farmhand walked a step behind them. Right behind Sofia, of course.

"Why is it so quiet here today?" she asked without looking back.

"She is sick."

"Sick? Who is sick?" Stupid question; the answer to it was obvious. Exhausted by the recent events, she was unable to control herself, and it somehow slipped out of her mouth.

"The Honorable Lady. The Padishah sent a lot of doctors to her. Everyone is with her now."

"Is it something serious?"

She didn't hear the answer because she started to run involuntarily. And maybe there was no answer.

While she waited for Safiye to receive her in her apartment, she imagined that she would find her as pale as her hair, scattered across the pillow. Her arrival would be greeted with a faint smile. She would probably ask her for a detailed report. And when Hatice approached her, she would immediately ask her about the ring: 'Did she put it on?' After all, she'd repeated to her a hundred times before leaving: 'Do not leave until she puts it on. And if you repeat everything exactly as I taught you, she certainly will.'

It turned out that she was right. Indeed, Handan finally did put the ring on her finger. Why was it so important to Safiye? She didn't know that answer.

As soon as the door opened, she almost ran into the apartment, and she realized at once how wrong she had been. She saw with her own eyes what the farmhand and Raziye had not told her – Safiye Valide Sultan was very ill.

Her once golden hair was almost completely faded. There was a purple spot on her right cheek. Hatice came a little closer and noticed that two similar spots also appeared on the left one. Her eyes were closed. It was difficult to tell if she was still breathing. One might think that years had passed since their last meeting.

And they'd said goodbye just four days ago. How could she have changed so much in such a short time? Four days ago, she was saying goodbye to a woman full of life and hope, and today the same woman now lay on her deathbed. Safiye was about to go away and leave her completely alone.

Suddenly, Hatice's hair bristled. It seemed to her that at the head of the Sultana's bed she saw Azrael, hiding his terrible face under a black hood. He held the sharp scythe of death in his bony fingers.

All her power and the power of the entire house of the Ottomans was useless. Death, uncaring of the division of the kings and the poor, was preparing to take the most powerful queen on earth in its arms.

Hatice boiled with anger. *God... you were silent when I was taken away from my mother. When I found shelter with Mirna, you separated me from her. You also took Şarazad from me. And then... then...*

This pain was still too fresh. *Then you turned a blind eye to the fact that Eftalya was killed instead of me. And now you're also taking Mother Safiye away from me... Why?!*

God was snatching from her, one by one, all the women she had ever loved, everyone she called 'mother' or 'sister.' All those who also loved her.

Suddenly she felt wetness on her hands and realized that a fountain of tears had been spilling from her eyes for some time. *Why, my God, why are you doing this to me?*

She tried to dry her tears with the back of her hand. *I know*, she continued in her mind, *I have a lot of sins on my conscience. How many times have I been against you...? You will not forgive me for that. But if I am such a big sinner, why did you take Eftalya instead of me? Why are you now taking this woman? Is this your justice?*

She already knew. As punishment, God first wanted to deprive her of all those she loved. And at the end, it would be her turn.

"So, let it be this way, God," she whispered. "Let it be done according to your will. But save her, I'm begging you!"

She crossed herself with growing repentance. "Lord Jesus," she prayed. "Please, plead for me with your Father, forgive me for my blasphemies. Please, beg him to keep my mother Safiye alive. Didn't you say in the gospel that He is always loving and compassionate? God, our Lord, forgive me. Blessed Lady, plead with God for the Sultana Safiye, let him call the Angel of Death away from her."

The Angel of Death has nothing to do here, her inner voice intervened unexpectedly. *He should take care of the Ice Queen instead. The murderess Queen!*

Hatice crossed herself again. She decided that very likely, nothing would save her from hell. Even while begging God for forgiveness, her thoughts were busy with cursing and death...

She approached Semiha. She looked at her quizzically – she needed to find out more about the condition of the ill woman.

"And the doctors? What do they say? They should make a mixture or something... They must know some remedy!"

"It's hard for them to tell anything. Her condition constantly changes. In one moment, it seems to us that she is dying, and then in the next, she recovers as if she has never been sick. We are happy that she came back to us from the embrace of death, but a moment later, she is getting worse again. And now also these spots have appeared... See for yourself."

Of course, she had already seen them.

"We noticed them this morning. There are more and more of them, and they keep growing..."

In just four days, the Sultana of the Sultanas, the powerful Safiye, had withered and wasted. She was now like a withered rose that could be knocked down from the branches by a strong gust of wind.

Hatice was very sad. She raised her head. *Why? Why are you doing this?*

Suddenly, she realized that she was shaking her fists at the sky. The question that struck her was like an echo: *Why? Why? Why? Why...?*

There could no longer be any prayers or begging for forgiveness. *After so many rebellions, neither Jesus nor Mary will hear me anymore*, she told herself. *Because how could they put in a word for me before God?*

Suddenly she thought she heard a whisper.

"Is it you?"

In one moment, everything jumped alert her.

She saw the woman's lips moving. "You're back?"

Crazy joy overtook her. God had to have heard her rebellion and prayers after all. Safiye had come back to life again. "Yes, it's me, My Lady."

"Pick me up."

She and Semiha helped her sit up, and the other girls pushed pillows behind her back. Safiye's eyelashes twitched slightly. After a moment, she opened her eyelids. Was it just a muffled gray shine that remained from the gaze that once charmed the Ottomans?

Never mind, thought Hatice. *At least there's that. As soon as her heart beats a little stronger, the sparks will sprinkle from her eyes again.*

"Let everyone else leave... Send them out."

Semiha immediately jumped to her feet. "Let's go," she said. "The Valide Sultan wants to be alone with Hatice."

As everyone present reluctantly left the room, Hatice suddenly shuddered with fear. Something caught her hand. Frightened, she wanted to withdraw it immediately, but then she realized what had happened – a bony hand had emerged from under the quilt and grabbed her wrist. It belonged to Safiye. Hatice felt sad. She took it between her hands and stroked it with tenderness. A smile seemed to run over Safiye's face.

"Are they gone?"

"Everyone left, My Lady."

The patient breathed very quickly for a while; she took one breath after the other. Her breast rose and fell like bellows.

"Did she put it on?"

"Pardon?"

"Did she wear it?"

Hatice moved away slightly, scared. The Sultana looked at her with wide eyes. "But who... what?"

"Sheeeee..." Safiye moaned. "She... The ring..."

Even while she stood at death's doorway, Safiye thought about revenge.

"She did," Hatice said slowly. "She put it on!"

A sigh resembling a groan escaped her lips. Hatice understood that it was a sigh of relief. Safiye smiled, and a glint briefly flashed across her eyes.

There we are, sparks have already sprinkled, Hatice thought. It pleased her very much.

"Good." Safiye took one more breath. "She's first... she grabbed its hand... but it will not... it will not take long!"

What?! 'She grabbed its hand...' What's that supposed to mean?

Safiye fell silent to draw air. After three wheezing breaths, she resumed, "After us... After us... she, too. Soon."

The Sultana's face strained with pain. She froze like that for a while. After a long moment, she revived again. She tried to rise, even more, pushing herself up on her elbows. "Come here..." she panted. "Closer."

Hatice fulfilled her order. Her ear almost rubbed against the mouth of the Sultana.

"Listen," Safiye whispered. "Listen to me carefully, my child. She killed... me. Killed!"

"Who?!" Hatice grew scared. She wanted to step back, but the bony fingers did not let go of her wrist.

"Listen!" repeated the woman. "Do not interrupt me. No questions..." She fell silent for a moment to rest. "First time..." she continued in a weak whisper. "The Great Sultana Mother... she was late for the first time. Even though she quickly got to work. She poisoned... me."

"Who, My Lady? Who?"

Safiye looked her in the eye. "She. Handan..."

"What? Oh my God! But... but how...?" She was shocked; she didn't know what Safiye was saying. Was it possible? Could the young Valide Sultan, with the beautiful face and kind eyes, be a murderess?

Naive, suddenly growled a voice in her head. *And didn't Mahfiruz try to kill you?*

She remembered how Handan had persistently asked about the health of her mother-in-law. As soon as Hatice told her that Safiye was a little pale recently, the Valide Sultan had muttered something under her breath, and a glow appeared in her eyes. She didn't think it was important then, but now she understood everything – it was joy. Handan was glad that Safiye was beginning to fall ill. Because she had her hand in it.

"Let it be her way," continued Safiye. "Do not be sad... You too, her..."

She could not finish it. A grimace of pain appeared on her face. She pulled her eyebrows together. She closed her eyes.

Chills ran through Hatice's body. *Me too? What does that mean?* The suspicion that formed in her head almost caused her to lose her senses. *Mother of God! It means... It means...*

"You too," Safiye gasped again. "You killed her..."

This time, Hatice could not stop the scream. "The ring! Something in the ring?"

The Sultana laughed. That laughter pierced Hatice to the bone.

"At night..." Safiye said suddenly. "He will be here. Padishah... In my chamber..."

All the Saints!

Hatice felt as if a thunderbolt hit her. A man struck by lightning would probably feel exactly as she did now – immediately turned into fire and then a rock, and his heart pops out of his chest and breaks into fine sand.

She was exactly like that. The recent events, everything she'd heard, made her dizzy.

The murderer sent by Mahfiruz was convinced that he was taking her life, but he killed Eftalya instead.

Safiye Sultan was close to death. And her groans: *'She poisoned me. Handan...'*

Hatice had not yet recovered from the shock of these words when the woman had consoled her. *'Do not be sad... You too, her...'*

Blessed Lady, did I, too? Does it really mean that I killed her, too? It couldn't mean anything else. She was the one who handed the ring to Handan. She persuaded her to put it on immediately, and not to take it from her finger. There was indeed a secret power in the ring. The power to take life!

Hatice didn't know what to do anymore; speak, or think. Her dream of becoming a queen made her a murderess. Also – the murderess of another queen!

And in the end, Safiye also said that... the Padishah would come. Here?!

She wondered if she had heard it right. Did she really say he would come here? Everything seemed to indicate that she had heard correctly. The Sultan was to visit his seriously ill grandmother. To see for the last time the woman who had been killed by his mother!

She watched Safiye Sultan for a long time. *This is another blow that destiny has prepared for me. Now it takes away the opportunity to enchant the Sultan. He will see me with his grandmother's body, but only as a mourning, unfortunate servant...*

Although she had spent so much time in the New Palace, she'd never had the opportunity to see him, even from afar. And the past four days? She'd seen the whole harem, not excluding secret passages and corridors.

Why didn't the fates bring him when I was there, to the rooms of his mother or his wife, the murderess with an icy look? If he saw me then – so beautiful, in all that splendor... And now?

She was indeed pale, depressed because of the deaths of two people close to her. How was she supposed to charm the Sultan Ahmed in such a state?

Safiye saw the dilemma and conflict play out on Hatice's face through her half-closed eyes. "It seems to me that with Ahmed" – it was hard for her to speak – "I think she will come here, too."

Another bolt to her head. "Ah! Who? Which one of them? The devil, who murdered Eftalya? Or the one who killed you?"

"Handan..."

She felt her brain swiftly go numb. The murderess was going to come here to see her victim?

It was hard to believe that all this was really happening. It was probably a nightmare. Yes, it looked like her dreams of becoming a queen had suddenly turned into a nightmare. Because how else to explain everything that had happened recently, what she saw and heard, all those secrets – secret passages, corridors, murders...

Safiye Sultan suddenly opened her eyes. There was no sign of the pain the distorted her face just a moment ago. She looked now as if she was well and strong. Exactly as Semiha said: 'She comes back from the embrace of death.'

"The Padishah," Safiye said clearly, "will take you with him from here. You must be ready, my child."

This time, it really chilled her. She raised her hand. She could not close her mouth. Even her eyes stopped blinking. Maybe even her heart stopped. She was not able to understand all this. *Is this a fairy tale or something?* Hatice thought mockingly. *The Sultan will come here to take me with him?!* She wanted to laugh. *Yeah... right... Is it possible?*

Of course not, she decided. It seemed that the disease had caused the Sultana to lose her mind. She tried to smile to show her that she believed these words. "But where My Lady? Where will the Padishah take me?"

"To the New Palace!"

"But it's impossible!" she blurted out.

"It is possible."

"I... I... I will never go back there!"

Bony fingers stretched toward her. They grabbed her wrist and jerked her closer. Hatice was surprised by the strength of this woman, who already stood in death's doorway.

"You will go back..." Safiye panted heavily.

Hatice shook her head. "Yesterday," she whispered in the Sultana's ear, "something terrible happened. You don't know about it yet –"

"We know!"

She knows? How come? I did not tell her anything!

"We're sorry for the girl."

And yet, she knew. But from where?

As always, when stupid thoughts appeared in her mind, her reason spoke: *Did you forget that she spent her whole life there? Who knows how many trusted people she still has there?*

Right. They probably told her immediately about the murder of Eftalya.

"Do you know who ordered it, My Lady? And why?"

Safiye nodded. "You were their target."

Oh my God! Although it wasn't a surprise for her, she was far from sadness, fear, or anxiety. Only anger grew in her. She wanted to break away and leave, but she gave up.

"Right, and that's why I will never go back there. Next time, they won't make a mistake..."

The Sultana straightened on the bed with great effort. Hundreds of torches now lit up in her eyes, where there hadn't been the slightest spark of life before. "They will not kill..." she panted. "Nobody... will kill... the Sultan's wife!"

The Sultan's wife? Whom?

First, the fates play with me at will, and now my ears and brain are also mocking me? She said, 'the Sultan's wife.' Who did she mean? Me? Or maybe I heard what I wanted to hear?

"Who, Lady? What Sultan's wife did you mean? Her?"

"You," Safiye hissed. "You!" Her eyes widened so much that their whites turned slightly pink. "It's you, my child. You will be the Lady of that palace."

Hatice wrenched her hand from Safiye's grip and stood up. Now she panted just as much as the sick woman did.

Don't listen to that nonsense anymore, the voice in her head thundered angrily. *Can't you see she's crazy?* "Please, do not mislead me," she said quietly. "How can a maid become a Sultan's wife? And... And besides..."

"What?" Safiye snarled.

Maybe I will regret these words for the rest of my life, she thought. She tried as hard as possible to look at Safiye with warm eyes. "I gave up my dreams and fantasies!" she began. "I swear. I will also forget about that imaginary prophecy of some stupid, blind beggar. I don't want to be a queen anymore!" She swallowed. She didn't notice how Safiye measured her with a threatening look. "Here I saw that queens live side by side with death. They kill to live. Either they die themselves, or they kill... Isn't it so? I... Oh God, I gave her the ring... I convinced her to put it on –"

"Shut up!" Safiye yelled. There was great energy in her voice and gaze. It was hard to believe that just a moment ago, she wasn't able to speak. "Do not talk nonsense."

"I almost lost my life because of this stupid dream. It's because of me that an innocent girl died... And I... I... My God, I've already become a murderess, too. To a smiling woman, who had been so good to me." She crossed herself. "No... A servant will never become a Sultana, My Lady..."

"Stop talking nonsense, I'm telling you!" Safiye's voice was sharp like a knife. "You cannot escape your destiny, child. What had been written for you will happen."

"For me, it was the fate of a maid..." She realized she was crying. "A slave... A stupid maid who believed she could become a Sultana," she said, sobbing.

"Don't provoke your luck. Believe finally in the destiny that brought you all the way here. Do not try to oppose the divine plan!"

Divine or yours? The thought crossed Hatice's mind.

"It will be as we said," Safiye said firmly, staring at her. "You will become a Lady, the Sultana of that palace..."

Safiye's face writhed again in pain. The bony hand went quickly to the chest, and it stayed there. She barely breathed again. She slowly fell back on the bed. She still tried to smile at Hatice.

"And now, go," she said. "Go and get ready. Padishah will take you from here."

"Are you going to have me killed?"

"Don't be afraid," she moaned. "Don't be afraid. I will entrust you to His Majesty. Until he makes you his favorite, you will remain under his protection. Nobody will harm a hair on your head. Even that cold highlander... And... never... never..."

She was breathing faster and faster. She closed her eyes. Hatice was scared that the Sultana was dying. She already wanted to run into the corridor and call for the doctors. But Safiye was determined to say what she wanted, to the end. Even at the expense of her life.

"Never... repeat my mistake..." she moaned. "Do everything at the right time... neither earlier nor later..." She fell silent. She drew air a few times. "And never again..." she hissed. "Never reject your destiny... Promise me this, Hatice... Swear!"

Hatice ran to Safiye's bedside again. She started crying.

"Your word?"

"My word!"

"You swear?"

"I swear!"

"Be patient... Until you become a Sultana. Promise?"

She knew it was stupid, but she repeated after her again through tears: "I promise!"

"Don't cry..." Safiye said in a weak voice. Talking was becoming more and more difficult for her. "My... revenge... Remember!"

She was breathing very quickly.

"Ring... Ring... She can't take it off! You understand?"

Hatice nodded.

"Promise me that..."

"I promise!"

"No taking off... Ring... no... ring..."

"She won't take it off!"

She is dying here, and you just sit and listen! Hatice's voice of reason reprimanded her. She wanted to get up. "I'll call the doctor, My Lady."

But Safiye did not want to let her go. "Relax. Until I see the Sultan and entrust the care of his future wife to him, I am not going anywhere!"

Hatice did not know what to do anymore. She did not even know if she was sad or happy. She was not sure if she believed all these unbelievable things. But despite everything, joy swirled somewhere deep inside her.

Joy at a dying person's bedside! She shuddered. That was unthinkable. What a great sin! But since she already felt this embarrassing joy, she must have believed the Sultana's assurances. Sultan Ahmed... The head of the Ottoman dynasty was already on his way... and he was to leave from here with her!

I must already be crazy, too.

"Go now," Safiye said suddenly. "Tonight... try to look beautiful. When the time comes... let everyone say that... Safiye Valide Sultan did not leave the Old Palace alive, but..." She fell silent. She'd run out of air again. "...she sent Hatice to the New Palace. The Ottomans called us a Great Sultana Mother, my child. Let them call you Kösem from now on, dear."

Kösem? She wanted to ask what it meant. But she did not manage to.

"Go!" Safiye said, trying to smile. "Get ready, Kösem. Go now!"

"They all have gone crazy," Hatice murmured.

And you haven't? Her reason mocked her. *You are the same, Hatice!*

She *was* crazy. Thinking about everything that had happened, what she had seen and heard, she could not disagree.

In one of the chambers of the Old Palace, the Sultana was dying. At the same time, in another one, the ladies of the dying woman's court went out of their way to make

Hatice look her most beautiful for the arrival of the Sultan so that she could enchant him.

There, people were busy around death, here around life.

"Faster, faster!" Semiha bustled among them. "You haven't even done her hair yet!"

She didn't understand anything that was happening around her. She was overcome with apathy.

If that's not madness, then what?

An innocent, young girl was killed, only because one woman was jealous of her – because she considered Hatice to be her mortal enemy.

And now, right before her eyes, Safiye Valide Sultan was being murdered... Safiye, whose name, fame and power had reached her ears even back on the Island of Milos. Worse, Safiye was being murdered on the order of her daughter-in-law, who did not want to share power with her mother-in-law. And on her deathbed, she'd made Hatice swear that she would carry through her revenge to the end. What kind of world was that?

Hatice had dreamed of the crown and a life in the palace only because it seemed to her that queens were always beautiful, that they sat on the throne in majesty, and that the glitter of the jewels in their crowns almost blinded the eyes of the beholders; she believed that queens were admired, loved, and respected by everyone. In her imagination, palaces were wonderful places that guaranteed all this splendor.

But now she had come face-to-face with a reality she had never suspected: the queens could also be ugly. And very much so. They looked around jealously, with an icy stare, from the height of their thrones. There was no glitter... She wasn't even sure if they were really admired and loved. She had no doubt, though, they were taken into account – because everyone was afraid of them – because, in the blink of an eye, queens could turn into murderers.

The alleged splendor of the palaces was also an illusion. Murderers circled their dark, secret corridors. There was an executioner behind every corner, just waiting for the nod of a king or a queen. No one who went to sleep at night could be sure that they'd see another sunrise. Not even kings and queens.

This was the reality here – fear and death. How could one come to terms with such a life?

And yet... Everything has its price. Apparently, the price of power was just that. To live constantly on the verge of death... And to live, you had to get rid of all scruples.

And you? spoke her mind again. *Are you ready to pay such a price?*

There was no end to the storm that had been raging in her heart for some time. One moment she'd say fearfully, "I don't want it, I can do without it," ready to give up her dreams, then in another moment, she would grip them again with all her strength. Sometimes, reason told her, 'Run away from here!' If, however, she was told now, 'Go away, you are free,' she' probably not be able to do it.

Well, but what will happen to me?

The Padishah was to appear here at any moment – assuming, of course, that this wasn't just the delirium of a dying woman. His icy wife, the mother of his only son, who seethed with jealousy, already waited for her with her executioners.

The Queen of Ice did not care that she was a Sultana, while Hatice was just an ordinary slave, a maidservant.

Hatice was more beautiful. Much more beautiful. She understood that Hatice could easily take Ahmed from her. So Hatice had to die.

That was the price she might have to pay. Life. She could die in pursuit of a dream.

And this was the time to decide.

The Sultan was already on his way. He was to take her from here to the New Palace. To the palace where death or a crown awaited her!

Hatice would either become scared of death and run away, betraying her dreams, or she would follow them.

Don't think about it anymore, said her reason. *Are you ready to pursue your dreams, even if the price for it might be your life?*

She felt so. "I'm ready," she whispered.

Have you considered death? You can die, but you can also kill. Will you be able to get rid of mercy completely?

What else could she do? Her fate called her. And from this, as Safiye Sultan said, there was no escape... Whatever is written for a man, will happen. But no one could know what it is before experiencing it. All she could do was to believe that a good God was preparing a great fate for her – the queen's fate.

And against all the odds, she believed it. Why else would the winds of destiny bring her all the way here? If she gave up her dreams and remained who she was, then what would she say to Eftalya when she asks her one day: 'So was my death in vain, Nastya?'

Yes. She was sure of it. She was ready. She decided to reject once and for all the ever-recurring doubt that disturbed the calmness of her spirit. She was ready to pay any price.

Maybe that's why the words of Safiye were still in her head: 'When the time comes... let everyone say that... Safiye Valide Sultan did not leave the Old Palace alive, but... she sent Hatice to the New Palace. The Ottomans called us a Great Sultana Mother, my child. Let them call you Kösem from now on.'

It is a pity that she did not explain what it meant.

Kösem. God, what a beautiful word.

She repeated it several times. *Kösem... Kösem...* The perfect name for a Sultana. *Kösem Sultan!*

It sounded so dignified. It inspired respect.

Kösem Sultan, she repeated once more. It means me! *Beautiful Hatice Kösem Sultan from Milos!*

What a pity that she didn't know what it meant. The Sultana did not give her the opportunity to ask.

"Go, get ready, Kösem Sultan. Go!"

She was just being prepared.

At first, she was taken to the hamam, almost by force. Petals of roses, jasmine, hyacinths, and many other flowers whose names she didn't even know were thrown into the water. The marble trough turned into a real floating garden.

Regardless of her objections that echoed throughout the vault of the bathhouse, she was not left alone. Warm water, taken from the trough with golden pots, was poured over her from head to toe. Leaves and flowers stuck in her hair and on her bare shoulders. She felt soaked by their fragrance. She almost felt dizzy from it as she was being wiped dry.

Then Hayganoş Kalfa appeared with her assistants. They were in an even greater hurry than usual.

"I said hurry up, don't you understand? Someone bring the purple bundle, run!"

The 'purple bundle' were a phrase she'd heard from time to time in the dressmakers' conversations, ever since Safiye Sultan had mobilized them to prepare for her wardrobe. It was the secret that had been hidden from her. There was probably some special kaftan in the bundle. One that she'd not seen or even tried before. It was shown only to Safiye Valide Sultan, then carefully folded, wrapped into a bundle, and put away for later.

And just now Hayganoş ordered her assistant to bring it. She was going to learn the secret of the 'purple bundle' this night.

I wonder what else will be explained today? Hatice thought.

It could be today, for example, that the thread keeping Safiye Sultan alive might be cut.

Or her dreams. Destiny surprised her when she was completely unprepared for it. She had just experienced an amazing fear – Azrael brushed her with his wings. She was panicked. Sad. Weary. Despite her unlimited ambition, both her spirit and body were tired of pursuing that prophecy.

And most importantly, because of the recent experiences, she'd lost some of her beauty... Perhaps even more than some. All the efforts of the girls who were now busy with her would probably be wasted. Sultan Ahmed won't like her, she was almost sure. He would probably wince his face, disappointed. 'So, this is the girl whose beauty even the fairies are supposedly jealous of?' He would abstain from taking her to the New Palace, and his grandmother's words would not be fulfilled. And even if he took her, it would only be to keep the promise given to a dying woman. He would put her away in some corner there and forget her completely. She would be one of those lonely and unhappy girls, of whom she saw hundreds in the palace.

"Death will make no mistake this time..."

"What are you mumbling there, my dear? What did you say?"

"What?"

"It seemed to me that you said something. Death...?"

"No..." she denied. She'd unconsciously spoke her thoughts aloud. "I'm just praying for health for our Lady."

"May Allah grant her life, may Allah..." Hayganoş picked up.

"May Allah return the Sultana to those who love her, and to all those she loves," the girl who was combing her hair added.

Those who love her and those she loves?

She'd never thought about it. *Indeed... Who really loves Safiye Sultan? Her daughter-in-law Handan, whom she suspects of assassinating her? Or maybe the daughter-in-law of her daughter-in-law – the Ice Queen? Her grandson the Padishah? The crowds of Viziers, Pashas, and Beys? Ladies of the court? People?*

Nobody, her mind answered. *None of them. In reality, nobody loves her.*

And her? Whom does Safiye love?

Nobody, either.

That's not true, she protested fervently. *She loves me! I don't know why, but she loves me...*

It's hard to call it love. She's doomed you.

Why?

You are her tool, that's why.

What nonsense... What tool?

A tool for revenge. A tool that, even after her death, will be faithful to her orders to never give up vengeance.

That's true... Maybe that's why she became interested in me so suddenly. When she secretly watched me, she had to see something in me. Something she had been looking for. That was the real reason Safiye wanted to make me a Sultana. She wanted a tool in the palace that would take revenge on her enemies.

Do you agree to that?

This time, it was not her reason that asked her a question. It was a strange, cunning voice she had never heard before. A dangerous whisper that resembled a hiss of a snake. *Agree? But to what?*

That Safiye will put you in the palace as a tool of revenge?

Who did that voice belong to? A voice of something, whose presence she had been feeling in her head for some time, but what she couldn't name in any way? It must be something dangerous, something terrifying, and cunning. Something restless. Something similar to a snake or a scorpion; something treacherous. Or something like the octopus she once saw in the hands of a fisherman at Milos, which terrified her from the first sight.

She shivered as she recalled that scene in her mind. *Yes, it must be an octopus! It's attached its repulsive tentacles to my brain and sucked out my thoughts. It's consumed my conscience, destroyed my mind. It wants to leave only hatred and ambition in my soul, sucking and destroying the rest.*

Answer me! the octopus hissed. It turned its spherical head with hideous, bulging eyes toward her. *Do you agree to Safiye placing you in the palace as a tool of revenge?*

Did she agree?

Anger raged in her.

If I am to be Kösem Sultan, then yes! Do you understand? Yes, if I am to become a queen! Leave me alone!

The octopus moved its tentacles. She could almost see its suction cups, how they opened and closed. *It's swimming away.* She was glad. It was indeed swimming away. But it would be back again; Hatice had no doubt that from now on, she would often have to endure its presence.

One day, someone will wonder, just like she does now: 'Who really loves Kösem Sultan?'

The answer will be the same – no one. That was how it worked. The queens were forbidden to love and be loved!

Hatice suddenly emerged from the stormy sea that had seized her for a while.

"Hayganoş..." she asked the Kalfa, who was rubbing her hands as she waited impatiently for the girls to bring the purple bundle. "What does it mean – Kösem?"

"Kösem?"

"Yes..."

"You said 'Kösem'? And you ask Hayganoş about something like that? Do you think she knows?"

"And she doesn't?"

The woman stared at one point as if she thought deeply about something.

"Kösem, Kösem..." she repeated several times. "This name probably means something. And something very beautiful. You understand?"

She didn't understand. Her unquenched curiosity only sharpened even more. She looked intently into the woman's eyes.

"Or maybe, you just don't want to tell me, Kalfa?"

"Finally, finally! Here!"

Hatice forgot about the secret of her new name for a moment and jumped to her feet.

"What? He has already arrived? Mother of God, I'm not ready yet!"

The women in the room giggled.

"I didn't mean the Sultan, honey. I was talking about the bundle."

Hatice blushed, embarrassed. She became impatient as one of the dressmakers unpacked the bundle. She was about to learn the secret of Safiye Sultan and her main dressmaker.

Hayganoş approached the bundle and put her hands on it with such tenderness as if she wanted to take a child from the cradle into her arms.

She took out from it the most beautiful thing Hatice had ever seen in her life.

"Oh my God! Hayganoş... That, that..." She did not have words to describe what she saw.

"This is the kaftan," the radiant Hayganoş began solemnly, "which Sultana Valide Safiye wore when she first stood before the late Sultan, Mehmed Khan."

She was ready. The Sultan could appear at any moment now.

The dressmakers did everything they could to make her look great tonight. Was she beautiful?

Judging by the cries of delight made by Sofia, the courtiers, and the dressmaker's assistants – yes. But she was not completely convinced. Hatice looked at herself in the silver mirror for a long moment but still couldn't decide.

It seemed to her that she looked much better the previous time.

No wonder... What I went through in the New Palace could not fail to affect my appearance, she thought with regret. *God be my witness, fear clings to my face like a mask. Shadows have appeared under my eyes... and my eyes are bloodshot from crying. But it will have to do,* she thought resignedly. That's what Sultan Ahmed would see her like. Not much could be done about it.

Perhaps she had reservations about her appearance, but as she regarded the outfit, she didn't have the slightest doubt – it was wonderful. She had not seen anything like it before.

It was like a dream.

Magical.

She stroked it. The whole kaftan was covered with hundreds, maybe even thousands of tiny, white flowers, crocheted on light-yellow chiffon. *Is this really happening? The kaftan of the golden odalisque Safiye Sultan on her; a slave from Milos... It's a pity my mother cannot see me now*, she thought. Her eyes glazed, and she sniffed. *And my father, Mirna Abla... And Şarazad... Mürüvvet... And... ah, my beloved, poor Eftalya!*

There was still no sight of the Padishah.

Maybe he wasn't going to come, after all. Maybe they only told Safiye he would, so as not to worry her on her deathbed? The day was over. The Old Palace looked as if it were covered with blue tulle. If the Sultan really were to come, he would've been here long ago.

Hatice felt unhappy. Fate was playing cat and mouse with her again. First, it whispered in her ear: 'Your king is coming. Your dreams will become true in a moment. He will come through this door and take you to his palace, where you will become a Sultana. Kösem Sultan. Hatice Kösem Sultan!'

And when inspired by this whisper, she was ready to spread her sails to glide out to meet her happiness, fate laughed in her face: 'Don't wait in vain. He will not come. Stupid servant... Did you really believe such a lie? The Great Sultan, bothering to come here, especially for you?'

Right. It was impossible!

There was going to be no continuation. She sensed it with her whole being. To get so close to your goal and suddenly lose everything... It was terrible. If the prophecy was to really come true, and she was to become Kösem Sultan, it could only happen during Safiye's lifetime. Otherwise, there will be no hope for her, and the fairy tale of a prince who arrives on a white horse for a beautiful girl and takes her to his palace was to end under this window. And no one would say: 'And then they lived happily ever after...'

While she waited for her prince here, Azrael might eventually lose his patience. Silently, he could enter the great chamber at the end of the corridor and take the soul of Safiye Sultan under his black wings, and carry it away with him. With her gone, all of Hatice's dreams and her future would also be lost. Who knows, maybe even her life? Because how long can the knight who'd lost his shield still stay alive? Safiye Valide Sultan had appeared unexpectedly on her path, and announced the wonderful news: 'Your dreams will come true!' But that was not all. Only now did she realize that Safiye was also her guardian angel. When she is no longer here, who will save her from the Ice Queen's thugs?

Semiha's reflection appeared in the glass.

Hatice turned to her. "How does our Lady feel?" Her heart went to her throat. She was afraid that she would hear the worst.

"She's holding on," Semiha replied. "At least she's better than in the morning. I hope she will get better."

Hatice crossed herself. "I am praying for it all the time."

"If only you could see how she's fighting... It's as if she has unfinished business here. She expects the Padishah. She wanted a hairdo. She chose the kaftan to wear and wanted us to move her onto the sofa, saying, 'We will not be lying down in front of His Majesty, even if he's our grandson!' Every now and then she also repeats the name 'Kösem.'"

Kösem!

"Do you know what it means, Semiha?"

Despite all the sadness and anxiety that the woman was experiencing, a faint smile crossed her face. "I don't know..."

"Please... I'm sure you know. Safiye Valide Sultan today gave –"

"I know, but I can't tell you."

"Why? Is it a secret?"

Semiha looked at her maliciously this time. Hatice felt the woman's index finger on her lips.

"Shhh... A little patience, my dear... First, let the Sultan come. You'll find it out at the right time, not sooner."

What was that supposed to mean? All this was absurd. The palace loved these kinds of secrets; meaningful half-words.

"Will he be the one to tell me what the name means?"

With her hand, Semiha acted out closing her mouth with a padlock. "For now, we wait for His Highness."

"He seems to be taking his time." She turned back to the window again. In the glass, she also saw Semiha's reflection next to hers. And behind her, the darkness of the night enveloping the capital. "He probably won't come; it's too late."

Nervous, she wanted to sit on the sofa, which stood to the side. The dressmaker's helpers panicked when they understood what she wanted to do.

"Stop! There is no sitting, no sitting!"

"Why? I've been standing up like a peg for so many hours, my legs are sore already."

"The kaftan will crumple if you sit down!"

"So, what? And to whom would I show myself in it? Why did you even dress me in it?"

One of the girls grabbed her hand and tried to pull her away from the sofa. Still complaining, she began to walk around the room. Out of the corner of her eye, she looked at the window in which her gorgeous kaftan was reflecting.

Indeed, she looked like a queen. Or a bride.

In the glass, she saw not a dream, but a real Sultana. *Hatice Kösem Sultan*. But there was no Padishah!

She approached the window. She wanted to look at her face again.

Suddenly, she saw something like a bunch of fireflies hovering in the dark.

At first, she was surprised that she could see them at all because they were quite far away. After a moment, she saw them lining up in rows. Two rows of fireflies, arranged in lines, one after the other. *So many of them*.

"Look at that!" she called to Semiha. "Hundreds of fireflies, heading in our direction..." Then Hatice understood what these fireflies were before the woman approached her. "It's torches!" she shouted. "Hundreds of torches!"

They all ran to the window.

"It's him, the Sultan is coming!"

"Padishah!"

Emotion took Hatice's breath away. She thought she would suffocate in a moment.

The torches were indeed approaching the palace. *He is there, too!* She wanted to scream with joy. *My beautiful prince comes here for me!*

Semiha rushed to the door. "I will inform the Sultana."

"Wait!" Hatice ran after her. "And I... what should I do?"

"You wait here!" she replied and disappeared at the door in an instant.

"You wait," she muttered under her breath, going back to the window. "Wait for the arrival of the fireflies."

The window now reflected the bright red-yellowish glow of the torches held by the soldiers who filled the courtyard. There was a clatter of horseshoes. Hatice's throat became dry from the excitement. In just a moment, she was about to see the Sultan for the first time.

She imagined him coming through the gate on a white horse. He'd lift his head, look up, and catch a glimpse of her through the window. He would see her and fall in love at first sight, then jump off the horse and run toward the stairs.

The scene, however, played out completely different. The courtyard was full of soldiers, but no one among them looked like a Sultan. Soldiers on the right side of the row held torches. The others held long spears raised up, with red, white, and green ribbons fluttering on them.

In the light of the torches, the red uniforms, white felt hats, soldiers, and horses looked like in a dream, but Sultan Ahmed was not among them.

"Where is he? I can't see him..."

Right, because if you see him, you will certainly recognize him, the little internal voice mocked her.

Of course, I will, she replied to it. *The highest, the most handsome of all, the most majestic...*

For weren't the kings like that in all the fairy tales she had heard in her life? The kings were always handsome in them, and the queens were beautiful like fairies.

"This girl will kill me someday," groaned Hayganoş. "She's looking for the Sultan in the backyard, among his servants..."

"His Majesty will not enter the palace from the back, will he? He will enter through the main gate, of course," one of the ladies of the court replied, trying to be smart.

At another time, Hatice wouldn't leave the wisecrack to hang without response, but right now she didn't care – the King had arrived. The fairy tale continued; nothing else mattered.

In a moment, the door would open, and he would come here. The Sultan would freeze for a moment, enchanted with her beauty, and then kneel in front of her. 'I came for you, fairy.'

And she would throw herself in his arms.

The Sultan would take her in his arms and carry her downstairs. There would already be a white steed waiting for them there, not tethered by grooms. Ahmed would jump on it, then he would pull her up behind him. The horse would stand up and gallop. The wind would blow its mane, and her hair would strike the Sultan's beautiful face.

And then... old women would tell tales about her to their grandchildren. All of them should end in the same way: 'Hatice fulfilled her dreams, and then they lived happily ever after. It's time to sleep!' And the little girls, as they place their heads on pillows, will look at the stars blinking above them, and dream about the fairy Hatice and her beautiful prince before falling asleep. And their mothers would beg God to let the happy fate of the Sultana Hatice also become their beloved daughters' fate.

In the glow cast by the torches, the reflection of her face in the windowpane also reddened. So, did her white and bright yellow kaftan. *I'm beautiful*, she thought. *Like a fairy*.

She slowly turned away from the window toward the door, through which Sultan Ahmed was surely about to enter.

Although the scene of the prince's arrival was different than in her imagination, the next one would certainly happen the way she'd imagined it hundreds of times – the first sight and encounter. She folded her hands on her stomach and stood sideways.

Sofia watched her, delighted. "My beautiful sister!" she said as usual.

She also heard a whisper from one of the girls: "What a wonderful silhouette, what a beauty!" Next, she heard the sounds made by Hayganoş, who spat in all directions, trying to drive away the evil powers that could cast a spell on her.

What she heard, and saw was of no importance. The most important thing now was something else. She wanted the door to open and let the Padishah stand in it and fall in love with her at first sight.

He should be charmed by her eyebrows and eyelashes, and her lips; her slender figure and full breasts, as well as her legs that were only covered with thin chiffon.

As soon as he saw her, he should throw himself, his body, frozen in ice, into her arms to warm his body with her fire.

What's that supposed to mean? Her inner voice spoke suddenly. *You only keep thinking about how he will like you. And what about you? Aren't you curious if you will like him?*

And what if I don't like him? Hatice mused.

What did she know about him? Only that he was the same age as her. *He's probably even a few months younger than me,* she added in her mind.

She wondered what he was like. What if he was short, thick, and with crooked teeth? Or scraggy and tall?

And what if his mouth smelled bad like Cyprian's, whom she bit on the ear in the carriage?

What if he was hairy?

What if she abhorred him?

She was surprised that she didn't care about the answers to those questions. How was this possible? It really didn't matter to her whether he was short or tall, fat or emaciated, blind or mute?

It doesn't matter, her mind reprimanded her. *He's the Padishah. If a man is a Sultan, it does not matter what he looks like.*

And if I don't fall in love with him?

Then don't. The most important thing is that he should love you. He has to worship you!

Yes, that was the most important thing. That's how it was supposed to be. *After all, I will not reject him just because I don't like him!* She even smiled at such a thought. After all, he had something that was much more important than appearance – the throne, crown, and power. Whatever he looked like, Ahmed was the only man who could provide it to her.

She regained hope again. It will be as the blind beggar foretold. She will become a queen.

It will be as Safiye Sultan told her. She will become the Sultana of the New Palace – Hatice Kösem Sultan.

She waited for the door to open.

Five minutes... Ten... A quarter hour... Half an hour... And nothing happened. Impatience, fear, and anxiety consumed her from the inside.

Come on, she called him in her mind. *Come here, sir. Open this door and see your Kösem*.

She almost fainted when footsteps sounded outside.

Behold, the king was coming. Sultan Ahmed was coming here for her. She stared at the door and stretched her lips into her most beautiful, most charming smile. The steps were very close.

Blessed lady, she began to pray. *Help your daughter!*

The knob at the door turned very slowly. It opened.

Semiha stood in the doorway.

Hatice did not even have time to curse in her spirit and become upset, because the woman immediately gestured at her. "Come. They are waiting for you."

As she walked, she fell deep into thought. *Who is waiting for me there... who?*

"What's happening, Semiha? For God's sake, tell me. Who is waiting for me... the Sultan?"

"This is not the time for questions. You will find all the answers behind this door."

Tall guardians stood on both its sides. Their heads almost reached the ceiling. They both wore hauberks and pointed helmets. The eyes of each of them, separated by a piece of metal covering the nose, resembled fireballs. They stood so still that it was difficult to say whether they were alive at all. They were scary, even though they did not have any weapons. It seemed strange to her.

Why would they need weapons? her mind asked mockingly. *Have you seen them? Do they look like somebody who needs a weapon?*

Of course not. They were walking weapons themselves, after all. She looked at their fists as big as a bunch of grapes. Certainly, it wouldn't be a problem for them to crush someone's bones into powder. It seemed that they could even kill with just a look. Hatice did not dare to look them in the eyes.

The door wings slowly began to open.

Her king waited for her just behind them.

Hatice silently ordered herself to do a lot of things: *Enter so that your very entrance will drive him crazy. Then smile so brilliantly that he thinks that it's the sun rising in the night. Look at him so that the ice that bound his masculinity in the embrace of Mahfiruz melts under your smoldering gaze.*

She saw several ladies of Handan Valide Sultan's court. She grew nervous, almost panicked. *So, she came. Is Mahfiruz here, too?* One to see the death of her mother-in-law, the other, the victim who slipped out of her hands. Hatice scanned the courtiers, looking for Taciser among them. She did not see her.

Instead, an elderly woman stood in front of her. In her youth, she must have been very beautiful. In fact, she still was. A white shawl fell from her head to her waist. The old woman stuck her little blue eyes on her.

But where is he? Where is my King?

Hatice was already almost inside, but she still did not see Sultan Ahmed. She took two more steps. The door opened wider, and a large sofa appeared before her eyes. They were sitting on it...

Two Valide Sultans – Safiye and Handan.

The Great Sultana Mother and Little Sultana Mother; the mother-in-law victim and daughter-in-law murderess!

Safiye was surrounded by a lot of fluffy pillows. One could get the impression that if the pillows were taken away, the Sultana would collapse without support. She'd put on a red kaftan for the occasion. A fur was thrown over her shoulders. Her head was almost completely exposed, with her hair partially covered by tulle in a golden color, pinned with a decorative ivory comb. She sat cross-legged with the long edges of the fur gathered on her knees.

Hatice remembered the words of her main courtier, who'd confessed that the Sultana seemed to have freed herself from the embrace of death for good. And she indeed looked like that. She was pale but happy. Hatice knew, however, that it was just an illusion.

The murderess stood right next to her. Safiye did everything not to be defeated and tried to savor the last game in which she had to face her opponent.

Handan Valide Sultan had looked toward the door with a big smile. Where was that smile coming from? Did she rejoice that she would soon stand at the grave of the woman whom she had earlier ordered someone to kill? Or maybe she was smiling at her?

Hatice crossed the threshold of the chamber. The beautiful elderly woman gestured for her to stop.

"Wait, my child," she said in a soft but firm voice.

She paused.

For the hundredth time, she began to repeat all the prayers she knew. *Our Father... Lord Jesus... Blessed Lady... Help your daughter!*

The old woman nodded slightly and invited her inside.

Hatice walked toward the door. As she crossed the threshold, the woman whispered to her, "On the right. Do you know how to greet His Highness the Padishah? Do you know how to behave?"

Ah! Finally!

His Highness... Padishah... King. So, Sultan Ahmed, who was to make her Hatice Kösem Sultan, was here. On the right.

"I know, ma'am."

The woman smiled kindly. "May Allah guide you, my child."

Bending over, she stepped over the threshold. For a moment, her gaze met the eyes of Safiye. She saw her tired face light up with a smile.

She noticed something else. A sign: Safiye was running the index finger of her right hand along her left ring finger. She wanted to draw her attention to the ring – the ring on Handan's finger.

As Hatice greeted Handan, she looked at her longer than she should. The Valide Sultan answered her with a smile. Hatice thought, however, that there was a surprise behind it. The ring! Good God... she had the ring on her finger.

Turning to the right, her eyes met Safiye's gaze again. The Sultana was weak but happy, and her lips moved as if to thank her. Or maybe she just prayed?

Focus! Hatice reminded herself. *You are standing before the Sultan. Focus only on this. Everything depends on this single moment now, do you understand?*

She understood, perfectly. She turned to the right.

The Padishah! Sultan Ahmed!

He was there – the beautiful prince from her dreams. Her king.

He stood in front of a high window, with his back to her. He did not have a turban on his head. That pleased her. She couldn't get used to those bizarre hats in any way. His hair was black and short. He was dressed in a sleeveless leather jacket with sleeves from a silvery shirt underneath, lined with a fur hem. He looked out of the window, with his hands resting on his hips.

So that's how he greets me? She suddenly boiled with anger.

Calm down, do not lose your temper under any circumstances, her sense of reason immediately responded.

But he hasn't even looked at me!

It's his right. He is the Padishah. What did you expect? That he would ask where you have been for so long and throw himself at your neck?

But he must see me. He should look at me. Otherwise, how will he fall in love with me?

"My Lord..."

Her hot whispering, said in a sweet tone, resounded like thunder in the silence of the Sultana's apartment.

The Sultan lowered his hands along his body and began to turn toward her.

The Blessed Virgin... He's turning this way. He will look at me in a moment. He will see me...

She bowed with dignity. She doubted for a moment... should she indeed just bow like that? Maybe she should fall to the ground completely? But it was too late.

Even if she wanted to, she would not be able to do it. The Sultan was probably already looking at her.

It's even better like this, she finally decided. If she fell to the ground in front of him, the first thing he would see would be her hunched back. At least like this, he had her wonderful kaftan in front of his eyes, her hair falling over her shoulders like a waterfall, her slender waist, and figure. She put one hand on her heart. *So that I can catch it when it pops out of my chest*, she thought. She had no doubt that this would be the case if this silence would last any longer. Her heart could not endure this tension any longer: it would either jump out or stop completely.

"Stand up; we want to see your face."

God, what a haughty voice, her pride spoke again.

That's how the Sultan is used to addressing his servants. You are a servant, she scolded herself silently. *A slave. It takes just one of his orders: behead her! And you're gone. Who do you think you are?*

She carried out the order of the Sultan. Slowly, she straightened up. She raised her head high.

She turned to the side in an imperceptible move because she knew that she was better presented in this way. She folded her hands and rested them on the kaftan below her waist. Now she stood as befits a queen.

Your fate is in the balance now, Hatice, she thought.

She could not see the Sultan, because her eyes were all the time pointed at the ground.

She guessed that he must be looking at her now. Evaluating her.

Did he like her? She didn't know.

No reaction. *Damn it! How long will this silence last?*

Come on, she prompted the Sultan in her thoughts as if he could hear her. *Say, 'God, I've never seen someone so beautiful. Ah, I fell in love with you, fairy!' Say, 'You've warmed me, you've freed me from the embrace of the ice!'*

But the Sultan remained silent. Suddenly she heard Ahmed move. The rustling of his robes sounded to her right. No, just behind her. And now to the left.

It means... it means he is walking around me! She panicked and prayed with all her strength. *Blessed Virgin, Lord Jesus, I am begging you, I want the Sultan to like me. Let the Padishah love me!*

"This girl is taller than us."

Chapter Twenty-Two

Old Palace
January 9, 1605

She thought the world had collapsed over her head.

'This girl is taller than us,' was all he said.

Wake up! the voice in her head cried. *It's time to get up. It's over now. End of the dream. The end of the fairy tale. The King doesn't like you!*

So, this was the blow that her destiny had prepared for her in the end! It put her before the king from her dreams, let her believe that the fulfillment of the blind beggar's prophecy was at hand, and then... everything, just like that, collapsed on her head.

He does not like you!

And? Hatice thought proudly. *I haven't decided if I like him, either. If he says I'm too tall, he's probably very short, maybe even a dwarf. A fat, ugly, and stubby dwarf!*

She slowly raised her eyes and looked discreetly at the Sultan.

Oh Jesus! He's still a boy! The prince was still a child. No facial hair. Even though he already had a little fuzz under his nose, it was too early to call it a mustache. What could she say – he was a child.

But this child has a son already, she added in her mind.

Well, well... This time, the playful part of her nature came to the fore and silently giggled. *He isn't that bad. Maybe not as handsome as Slobodan, but he's not ugly either.*

They both looked at each other now. She sighed. Her eyes should now send sparks at him. She asked God to put the most captivating of her smiles on her face.

The behavior and the voice of the Padishah were haughty, but there was no trace of contempt in his eyes. He looked rather surprised. The reason for this growing amazement apparently was not the fact that the girl standing in front of him was taller than the ruler. His gaze was distracted, even dreamy. In his eyes, initially expressionless, a luminous rain now raged.

"The height of your humble servant does not stick out above the ground you tread on, My Lord."

She regretted her words as soon as they sounded. She hadn't planned them at all. Where did they come to her head from? Hadn't she been warned thousands of times to not speak without the Sultan's express permission?

However, she didn't stop at that. "And besides, isn't intelligence the most important thing?" she blurted out.

"Is it so?" Sultan Ahmed asked politely.

She was glad. She had rather expected an outburst of anger and words like, 'How dare this girl talk to us without being asked?!'

"In my country, people used to say that beauty is something temporary. It is here today; it will be gone tomorrow. Meanwhile, intelligence – reason – stays with a human throughout of his life. This is the greatest gift we have received from God. He gave some people less of it, more to others. A wise man is a rich man. And how rich he is – that is, how much intelligence he has – one can read in his eyes. Looking into the eyes of Your Majesty..." She was surprised that she was able to make such a speech without a single stumble.

She paused. This, in turn, had been planned. She looked down as if she were ashamed. She clenched her teeth firmly. She hoped that it would make her face red.

"Yes? Looking into our eyes..."

Ahmed must have been very close now, for his voice was right in front of her. She could see the tips of his shoes, very close to her feet. They almost touched.

"Go on."

"My Lord, forgive me that I have dared to look into your eyes," she whispered, close to fainting. This time it was not a game. She really felt that way. She was close to fainting at any moment because of fear and other strong emotions.

Suddenly, the Sultan's hand appeared in her sight. A nice, white hand, almost transparent, with slender fingers. Sparks from rubies and emeralds in a big ring hurt her eyes. The Sultan's hand slowly went to her chin.

It meant only one thing.

Hurray! He likes me, he likes me, he likes me, repeated in her head. *He likes me, he likes me!*

Sultan Ahmed lifted her chin. Embarrassed, she looked into his eyes.

"Go on," he repeated. "Do not be afraid. Anger is not deserved by one who dares to look straight into the eyes, but rather by one who is afraid of it. There might be a suspicion that he may be hiding something. Eyes are not good guardians of secrets; they will always tell the truth. This is what is said in our country..." He paused for a moment. "Besides, you should finish what you started. Looking into the eyes of Your Majesty... What's next? What is it in our eyes?"

They stood there staring at each other. Her breathing fast; she didn't want to hide her emotions.

"Looking into your eyes, My Lord," she began slowly and clearly, "I saw the most precious treasure in the world. Its glow blinded me. I thought then that the intelligence of Your Majesty cannot have an equal in this world."

Sultan Ahmed nodded thoughtfully. *Really?* he thought at the same moment.

He likes me! Hatice continued to triumph. It was clearly seen in his gaze. He was thinking and looking at her. She had no doubt that he was watching her closely. Her hair, eyes, lips, and neck – of which swans could be envious. Her narrow, round arms, her bosom – with her breasts defiantly marking their presence under the chiffon – a slim figure, hips, and her legs, not completely covered by tulle.

Hurray! He likes me... He likes me... He likes me!

And he? Do you like him? True, he was shorter than her. The ribald voice spoke again: *Well, well... He's not bad. You can actually say he is handsome. Slobodan was great, but he was just a groomsman. And Ahmed is both handsome and...Oh, God... He is the King... your King!*

His pale skin was surely inherited from his mother. Other than that, she could find no other similarity to Handan. His hair, as she had seen before, was short and black; his forehead was narrow. She noticed a red line passing over the eyebrows across his entire forehead. She immediately guessed it was a mark from the turban. She thanked God that for their first meeting, God had put him in front of her without a turban. She just couldn't get used to them, especially to the tall ones.

She caught herself wondering what Ahmed's turban looked like. A murmur in her head sounded instantly.

What do you care? Whatever it looks like, it's none of your business! She, however, kept thinking: *He would look better in something oblong.* One could not see then that he was shorter than her. She decided that when the time came, she had to persuade him to get something like that.

"And the beauty?" the Sultan asked softly. He did not take his eyes off her. Breathing was clearly difficult for him.

"Pardon, My Lord?"

"I asked about beauty. Did your fathers say nothing about it?"

Her face lit up with a smile. "About beauty, right?"

She hoped her cheeks were red again. She wanted to lower her head again, but he wouldn't allow it as he held her by her chin.

"Of course, they did, My Lord," she answered quietly. "They said that..." she paused as if she hesitated to continue. This time she did not give him the opportunity to make her continue. She looked at him closely. "Beauty," she spoke again, "deprived of reason is an illusion that can dissolve."

"There is no doubt that you had wise fathers!"

She looked at him through her eyelashes to check if he wasn't making fun of her. No, she saw only fire in his eyes.

"What if beauty goes hand in hand with reason and intelligence? Did they say something about that, too?"

This time, she couldn't stand his look and lowered her head, even though the Sultan's fingers were still on her chin.

"My Lord..." she whispered like an embarrassed girl. "Forgive me... This... this... me..."

Sultan Ahmed suddenly turned to his mother and Safiye Sultan. "You were right, Grandmother. The mind of this girl matches her beauty. You cannot fault them!"

She heard Safiye say something in a weak voice, but Hatice didn't understand what.

It did not matter anymore. At the moment, only one sentence rang in her ears: 'Her mind matches her beauty.'

Hurray! She was happy once again. *He likes me, he likes me, he likes me! He likes me... I'm both beautiful and smart... I'm beautiful and smart!*

The Sultan touched her face again. This time, it was more of a brush. A small caress. "What's your name?"

Oh no... she moaned in her heart, as always when she was asked that question. *What should I answer him?* Should she give the name Hatice, which was given to her the first night in the Novice Courtyard? She'd disliked that name from the beginning. And since she had learned that the Ice Queen's name was the same, she had even started to hate it. What was she supposed to answer the Sultan? That she had the same name as his wife, the icy murderess? Or maybe, without looking at anything, she should introduce herself with her real name?

Don't push your luck! her mind warned her.

"Am I to understand that you will not tell us your name?"

"Hatice," she answered reluctantly. "My name is Hatice..."

"Did you hear that Mother?" he asked, turning to Handan. "Fate put another Hatice in our path."

"Coincidence," she replied. "I noticed that, too..."

Ahmed turned back to her with a smile. "Did you know that the mother of our firstborn also has that name?"

Come what may... Rebellion grew in her. *He won't order someone to behead me for this, after all. He likes me. Whatever, if they want to behead me, they can go ahead and do it.*

"But my real name is different," she said boldly. "My Lord," she added immediately when she realized that she had forgotten the honorific.

"So, what is your real name?"

"Anastasia, My Lord... Anastasia. But everybody called me Nastya."

"Nastya..." the Sultan repeated after her. He was thinking. Their eyes met again. "You should have a different name. Doesn't such a beauty, shining like the moon, deserve of a name equally luminous and shimmering with glitter as herself?"

There were whispers in the chamber: "Deserves, deserves."

Torches burned in the eyes of Sultan Ahmed. It was the first time that a man had looked at her that way. She flinched. She was sure of it already. She'd charmed him. He was captivated by her.

"Well, then," he said almost affectionately. "One Hatice in our harem is enough. So, you are no longer Hatice or Anastasia. From now on, we will call you Mahpeyker. Everyone will know and remember you by this name. It describes you well, I think. It means 'beautiful, with a moonlike face – light, pale, and full.'"

Mahpeyker?

Mahpeyker!

Mahpeyker Sultan!

Wonderful, she thought. Mahpeyker counters Mahfiruz. Just as the Ice Queen has a face of stone, hers shines like the moon. She is the Queen illuminating the darkness... Mahpeyker Sultan.

"Do you like it?"

"My Lord..."

The Padishah turned suddenly toward the door. "Daye?"

Who is that?

The woman, who had wished her luck before entering the room, appeared next to her. "At your services, My Lord."

"Mahpeyker will immediately move to the New Palace. Send a message; let them prepare a suitable place for her in the Haseki Hall even before she sets off."

What is all that supposed to mean? Is it good or bad? Judging by the fact that Ahmed isn't taking his delighted eyes off me, it should be good...

But was it really? Who was she supposed to become now? She'd dreamed of becoming a Sultana, but was she going back to the palace as a maid again? Apparently, yes. *Damn it. It was not supposed to be like that...*

The Sultan's words still rang in her ears: '*Let them prepare a suitable place for her in the Haseki Hall.*'

'A suitable place!' What is behind those words? It's obvious. Ahmed meant: 'Prepare a place suitable for a maid.' Oh God, what if he assigned me to the servants of this murderess? No way! I will never agree to that!

The woman he called Daye was also surprised by the Sultan's words. "Whatever you order, My Lord," she replied.

"You'll be with her from now on, Daye. Take care of her. Make sure she will have everything she needs."

The woman looked at her, indicating that they should leave now.

"My Lord..." Mahpeyker began in a whisper.

She knew what she wanted to say to the Sultan: *I'm not going anywhere. I cannot serve this viper. Your son's mother... she will kill me! Besides, I cannot leave here.*

Safiye Sultan is dying. She is convinced that your mother poisoned her... and your icy wife killed my Eftalya instead of me. There... there is death in those corridors... You called me Mahpeyker, Lord. Please, let Mahpeyker shine with her glow here. I cannot become a Sultana like I dreamed, so at least let me stay alive."

She hesitated, however, after his last words: 'Take care of her. Make sure she will have everything she needs.'

Why would an elderly woman look after her? Was she supposed to make sure she didn't run away? After all, there was a whole army of guards for that.

And even if so, why was she supposed to make sure that the maid has all she needs? The darkness that overwhelmed her soul so suddenly disappeared just as quickly.

In that case, the words of the Padishah must be understood differently, she concluded.

Her eyes ran toward Safiye. She must have certainly understood what his words meant. Triumph shone in her eyes. Her gaze said, 'Go! Go, Sultana Mahpeyker Kösem!'

Padishah touched her cheek gently.

"This night," he began in a soft, sad voice, "sadness, bitterness, and fear fall on us, Mahpeyker. You know that our grandmother is seriously ill. The doctor says that she will not see the morning. We are lucky we have listened to her and sent for you. We forgot about our sadness for a moment. You brightened the darkness that enveloped our soul. However, we do not want this sadness, bitterness, and sorrow to cast a shadow on your radiance. And now, go..."

Her destiny was commanding her to do it. She had to submit to it. No matter how the whole story would end.

Go, Mahpeyker, she repeated in her mind. God, how much she liked her new name. *Go, Mahpeyker Kösem. Your destiny is calling.*

As she crossed the threshold, she looked once again at Safiye.

She read a farewell in her eyes. She understood that she was seeing her for the last time. The Sultana was still running her fingers of her right hand along the ring finger of her left hand. The ring!

The smile on Handan's face, in turn, she took as a sign of surprise. But for what reason? She wasn't able to wonder about it for now.

She had seen the Sultan.

He liked her.

He gave her a name that praised her beauty. And from now on, she would be Mahpeyker.

She still didn't know what the name Kösem meant, though.

She was sure, however, that she would solve this mystery, too. When it was time.

"Come on, child. Come with me," gently urged Daye.

She curtsied on leaving. Both the Padishah and Valide Sultan Handan decided that the bow was addressed to them. They were wrong, however. She bowed to Safiye Sultan. With gratitude.

She turned away and went to meet her destiny. She could feel joy growing in her. And fear.

She didn't see Handan approach her son, or hear her words: "We thought you would entrust her with the girls in the harem. In fact, we are very surprised by your decision, Son. I am afraid Mahfiruz will not be happy about it."

She didn't hear the Sultan's answer either: "We have been chilled to the bone, Mother. We need a fire that will warm us from within."

Chapter Twenty-Three

New Palace, Haseki Hall
January 9, 1605, Midnight

Three people sat in the carriage – Hatice, Sofia, and Daye. Daye and Sofia took their seats opposite her. The older woman didn't let it show, but she was aware that Mahpeyker eyed her from the top of her head to the pompons on her shoes. Sofia, on the other hand, was silent. The girl succumbed to the magic of these constant trips to the New Palace. This time, however, more than curiosity, one could read anxiety in her eyes.

Isn't she right? Hatice thought. *You don't even know where they are taking you.*

Of course, I do, she protested. *To the palace.* Suddenly, she remembered the words of Safiye Sultan. *To my palace... I will soon be a Sultana in it!*

*Oh, I se*e, her reason said, mocking her. *In the same palace that already swarms with Sultanas?*

The glow of torches held by the guard, which rode on both sides of the carriage, penetrated inside, dispersing the darkness there with an ominous bright red light.

God only knows how much she liked this new name. She could lose her head for the Sultan just because he called her that way. The words of Ahmed kept ringing in her ears: 'From now on, we will call you Mahpeyker. Everyone will know and remember you by this name.'

Even I've already gotten used to it, she thought. She decided she would not think of herself other than as Mahpeyker from now on. She would soak that name down to the marrow of her bones. Mahpeyker! This is it! Everything inside her was mad with joy. The King gave a new name to his Queen. Mahpeyker... Mahpeyker Sultan.

Her mind, however, told her otherwise. *Do not fool yourself... what Sultana? There is already Handan Valide Sultan in the palace. And... the murderess Queen Mahfiruz...*

She only shrugged her shoulders in response. *Let them be. They will pass sooner or later. Only Mahpeyker will stay.*

"Yes, my child?" Daye asked from her seat, leaning slightly toward her. "Do you need something?"

"Me? No... why?"

The calm smile on the woman's face disappeared for a moment. "In that case, I had to have heard wrong. Oh, the old age... It seemed to me that you said Mahpeyker."

The sadness that appeared on the woman's face caught her heart. She liked her. "You heard it right," she answered immediately. "Indeed, I said Mahpeyker. I'm trying to get used to my new name. That's why I keep repeating it to myself..."

The smile returned to Daye's face in an instant. "Do you like it?"

"Very much! I hated Hatice!"

"Shhh!" Daye whispered nervously. "Do not say that, child. You know that name is the first name of the Sultan's wedded wife."

"It may as well be," she replied with a smile. "I can't help it... I won't like it just because she also has it. Besides,

I never got used to it. When somebody called me Hatice, I never reacted to it. I was still Nastya. I couldn't erase the name given to me by my parents from my memory and heart. But now..."

"Admittedly, Ahmed chose a very proper name for you, child."

Mahpeyker was surprised that the woman called the Sultan by his name. She didn't say anything, though. Even his mother did not address him like that. She heard her say about him, at most, 'our son.' Daye broke away from this tradition. *I wonder if nobody blames her for that. Who knows, maybe they tolerate it because of her age?*

"Mahpeyker fits you very well," Daye said, stroking her hand. "Do you know that this has been the first time that Ahmed has personally given a name to a girl?"

She said it again! Mahpeyker decided that if she didn't ask, she would probably go crazy with curiosity.

"I..." she began timidly. "I'd like to know so many things, ma'am..." She was not sure she did a good thing by addressing her like that. She did it instinctively. The old woman's face inspired respect. There was so much warmth in her eyes, and her voice was very pleasant. "Can I ask you about them right now, ma'am?"

"Of course, my child."

"All I know is that your name is Daye. What do you do in the palace?"

"Ah, Allah bless you!" she said, exploding with almost silent laughter. Everyone probably laughed this way in the palace. "So, my name is Daye, right?" The woman laughed hard. Mahpeyker laughed, too, although she understood that she had said something silly because the old woman looked very amused. Sofia followed them.

"My dear Mahpeyker... May you often have the opportunity to laugh so much," the old woman said after a long moment and moved closer to her. "Daye is not a name, it's the job I do. Don't think I haven't noticed how surprised you were when I called the Sultan by name. I took him in my arms for the first time when he started crawling. Since then, I have always been with him. As you probably already guessed, I am the Sultan's nursemaid. Daye is how the women who feed and take care of the education of princes are called; those who fulfill all their whims, and prepare them for life... A nursemaid is kind of a second mother."

She paused and leaned close to her ear. "To tell the truth, I put a lot more effort into his rearing than the Valide Sultan."

"Please forgive me... And I thought that... There are so many things I don't know yet. What to do... if I've offended you..."

"But of course not, what are you talking about... You just amused me. I am grateful to you for that. I have not laughed like that for a long time; I've missed it."

"In that case, what's your name? How should I address you, My Lady?"

Daye's face became instantly serious. "First of all, do not call to me 'My Lady!'" She looked out the window and was quiet for a while. She watched the stirrups at the saddle that held the shoes of one of the riders who escorted the carriage. "And as for my name..." she slowly continued. "I don't remember it anymore... It's been so long since the last time I was addressed by name. I'm simply Daye. And you too can call me that, okay?"

Mahpeyker nodded, but it was clear that something still bothered her.

"Tell me what you are thinking about," the woman said to her.

"I... I'm thinking about what you said, Daye. I am Anastasia. It's true, I really like my new name... I love it. Ever since I heard it, I can't stop repeating it in my mind. Mahpeyker... But Anastasia will also live in some corner of my heart. How can a person forget about their name?"

Daye straightened up. "You can..." she said in a sad voice. "The palace makes it possible. It's even better to forget about it, my child. The past is a dangerous burden. If you don't throw it off your back, it will crush you."

"Not me!" she said firmly.

Daye looked in her eyes with a silent seriousness. In the end, a smile appeared on her lips, which fit her face so well. "Can I tell you something, Mahpeyker? Stay as you are."

"As I am? And what am I like?"

"Honest. Truthful. And very beautiful."

"Am I really beautiful, Daye?"

"Please, don't tell me that you do not realize how you have enchanted Ahmed. You hit him right in the heart!"

"Really?"

The woman nodded. "Is that all you wanted to know?"

"No... Where is this Haseki Hall? What is it like there? Very bad? Like in the Novice Courtyard?"

Daye did not expect such a question at all. "The Novice Courtyard?" She froze and eyed the girl in front of her. *Is she really as innocent as she looks, or is it perhaps the Safiye Sultan's schooling?* "You really don't know that?"

Mahpeyker shook her head.

"I was told you visited the Valide Sultan in her apartments."

"Yes, it's true."

"Well. Do you remember the long corridor? To the right of it, there is a spacious hall that leads to the Sultan Gallery. It's there. The rooms are connected by doors with the Sultan's apartments." Daye gave up on sitting back and leaned toward Mahpeyker again. "It seems to me that you have not yet asked about what is most interesting to you..."

"Of course, I haven't asked... I don't know how. I'm afraid. And I'm ashamed." She looked at the woman. She tried to smile. Finally, she leaned her head toward her. "Haseki... what does it mean?"

Daye wanted to laugh again. She refrained from that, however, seeing – despite the darkness of the carriage – how Mahpeyker blushed with shame.

"Haseki..." she began in a serious tone, "is the Padishah's woman."

A hot wave flooded her instantly. Something broke in her heart. What she was most afraid of had happened. *Mother of God, they want to make me a concubine... They are taking me to the palace not as a Sultana but as a mere concubine!*

I warned you, said the voice of reason. *You were too fast with your joy. You already thought of yourself as a queen... and meanwhile, you have become a slave. You will spend two, maybe three nights by the Sultan's side, and then they will move you aside like they do with most odalisques. Oh well, but you can still rejoice that the King named you Mahpeyker...*

She suffered. She felt that her wings had been cut. Not a single word that could deny it came to her mind. The Ice Queen, as the legitimate wife of Ahmed, will proudly parade through the bright corridor of the Valide Sultan's suites, where even the ceilings are made of gold, and she would be stuck in one of the rooms for the odalisques.

Of course, no one will tell you face-to-face that you are a murderess, not a Sultana!

She, in turn, will be called by the agas in the harem as 'Concubine Mahpeyker.'

Who do you think you are, girl – a Sultana? You are just a concubine, Mahpeyker, a concubine!

Mahpeyker? The little voice in her head chuckled. *Do you think that after the Sultan gets bored with you, they will still call you that? Is Hatice not enough for you? A name that is just right for an odalisque!*

Tears filled her eyes.

Daye immediately grabbed her hand. "Why are you crying? What happened? Did I say something wrong?"

She sniffled. "I'm not crying." To stop the tears, she opened her eyes wider. It didn't help. So, she let her emotions run free. "Odalisque," she moaned. "I will be a concubine, Daye."

The old woman felt awkward. *In fact, she is right...* she thought. But it really was like that – everything depended on the whim of Ahmed. True, he didn't hide the fact that he liked her very much. He made her his favorite girl, whom his mother wanted to accept into the service of the harem as a Chief of Girls. It was difficult to say whether this infatuation with Mahpeyker would pass at all, sometime in the future. And if it did... when? Ahmed was, after all, the Sultan. He saw a beautiful flower bud on the branch, so he picked it. He will enjoy it until his attention is attracted by another one. Then he will reach for the other one and throw this away. And no one will say a word to him... The powerful Sultan could not content himself with just one flower!

Daye sighed. Meanwhile, Ahmed had not just one, but hundreds of flowers in the harem. She thought about the odalisques that lived there. Beautiful quails, robust gazelles with beautiful eyes, swarthy girls who bounced like partridges, ebony girls, seductive Greek beauties, and fair-haired Serbian dolls...

They all wanted the same thing: get to the Padishah's bed. If she is sufficiently flirtatious to sneak into the Sultan's favor, if she knows how to please a man, if she turns out to be skillful, and above all, the fates favor her, then her 'Sultanate' will last longer than a few nights. She will attach the Padishah to herself; enjoy his favors. Of course, it won't change the fact that she will still remain a concubine... Although as the haseki, she was to be respected. She would eat together with the Sultan. But if she fell out of grace... Daye sighed again. Well... Only Allah is eternal. Then the future of an ordinary slave awaits her.

Daye thought about Ahmed's wife. She was someone more important than the haseki. She turned to the window to not let Mahpeyker see the shadow on her face.

Hatice had come from the Ajar's palace to become Ahmed's wife and Sultana. She had powerful Ajarian beys, Georgian agas, and Caucasian tribes behind her. Also, she'd already given the Sultan a son. She was the mother of the heir to the throne. In time, she was to become the Valide Sultan.

Daye looked at Mahpeyker, who sobbed with her head on her chest. *And her?* Something squeezed her heart. *Poor girl, she has nothing but beauty and freshness. And they will fade with time...*

"You're quiet, Daye. I'm already an odalisque, right? I will live with others –"

"Stop crying," the woman grumbled warmly. "Instead of enjoying yourself, you are crying! Didn't you hear what the Sultan said? He ordered a separate room for you to be prepared – the haseki apartment. He said that you should have everything you need. Yes, you are an odalisque, but so what?"

"Haseki... Okay, but what does it mean?"

"Haseki is the first woman of the Padishah. The Sultan's favorite. From now on, you will be Mahpeyker Haseki, his beloved Mahpeyker..."

Her heart went to her throat. She wanted to jump from joy. She almost flung herself on Daye and choked her in her arms, showering her with kisses. *The first woman of the Padishah!*

So, she was to become the King's woman. And the first one... his wife. And that means... Wait, isn't the King's wife the Queen? In that case... she was to become a queen. *Oh God, I will be a queen!*

Her reason quickly suppressed her joy. *Daye said 'Mahpeyker Haseki.' If you were to be the wife of the Sultan, shouldn't she instead call you 'Mahpeyker Sultan?'*

That's true. She sighed sadly. *After all, he already has his Hatice and she's the first and most important woman of the Sultan...*

Another word almost slipped out of her mouth: *Murderess!* At the last moment, however, she held her tongue. But she couldn't resist and whispered, "Ice Queen!"

"What now? What is it?"

Mahpeyker looked at Daye suspiciously for a moment. *Will she tell on me?* It didn't matter to her anymore, though.

"I said: Ice Queen... Ice Queen!"

The woman covered her face with her hand and burst out with sincere laughter. "Ice Queen? Ha, ha, ha.... You.

One day I'm going to die of laughter because of you, child. I got it. Ice Queen! Hahaha..."

"Isn't it true? Isn't she ice cold?"

Daye couldn't admit it, even if she thought the same. "Be quiet," she pretended to scold her. "Mahfiruz Sultan will now be the neighbor of Mahpeyker Haseki." *You will even share a man*, she added in her mind.

As soon as she said her name, fire appeared in the girl's eyes. Daye flinched. She had no doubt that a war with fatal consequences would soon begin in the harem. A war in which everyone will have to join one side.

And you? Whose side will you be on? asked the voice in her head. She couldn't answer that. The only thing she knew was that black clouds were gathering over the harem. A battle for life and death was going to happen. She didn't want to think about it. The riders provided the excuse for this. They'd clearly accelerated. She looked out the window.

"We're here. We'll see if you'll like your new apartment!"

Did she like it? She was delighted with it.

It consisted of three rooms connected to each other. Velvets and silks. Side tables inlaid with pearl. Two huge cabinets. And a whole lot of other things. She didn't even try to count the oil lamps and candlesticks. She ran to the window. She saw nothing but darkness.

"My window doesn't look out to the sea?"

"Wait until morning," Daye said. "The sea will embrace you then."

Sofia ran from room to room and breathlessly told Mahpeyker of all the magnificence she saw.

Daye provided appropriate explanations. "For now, the three girls you saw in front of the door will serve you. With time, we will choose new servants for you. And here is your bedroom."

Sofia ran into it immediately and threw herself on the high bed.

"Of course, you," Daye said to Sofia, "will not sleep here. Your bedroom is in a side room." She turned back to Mahpeyker. "This is a chest for your kaftans. Starting tomorrow, we'll put together your wardrobe. The bathhouse for the haseki is behind the fourth door on the left... But behind your bedroom, here, there is also a place where you can wash. And behind that door..." She opened it. "Toilet... and –"

"Daye?"

"In the morning, the dressmakers..."

"Daye?"

The woman pretended not to hear again.

"Where is her room?"

"At the other end of the corridor."

"Which of us lives closer to the Sultan, her or me?"

The woman thought for a moment how to answer, so as not to offend her. Nothing came to her mind. "She's a Sultana," she finally said. "It will be better for you to come to terms with that thought, child. She is the Sultana!"

"She's ice... she..." Mahpeyker bit her tongue. "Eh..." She sighed suddenly. "There's no other way. It seems that to live closer to the Padishah, one must first become a Sultana... We will become one then!"

Ah, thought Daye. *I feel sorry for this girl. It seems that she has no intention of coming to terms with the existence of Mahfiruz Sultan... Well, the other one probably will not be delighted either*. "I am not young anymore, I cannot stay on my feet all the time. If you don't have any more questions, I'll lie down. Good night!" she added, not waiting for an answer.

As she was leaving the room, Mahpeyker called after her, "Daye!"

"Do you need anything?"

"I feel a bit uncomfortable calling you Daye... Please, let me call you mother."

She saw the woman sway and hold the doorframe.

"Mother?"

For fifty years, she had been raising princes, none of whom, however, ever called her so. She was always Daye – a nanny. 'Nanny this, nanny that.' Tears stood in her eyes.

Well, now you know, whose side to stand on, Daye, she thought. *You will not go against a girl who calls you 'mother,' will you? Did anyone see a mother join her daughter's enemies?*

She managed to smile.

"Well..." she whispered with difficulty. "Yes, you can call me mother. And you will be my little daughter..." She couldn't control the trembling of her voice. "But we must be careful... It will be better if you don't call me that in the presence of other people. But in private... Every time you say to me mother, I will answer, 'Yes, my dear daughter.'"

Daye turned her head to hide the tears that appeared in her eyes.

After Eftalya, this is my first ally in the palace, thought Mahpeyker. She walked over quickly to Daye. She took the hand of the woman standing in the doorway, kissed it, and placed it on her forehead.

"Will Ahmed come back tonight, Mother?"

Good God, Daye groaned in her thoughts. *The old lady is dying, and she asks me about such things... Is it proper for Ahmed to take a woman at night in such a situation? Why are you in such a hurry, child? You better pray for Safiye not to die. Because otherwise, for forty days of mourning, you won't see him even from afar*.

Instead of answering, she made a gesture that she wouldn't be able to interpret. "We will have a busy day tomorrow," she said. "It will be best if you lie down, my daughter."

"This night, I won't close an eye, Mother."

Daye's heart grew warmer. *This girl will finish me off. One day I will die, either with laughter or from crying.*

"And in the morning, your beautiful eyes..."

"I will pray for Safiye Sultan to recover!"

She prayed all night. "Lord God, don't let Safiye die. Blessed Lady, make the King come back to his Queen already."

Neither of those prayers were heard.

Safiye Sultan gave up her spirit even before dawn. The King did not return to the palace. And even if he did, he did not come to see his 'Queen.'

She understood at dawn that a misfortune had happened. Anxious voices called from outside her apartment. In one moment, the whispers turned into screams.

Just as she wanted to jump up and run out of the room to find out what was going on, the door opened, and Daye came in. With her, the shouts, "She's dead, she is dead!" got inside.

"Get up, child. Safiye Sultan has died!"

Mahpeyker was very saddened by this message. The fact that she was here now, and not in another place –

though she did not know exactly where she was – she owed only to Safiye.

The beggar-slash-fortune teller was gone.

The woman who swore to fulfill her dreams was dead.

Eftalya was killed instead of her.

The Ice Queen's executioners were probably already preparing to correct their mistake. She crossed herself. She knelt. She put her hands to prayer, resting her chin on them.

Lord God, she began. *Why haven't you heard my requests? Why didn't you call the Death Angel back? Why did you take from me the only support I had in this huge palace?*

She fell silent as if waiting for a voice from heaven. She felt her cheeks grow wet. After a moment, she sighed.

Blessed Mother. Ever since I went against him, God no longer listens to his daughter's prayers. He ignores her... Sobbing stuck in her throat. *The Ice Queen will not let me live for too long. I am alone here. There is no one left I can trust.*

"Mahpeyker!"

She shuddered at the sound of that voice. It came as if from far away, from the depths. *Maybe from paradise*, she thought. Only the voice of angels in paradise could be so warm, captivating, and full of love.

"Mahpeyker..."

"Blessed Lady!" She fell to the ground with a sob. "Blessed Lady..."

"It's me," said the voice. "I think your Blessed Lady heard you. Who knows, maybe she just chose me to give you her answer? She wants me to tell you one thing: do not be afraid, child. Even if Safiye Sultan is gone, your Mother Daye is still with you!"

Chapter Twenty-Four

New Palace, Mahpeyker Haseki's Suite
January 12, 1605

The next day, Safiye Sultan's body was put to rest. As Mahpeyker couldn't attend the funeral, Daye made sure she wouldn't have time for sorrow.

First, she ordered the servants to make a fire in the bathhouse. The hamam for the haseki was nothing like the one she'd been taken to before her first visit to Handan Valide Sultan. It was crowned with a huge dome with many round windows. As the steam from the glowing marble rose to the dome, the light that came through these holes tinted it yellow, red, and white.

Along one of the walls, there were two huge marble troughs. A wide stream of water poured into them from the taps. There was a small pool by the wall opposite them, where hot water fell into it from the mouth of a lion above.

"Does Hatice take baths here too?" she suddenly asked the girl who helped her to undress. The maid's face turned red.

"Who?"

"That one, the Sultana..."

"The Wife," she whispered fearfully. "You mean Mahfiruz Sultan?"

"Whatever you call her, yes, that one. Does she also bathe here?"

"Of course not! Would anyone see the Sultana bathing in the bathhouse for the haseki?"

Damn it! She stamped with anger. She had to face this unpleasant truth at every step. She was just the haseki. In other words – a concubine!

And that... that one was a Sultana. A real queen.

The Sultan said that from now on she would be called Mahpeyker, and sent her here. He sowed hope and joy in her heart, and immediately afterward he vanished into thin air.

Almost half a day had passed, and he never even ask about her. Daye was silent, too, and just smiled. Mahpeyker decided not to ask any questions. She repeated to herself: *Let him come when he wants to himself,* but the poison had already begun to seep into her brain.

Does she know about my arrival? Probably.

The murderess who sent the executioners to me surely ordered someone to follow my every step.

Maybe it was the Ice Queen that discouraged him from coming?

Maybe she reproached him like: 'You have nothing to look for at this maid's side.'

Maybe she was nagging at him now: 'Chase her out of here, My Lord. You do not want to offend your son's mother, do you?'

But... perhaps it was the Sultan Ahmed himself who quickly regretted what he'd done, and was now ashamed to send her back?

Maybe they'll tell her that Valide Sultan wants to see her, but it would really be a falsehood, and in truth, they'll put her in a carriage and take her away, God knows where. After all, after the death of Safiye, she had nothing to look for in the Old Palace.

How many of these 'maybes,' how many question marks and doubts were present in her life? She felt that she'd reached the edge of the abyss, and now she was sliding down to the bottom. How was she supposed to live here, constantly thinking about all this? Trembling at the sound of every step? Afraid of every shadow?

But it's not just you... her inner voice whispered.

It was right. Everyone was afraid of something here. Death lurked around every corner; the only thing that was unknown was when and whom it would visit. Getting up in the morning, you couldn't be sure if you would ever see the stars again. Going to sleep at night, you couldn't be sure to welcome another sunrise. Safiye Sultan had been afraid... Handan probably was, too. Also, the Ice Queen... or would she try to get rid of her?

This was really what they call the 'palace life.' She finally understood it, but it was too late. That was the price of power: to live in constant fear, to live as much as you can, to rise as far as possible.

Yes, yes... It's an abyss. Once you fall into it, you go down like a stone. Gold, diamonds, and silks were just a shimmer for the eyes, to distract them from this terrifying limbo.

She'd learned the secrets of the palace life, not even realizing when it happened:

Firstly, you should stop listening to the voice of conscience.

Secondly, live in today while designing the future.

And the third rule, to not only think about her own plans but also to keep in mind those that others were making for her.

She'd already learned that what other people think is often more important than her own plans. It didn't matter what she thought about the Ice Queen, the Valide Sultan, or Ahmed himself. What really counted was what they thought and what they intended. That was the whole secret. The secret of being a queen and even the secret of survival.

She decided that as soon as she became queen, she would send Mahfiruz to the Old Palace. This iceberg with her child had nothing to look for in the bedroom of the Padishah. It should belong to her now. Only to her.

In fact, she'd already given a death sentence to Mahfiruz as soon as she understood what had really happened to Eftalya. She had to avenge her. This thought never left her, even at night, not even when she went to the haseki apartments for the first time.

Can you hear the steps of the coming death already, Ice Queen? Prick up your ears and listen to them well. Azrael is already coming for you.

Think carefully! her inner voice whispered. *Watch out, Mahpeyker, Hatice, Nastya, or whatever your name is. Be careful! Do not let the ambition take you over!*

It didn't want her to take on something that she would not be able to bring to an end. There are also things worse than death in life, it instructed her. Living in constant fear, for example. Who could know that better than her? She had lived that way until now, and she would have to live like that from now on, too. It was sad, wasn't it? If it was going to be that way, she should prepare the exact same fate for the Ice Queen.

Get rid of her, Mahpeyker. Light a fire of fear in her heart and watch how the ice begins to melt. She should tremble at every clatter of horseshoes, or squeaking of wheels, wherever she will be. Here was a death sentence delivered for her. Let her believe that an executioner waits for her behind every corner. Let her taste poison in each swallowed bite, and in every drop, she drinks. Let her see a potential murderer in anyone who comes close to her son!

"Oh God," she sighed as she sat in the bathing pool. How awful these whispers were...

And a quick death will save her from all this. You should first drive her to such a state that she would beg for it herself!

She'd taken up the direction already. Now she just had to set the rudder toward it and put her sails up.

She finished bathing. When she returned to the Haseki Hall, all the passing pages, servants, and farm workers watched her. She had grown used to this already. But this time, there was more in their eyes than jealousy or admiration - Respect.

Of course, they must respect you now. You are the haseki of Sultan Ahmed, after all, do not forget about it. True, you have not yet had the opportunity to spend the night with him, but that's fine.

When she came to the door of her apartment, two servants got up to open it. They gave her a slight nod and moved aside. She felt that if it were only possible, her heart would break free from her breasts and fly away, that's how excited she was.

She felt dizzy, just the same as she did long ago, back in the family village of Hagia Eirene, when she secretly drank two goblets of wine in a row with other girls on a Christmas night.

She liked it very much – not to greet, but to be greeted. For the first time... For the first time, someone bowed to her and opened the door for her. God... she thought she would go crazy with happiness. Without looking the girls in the face, she raised her head high and walked past them. She entered the room.

The sitting room was packed like a bazaar. It was filled with a crowd of women. Suddenly she caught a familiar voice in it: "I've told you so many times that she's beautiful like the full moon, and you didn't believe it. His Highness, as soon as he saw her, immediately gave her a new name... Mahpeyker. And our Master is no longer talking about anything else..."

Hayganoş hugged her, while at the same time trying to keep an appropriate distance. She might not be a Sultana, but a haseki, is a haseki. The Sultan's favorite woman, Mahpeyker Haseki, who swore to change the life of his wedded wife into hell.

In addition to the dressmakers, there were also fabric sellers with their bundles here. They stretched all sorts of fabrics before her. While Sofia chirped and laughed like crazy among all the chiffons, silks, satins, and velvets, the women praised their products as they tried to persuade her into one or another color.

Her thoughts were with purple. She loved carmine. She also loved orange, in a bright yellowish shade. And blue and green... But this color she had chosen for herself a long time ago.

Her wardrobe would be all black.

She will be a Sultana in black. She will give herself completely to this color. Her beauty, bathed in black, was supposed to shine like the sun that suddenly rose in the middle of the night. In this color, she felt happy, invisible. However, it was not the color of innocence. She rejected the clarity of the blue, the spark-striking vitality of the yellow, the innocence of pink, and the naturalness of the orange. If necessary, she should be dark like a guardian of hell, dark as the Angel of Death himself. The face of the fairy should hide a monster. This decision was frightening, even for herself, but that's what she'd decided. And now she could proceed to implement her plan.

The first step was to complete the black wardrobe. She was to tie a gold sash at her waist. She ordered the dressmakers to fasten black chiffon to the cap she wanted to put on her head, to which a carmine shawl was tied, falling all the way down to her waist. And that was all. She was already Mahpeyker, shining in the darkness of the night like the full moon.

The dressmakers worked day and night. In three days, her chests were filled with kaftans, one prettier than the next.

In Sofia's wardrobe, standing at the headboard of her bed, also hung gorgeous kaftans, made especially for her.

On the third day in the early afternoon, two black slaves smeared her arms and legs with a sticky, warm paste. She cried out when they removed the wax from her body with a quick movement. Another slave sat down opposite her and took care of her eyebrows. When she got up, two younger servants blackened her eyebrows and eyes.

They put something on her cheeks, then put the powder on it and rubbed it in for a few minutes.

After all those treatments finally came to an end, they stripped her naked and applied fragrances to her with long, thin fibers dipped in cups that spread the aromas of jasmine and rose.

Finally, her patience ran out. "Dress me," she ordered. "That's enough."

Her order was immediately followed. First, a chemise made of black, impossibly thin chiffon was put on her, and over it, a satin shirt with a bateau neckline. Then the galligaskins were put on her, whose legs were fastened with black pearls. The chiffon, stroking her legs, wrapped around her body. The pearly white of the galligaskins, visible through the cut, enlivened the blackness of the kaftan a bit. The striped shantung jacket was adorned with a large collar that none of the women had ever seen in this palace.

While the dressmakers and their assistants dressed her, Hayganoş and Daye stood opposite whispering something to each other. Mahpeyker was quiet and obediently did everything she was asked to do. She leaned forward. She reached out her hand. She lifted her leg. She pulled her coat flaps back so that a gold sash could be tied around her waist.

At some point, everyone gathered around her.

"Finished?" she asked. "Well, let's see if I look the way Safiye Sultan wanted."

Two pages placed a tall silver mirror in front of her. They moved aside.

Mahpeyker stared at the floor for a while. After a moment, she began to slowly look up.

First, she saw the slippers. Then, white-pink calves appeared in her sight, shining flirtatiously through the cut in the kaftan. Further up, a gold sash with a fist-sized button, then full sleeves of the shantung jacket with an extremely large collar. The tempting freshness of her breasts gushed out from under a satin shirt. Finally, a tiny, proudly upturned nose, the innocent pink of the cheeks, and black eyes in which a fire smoldered.

For a moment, she wanted to look back to see who stood behind her. *Stupid*, said her pride. *Of course, it's you. Mahpeyker Haseki.*

Mahpeyker Haseki... Mahpeyker Haseki... Mahpeyker... Mahpeyker...

Yes, it was her.

There was a girl in front of her that she had never seen before – because she had never looked so wonderful before.

She didn't know if it was the black color that so emphasized her beauty, or maybe she alone made the black so charming. In any case, she looked wonderful.

Yes, she thought. *That's exactly what Safiye wanted.*

"Ah, to not attract the evil eye... I will say nothing more!" Hayganoş chirped cheerfully.

Sofia wanted to throw herself at her feet, but one of the girls stopped her. "My beautiful sister!" she only shouted. "My abla, the Sultana of Sultanas!"

Mahpeyker liked those words: "My abla, the Sultana of Sultanas." That was the truth. She stood out even against the Sultanas.

Only her Sultan had still not shown up.

Three days had passed since her move to the Haseki Hall, and no one had come to her except for the servants and dressmakers.

All right, for some reason, Sultan Ahmed had not come. But shouldn't at least his mother visit me? Come in for a moment; find out how I am doing?

Although she often walked the corridor, she had not seen that other one yet. She didn't really care about it at all, so she just suppressed her laughter. *The Ice Queen has been hiding for good since she heard about my return to the palace*, she thought with satisfaction.

They all outdid each other in the praise of her beauty and told her how well she looked in black. But her eyes searched for Daye. She didn't see her anywhere. *She was here just a moment ago; where did she go?*

Suddenly Daye appeared in the doorway as if she'd heard her thoughts. She moved toward her with verve hardly expected from a person of her age. She held her hands behind her back, with a happy smile on her face.

"Help me," she told one of the dressmaker's assistants. "Take off this cap," and she pointed to the magnificent carmine chiffon that hung from its pointed apex, all the way to her waist, like a veil. The girl took off the cap and gave it to Daye. Daye turned around and did something to it for some time. Then she placed it back on Mahpeyker's head so that the girl would not see it too early. The dressmaker's assistant adjusted the chiffon, which fell back on the black of her kaftan.

"Bring the mirror, we'll see you now!"

Once again, the mirror was set in front of her.

"A gift from the mother-nanny for her beautiful daughter," Daye said quietly, smiling.

A crown! Oh God, a crown!

Mahpeyker could not hold back an exclamation.

An intricate crown glistened on her hair, spreading golden sparks from its sharp tips. It surrounded the cap, which seemed to be growing out of it.

"Do you like it?"

She was almost mad with happiness. Even if she wasn't a queen yet, she already had a crown on her head. She threw herself into the embrace of the nanny.

"I got it," the woman said quietly, "from Valide Sultan Nurbanu, on the occasion of the circumcision of her grandson. Since that day, I have been waiting for somebody worthy of it to appear. It looks like it has been waiting for you, Mahpeyker.

Mahpeyker had heard of Nurbanu before. She was the mother-in-law of Safiye Sultan. She wanted to kiss Daye's hand, but she thought it was not proper in front of everyone. Daye sensed her dilemma and moved a bit to one side.

"Thank you," Mahpeyker said, beaming with happiness. "Thank you very much, Daye..." She approached her only when the crowd of women began to disperse. "Daye?"

"Would you like something, my child?"

"I will have a great request for you, Mother." She leaned over and whispered something in her ear. Daye immediately stepped back and looked at her with surprise. "Please, Mother! For me, it's very important. I must do it. I owe it to them!"

Chapter Twenty-Five

New Palace, Apartments of Handan Valide Sultan
January 13, 1605

When Nevcihan entered her chamber, Handan Valide Sultan was lost in her thoughts.

The Padishah was nowhere to be found. He'd disappeared somewhere right after the funeral ceremony of Safiye Sultan. Also, several other people were missing.

There was still no news of that girl, Eftalya. It was as if she'd disappeared into thin air. No one even knew whether she was alive – gone like a stone in water. Nothing indicated that she'd escaped. Handan had personally interviewed all the court ladies, one after the other. She didn't learn anything from them that would suggest a secret relationship with a man. Every courtier told her almost exactly the same thing: 'A quiet, calm girl. She didn't have anything to hide.'

She really wanted to believe it, but it was hard for her to imagine the existence of someone like that in the palace. Everyone had something to hide here, some kind of secret tailored to their own measure. Some stole food, others fabric. Some took bribes, others gave them. They intrigued to achieve their goals – one wanted to become a Vizier, another lay in wait to get the title of the second or third Vizier; somebody else played for the highest stake – for the office of the Grand Vizier. Everyone pretended to be friends, while everyone – including her – was the enemy of everyone else.

Bored, she put the needlework aside. How could this girl just one day never be heard of again? It troubled her that she couldn't explain this matter. She even began to wonder if the story had another side to it.

And what about the rest, Handan? her conscience suddenly said. *You forgot about the other two? You don't know what happened to that girl, but what about those two unfortunates?*

On her first day in the palace, she already understood that to live in it – and most importantly, to gain and maintain power – one should forget about their conscience. She tried to behave like that, but she couldn't do it. Her conscience reminded her of itself at the least appropriate moments.

"How can I forget," she murmured to herself. "After all, I was her daughter-in-law."

An unpleasant smile appeared on her face. *The fish had a nice feast on them...*

Why did you kill them? They did exactly what you wanted. One girl prepared the sorbet and the other added death to it. Everything went according to your plan. Slowly and without unnecessary hustle. No one's suspicions were aroused. Safiye suddenly fell ill and left us. Nobody guessed anything, maybe even she was not aware of what was happening to her. And what did you do? How did you pay back to the two girls, thanks to which you, Handan, are now the most powerful woman in the Ottoman Empire?

Silence! Was I supposed to leave them alone, and live with the knowledge that the possibility of a death sentence for me rests in the hands of two servants? Allah has assigned a task to everyone in their earthly life. They did their job so they could leave this world peacefully. That's it.

She should finally stop thinking about it.

Safiye Sultan was where she should be. Her killers, too. Now Handan must look ahead.

The empire resembled a cauldron set on the fire; it boiled inside. And her son, the Padishah, had not given a sign of life for several days. *Where is the boy?* Handan thought feverishly.

Maybe she didn't know where he was, but she knew perfectly well what he was doing. After his grandmother's funeral, Sultan Ahmed went hunting. She had no doubt about it. It was his way to escape trouble and responsibility. While he tracked gazelles and deer, the child could forget about the problems troubling the state.

"It's strange, too," she said under her breath. The 'child,' as she thought of him, was her son. The indivisible ruler of three continents and seven climates. He didn't care about it, however. It was hard to admit it, but she was beginning to conclude that Safiye had been right. A husband, a son, or other dignitaries, all of them only enjoyed the pleasures of power, but the burden of responsibility for the state fell onto the women's shoulders. There were no Sultans like Suleiman – still talked about by the old men who can still remember him – anymore.

Her husband and son were cast from a different mold entirely. Yet they came from the same family!

As for her, long ago, she'd taken this burden upon herself. Now she was supposed to lead the Sublime Porte; to stifle rebellions of the robbers, poison the lives of the giaours, deal with the families on the borderland using the hands of the Pashas. *And the credit for everything will go to Ahmed,* she thought bitterly. *What can you do? That's how the world works, Handan. Women determine the course of history, and men get immortal fame.*

There was nothing she could do about it. History would forget about the Valide Sultan, Handan, while it would always remember the name of her carefree son – Ahmed I – a powerful Sultan of the Ottomans.

She couldn't even ask anyone where he was now.

She suddenly thought about that girl. Nastya! She knew immediately how it would all go when she saw her that night at the Old Palace. She had not seen Ahmed look at a woman with such dreamy and passionate eyes before. Many girls, beautiful like houris, had been sent to his bedroom to prove to the world that he was a real man. Ahmed, however, was not very interested in them. In fact, when Mahfiruz was brought to him, he was not too eager, either.

Deep in her heart, she thought he was right. She'd reproached herself many times. 'If only I knew... I would have never chosen her for him.' Could a woman be so very expressionless, so cold? Apparently yes... Especially her eyes.

Oh well, she thought resignedly, nodding. *At least he got interested enough in her that she gave him a son. That's enough.*

Ahmed had a small heir to the throne already.

And now he'd disappeared from everybody's sight.

Nevcihan asked about him wherever she could. She'd learned that the Sultan had not yet visited the new haseki, whom he named Mahpeyker on an impulse. It didn't surprise her too much – she never expected the Padishah to rush into the arms of the maid immediately after his grandmother's funeral. However, this thought alone was enough to throw her out of balance.

It irritated her that she had thought so. *A servant... so what? And was I any different?* A simple peasant woman from Thessaly, Helena. And now?

But she could sense danger. It was due to this gift that she was still alive.

The doubt that sprouted in her bothered her. She remembered the tenderness with which he looked at the girl, even though his grandmother was dying next to him. She was afraid that after he gave her a new name and took her to the palace, he would go even further.

That's why she was greatly pleased by the news brought by Nevcihan. Her son behaved decently!

She decided not to think about it anymore. She was afraid that otherwise, her conscience would wake up again. *What? You worry that the Sultan could sully the memory of his grandmother?! Have you forgotten that it was you who sent her to the other world?*

She took the loom in her hands and carefully examined the needlework. She tried to think about something else, but that girl still came to her mind. *My countrywoman... Whoever you ask, they are delighted with her beauty.*

Suddenly, she felt as if someone had sunk a knife blade in her brain. *Safiye!* Suspicion crept into her heart. The girl looked so beautiful that night. It was as if someone had specially prepared her for the meeting with the Padishah.

Meanwhile... it was true, she had succumbed to Mahfiruz's persuasion before and sent her to the Old Palace. But later, she wanted to take her back into her service. She thought about making her the Head of Girls. The same blood flowed in their veins after all. She wanted to take care of her, from her heart. Ahmed also agreed. 'It's not us who decides who will rule in the harem, Mother. You praise this Greek girl so much that we would like to see her.'

She recalled that moment. Her outfit, hair, face. Her posture, her gaze... She was charming in every way. And Ahmed quickly let himself be charmed by her. Could Safiye have arranged the meeting? That outfit, the silks. Her behavior... gestures of her hands... you could think that someone had taught her how to seduce men before. Was it really Safiye's doing? Perhaps she had used the girl so that the power would not pass to her, Handan? So that she would ensnare Ahmed and remove him from his mother? She considered it for a moment. Eventually, she burst out laughing.

Of course not! I think I've become too suspicious... she thought. *The poison was circulating in her royal veins, and she would plot against me?*

Just in case, however, it was necessary to keep an eye on Nastya, Mahpeyker, or whatever her name was. Besides, she should also understand her son's feelings. Was the fire in his eyes that she saw that night only a sign of a brief whim? She knew that Ahmed tried to stay away from Mahfiruz and preferred to sleep with his concubines. Until recently, he'd had a pretext – she was pregnant. But now? Evidently, he found nothing appealing about her. No wonder such a shapely, fiery girl got into his head.

Leave it alone already, Handan, she reprimanded herself. *You'd better think what to do about this rebellion.*

Yes, it was indeed the most urgent matter. Kaymakam Sofu Sinan Pasha told her just two days ago, 'The rebellion also engulfs the ranks of the cavalry, ma'am. Gödöslü Ali and Mad Derviş are the main ringleaders. They incite soldiers to rebel. Allah forbid, but I am afraid that they will soon give us trouble. Therefore, appropriate steps must be taken now.'

"Alright," she said as if he were standing in front of her now. "You're the kaymakam, right? Do what you think is right. Order to have a few heads fallen and let it finally end!"

She knew, however, that all this was not so easy.

And as if that were not enough, she'd also heard rumors of the poor health of Lala Mehmed Pasha, the Grand Vizier. He did quite well in Austria; he'd put the issue on better tracks with a single agreement. Who would she appoint in his place if something happened to him? Sinan Pasha?

Eh, she smiled maliciously, imagining the situation. *Before he would place the Sultan's seal to a document, he would run over to us first: 'There are no obstacles to approve it, My Lady. So, what should I do, put a stamp on it or not?' And he would wait for my decision, stroking his beard behind the screen.*

Suddenly she heard the door rattle. She turned back. The main lady of her court, Nevcihan, stood in the doorway. Bowing, she waited for the Valide Sultan to let her speak.

"Has something happened, Nevcihan?"

"Taciser came. Mahfiruz Sultan sent her. If you agree, the Sultana would like to bow before you."

"To bow," she murmured discontentedly under her breath. "She's is probably going to badmouth that girl again..."

"Let her come," she said without enthusiasm. "First, however, we must make another visit that we have put aside and which we can no longer postpone. After the death of the Sultan's Grandmother, we had absolutely no head for it. It was totally out of our way... We must finally visit Mahpeyker Haseki. We would not want our neglect to affect the Sultan. I will see how his beloved is doing. I will not be there for long. Then I will send for Mahfiruz."

She looked meaningfully at Nevcihan. The courtier hesitated. The reply of the Valide Sultan was unambiguous. She had guessed that a lot would change with the girl's return to the palace, especially since this time she lived in the Haseki Hall. However, she didn't expect it to happen so soon.

It looked like the balance had shifted to the haseki...

Well, but will Mahfiruz Sultan allow for it? Nevcihan wondered for a moment. *Only a fool would think so, that a woman who had hatred even toward servants and farmhands would leave the haseki in peace, with whom she would have to share the Sultan's favors? If so, we will soon witness their clash. Or should I rather say – a war?*

Nevcihan moved to the door to pass the answer of Valide Sultan to Taciser.

"Nevcihan!" Handan called after her. "Mahfiruz may also come to see her if she wishes. We will stay there for fifteen minutes and come back together."

That was the solution to her doubts. *So, it is a war!* Nevcihan thought as she left the room. She realized how wrong she'd been, thinking that there would be peace in the harem with the death of Safiye Sultan. The real problems were only just beginning.

Handan Sultan, despite the rules of etiquette, did not announce her visit. She walked quickly, with the skirts of her kaftan flying sideways. Only Nevcihan, who was just behind her, knew where her Lady was going. Suddenly, she turned and found herself in the corridor leading to Haseki Hall. She was glad when she heard the whispers of the courtiers that followed her. *Just look at this, Safiye Sultan!* Handan told herself. *That's how an attack in the palace is carried out. You must surprise your opponent, suddenly changing the direction of the attack. When he is expecting a blow to the right, you put it on his head from the left.*

The first one to notice her was a little girl with curly hair. The same girl whom Nastya had said that she would not stay here for a single moment without.

As soon as Sofia saw that the army of girls headed by the Valide Sultan approaching them, she instantly put everyone on their feet. "Abla, abla!"

Suddenly, a woman whom Handan had never seen in the harem came out of Haseki Hall.

"Şarazad abla!" the girl talked to her. "Look... see who is coming!"

Şarazad? Who is this? Anyway, what do I care? Handan thought.

The woman glanced at her and hurriedly returned to Mahpeyker's room. It was as if a bomb was thrown inside: "Attention girls, the Valide Sultan, is coming!"

The sounds of confusion that reached Handan's ears clearly made her happy. She imagined what must be happening inside now.

"Quick, clean it!"

"Take this skillet from the fire!"

"Instead of talking so much, you'd better clean up these bolts of fabric on the ground!"

"Mürüvvet!" a firm voice came suddenly. "Notify the haseki, immediately!"

Handan Valide Sultan recognized her voice immediately. *Daye! I see you took the order of my son seriously. You have settled in at her side quite fast...*

She caught herself, as she realized that she wasn't upset by that at all. It didn't worry her whatsoever, although it should. *You behave strangely today, Handan,* she reproached herself silently. *First, you turned away your daughter-in-law, for no reason, and you come here instead. You calmly accepted the move of this girl, and how the servants are lackeying to her. And now you also don't mind that the Sultan's nanny has also begun to serve her. What's going on with you?*

She did not know. She was aware, however, that she had to find the answer to this question. And as soon as possible.

Nevcihan gestured to the two courtiers watching at the door of Mahpeyker's apartment, indicating for them to move aside. She opened the door and poked her head inside. She looked around the room. She swallowed three times, giving some time to the women who were busy there, then announced the arrival of her mistress in a solemn voice:

"The Honorable, Bountiful, Serene Great Sultana Mother, Her Highness Handan Valide Sultan!"

Daye greeted her on the doorstep. "My Lady," she said, bowing. "It's an honor for us!"

"We thought that it would be better if we showed up without any announcement. We didn't want to make the girl unnecessarily nervous..."

Daye greeted her once more and curtsied. This time, it was supposed to mean gratitude for the Sultana being so gentle with them. But the thought crossed her mind: *What a pig. She didn't want to make us nervous unnecessarily...? Right, would anyone believe that? Just say that you wanted to take us by surprise.*

Handan expected to find the parlor in a mess, as indicated by the confusion that erupted at the news of her coming. Now she understood that she was wrong. There was order in it; everything was in place. She didn't see the slightest trace of any recent bustle. *They really have to care for their mistress,* she thought. *Otherwise, no servant would be so orderly and quick to bring order here.*

Daye was at the front. Girls stood in a line behind her, all of them very beautiful and neat. Dressed almost in the same way, they looked like flowers on the same branch. There were two slightly older servants standing to the side. One of them was the dark-skinned woman whom the girl in the corridor called 'Şarazad.' The other one was portly, with curly hair. Behind them, she saw four more. She immediately recognized the plumpest of them – she was Safiye Sultan's Armenian seamstress. She guessed that the others were probably her assistants.

Sofia waited at the door leading from the drawing room to Mahpeyker's bedroom. There was an indefinite smile on her face. She wore a blue tulle kaftan. In the light of the day, she looked like an angel: a guardian angel who makes sure that no one gets inside without her permission.

The living room was decorated exactly like the rooms of the Sultanas. In just a few days, the haseki apartment had assumed a staid look. Curtains, carpets on the walls... literally, everything was changed here. Instead of sensual colors, which were supposed to light a fire of desire in a man right at the doorway, calm colors prevailed. Someone from outside would never believe that he was looking at a room that was to be the love nest of the Sultan and his chosen girl. It might instead be considered as a room in which issues of national importance were discussed. One could feel Daye's hand in that. Mahpeyker had been here for a short time, so it was not her work.

But she was a servant until recently, her inner voice whispered.

She ignored it.

"I assume that the haseki has been informed about our coming?" Handan asked haughtily when Daye indicated to her a place where she could sit down. These words meant: "I will sit in her room, not here!"

"Of course, ma'am," Daye answered. Handan caught right away the anxiety in her voice.

So, the girl was not ready to show herself to her. Deep down, she was glad of it. She wanted to see her just as she was, without all the clothes and decorations she had put on for the previous meetings with her. It was thanks to this shell that she'd charmed the Sultan. Handan was afraid that she would be charmed by her, too. That is why she came here unexpectedly – she preferred to see her former servant.

She had no intention to give her more time, so she headed for the bedroom door. Only a few minutes had passed since her arrival, so the servants probably did not even have time to put a chemise on the girl.

Smiling, she turned to Sofia. She noticed that Daye moved uneasily. *So, it's true!* Handan thought with satisfaction. *The girl is not ready!*

At the same moment, one wing of the door in front of her was opened.

Semiha!

The main lady of the court of her late mother-in-law appeared in the doorway. In order not to show her surprise, she bowed her head, pretending to adjust the collar of her kaftan. At the same time, she heard Semiha's voice. "My Lady..."

What was that supposed to mean? What is she looking for here? How is it possible that without my knowledge, former servants of Safiye had gathered around the haseki? Anger grew in her. *That... what brazenness!* The recent suspicion came back to her: *Was she really a spy of the deceased?*

She did not have much time to think about it.

"My Lady!"

It was her voice.

Handan looked at her. She was speechless. It was not a haseki standing before her, but a real Sultana!

Nastya Sultan, her inner voice told her. *No... It's Mahpeyker Sultan!* Handan corrected herself.

The girl was dressed in black from head to toe. The only exception was the carmine chiffon attached to the cap on her head, and a gold-embroidered sash tied at the waist, whose ends hung down to her knees.

If any of her dressmakers tried to sew anything black for her, she would personally nail the needles into their hands. And if someone said that black is beautiful, she would probably order her guards to tear out that person's tongue. *Oh, Allah*! She sighed heavily. Can black really be so wonderful? Can it make a woman so beautiful, so alive?

Or was the secret rather in the beauty and freshness of this girl? In the fiery gaze, the pinkness of her face, in the smile that touches her lips?

The Sultan was right, she said inwardly. *Yes, he was right.*

She spoke to the girl in a voice full of sympathy, to mask her delight, "Nastya!"

The girl immediately came up to her. She almost seemed to float in the air.

Mahpeyker immediately noticed that although she'd not had enough time to prepare, she'd still managed to make exactly the impression she wanted on the Valide Sultan. *See well, ma'am*, she said to her in her mind. *The servant you once drove from here came back to take your son away!*

"My Lady," she said aloud, while at the same time she bent her head and kneeled on one knee. Suddenly, Safiye's moan resounded in her ears: *'She poisoned me!'* Mahpeyker leaned over to kiss the murderess's hand.

The ring!

The death gem was on the Sultana's finger.

She took her hand. "My Lady..." she whispered. "You give us great joy..."

And she meant it. She really enjoyed her coming. The visit of the Valide Sultan in her chamber was the official seal to her move to the New Palace. And besides, Mahpeyker expected the Ice Queen to go mad with jealousy!

She kissed the top of the visitor's hand and put it to her forehead.

"You look wonderful," Handan said. "I didn't think anyone could look good in black! Apparently, one must have your beauty for this... Houris could be jealous about it!"

Mahpeyker lowered her head as if she were embarrassed by those words. "You have your part in it, My

Lady. When we look at our Valide Sultan... Your beauty is reflected in my face, My Lady."

As soon as they heard these words, Semiha and Daye discreetly exchanged glances. They expressed the highest surprise and admiration. Daye almost burst with pride: *Well done, daughter! Where did you learn to speak so beautifully?*

"The crown on your head," Handan added. "Is it also from the Old Palace?"

Daye pricked her ears. *Nothing escapes her attention,* she thought. *She will not miss the slightest opportunity to needle someone...*

"Oh, no," Mahpeyker answered shyly. "It's a memento of your mother-in-law's mother-in-law."

"Nurbanu Sultan? I don't believe it..." Handan was surprised. In the polite language of the court, it simply meant: 'What is her crown doing here with you?'

Mahpeyker pretended that she hadn't guessed the true meaning of her words. "She presented it to Daye as a gift for the circumcision of Mehmed Khan, the late father of our Sultan. And Daye gave it to me," she explained, all the time smiling.

"It suits you very well," said the Valide Sultan, giving Daye a stealthy look. *This old woman again...* she thought.

"A crown gifted to an ordinary servant is not worth your attention, My Lady," Mahpeyker said slowly. "You probably noticed right away that the stones in it are not very valuable... But even if there were diamonds and rubies in it, they would not do much good. Next to the sparkle of your eyes, even the most valuable jewel looks pale!"

I give up, thought Daye again. The girl has an answer to everything. If she's not a gift from Allah, then what?

Mahpeyker's words had no less impact on Handan than her beauty. She was enchanted with them. She didn't expect at all that their talk would take such a turn. During their previous meetings, she'd found her beautiful, but now a completely different girl stood in front of her. Beauty was not her only asset. She bubbled with youthfulness. She knew how to behave. She was smart and eloquent. She had also learned the art of winning people over, using words. *Who would have thought...? Her sweet words have captivated even me. If she's doing equally well with other things...* It was already decided. If she was equally talented in bed, she already had the Padishah in her hand.

Handan was not sure if it was good. Sultan Ahmed should be in the grip of just one woman: Handan. He should listen to one woman only: Handan. Only one woman should rule in the palace. Handan. The Great Sultana Mother Handan.

This girl was a threat to her. She understood, however, that if she declared war on her, she would lose.

She was only the mother of a Sultan.

And the haseki was a flirtatious, full of life, charming girl with curly hair. No man would resist such a woman... Why should Ahmed's heart remain unmoved?

She should be your ally, not your rival, her inner voice told her.

I think so, too, she agreed with it. *No doubt, I should have her on my side. This is the best way to avoid losing influence on the Sultan. At least for now...*

"Ah, you are still kneeling?" Handan leaned forward to her with care. "Get up, honey." She gave her a hand and helped her to her feet. *Mahfiruz was rightly afraid of her.*

She felt that she could take Ahmed away from her. And it has happened, she thought.

"First," Handan began, as they moved toward the sofa in front of the window, "we have to explain something to each other, my child. How are we to address you? We cannot decide – Nastya or Mahpeyker?"

Mahpeyker looked at her with a hearty smile. Handan helped her sit down. She put pillows behind her back even before the servants could do it. She just looked at one of the girls, and the maid immediately served them sorbet.

What do you choose? What name do you choose for this black-dressed beauty?

"My parents called me Anastasia, My Lady. For them, I was always their little Nastya. I liked that name very much..."

Handan listened to her words, nodding.

"You probably also liked the name Helena, which you had as a child, didn't you?"

Well, well. What a little devil. Isn't she bold? Handan thought.

"But it was Handan who received the crown from the hands of the Ottomans. It was under this name that they love and respect you; first as the wedded wife of the deceased Sultan, and now as Valide Sultan..." Mahpeyker paused for a moment and looked straight into her eyes. "I want to be honest with you, My Lady. With me, it is like this – what is in my heart, is on the tongue. I regret that I could not remain Nastya, but when My Lord found me worthy of the name Mahpeyker, he delighted me greatly, calling me 'His Mahpeyker.' There is no room for Nastya in this world anymore. Whatever His Majesty deems appropriate for his servant, it will be so for her, too..."

Daye and Semiha once again looked at each other. Semiha made a face that expressed genuine admiration. She nodded slightly in her thoughts. *Ah, if only Safiye Sultan could hear that! She would be proud of her pupil. I hope that it will reach her wherever she is... Or maybe her spirit is right here, by Mahpeyker, and it is telling her what to say?* She shuddered at the thought.

Handan Sultan was also utterly astonished. The girl behaved as if she had spent her entire life in the palace. It was something totally unbelievable.

Safiye had turned the servant into a Sultana of blood and bones in the Old Palace. And in just a few months!

"We've already decided, my child," she said with a smile. She took her hand and pressed it to her breast. "You will be both Nastya and Mahpeyker for us."

Mahpeyker thanked her with her most beautiful smile.

They drank sorbet. Then the skillets were placed on the hearth to prepare coffee.

Handan, who was supposed to stay here no more than fifteen minutes, could not bring herself to leave.

"I can't believe it!" she shouted, surprised when she found out that Mahpeyker's entire wardrobe was the same color. "But why black?"

"Just like you, I noticed that black emphasizes my beauty, My Lady."

You should watch out for her, her inner voice warned her immediately. *This girl is a seasoned hunter. Nobody knows where she will release her arrow from. Keep that in mind. I know... I understood that today when I saw her in this black kaftan.*

"I see that you brought Semiha with you," she said at one point. "Did you take others from the Old Palace, too?"

A sly vixen, thought Mahpeyker, amused. *She's trying to lead me into a trap.* "Oh, yes, My Lady... That was the last will of your late mother-in-law. She told me to take care of Semiha after her death. But there are two other people..." She looked at Handan with the gaze of a child who is aware of having done something bad and is counting on the leniency of their parents. "There are also... my two devoted friends. They helped me in the Novice Courtyard. Şarazad and Mürüvvet... I owed them..."

Two terrified women stepped forward and fell at the feet of the Valide Sultan.

"I begged Daye to move them here. Thank God she let me persuade her..."

Handan looked at the backs of the women at her feet. "I see..." she said quietly, not quite realizing what she was saying. "After all, you could not stay here longer without them..." The women, listening to this conversation, held their breath for a moment. Fortunately, Handan Valide Sultan laughed happily. They breathed a sigh of relief.

"Now I only miss one thing," Mahpeyker said, sighing sadly.

"Can I help you somehow?"

Mahpeyker shook her head negatively, turning her moist eyes to her. "Unfortunately, no, My Lady. Even the Great Sultana Mother Handan cannot do anything about it."

Handan smiled, not showing that these words hurt her pride somewhat. "Why?"

"Because she died, My Lady."

Handan panicked. *What is this girl talking about? Does she mean Safiye?* she thought feverishly. *If so, you signed your death sentence yourself, my child.* She had to find out what was behind Mahpeyker's tears.

"She died?" she asked sharply. "Who?"

"Eftalya."

"Eftalya?" Indeed, she had not been seen anywhere for several days, but...

Mahpeyker nodded her head decisively. "She died. Eftalya has not gone missing. She is dead!"

Handan was still terrified. After returning to her apartments, Handan Sultan couldn't shake off the dark thoughts. *How did she come up with the idea that Eftalya was dead?* She didn't have any evidence. There was neither a body nor blood. Nobody saw or heard anything, there were no witnesses.

Only her firm statement: 'I am sure of this, My Lady. My beloved Eftalya is dead. Now she is already in heaven.'

How could she talk about it with such confidence? What does it mean... she died? Was she sick?

Handan remembered the mysterious smile that appeared on the girl's face when she asked.

'I said it wrong, My Lady. She did not die... Eftalya was killed.'

Hearing this, she'd jumped to her feet. 'It is impossible!' She almost said, 'No one can be killed in the harem without my knowledge!' Fortunately, she quickly pulled herself together and only asked, 'Who could have done something like that? Who would dare to do such a thing?'

She didn't know. There was something in Mahpeyker's attitude and gaze, however, that – without admitting it to herself – she began to believe it. *There are reasons for that,* she thought. *The girl vanished without a trace.* If she'd run away, she would've left some kind of a trace. And she disappeared into thin air. So... but who could do it? Why would anyone kill her? Did she have any enemies they didn't know about? *I should probably take a closer look at this matter...* she decided. Her reason immediately protested: *No! Leave it alone.*

But even if she left it alone, the girl won't leave it that way. Something... someone obviously stood behind this.

There's no other way, Handan, she told herself. *Nobody will stop this girl.*

Except death, her mind prompted.

Do not confuse me now! she rebuked it. *I need her alive. She will not be satisfied with Haseki Hall for long... Have you seen how beautiful and smart she is? I set so many traps for her, and she didn't fall into a single one of them.*

She remembered the moment when they were left alone. She then whispered to her, bending close to Mahpeyker's ear: 'Eh, now it will be a bit difficult, with two women... I'm talking about you and Mahfiruz. We are thinking about suggesting to our son to send his wife to another palace for a time. For better or for worse, Mahfiruz is already a mother. She has some duties with Prince Osman. He is still a baby; there will be lots to do around him... Do not get me wrong, I just care about the peace of His Majesty. Let the prince grow up a bit. They can come back after some time.'

She expected Mahpeyker to pick up this idea eagerly. And yet, she didn't.

She protested immediately, worried. 'I wouldn't want to be the reason for such a separation, My Lady...'

There was genuine sadness in her eyes!

‘I don’t think it is appropriate to separate the Padishah from his son, and the little prince from his father. God forbid me to interfere with the happiness of others, minding only my own convenience and peace of mind!’

Even now, remembering those words, Handan nodded appreciatively. Yes, there was no other way. The girl was to continue along the chosen path. Of course, on her leash. Let her go wherever she wants; she will keep the leash long. And if she doesn’t know where to stop, she will not hesitate to remind her. She will pull on the leash.

When she returned to her apartment, there was the call for evening prayer.

“Let Mahfiruz know,” she said to Nevcihan. “She may come.”

However, instead of her, a message came: ‘The Sultana is very sorry, but unfortunately, she suddenly feels unwell. She said she would allow herself to take your time at another date.’

The girl understood, she thought. *The Caucasian origin makes itself felt. Look at her, she’s immediately grabbed her weapon.*

Let her grab it, said her inner voice. *In any case, you do not deviate from the chosen path.*

That’s exactly what she was going to do. While Mahpeyker and Mahfiruz wage war with each other, she will calmly rule.

Mahfiruz did not announce any more visits. She didn’t knock on her door, either.

The first crisis occurred on the seventh day after the death of Safiye Sultan. Mahfiruz declared that no one without the honor of being a Muslim would be able to participate in the prayer for the peace of the soul of the dead Sultana.

Neither Sultan Ahmed nor Handan Valide Sultan could fault this decision. Sheikh Al-Islam, Haji Sunullah Mustafa Efendi also considered that the participation of someone unfaithful in such a ceremony would be inappropriate.

It was not a place for a non-Muslim. After all, she could not listen to the recitation of the Noble Qur'an without having completed the ritual of ablution.

Everyone agreed with Mahfiruz Sultan. In fact, no one in the harem really cared about this issue.

Except for one person. Mahpeyker Haseki.

It's that viper's doing! Mahpeyker thought as she charged around her chamber. *She doesn't care about Muslims, Christians, or Jews. Her only problem is me. She doesn't want me to attend a church service for Mother Safiye.*

There was consternation in the harem when it was understood that Mahfiruz was not motivated by religious motives, but rather by the desire to tease a new rival. Mahpeyker did not leave anyone alone that day.

"So, we are not allowed to enter the mosque to pray for the deceased, and meanwhile, the presence of this devil there will be fine for everyone, right?!"

Semiha and Daye tried to calm her down and asked her not to talk like that. Sunullah Efendi regretted the fatwa he published; the inhabitants of the palace did not give him peace. "Advise something, Hodja Efendi! Make an exception for the Sultan's haseki. If the Padishah becomes furious, Allah is our witness, we will not be able to save you from his anger. Have you already forgotten what happened to Kasim Pasha? You can be sure that he will not spare you. Help us!"

Shaykh al-Islam shivered all over his body at the memory of that scene. "But I'm right!" he tried to defend himself. "From the point of view of Sharia and the religion, a non-Muslim cannot participate in a prayer!"

Mahpeyker wondered all night how she should behave. "Dear Mother, advise me what to do?" She turned to Daye. "To obey this fatwa and not go? Or is it better to accept your religion?"

"It is a sin!" Daye objected. "You want to cheat Allah, just to rub it in this woman's face? If you are to become a Muslim, then this should only be done with Allah's permission when the light of Islam is lit in you, and you hear the inviting voice of Prophet Muhammad. I will not let you do it, my child, in any other case!"

"So, do you want to tell me that this time Mahfiruz has defeated me with her mind? I can't take it, I can't take it!"

Daye looked straight into her eyes for a long moment. Finally, she spoke to her in a whisper as if she revealed a secret: "And you will defeat her with your courage!"

Mahpeyker listened carefully to what Daye whispered in her ear.

"Will you find enough courage for it in yourself, daughter?" she asked after she had laid out the plan for her.

The prayer was to take place before the afternoon ezan. Pots full of sorbet with roasted pistachios were brought from the palace kitchens. A few pitchers of rose water were poured into them. Tinned cups and glasses were also prepared. After the prayer and after the solemn invitation of Hodja Efendi, the drink was to be distributed to everyone gathered.

Amid all this bustle, nobody noticed a woman in black entering the mosque. Mahpeyker sat down to the side, her face covered with the black scarf she wore. Her attention was focused on the storm that raged in her heart. She kept repeating half-consciously: *Blessed Lady, Blessed Lady...*

When the mosque began to fill up slowly, she no longer had any doubts. What she was doing was not a sin. If she believed in the only God, could it be important in what language, according to which religion she prayed? All the more, in the House of God. She was surrounded by many women of all ages. They all sat cross-legged. Some were servants, others the daughters of Pashas. They all sat here next to each other, shoulder to shoulder, all equal before God. *It should be like this not only in the mosque,* she thought. But it was not.

One of the women began to recite the Qur'an in a poignant voice. The Arabic words, incomprehensible to her, reflected from the walls of the mosque in the distance. Their divine harmony filled her heart. She felt like she sat on a cloud, which, as it rose to the sky, it brought her closer to God.

Suddenly, she felt a chill. She realized that it was the Ice Queen even before she saw her – the ice blue of her eyes, the ice blue of her outfit... Mahfiruz sat at the very front. Six court ladies surrounded her. She recognized one of them at once, despite the shawl lowered all the way to the eyebrows – Taciser. *A viper,* thought Mahpeyker. *Devil's spawn!*

Handan Valide Sultan appeared last. She noticed that while Handan passed the women sitting on the ground, she greeted some of them in a strange way. First, she took their hands between hers, and then, letting go of them, she made a gesture as if to wash her face.

Handan and Nevcihan approached six female clerics in white scarves, who sat behind sloping desks. The figures in their path moved aside, without showing any special signs of respect. It struck Mahpeyker: *Rightly... why should they get up and bow before her? Here, everyone is before the face of God. No one is important enough to make others bow down before her in his home.*

From her place, Mahpeyker noticed that Mahfiruz did not sit next to her mother-in-law... she counted four female heads between them. The Sultanas did not even look at each other. *Had they had an argument?*

The moment came that she'd been waiting for. She stood up and headed across the crowd toward the front rows. Daye and Semiha also rose and followed her. In turn, Mürüvvet and Şarazad stayed in the place indicated by Daye.

The eyes of the women gathered in the mosque immediately turned toward the black figure. They were curious to see who dared to come after the Valide Sultan, but only saw the face tightly covered with a shawl. It was evident from their faces that they were shocked by such behavior.

If Mahfiruz was in front, she also had to be there. She passed Nevcihan, who raised her head, wondering who was trying to get to the row occupied only by the Sultanas and the wives of the Viziers and Pashas. She squeezed between the two women sitting next to her. She was now exactly behind Handan. The Valide Sultan did not turn to see who next near her. She wanted to show everyone that she was in grief after the loss of her mother-in-law, and completely indifferent to everything that was going on around her.

But Nevcihan recognized Mahpeyker. The girl almost screamed in surprise. She thought she should whisper in her ear, 'You should not be here!' She met Daye's gaze, though, which seemed to say, 'Don't do it!' She gave up, but she couldn't help but think that the haseki had lost her mind. She couldn't find another explanation for her presence here. In a moment, everything would come out, and she would be thrown out from the mosque. Maybe Mahfiruz would be delighted, but when the Padishah found out about it... real hell will break loose.

Fortunately, one of the clergies had resumed the recitation from the Qur'an anew.

Mahpeyker froze like a stone, letting her soul absorb the soothing harmony of God's words. Her shawl was supposed to 'accidentally' fall to her shoulders, but for now, it was still too early. She was to wait until the end of the prayer and reveal herself only when all of them were to get up from their places.

However, everything happened differently than she and Daye had planned. In their calculations, they had not included Taciser, who was very interested in this newly arrived woman in black. She lifted herself slightly on her knees as if changing her position. She did everything to see the face of the stranger. When their eyes met, Taciser lost her breath for a moment. She immediately whispered something into the ear of Mahfiruz, who sat in front of her. The woman suddenly straightened up, as if an arrow had hit her in the back.

I'm here, you, icy witch, Mahpeyker mocked her in her thoughts. *You failed again. Again, you weren't able to stop me. You will never manage to do it!*

Sultana Mahfiruz paused for a few seconds to assimilate what she had just heard. After a moment, she said something to Taciser, and the woman nodded in response.

In addition to Mahpeyker, three more people were aware of the coming danger: Daye, Nevcihan, and Semiha. They could not do anything, though. Semiha wanted to warn Mahpeyker, but Daye stopped her. "Leave it," she said quietly. "Let's leave it to Allah."

Taciser waited for the Hodja to finish reading the fragment of Qur'an. She only spoke when the other clergywoman was about to start the proper prayer: "Hodja, please stop for a moment!"

In the face of these unexpected words, all the heads turned to her.

Go ahead, do what you have to do, you devil's spawn, thought Mahpeyker.

Taciser raised herself on her knees. "It is not too late to prevent a sin!"

There were murmurs around. "What's that supposed to mean? What sin?"

Mahfiruz sat unmovable like an ice sculpture, not taking her eyes off the mihrab, the niche in the mosque that indicated the direction of Mecca, exactly in front of her. Meanwhile, Taciser's eyes almost threw lightning bolts.

"There is someone unfaithful among us," she said. "We cannot start the prayer until she leaves the mosque!"

The murmurs turned into noise.

"What is going on? What is it about?"

"She says there is an infidel here."

"Aaaah..."

The Hodja raised her hand, trying to silence the women. "Who?" she asked.

"Over there!" Taciser answered, and she pointed her finger directly at Mahpeyker. "And she even had the audacity to sit next to Her Majesty Handan Valide Sultan!"

Handan turned to the left with a great surprise. "Child, is it you?" She was so surprised she could barely get the words out of her throat. "Mahpeyker?"

The Hodja did not know what to do. To gain time, she repeated the question, "Who? Show yourself!"

The Valide Sultan wanted to stop her, but Mahpeyker got up. "It's me they are talking about, Hodja Efendi!"

She raised her head. Her gaze, suspended between heaven and earth, seemed to be seeking Allah.

Amid the exclamation of surprise, the veil covering her face fell to her shoulders. She shook her head to adjust her hair and immediately took on the Sultana pose she had studied. She tilted her head slowly to the right shoulder and crossed her arms over her stomach. She brought her most beautiful and innocent smile to her face. She turned slightly sideways so that both the clergywomen and the women sitting behind her could see her better.

Those who did not know her, prodded each other, asking, "Who is that?"

"I have no idea. I've never seen her before."

"Look at her. It is as if the late Safiye Sultan stood here..."

"Ah, indeed!"

"And how pretty she is! Who can it be?"

"Allah did not spare her beauty..."

Those who knew her froze with their mouths open.

The Hodja who sat in the front, a woman with a noble face, could not take her eyes off her for some time. "Who are you, child? What's your name?"

"My real name is Nastya. Anastasia," she said boldly. "But His Majesty the Sultan Ahmed honored me with the name Mahpeyker. So, since then, I am Mahpeyker."

"Ooo!" The whispers could be heard again "So it's her... The favorite of the Sultan Ahmed!"

"Can't blame him..."

"What a beauty, what posture!"

Most of them thought of one thing at the same time: *unlike Mahfiruz...* but none of them dared to say it aloud. True, the Padishah's wife also had everything in its right place, but she was extremely cold and haughty. And this girl radiated warmth. She was beautiful, hot, adorable, and fresh.

The Hodja had also heard bits and pieces already. Apparently, the Sultan brought a girl from the Old Palace who immediately settled into the Haseki Hall. It was also said that nothing had happened between them yet. *Nastya...* thought the Hodja. *So, she is not a Muslim. And what should I do now? Throw out the haseki, whose name was given by the Sultan himself, from the mosque?*

"Is it true that you are not a Muslim, my child?" she asked, at the same time trying to read something from Handan's eyes. The Sultana, however, was still shocked, and frozen with her head raised, staring at the girl next to her as if enchanted.

"Yes!" Mahpeyker answered without thinking. "It's true, Mother."

*An infidel, but she knows how to spea*k, flashed through the clergywoman's mind. She remembered the fatwa of Sheikh al-Islam Sunullah Efendi. Undoubtedly, he must have known that it would affect the Sultan's favorite...

"You've heard it yourselves," said Taciser, who grew more and more impatient as the whole thing lagged. "She confessed. Mustafa Sunullah Hodja Efendi officially announced that it is unacceptable for a non-Muslim woman to be present in the mosque during this prayer."

Mahfiruz shifted uneasily. *What is she still thinking about? Why the delay?* She decided she wasn't going to look idly at this scene any longer. "Throw her out of here immediately! Besides," she spoke in a voice as cold as ice, "her outfit alone is enough to throw her out. Isn't she aware of the great loss we've suffered? Has she especially dressed in black to offend our mourning?"

What?! What is this ice-cold witch saying? Mahpeyker felt her face taken by fire. Only now did she notice that all the women filling the mosque were dressed in white. Servants, who did not have white jackets or vests, at least draped white shawls over their heads.

So, for the Ottomans, white was the color of mourning. But it was already too late. Among this snow white, she was the only one black as a crow.

"She is openly showing her disrespect!" Taciser said. Mahfiruz's courtiers began to murmur something under their breath.

"Ah, Sultana Safiye," one of them said. "It's good that you can't see this insolence!"

"She has just left us, and that one is dressed as if for a holiday!" another murmured. "Shameless, shameless!"

Mahpeyker was close to crying. The Ice Queen had defeated her.

Suddenly, she felt a movement beside her. It was Handan, who rose from her place. "Enough! Enough of this!" She scowled at the place where Mahfiruz sat. "The real insolence, shamelessness, and disrespect," she pronounced every word slowly and clearly, "has afflicted the haseki of Sultan Ahmed!" Handan pointed at Mahpeyker.

There was dead silence. Mahpeyker saw Mahfiruz's eyes freeze into ice. Fear appeared in Taciser's eyes.

Mahpeyker looked only briefly at the Padishah's mother. She lowered her head, still smiling. She bit her lip as if she wanted to disperse the rain clouds that flowed to her eyes. The thick silence was suddenly broken by a soft sob. A moment later, similar sounds could be heard from further rows.

Daye also cried. "Thanks be to Allah!" she whispered. She was right. Mahpeyker had enough courage to risk even death!

Şarazad and Mürüvvet, sitting in the back, could not control their emotions, either. "Shame and sin!" muttered one under her breath. The other prayed for Handan Valide Sultan: "Allah blesses your reign! You stood up for the oppressed girl. May Allah be with you always!"

The defeat almost turned into a great victory.

Handan was as aware of it as Mahpeyker. She addressed the clergywomen with dignity: "We would like to state clearly that there is nothing scandalous about it! Let those who do not know learn, and not repeat similar nonsense again. Where we come from," and she indicated herself and Mahpeyker with her finger, "when someone close to us dies, we wear black as the sign of mourning. That's what the tradition says. A black outfit is not a sign of disrespect, but rather talks about pain, attachment, and loyalty." She paused for a moment. She looked around proudly and turned back to the clergy. "You ask what to do with a dissenter?" She waved her hand dismissively as if it were of no importance. "Judge for yourself, do you really have to be a Muslim to stand in front of Allah and be able to reach out your hands to him in prayer?"

For the Hodja, this performance tipped the scales. The girl was the favorite of Padishah... and the Valide Sultan stood up for her in front of everybody, in a direct action against her daughter-in-law. And besides, she'd liked this Mahpeyker from the first moment. She was beautiful and smiled so warmly, even when she cried. It is said that the beauty of the spirit is visible on the face. That was exactly how it was in her case. She'd never liked the other one. She was so haughty and cold, and the haseki was her exact opposite. *Eh,* she thought and sighed. *Nastya or Mahpeyker, it doesn't matter. My heart tells me that I should speak in your favor, angel.*

She exchanged a meaningful look with the other Hodjas. She understood that they all thought the same.

"My Lady," she said in a respectful voice. "All judgment belongs to Allah. There is no need for his servants to comment on it... No one has the right to banish someone who comes to his house to meet him; someone who humbly prostrates before Allah and wants to brighten his soul with the light of the Noble Qur'an..."

Hurray! Mahpeyker thanked her with her eyes full of tears and the most beautiful smile that she could give at that moment. She also squeezed the hand of Handan, who still stood beside her.

"Sit down, my child," said the Hodja, smiling at her kindly. "Each of us knew the late Safiye Sultan. You used to serve her, too. Even though you are not a Muslim, you came here to pray for her soul. Let thus everyone pray in whichever way she can, and it flows from her heart; according to what she believes and according to the principles of her religion. Allah will hear us all, and so will our late Valide Sultan."

Mahpeyker sat down and closed her eyes. She absorbed intensely, the harmony of the Qur'an's verses, and the beauty of the words of prayer, incomprehensible to her.

When the sorbet was handed out after it was over, she looked at Mahfiruz from the corner of her eye. The iceberg was smashed into powder.

Her gaze suddenly met with the eyes of Handan. She watched her, holding a glass to her lips. They exchanged smiles.

They both realized that their smiles did not express their true feelings. In Mahpeyker, everything shouted: *Have you seen? I defeated your daughter-in-law!*

In turn, Handan Sultan, looking at the haseki, thought: *So that's it... It looks like you are not even afraid of death, Mahpeyker. You took it into account, aiming at your goal, didn't you?*

To be continued in Part II of Sultana Kosem
The Black Queen

GLOSSARY

Abla: Big sister; used as a polite expression for women respected by the speaker.

Ajars: An ethnic group within the Georgian nation.

Aga: The title of officials and commanders in the army and harem, also used as a polite phrase, meaning 'Mister.'

Akçe: Silver coin in the Ottoman Empire.

Akinji: An irregular light cavalry in the Ottoman Empire. They attacked the lands of enemies on their own, their purpose was to recognize and plunder the enemy; they had the right to detain war spoils for themselves.

Alim: A Muslim scholar.

Azrael: The angel of death.

Baksheesh: A usual tip, alms, given in return for doing some minor activities.

Bey: A senior civil servant, as well as a courtesy in the meaning of 'Mister.'

Beylerbey: (Turkish: bey of the beys) The governor of the Ottoman province.

Börek: Filo pastry, usually stuffed with meat, cheese, potatoes, or vegetables.

Celali Rebellions: Rebellions in the 16th and 17th century Ottoman empire.

Damat: (Literally son-in-law) A title vested in dignitaries married to Ottoman princesses.

Dervish: A Muslim mystic.

Dirhem: An old unit of weight corresponding to 1 to 3.25 grams.

Divan: Sultan's council, acting as a kind of government.

Efendi: A title of nobility, which follows the given name, the equivalent of the English 'sir' but can also mean Lord or Master. The title was usually given to educated people, dignitaries, clerics, and military officers.

Enderun: School of elite clerks and military in the Topkapi palace, also the inner part of this palace.

Ezan (Turkish): A call for the followers of Islam to a prayer, which is a duty of every Muslim. The prayer is said five times a day.

Falaka: A torture instrument, used to administer a punishment in the form of whipping the feet.

Fatih: Conqueror, the title of Mehmed II, the Sultan who won Constantinople.

Fatiha: Sura (prayer) opening the Qur'an.

Fatwa: Official instruction, issued only in writing by the learned theologian, settling a legal or theological controversy.

Ferace: Long top coat worn by Muslim women.

Firman: An official document; an ordinance issued by the ruler.

Friday Greetings: On Fridays, when heading to the mosque for prayer, the Sultan greeted his subjects.

Ghazal: A lyrical poetic work.

Ghazi: Title granted to Muslims triumphing in the war.

Giaours: An abusive description for non-Muslim, especially a Christian.

Grand Vizier: The Prime Minister of the Ottoman Sultan,

with absolute power of attorney and, in principle, only dismissible by the Sultan himself.

Grate: Women could not meet men from outside the harem face-to-face. Conversations took place in a room separated by a latticework screen through which the talks were held.

Hagia Eirene: In the Turkish version, the name of the protagonist's family's village is Aya Irini. The Greek variant of this name has been used in this text.

Hajji: Honorary title of a Muslim who completed a pilgrimage to Mecca.

Hanim: Lady.

Hamam: Turkish baths.

Han: A caravanserai – a roadside inn with a central courtyard, rooms, shops, and a mosque.

Haseki: The preferred concubine of the Sultan, a favorite.

Hatun: A woman, lady; title awarded to women in high positions.

Hodja: A Muslim schoolmaster. A polite title used for teachers and clerics (including women).

Hotoz: A kind of high women headgear in the Ottoman Empire.

Hüdavendigar: The nickname of Murad I, successor of Orchan, meaning the ruler. Murad I was the first of the dynasty who used the title of a Sultan.

Houri: An eternally beautiful and young virgin of paradise.

Janissaries: The elite infantry units that formed the Ottoman Sultan's household troops and bodyguards, from the fifteenth to the nineteenth century.

Jatagan: A single-edged Ottoman knife with a double curvature of the blade and a characteristic handle. Also known as Yatagan.

Kafes: A designated place for women in the mosque; cage; rooms of Ottoman princes, after eliminating the rule of fratricide.

Kalfa: Apprentice; supervisor of white slaves in a harem.

Kapudan Pasha: Ottoman counterpart of an Admiral.

Kavuk: Turban-like headgear of Ottoman dignitaries. Its size and shape varied depending on rank.

Kaymakam: An official who stood in for the grand vizier during the absence of the grand vizier, due to illness, travel, or during the interval between the dismissal of one and the appointment of another.

Kazasker: One of the chief military judges of the Ottoman Empire.

Khan: The feudal ruler or provincial superior; here: one of the many titles of the Sultan.

Khutba: Friday sermon in the mosque, during which the name of the reigning ruler was mentioned.

Lafa: (Turkish: Ulufe) Military and civil salary in the Ottoman state, paid every three months.

Mace: A blunt weapon with a metal head mounted on the shaft.

Mahpeyker: The name Mahpeyker comes from the Persian language, where it literally means: “Beautiful, with a moonlike face.” In the harem, girls were usually given names related to some feature of their appearance. The moonlike face in the eastern sense means a face that is light, pale, and full.

Meleki (Turkish): Angelic.

Mihrab: A niche in mosques indicating the direction where Mecca is located (that is, where to turn when praying).

Miskal: A former measure of weight corresponding to 4.5g.
Muska: Triangular amulet, usually made of leather, with spells or prayers locked inside.
Namaz: Muslim prayer recited five times a day.
Nemçe: In Ottoman times, the name used to describe Austria.
Night of Innocence: (Turkish: Berat Gecesi) the holiday of remission of sins, celebrated on the night from 14th to the 15th day of the month of the Shaban.
Night of Destiny: (Turkish: Kadir Gecesi) a celebration commemorating the revelation of the first verses of the Qur'an, usually falling on the 27th night of Ramadan.
Odalisque: A female slave/servant in the harem; sometimes also denotes a concubine.
Okka: Measure of weight in the Ottoman Empire equal to 1283g.
Orchan Gazi: Son of Osman I, continuator of his work.
Osman I: Actual founder of the Ottoman dynasty.
Padishah: A Persian term for the Sultan; Emperor.
Pasha: High rank in the Ottoman political and military system, typically granted to governors, generals and dignitaries as an honorary title. Similar to a British peerage or knighthood.
Rumelia: Area of the former Byzantine empire.
Sadrazam: The Great Vizier.
Sanjak: A military and administrative unit; the sons of the Sultans were sent to Sanjaks as administrators, which was supposed to prepare them to rule the country in the future.
Sayyid: The honorary title granted to the descendants of

the Prophet Muhammad.

Sela: A prayer accompanying Ezan, often used to remember the dead.

Selim I: Warlike ruler, thanks to whom the empire acquired the holy cities of Islam Mecca and Medina, Jerusalem or Egypt.

Serdar: The title of commander-in-chief in the Ottoman army.

Shah: The title of rulers of Persia and other monarchs of the Muslim East.

Shahada: Muslim profession of faith, one of the five pillars of Islam.

Shahid: A person who died for faith; it may refer to the person deceased during the plague or in childbirth, or a warrior who died in the fight against unbelievers. It is believed in Islam that Shahids go straight to Paradise.

Shaikh al-Islam: In the Ottoman Empire, the title given to the great mufti: a lawyer and theologian issuing official interpretations on private life and national issues related to Islam; he declares his decisions in the form of a fatwa.

Sherbet: A refreshing drink of sweetened fruit juice and water.

Sipahi: An Ottoman cavalryman.

Spahis: The Turkish irregular cavalry. The feudal army troops of the Ottoman Empire; they were vassals of small estates.

Sublime Porte: One of the names of the Ottoman state (as well as its court and government), originating from the gate leading to the Grand Vizier's residence.

Sultan: A title used before the name by the actual Sultan, or after the name by the son of a Sultan or by the wife, mother, and/or daughter of a Sultan.

Tambur: A stringed instrument with a rounded resonance box.

Tespih: Muslim prayer string that consists of 33 beads (smaller) or 3 pieces of 33 beads. It helps in pronouncing all the names of Allah.

Ud: A stringed instrument with a pear-shaped resonance box.

Valide-i muazzama: A great Sultana Mother, a title belonging to the Sultan's grandmother.

Valide Sultan: Title held by the 'legal mother' of a ruling Sultan. The most influential woman in the Ottoman Empire.

Wilayah: Administrative and territorial unit in the Ottoman Empire.

Yatagan: A single-edged white weapon with double curvature of the blade and a characteristic handle. Also known as Jatagan.

Zittau Agreement: Signed between the Habsburg monarchy and the Ottoman Sultanate, considered one of the symbols of the fall of the empire.

About The Author

Demet Altınyeleklioğlu was born in Ankara.

She obtained a degree from Ankara University's Faculty of Political Sciences and Journalism and a master's degree from Haceteppe University in Educational Communications.

From 1980 onwards, she worked as a producer for TRT Turkish Radio and Television Corporation and was a director on various levels. She has translated a few novels and continues to translate. Demet Altınyeleklioğlu lives in Istanbul with her family.

About The Publisher

Royal Hawaiian Press is a publishing house located in Honolulu Hawaii. It was established in 2005, primarily to promote the works of author and founder, Maria Cowen. Since then, it has expanded to encompass an assortment of other authors from around the world.

Royal Hawaiian Press specializes in providing books in a variety of languages and genres, including translating and publishing existing European-language books into English for the English-speaking market.

To learn more about Royal Hawaiian Press and the books it represents, please visit:

www.royalhawaiianpress.com

To receive an alert when new books are released, subscribe to the Royal Hawaiian Press Mailing List:

http://tiny.cc/rhp

Printed in Great Britain
by Amazon